TH

Frank began to count down the paces that still separated him from his two wives, which he estimated at only fifteen.

Fourteen, thirteen …

Wheeler was right — Hilda *was* a handsome woman.

Twelve, eleven …

And dignified, too. Look at her standing there, not a twitch in her features, not a hair out of place.

Ten, nine, eight …

And Teresa! A sight to melt a heart of stone.

Seven, six, five, four …

How could anyone, looking at her, seeing that wild, audacious beauty — how could anyone blame him?

What *was* he going to say to her?

Three, two …

Hilda stared at him — what was he going to say to *her!*

One …

Teresa stared at him. Hilda stared at him. He drew breath to speak …

THE CAPTAIN'S WIVES

Malcolm Macdonald

CORONET BOOKS
Hodder and Stoughton

Copyright © 1991 by
Malcolm Macdonald

First published in
Great Britain in 1991 by
Hodder & Stoughton Limited

Coronet edition 1992

Laserset by the author using
Spellbinder DTP®
in Glyphix® Palatino fonts
on a Hewlett Packard Laserjet III®
printer

British Library C.I.P.

Macdonald, Malcolm 1932-
   The captain's wives
   1.Title
      823[F]

ISBN 0-340-56235-8

Printed and bound in Great Britain
for Hodder and Stoughton Paper-
backs, a division of Hodder and
Stoughton Limited, Mill Road,
Dunton Green, Sevenoaks, Kent
TN13 2YA (Editorial Office:
47 Bedford Square
London WC1P 3DP) by:
Clays Ltd. St Ives plc, Bungay

till

Maj-Lis

ett minne blivit i min hand

PART ONE

Old Flame

CAPTAIN MORGAN WOULD NOT even let the gangway near the ship until the second mate had confirmed that the after breast rope was secure. He was a stickler, Morgan. Any other captain of a five-masted barque with a fast cargo for Boston would risk head and stern lines only, with perhaps a forward spring; and he'd raise the gangway the moment any one of them was fast. But not Morgan. Not even with this onshore wind to pin the ship to the quay.

The shore gang was annoyed. The raising of the gangway was the last chore of their day. They had the afternoon off — or they were going to take it off, anyway, to watch Cork play Youghall in the most important match of the season. One of them gave a sour nod in the Captain's direction. They all knew Morgan and feared the reach of his temper. "That fella," he said, "wouldn't give you the ..." He was about to say, "the steam off his own piss," when he realized that a group of females was standing within earshot. "Wouldn't give you the time of day," he concluded lamely.

They nodded and heaved their shoulders and contained their impatience as best they might; sure, what could anyone do about it, anyway? A captain was a captain; the next one up was God. Not that Morgan looked like anyone's idea of a god. Declan Kennedy, the oldest of the dock porters, who'd served in the Royal Navy long ago and had mounted guard on Elba, always said Morgan was the nearest thing to Napoleon he ever met. The others couldn't see it, of course, because all they knew of Old Boney's appearance was from prints; and, apart from the fact that both men were small in stature, the outward resem-

1

blance was slight. But when you drew near to the man you began to *feel* what old Declan meant — and to know something of the powerful and frightening magnetism of the old dictator of Europe.

For Captain Morgan, Captain Francis Brandon Morgan, seemed to carry about with him a kind of lethal electrical charge; the air immediately about him held an indefinably vibrant quality that kept you at bay — like the bars around the tiger cage in the zoo. Indeed, the comparison is apt, for there was something very tiger-like about the man. His head was sleek, close-cropped and clean-shaven, with curiously pointed ears that lay back against his skull. His eyes, which were deep and piercing, seemed never to rest; and even when his back was turned you dared not slacken your effort, for, like the tiger, he could turn and pounce in the blink of an eye.

The porters stared up at him until his merciless gaze fell upon them; then they looked away, shuffled their boots uneasily in the mud of that damp March day, and hankered after something, anything, at which they could seem busy. Happily for them, the group of females caught Morgan's attention next. Steerage passengers, of course. The only sort that ever seemed to emigrate from this wretched country. He eyed them with that impersonal curiosity all old seadogs acquire when they stare at females ashore. Not that he considered steerage women to be fair game. Indeed, he'd keelhaul the man who laid an unwelcome finger on any one of them. But they weren't like ladies; you could look them over easily, and without impertinence.

"I'd take a hose to that lot, Cap'n," Tony Wheeler, the First Officer, commented. He had the reputation of being the one man aboard *Pegasus* who did not go in fear of Captain Morgan; in fact, he was just as terrified as everyone else, but he masked it with a respectful bonhomie that deceived them all, even Morgan. Indeed, it was Morgan who held Wheeler in slight awe — one of the few men he'd met in his long career as ship's master who knew how to stand up to him, and not in any pugnacious way but simply by behaving as if there were nothing there that especially *needed* standing up to.

"You've Irish blood yourself, Mr Wheeler," he growled, still running his eye over the females.

But whatever the officer may have replied, Morgan heard none of it. Suddenly his blood stood still, his heart dropped a beat, and his knuckles whitened on the rail.

It couldn't be. It was. Yet it couldn't be. His mind teetered in a daze between what he saw and what he knew. She was dead — surely she was dead? Anyway, she'd be ... what? Twenty years older than *that* one. But he could not take his eyes off the girl down there on the quay. Jenny to a T, to the last curl of her rich red hair. Trick of the light. It must be.

At that moment the girl herself looked up at him. Or perhaps she was merely surveying her home for the next two weeks? Telepathy or chance? Dear God, what did it matter? Those eyes transfixed him. Pale green eyes, languid, intelligent, just like *hers*. It could not be chance, or life itself was all chance. If this were an accident, then so was his very existence.

"Cap'n?" Wheeler prompted at his elbow. The after breast was secure — had been secure for the past minute or more.

"Oh ... yes," he muttered. "Raise the gangway."

Wheeler and the young cadet exchanged bemused glances.

3

The familiar routine of the ship crept between Morgan and … he would not call her Jenny, he would not even think of her as Jenny. The familiar routines crept between him and that *apparition* on the quay. "And bring to me any man who lets it foul the side."

The threat brought an odd sort of ease to the quarterdeck; whatever excursion Cap'n Morgan had taken, he was now back. The world, like *Pegasus,* was on an even keel again. Then it was "Is the leadsman in the chains?" and "Aye, Cap'n!" and "Is his line freshly marked?" and again, "Aye, Cap'n!" — as if they didn't sail in and out of Queenstown a dozen times a year.

He gave the new passengers no more than half an hour to come aboard, get stowed, and say their farewells — all those well-intended promises to write soon and come back one day, from people who would probably never set pen to paper nor glimpse the Atlantic again.

He needed every minute of it to prepare *Pegasus* for getting under way, what with a stiff "soldier's" wind on her port beam, pressing her to the quay, and an adverse tide that would have her fouling a naval cutter astern within minutes. A less skilled captain, faced with such a tight departure, would warp her between the quay and two of the buoys in the tideway; but not Morgan. He knew he could take her out under shivering canvas to open water, and the crew would expect no less of him.

Pegasus was the very latest design for a fast merchantman, with five masts and split sails all the way to the top; and even her topsails could be reefed from the deck. Shaw & Eggar, owners of the line, had put Morgan in charge because no other captain would test a ship to the limits without hazarding a single life

— much less the ship and her cargo. On this run that cargo consisted almost entirely of cheap, machine-carved furniture for the American West, so she was heavily ballasted with casks of ale, sent round the world to age and mellow.

"All set, Cap'n." Wheeler waited for the command

Morgan ran an eye over the sails. Every yard was braced abox, sharp up, and every square foot that could safely be set was carried. She was now moored only by her head rope and after spring. He grunted approvingly. "Let go forr'ard."

The order went forward. They had to wind in double-quick time to get enough slack to slip the rope off the bollard on the quay. The moment she felt herself free she tried to run aback, but the after-spring hawser held her and the tiderace got in against her starboard quarter and swung her closer to the wind. Soon she was facing the Queenstown roads. Her canvas shivered as the wind began to spill from a sharper angle. "Set jib and spanker," Morgan ordered. "Let go aft." To the quartermaster he added, "Keep her helm alee."

From the calm of his voice and the quiet, measured response of the men, the casual onlooker might have assumed this was the easiest routine in the world for getting under way. One would have needed to look very closely to see that half the crew was either holding its collective breath or mouthing a prayer in silent unison. For one long agonizing moment an equal battle waged between wind, water, and the Captain's will. The sails quivered, the tidal rip curled against her starboard timbers like softwood passing beneath a planing machine, and Morgan stared out, down the estuary, looking for a contradiction in the wind that might yet upset all his fine calculations.

"By the mark five!" sang the leadsman.

It was almost as if *Pegasus* had been waiting for some such news — that there was a good enough depth beneath her — for she now answered to the wind. She nosed forward so that her stern, no longer pinned to the quay, began to dip and slew. At once the bow moved off the wind. "Starboard your helm," Morgan barked, but Abe Rogers, the quartermaster, was already there, bringing her alee again; having steered *Pegasus* through her trials in the Solent and then most of the way to Ireland, he now knew how she would respond even before she herself had quite made up her mind. She cleared the quay by inches. He checked her when she was still a point or two off her true course and she steadied perfectly. And then she really began to move.

"By the deep six!" sang the leadsman, now from the starboard bow.

"Brace round the head yards," Morgan commanded. And again he was anticipated, with both watches ready to haul on the sheets the moment the command came. "Port your helm, Mister Quartermaster. What's her bearing?"

"South-east by south, Cap'n."

"Steady at that!"

For a moment she was taken aback but as the head yards swelled she leaped forward once more, eager to clear the point of Haulbowline Island and race for the ocean again, her one true element. Her masts strained, the timbers lifted beneath their feet ... she was like a mighty horse, her namesake, galloping in strides a mile long. The thought was on Wheeler's mind as he relaxed and said, "She was well named, Cap'n."

"Who?" Morgan grunted, staring hard at the passengers; they were being allowed back on deck now that the sailing was plain.

"Pegasus." Wheeler was embarrassed at needing to explain.

"To be sure." The Captain's tone of voice was absent minded.

"Leave to stand down the starboard watch, sir?" the bosun asked; that, too, should not have been necessary.

"To be sure," Morgan repeated, never for one moment taking his eyes off the emerging stream of passengers.

T HE LIFE HILDA MORGAN now enjoyed was exactly the life she had planned from the moment when, sometime in her fifteenth year, she had been capable of planning anything beyond her immediate future. Its elements included: an adoring husband who was away most of the year; three dutiful children, two sons and a daughter; a decent house in one of those delightful, leafy, urban villages that surround London; half a dozen loyal and trustworthy servants; and a goodly circle of respectable and amiable friends. And now she had it all. Why, therefore, did she so often sit at her boudoir window these days, gazing out at the houses opposite, feeling herself possessed by the notion that the lives *they* enshrined was in some indefinable way richer than hers? What ingredient, if any, had she failed to incorporate into her wonderful scheme of things?

None that she could think of; on the contrary, time had fleshed out its elements in a most satisfactory manner.

The adoring husband was a sea captain — and not just any old sea captain, either. In fact, she had been told on more than one occasion, and by more than

one who should know, that Francis Morgan (she did
not like the bluff "Frank") was probably the finest
captain in the entire British mercantile fleet (which
automatically made him the finest in the world, of
course). Even twenty years ago, as a mere second
officer, he was already talked about on "the Baltic" as
a man to mark; otherwise, to be sure, her father would
never have invited him to dinner. How flattered she
had been when he began paying her court. Never
mind her friends' sneers — that any young officer
who *failed* to court the daughter of the chairman of
the Baltic Exchange would be a fool — she knew,
from the tremor in his voice, the anguish in his eye,
the utter awkwardness that replaced his normally
brusque and jaunty manner when in her presence ...
she *knew* that a bewitchment more ancient than
ambition bound Francis to her.

Not that she understood it, that strange magic
which held the sexes in thrall to one another, often
against their better judgement and self-interest.
(Though happily such degrading mutual slavery was
not the case with her and Francis.) She was not sure
she even wanted to understand it. She regretted those
necessary little rituals by which men refurbish their
adoration and the race renews itself. Ever since
Daphne Troughton, as she then was, had whispered
the Awful Truth to her, the day they flew their kites
on Highbury Fields, she had been terrified of marrying a man who was not of the very finest type — by
which she meant one who would trouble her as
infrequently as possible; her family's connections
with shipping had naturally made the choice of a
seafaring man doubly desirable, given her feelings on
the matter.

Francis had been very good about it. And she had

rewarded him with three fine children — or youngsters they were by now. In fact, Neil, at twenty, was
really a young man; and as for Lawrence, why it
seemed only yesterday he had started shaving — and
here he was, eighteen next month already. How
swiftly childhood fled, even though some particular
days of it had dragged like centuries!

They had even arrived in the order she had planned: two boys and a girl — Neil and Lawrence, the
apples of their father's eye, and Kathleen, her mama's
own little darling ... For some reason her contemplation of her perfect little family (such a *sensible* number
for an intelligent couple to have, such an *example* to
the poor) failed to bring its usual glow of satisfaction.
Clouds were beginning to intrude upon that hitherto
sunstruck scene.

Neil should not have been quite so reluctant to take
up his cadetship on the *Orestes*. That had wounded
Francis, though he hadn't said so openly. *Orestes* was
the flagship of the Union Line and Neil's father and
grandfather had put their own credit in the balance to
get him the position; in the circumstances he might
have shown just a little more gratitude. (Also, to be
fair, the Union Line could have shown just a *little*
more understanding. True, Neil's mistakes had been
costly, but a beginner can't be expected to get everything right from the word go, can he?)

When it came to filial gratitude, Lawrence had
behaved little better. All his life he'd known he was
intended for the Baltic; one day he'd be chairman
there, too, like his grandfather — just as Neil would
one day inherit his father's reputation as the finest of
masters in the Mercantile Marine. It was all very well
for Daphne to wax philosophical and say airily,
"'twas ever thus ... ever since the Ancient Greeks,

anyway." (Oedipus, was it? Daphne had spent far too much of her youth reading the most unsuitable literature — and still did, come to that.) One more episode like last Saturday, when Lawrence and his unsavoury chum Billy Attwater had spent the afternoon in the dinghy they'd built, racing the *Hansa* down to Tilbury (the very ship whose manifest Lawrence ought to have been tallying!) ... one more drama like that and Lawrence would be out on his ear. What was so difficult about being at your desk at the appointed hour on the appointed days and carrying bids to agents and owners and bringing back their replies and keeping proper records of everything? Yet to hear the lad talk about it you'd think they were asking him to leap over St Paul's every day and twice on Sundays.

Thank God for daughters! Kathleen at least was the one nugget of unalloyed gold among her children. She had more faculty than both her brothers put together, if truth were told — and why should it not be told in this day and age, Hilda wondered? There seemed to be nothing the girl could not pick up once she set her mind to it. In fact, the difficulty with Kathleen — the *only* difficulty — was in steering her away from unsuitable things for a girl to pick up, like navigation when Neil had all those difficulties in understanding it, or obscure systems of weights and measures when Lawrence had come home complaining about "tons-tallow and tons-cubic and tons-my-eye-and-Mrs-O'Grady." You only needed to watch her looking up things like that in *Parnall's Handy Household Reference* and you could actually see her eyes darting here and there about the page, sorting it out at a rate of knots, like a card player's eyes when arranging a new-dealt hand. She always beat her brothers at cards, too, because she had memorized all the mathematical chances of getting this or that winning combination — until Lawrence had twigged, of course. Now he usually scooped the kitty.

And yet, for all her cleverness, Kathleen remained so modest and biddable, so unspoiled, such a *sensible* girl, as everybody said of her. Not even Daphne, who always thought the jovial worst of everyone, could fault Kathleen. She had to content herself with vague warnings like, "one day that girl will confound us all. Wait till she turns sixteen!"

Only three months to go now!

But Daphne was wrong. Kathleen wouldn't change. Yes, thank God for Kathleen. And thank God, too, that the remainder of her girlhood vision was intact: the fine home, the loyal servants, the good friends.

Highbury had been a natural choice for the Morgans, quite apart from the fact that Hilda herself had grown up there. For some reason, without anyone on the Baltic convening a committee and deciding it should be so, this particular village on the fringe of London had attracted large numbers of people "in shipping." Not *Old* Highbury, where Daphne and Brian Dowty lived — up around Highbury Fields. That area had enjoyed its heyday a century earlier and was now past it, a little raffish, in fact. Not absolutely raffish, of course, or not even Daphne would live there, but relatively so, when contrasted with the extremely respectable people who lived in Highbury New Park. It was a wonderful sight on a warm Sunday in summer to see them all parading to and from St Augustine's to hear that fine preacher, the Rev. Prebendary Gordon Calthrop preach his impressive sermons. Up and down they went, with

11

their tall toppers ironed and polished, their black tail coats brushed and brushed again, their lovat-grey trousers still warm from the press, set off by the blinding white of their ties and waistcoats, and their yellow or mauve gloves spotless, their black boots vying to outshine the silver knobs of their canes, and the flowers in their buttonholes fresh snipped from the conservatory on their way out ... it was a brave and beautiful sight. One wag had called it, "the Baltic at prayer."

Highbury was far enough from the West End for its decadence and "Fashion" to hold no influence; and it was near enough to the City for a gentleman to walk it in half an hour, as many of the younger ones did, gaining in both health and purse thereby. Hilda's father, of course, kept to the old tradition, riding his mare the half mile to Canonbury Station, followed at a respectful distance by his groom, who would then lead the horse home again. People could still set their watches by "old Victor Watson" each morning. But it was still sufficiently apart from the great wen of London, City or Westminster, to support a life of its own. Anyone who was anyone belonged to one or other of the two big societies — the Philharmonic and the Dramatic; Neil had sung in the former before going away to sea, and Lawrence was one of the great back-stage stalwarts of the latter. The Highbury Athenæum was jam-packed when either group put on a performance, and people came from as far afield as Hampstead and Walthamstow. Charles Brightman was chairman of the "Phil" and his brother Fred took the lead in the Dramatic; Brightman Bros was one of the leading shipping lines — so it just showed there was no better place than Highbury in all the world for a family whose interests lay in mercantile affairs.

Hilda, at her boudoir window, looked up and down Highbury New Park with quiet satisfaction. For all that it was a small, self-contained community — perhaps even a little tight and inward-looking (she would allow Daphne that much of a sneer) — it was also undeniably cosmopolitan, even more so than the West End, which liked to boast of being the ultimate in that line. Why, at that very minute, Mr Camille Abbati and Mr Franz Hinzer drove by in an open gig — brave men, considering the rawness of the day. They were the two leading chartering agents in the Azoff, Black Sea, and Danube trades. She gave them a dignified nod but, though they seemed to be looking at the house, they were talking and gesticulating in that endearingly quaint, foreign way of theirs and did not notice her.

She glanced at her clock; gone eleven. Rather late for them, surely? And Abbati's house was up in Aberdeen Park, so why was he driving down this way? She must mention it to Daphne at choir practice tonight; Daphne loved to spin grand and impossible conspiracies out of such chance sightings.

Thoughts of the choir, and its offshoot the Phil, brought her to the last item in her *tour d'horizon* of achieved ambitions: good friends. Most people were lucky if they could number them on the fingers of one hand — really good friends. But Hilda would need all her fingers and all her toes for the task, and still want more for the tally. First there was the choir and the Phil, on Tuesdays and Thursdays, respectively, where her clear and reliable soprano earned her the occasional solo part; there she had at least half a dozen close friends. Then, on Wednesdays, came the Dramatic, where her green eyes, fair hair, and aesthetically dreamy expression brought her parts a good ten

13

years younger than her true age; and there, too, she had several close friends of both sexes. Other days brought her into yet other circles. On Mondays it was the Highbury Missionary Society, which supported two missions, one in Darkest Africa and the other in even darker Whitechapel, just down the road. On Friday afternoons it was Clothing for the Poor, after which she always needed a good bath, and then — the one sheer indulgence of the week — the whist drive in the Meeting House at the bottom end of Highbury Crescent. It was mostly ladies who played there, with a sprinkling of a few retired gentlemen; the husbands were either away at sea, like Francis, or "on the Baltic," and Friday evenings were busy ones for anybody in the City, being the traditional evenings for banquets and testimonials.

It was amazing, really, how few of the friends in one circle overlapped with those in another. Only Daphne. She was in everything except Clothing for the Poor; her pet charity was Distressed Gentlewomen, where she claimed to be picking up tips for her own old age. Otherwise there were fewer than half a dozen duplications among all Hilda's various circles of friends — and yet all lived within less than one square mile of each other! She often wondered what would happen if she gave a grand garden party one summer and invited all of them to mingle. Of course it was impossible; there were ladies, or females, in all her circles with whom she got on splendidly but with whom it would be unthinkable to mix socially. Hilda prided herself on her ability to get on with people, especially those with whom it was inconceivable she should mix; she wished there were some way of drawing more attention to the fact, so that the members of all her various circles would

14

understand how extremely progressive and tolerant she was. Most of them, she felt sure, assumed it was some especial quality in themselves, rather than in her, that forced her to accept them.

She rose from her chair in the bay window and was just about to cross the room to the door when a movement along the street caught her eye — a young girl walking along hand in hand with an older woman. A second or two later they resolved into Kathleen and Miss Kernow, her teacher at the Highbury Grove Academy for Young Ladies. With a quick, guilty glance up and down the street, she raised her binoculars to her eyes; normally she did not use them until the evening twilight rendered her invisible to other binocular users among her neighbours, of whom there were many.

At least Kathleen did not seem ill, though her face had an unusual pallor and she walked with a strange, almost mincing step quite unlike her usual, confident stride. They halted. Miss Kernow said something to her. Kathleen shook her head and gave a brave little smile. The teacher linked arms with her and they resumed their walk at an even gentler pace. But now they were no longer teacher and pupil; they were woman and woman.

A dread premonition seized Hilda in that instant; the unalloyed gold, she felt, was about to show the first sign of tarnish.

ORGAN STIRRED IN his bunk, harried by a dream in which he was left single-handed in charge of a vessel very like *Pegasus* except that it kept growing new masts behind his back. At length he awoke, filled with a sense of unease. The masts. There was something about the masts. When he first went to sea there had been little difference between the construction of a merchantman and a man of war, at least as far as their solidity was concerned. The masts on both would stand firm even in a collision. But now, with each new merchantman they built they shaved her masts, split her sails, and cut her crew — all to make her lighter, leaner, and better able to compete with steam. The five slender, graceful masts of *Pegasus* worried Morgan out of his dreams.

He lay in his bunk and listened as they creaked in their stepping, not the deep bass creak of the mighty oak trunks of yore but the shrill contralto of …

The word contralto made him think suddenly of Daphne Dowty, a name that added naught to his comfort. Just because she was Hilda's childhood friend and lived so near to them in Highbury, it did not make a suitable companion of her. Fortunately, dear Hilda had a mind of her own but even so, a dripping tap could wear down stone in time. Daphne was to blame for the unruliness of both Neil and Lawrence; he couldn't prove it in a court of law, but her disparaging little remarks about Duty and Authority all through their childhood cannot have failed to leave its mark on their impressionable young minds. Thank heavens for Kathleen. She had more sense than …

How had he wandered from masts to Kathleen? He shook his head as a man may jiggle a faltering timepiece. Masts. Stick to the masts.

Faculties within him that persisted through his slumbers told him *Pegasus* had not tacked for an hour or more. Her slight but steady list to port said she was running before a half-gale, fine on her starboard quarter. Not much for the watch to do but show as much canvas as she'd bear and, keeping all yards braced round, hold the tension in her sheets within limits. "Farming," as they called it. Must be close to the upper limit now, he thought. Every time she checked at the foot of an adverse swell, he could hear her masts groan at the strain. Four bells rang. But which watch? He reached for his chronometer, intending to carry it to the moonbeam at the porthole, when he heard McLennan, the First Mate, cry, "Haul up the mains'l weather clew!"

Six o'clock, then. Dawn soon enough — and the wind obviously getting up. He should do the same. Little point in trying to snatch another half-hour.

He rose, shaved in ice-cold water, and dressed, wincing as the imperfectly removed stubble on his adam's apple grated against the stiffly starched collar. The glass stood at thirty-two inches — nothing ominous for the time of year, except that yesterday it had stood at thirty-three.

"Morning Number Two," he grunted as he went on deck.

"Morning Cap'n. All's well." Feehan, the Second Officer, moved to the starboard rail. Like many new ships of that time, the *Pegasus* was commanded not from the quarterdeck (except in harbour) but from a bridge, amidships.

Morgan noted with approval that all topsails and t'gallants were already taken in; he put his binoculars to his eyes and scanned the horizon. The sky, though cloudless above, was ominous on the port bow; there a huge black hole in the sky was just starting to swallow the setting moon.

It looked as if they might be heading just north of a big one — which the strengthening wind confirmed. The only other vessel in sight was a steamship, a huge merchantman of about five thousand tons, hull down on the starboard quarter. A heartening vision, with a sky like that coming up.

He lowered his binoculars and went down the companionway to the foredeck; as he made his way forr'ard he checked the occasional wedge in the cleats on the hatch combings. None was loose, of course; if it had been, the cook would already be frying some-one's liver for breakfast. Morgan used the heads and then went up to the "policeman" on the fo'c'sle deck.

"Davidson, isn't it?" he said, knowing very well that it was. "How long have we had her for company?" He nodded toward the merchantman astern, now visible only by her smoke.

"We picked her up just after one bell on this watch, Cap'n. Then she was a few points to starboard." He gestured almost dead ahead.

"So we've gained about sixteen miles on her in ninety minutes, even with the wind behind her. We must be moving." He peered over the rail, but with a following wind and the sea running with her, *Pegasus* seemed to plough no more than an average furrow.

"'Tis a contrairy sea, Cap'n," Davidson volunteer-ed. "There's a rising swell forward of her port beam."

"Not on her port bow?" Morgan asked sharply.

The man shook his head and sucked a tooth. The difference was important for it revealed that the centre of this storm was still a long way off.

"There's one now," the man warned. His eyes, long adapted to the dark, picked out the black-on-black trough and near-black-on-black flank of a vast swell, about half a mile off on the port beam. "We had another like that just before four bells," he added.

Morgan knew then what had awakened him early. They stood and watched, powerless, as that mighty wall of ocean continued its remorseless advance toward them. No, not toward *them*, not toward anything in particular. That was what made it so awesome: It did not even acknowledge their existence. It would roll thus across the face of the deep whether they were there or not. It turned their very being into an irrelevance.

The long toe of it got in under their keel and began to lift her while the crest was still so far off it was only just beginning to form a new horizon. The two men held their breath; Morgan's gloved fingers tightened on the rail as *Pegasus* rose and rose, and — incredibly — continued rising as the long wedge slid beneath her. The very length of it was a relief in one way, for, like its direction, it implied that the storm centre was still far off; but in another way it was the most ominous sign yet, for it confirmed this particular storm as one of Atlantic proportions, which made terms like "far" and "near" seem quite meaningless in the long run. Wherever you might seek to hide between the Aran Islands and Cape Cod, this one would find you out.

When the crest of it reached them he looked nervously up and watched the masts go racing northward across the sky, shrieking their protest as they dipped. The sails, though braced right up to the weather, shivered as the sudden motion spilled their contents — which was as well, he reflected, for he could hardly believe that masts so slender could withstand both forces at once. The vessel herself checked and shuddered as the oblique crest of the wave took her aback; the canvas barely had time to fill before they were falling down the back of the swell and the masts raced once more across the dawning sky, this time to the south. There was a long moment of contradiction as the running sea and the afterswell contended for her keel.

"Mr Feehan," Morgan called across the space of the foredeck. "Turn out the forenoon watch. Set by the wind. Reef all courses. Close-reef main-tops'ls, fore-stay-s'l, and mizzen-try-s'l. Prepare life lines."

"Aye aye Cap'n!" came the reply. A few minutes later the decks were swarming with both watches as they jumped to reduce her head of sail. Not a single man needed to set foot to a single ratline; it was all done from the deck, in half the time and ten times the safety of the old way.

The Bosun was waiting for Morgan at the foot of the forward companionway. "Three good men and the carpenter to inspect the battens," the Captain told him in passing.

"Aye aye sir."

Morgan was a few yards past the man when he heard him add, "You'd best stay below there, miss. This is no weather for a Christian."

He turned and saw the light of the man's lantern falling on *her* — Teresa O'Dee, as he now knew her to be called. A power he could not gainsay made him turn and say, "All right, Bosun, let her on deck. She won't be in the way there." He pointed to the space between the companionway and the scuppers, just forr'ard of the foremast shrouds.

She screwed up her face and took an aimless step or two, feeling around her for something solid. He realized she was too blinded by the light to see where he had pointed; he took her gently by the elbow and guided her into the little arbour of safety. The touch of her arm was electric. An impulse within him to drop her like a hot coal fought with an equally powerful urge to hang on to her as long as he could — forever, if possible.

The bosun stared at him in amazed disbelief before recollecting himself and jumping to his orders.

"We're carrying too much sail for this wind, Miss O'Dee," Morgan explained. "We're going to take some of it in — and just make sure the tarpaulins are well secured over the cargo hatches."

The place he had chosen for her was so well sheltered that he hardly needed to raise his voice — nor to draw so close to her as he now did. The air around her had a special, vibrant quality that captivated him.

She, for the moment, had no voice to raise, being too astonished to learn that the great Captain Morgan actually knew her name.

"Nothing to be alarmed at," he added, "but the sea's getting up and she's a new ship — a bit of an unknown. Best to play safe, don't you know."

Go, he told himself. *What good can you do here?*

"You know my name," she said at last.

"I make it my business to know as many passengers' names as possible, young lady," he replied; it was more than half true, anyway. But then, feeling it sounded a little impersonal, even ungallant, he added, "Yours, to be sure, was one of the first." Then he could have bitten his tongue off. What was the point of saying such things? What good could ever come of these idiot notions that now hovered at the rim of his mind?

21

But far below this superficial annoyance a great calm had descended upon him. The strengthening daylight was yet weak enough to blur those lines that were peculiarly hers and leave a blank into which his memory could paint those features once so dear.

She smiled demurely at his chivalrous compliment and retreated into the fastness of her self-sufficiency — that unreachable femininity which still had powers to drive him distracted. She rearranged her shawl. For a moment the line of her breast was firm against the darks of shadows beyond; his hand stretched out in fancy and touched her there. He closed his eyes in shame but, like his earlier annoyance, it was a most superficial burden; inwardly he exulted once again.

He followed her gaze out to sea, aft toward the plume of smoke off the starboard quarter. "A steamship," he told her. "A merchantman like us, with a thousand tons more in ballast to steady her. I expect you'd rather be aboard her at this moment."

She faced him then and smiled. "Begod, Captain Morgan, by no means."

Her smile — the sweetness and pain of it — succeeded where conscience and dignity had failed. It drove him from her. "Let the forr'ard steward know if the sea comes down the ventilators," he said in parting. "We'll plug them with hessian, but there's no sense in suffocating till then."

Teresa O'Dee followed him with her eyes. Though he no longer struck fear into her, as he had done when he was just a name, a remote, gruff figure on the bridge, she could understand even more why the men spoke of him in such awe and why scarce two minutes had elapsed between his turning out the watch below and the taking in of sails by that selfsame crew.

She watched them now as they finished their work, all looking as if they'd been alert for hours; and a great feeling of confidence surged through her. It was plain from his orders that they expected a storm, and a severe one at that, but the smooth and busy seamanship in progress all around her left no room for alarm. And it was all because of him, she realized. He was making all this happen. No matter what the storm might hurl at them, he would bring them safely through — of that she was utterly confident. There was some quality within him mightier than the mighty Atlantic Ocean itself.

And among all the passengers, he had taken care to learn *her* name first!

When the Captain was well clear, the Bosun came forward again, with the First Mate at his side. She shrank back as the light of the lantern fell upon her in the nook where she sheltered. "Captain Morgan said I could," she began defensively, but the Bosun cut her off with a laugh, not unfriendly.

"That's all right, miss. You stay there as long as you like. Well now, Mr McLennan," he said to the mate, "you've seen Morgan's daughter. What d'you say?"

The man peered intently at Teresa, as if she were a specimen in a case. "Nothing like the girl," he said at last.

"Then the mystery thickens, eh!"

The lantern vanished, and the two men with it, leaving her world newly darkened — and in more ways than one.

Morgan's daughter! The Captain had a daughter! Her euphoria shrank to one small point.

Well, what else had she expected?

Nothing. Only hoped.

Not even hoped. Daydreamed.

The single small point of her happiness began to swell once more as a new thought struck her: If Morgan's daughter were old enough to resemble her (or not, as it now turned out), then the Captain might well be a widower!

She stayed on deck an hour or more, waiting for the chill of the strengthening wind to drive her back below; it was a bleak choice, between the bitter blast on deck and the nauseating stench of the female dormitory. If only she'd known what it was going to be like, she'd have begged or borrowed the extra and travelled second, instead. What with women who smoked pipes, women who chewed tobacco and spat their quid where it pleased them, and women who had never heard of soap and water, it was purgatory for a well-brought-up young woman down there. The only compensation was that the reek from the men's dormitory, on the other side of the iron grille, was even worse.

There were six cabins for second-class and no firsts. But as they were all at the back end of the boat, separated from the steerage by the bridge, they might as well have been on the far side of the moon as far as Teresa was concerned. One of the ladies there might want a companion or a maid or something, or they might have a child with the measles who'd need nursing — anything to get out of this purgatory. Frank Kelly, one of the seamen, who seemed a bit soft on her, said only four cabins were taken. She wondered would they let an empty one go a bit cheaper now the voyage was half over? She should have asked Captain Morgan when she had the chance.

Dreams! It was all dreams. Going to America was a dream. Who said life there would be any better than it had been in King's County? Well, to be honest now, it couldn't be worse. It was her father's dreams had left her without a penny and brought her this low in the world. Still, fair dues to him, if he'd succeeded, they'd be living like pigs in clover. You couldn't say the dream was wrong, only the man who dreamed it. Her thoughts strayed back to Captain Morgan.

There was a man to strike passion in your heart! One minute you'd be looking at the sea, filled with the fear of it; next moment you'd see him on deck and the fear would just fly out of you. That wasn't just her idea. Frank Kelly said the same. He said that sailors talk of lucky ships and unlucky ships, but the only luck a ship needed was a good captain — and that made *Pegasus* the luckiest vessel afloat.

Was he a widower, she wondered? And why did he look at her in that special way, as if he, too, was soft on her? There was *something* there, you'd be a fool not to see it. All those times when the weather had been better and she'd been promenading up here on the deck, round and round the hatch combings, and she'd look up at the bridge, very casual, and catch his eyes upon her. The men must have noticed it, too, else why would they wonder was she like his daughter?

Thoughts of Captain Morgan's daughter brought a brief pang of envy. Ships' masters were rich and lived in fine houses in the country; their wives had their own gigs and did nothing only go to At Homes and balls, and they wore long gloves always, five or six pairs a day, Mary Quirke said. She could see the Captain's daughter now. Arabella, her name would be, and they lived in a grand villa on the edge of one of those cathedral towns like Barset. What time was that in England? Mid-morning, probably. So Miss Arabella would be off in her gig, all wrapped up against the winter wind with her hands sunk snug in her muff, and a haybox of soup for the deserving poor at her feet. Perhaps her mother would be the Honourable something or other from a titled family and the deserving poor would be their ancient retainers. Lætitia. The Honourable Lætitia Morgan. She'd be deceased, of course, which was why young Arabella, who looked nothing like her, Teresa, was doing the charitable round.

On second thoughts, she didn't envy the daughter at all. When it came to matters of solace, of comforting the loneliness of a poor widower man, the unattached spinster had the daughter bet hollow. With that thought kindling at the cockles of her heart, Teresa O'Dee withstood the raging blasta full ten minutes longer than she might otherwise have done — which was why she was still on deck when the Captain sent for her.

CAPTAIN MORGAN GOT A good fix on Venus before the dawn effaced her; with the sky closing in, it might be the last they'd get before landfall. A few swift calculations, automatic to him by now, put them at just over 29°W by just under 49°N, or almost exactly halfway to Newfoundland. From now on it would be dead reckoning all the way.

The *non*automatic part of his mind was still appalled at the way he was behaving over Miss O'Dee. He could not understand it. No man living had greater cause to philander, nor better opportunity, either; and yet during all the years of his marriage he had resisted those siren calls — only he knew at what cost to his nerve and self-esteem.

"Oh, Francis, darling, it's not as if you've been away for years. Only a month ... oh, very well, six weeks. But surely you can restrain your animal lusts

26

for a *little* longer when you know how much it upsets me?" How many times had he endured such homilies, spoken with all the impregnable sweetness of a woman who knows her mission is to civilize the world? How often had he been faced with tantalizing offers from silken-thighed senoritas and big, pneumatic black women — only to find within himself, and often at the last minute, the moral courage to resist them? And now here was Miss Teresa O'Dee, plaguing him night and day, all because she bore a passing resemblance to ...

Well now that was another odd thing. A few minutes ago, when he'd actually summoned up the courage to address her at last (Captain Morgan, terror of the seven seas, having to summon up courage to talk to a chit of a girl!), he hadn't even thought of Jenny Bright. Yet it hadn't changed his feelings for her in the slightest. His innards had still gone hollow at the sight of her; his hands still longed to caress her; his lips still yearned to feel the touch of hers — but it no longer had any connection with her likeness to his long-dead sweetheart. That might have been the initial spur, the trick that let the thorn of her beauty get under the armour and into his flesh. But now it was the girl herself who captivated him so. And worst of all, he felt no shame.

With the senoritas and the negresses there had always been his shame to hold him back; with Miss O'Dee, on the other hand, there was none. There was prudence, of course; a nice calculation of appearances in front of the officers and men in his command; but morally, inwardly, in the profoundest corners of his soul, not the faintest twinge of conscience held his imagination in check. What on earth was he going to do about it?

He watched his fingers grasp the pencil and draw a line across the Atlantic chart and he asked them what he was going to do about it.

He set his dividers to the distance he estimated *Pegasus* would cover in the next twenty-four hours — a little game he liked to play with himself each day. If he got it right, he would allow himself three fingers of whisky on retiring that night; if wrong, only two. Now he pushed the two sharp points into the back of his hand. The pain was not so sharp as he had imagined it would be. Was he losing touch with his senses in more ways than one? He watched the blood form two crimson globules, which congealed almost at once. He had never done such a thing before in his life.

Yes he had. Yes he had — at school, to show that bully Bulgin how indifferent he was to pain. The long-buried schoolboy sniggered at him a moment and then fell silent, mourning his own death.

"What *am* I going to do?" the adult Morgan repeated aloud, feeling himself at a loss for the first time in almost twenty years.

The boy within pricked up his ears; perhaps death was not quite so permanent as rumour would have it! Together they went back up on deck.

Miss O'Dee was still there.

By now the sky was black from horizon to horizon and the wind a full gale. Wheeler had reduced canvas yet again and *Pegasus* was now sailing under a close-reefed main-topsail and storm stay-sails only. Morgan considered reducing still further and decided to leave things as they were for half an hour or so. The wind had backed a point, which was a good sign, for it suggested the storm was tracking east — west rather than coming straight at them on the usual sou'westerly course. If that were so, they stood a chance of riding round its centre, with the storm growing no worse than this all the way.

"Rogers was just saying, Cap'n," Wheeler broke into his thoughts, "she handles well before the wind."

Morgan nodded. "We'll run west by south for Newfoundland as fast as we dare. With luck we'll miss the worst of it." He checked the pennant at her stern and then ran his eye up the mainmast, directly overhead. "Brace up that yard another three degrees," he said. "We'll get a knot or two more out of her yet."

Wheeler relayed the order and then followed Morgan's eyes down to the foredeck. "All battens tight, sir," he said, though he knew that was not what Morgan had on his mind.

The Captain grunted.

The First Officer decided to risk something more direct. "I hope she's not got a fever or anything, Cap'n," he added nodding at Miss O'Dee. "She's been standing there almost an hour now."

To his horror Morgan heard himself replying, "There's something about her that I ..." He bit his tongue off and wondered desperately how to finish the sentence. "I feel sure I've met her before," he said brusquely. "D'you remember old Cap'n Bright? Billy Bright. Owned the *Hiawatha*. Used to ply between Tilbury and the Baltic, mainly. I was cabin boy on her all my first year at sea. Wonderful man. He had a daughter the living image of Miss ... whatever her name is down there."

"O'Dee," Wheeler said, thinking it odd that Morgan had known her name yesterday and forgotten it again today ... or then again perhaps not so odd, when you came to consider it.

The Captain gave no sign of having heard. "She went down on the Goodwin Sands, the old *Hiawatha*," he said. "With all hands. And ... Bright's daughter. I'd have sailed with her if I hadn't had the chicken pox."

"Ah!" The First Officer shook his head at the vagaries of fate — and refrained from making the obvious comment that Miss O'Dee and Miss Bright could hardly be connected, if that were the case. So why had Morgan brought it up at all, he wondered? "She's not our usual steerage type," he offered.

Morgan nodded. "She should go below. She'll catch her death out there."

The other spoke rapidly, before his misgivings could restrain him: "I'll bet she can't tolerate the fug down there, especially now we've stoppered the ventilators. It must be unendurable for a woman with any sensibilities ... like the Black Hole of Calcutta."

In those superficial levels of his mind where Morgan made purely social calculations and looked after his own reputation and self-interest, he knew this was something of a test. The Morgan of yesterday, the Morgan with whom many of this crew had sailed before, and more than once, the Morgan they all knew and feared in their very bones — *that* Morgan would never have concerned himself with the comfort of one poor steerage passenger — most especially one who was young, female, and pretty. No more practised hater of women ever paced the quarterdeck. Wasn't it his proudest boast that he was bigamously married to his legal wife — since his first and only bride was the sea!

But such considerations were far too superficial to stop him now; Wheeler had opened a door for him, and the strength to slam it in the man's face was simply not there. "She may have a fever," he said angrily, clutching at the man's opening words. "Lord, isn't this storm enough to try us! A blasted female down with a fever! See she's isolated in one of the empty cabins aft. Say nothing about fever to the other passengers, of course — just make out she paid the premium and moved."

"Very well, Cap'n. A wise precaution, if I may say so, sir."

"You may not, sir!" Morgan snapped. "I am not used to having my decisions commented on by my juniors. What are you waiting for?"

Wheeler, outwardly calm, inwardly in a muck sweat at his own impudence, cleared his throat delicately and, avoiding his captain's eye, said, "You have the medical books, sir."

Morgan turned on his heel. "You look at her," he snapped. "You know as much about it as me, which is damn all. Just get her out of my sight."

He stormed off aft to check the battens on the rear cargo holds.

"That's more like his old self, sir," the quartermaster commented when Morgan was safely out of earshot.

"Very *like* his old self, Mr Rogers," Wheeler laid an ambiguous stress on the word, at which the other smiled. Then he went forward to relay the good news to Miss O'Dee.

BUT REALLY, 'CLARE TO GOD, I'm fine," Teresa protested for the third or fourth time as Wheeler flung open the door to the empty cabin. But the First Officer ignored her assertion, gave a quick, conspiratorial glance all about them, and urged her with a peremptory nod to enter. "Excuse my closing the door, miss," he said as he followed her in, "and don't take it amiss now, but there's a thing or two I ought to tell you. First, don't ever let Cap'n Morgan hear you say you haven't a fever. You see this neck?" He thrust his head forward awkwardly.

Taken aback, she stared at his adam's apple and nodded. "Yes."

Wheeler licked his finger and drew an imaginary line around it. "He'd sever it there if he heard you say that — and you'd be back in steerage without your feet touching the deck. D'you want that?"

"No!" she exclaimed fervently.

"I didn't think so." He gave a self-congratulatory nod. "When I saw you lingering there on the foredeck, despite the storm, I said to myself, she's loth to go back below to that Black Hole of Calcutta. And so, when the Captain asked what the hell you were still doing there — pardon my French — I used my wits and suggested perhaps you had a fever. That's the only reason you're in this cabin, you know — he wants you isolated."

"Oh." She dropped her pathetic little bundle and leaned against the upright of the bunk. "Was that it?"

"What did you suppose?" the man asked.

She shook her head.

"Little you know of Captain Morgan," he went on. "When they gave out sympathy he was playing marbles over the hill."

"He was very kind to me," she said stoutly. "When the mate ordered me below, he said I could stand by that staircase and be out of the way. And he spoke very softly to me."

But Wheeler shook his head. "Don't you be deceived by him. That man hates all women with an intensity you could carve up and sell to a seminary."

"Are you a Catholic?" she asked suddenly.

He ignored the question. "And the prettier they are, the worse it is for them. I've seen him reduce them to tears. And the light of pleasure in his eyes! You'd have to see it to know what I mean."

"But he's married," Teresa objected. "Or," she added more hopefully, "he was, once upon a time."

"To the sea," the other confirmed.

"He has a daughter. I heard the bosun say it."

Wheeler shook his head. "That man's only wife is the sea. I know."

She wanted to press her question to an absolutely unequivocal answer but something restrained her. She had the information she desired more than all the world to hear: Captainn Morgan was a widower, just as she had hoped.

"So my point is," the First Officer concluded, "if you want to stay here, you'll develop a fever, or an ague, or an ache or pain of some kind. D'you understand what I'm saying?"

The porthole turned dark green; she had a brief glimpse of a startled fish.

"Or d'you want to go back to steerage?"

"Yes." She sighed and squared her shoulders.

He was flabbergasted. "But why?" he asked feebly.

"Because he'll come to see how bad it is," she said resignedly. "And he'll know at once I'm lying — and sure I couldn't bear that."

Wheeler gave a little whistle; the business was deeper and even more intriguing than he had realized. He'd suspected that the girl had somehow got past the Captain's well-known misogyny, but he'd never imagined it might cut both ways. He changed tack at once. "The sentiment does you credit, Miss O'Dee, but see here now." He eyed her cannily. "There's one way he might let you remain on board. Are you willing to risk it? "

"And what is that, sir?" she asked. "I needn't tell you, I'd liefer stand on deck all the way than go back into steerage."

"I'll tell the man fair and square. He's always swearing there's no such thing as an honest female. Let's see what he does when he can't deny it in *you*."

She slumped onto the edge of the lower bunk. "I have no choice," she agreed glumly.

An exultant Wheeler returned to the bridge as fast as his dignity would allow. "Permission, sir?" he asked perfunctorily.

"Well?" Morgan barked.

"The ship's log, sir. I doubt we'll get a true reading, the way it is. I think the carpenter should have a look at it but I believe you should see it first."

"Lead on." A curt nod of the man's head sent him down the after companionway, with the Captain hard on his heels.

"What's all this?" Morgan snapped the moment they were alone on the afterdeck. "Ship's log? Never heard such flannel in my life."

Wheeler gave a rueful smile. "I'm sorry, Cap'n. I should have thought of something better, but I didn't want the quartermaster to overhear. The fact is, Miss O'Dee has not the slightest degree of fever and is unwilling to accept the cabin under false colours."

"Well, why didn't you send her straight back to steerage, you fool?" the Captain asked.

The officer turned from him at once. "Aye aye sir. I just thought that as the decision to send her there had been yours ..."

"Oh, for God's sake leave the little bitch where she is!" Morgan shouted after him. "She'll only moon around on deck and get in the way."

Wheeler, now more committed to the game than was good for either his skin or his career, took his courage in both hands and said, "I think you'll have to tell her that yourself, sir."

"Damned if I will!"

"She's a highly principled and strong-minded young lady, Cap'n."

"Tell her she's in irons. Tell her anything you like — but keep her off my quarterdeck, d'ye hear?"

The officer hesitated just long enough to give Morgan the excuse to explode. "Damm your eyes, Mr Wheeler, but I'll do it myself! I'll give her such a tongue-lashing she won't show her face on deck this side of Boston. But mark'ee now, sir — this will go ill with you in *my* ship's log."

Wheeler responded with an embarrassed shrug. "I'm sorry, Cap'n. I seem to have made a mess of this from start to finish. I can only offer my sincerest apologies, sir."

"Humph!" Morgan strode exultantly past him to the after deckhouse and the companionway down to the second-class quarters.

This was the decisive moment, Wheeler told himself. If Morgan turned and hurled more abuse at him, he was genuine. If not ...

The Captain reached the bulkhead, opened it, turned, saw his First Officer still standing there, looked somewhat surprised — maybe a little abashed — and vanished below without a word.

To his surprise, Wheeler felt the unaccustomed pressure of tears, the merest incipient tears, but tears nonetheless, behind his eyelids. "Dear God!" he murmured. "You stupid ... magnificent ... old man!"

Frank's knock was hesitant, almost boyish; when Teresa cried, "Come in!" she half expected to see a deferential youth there, twisting his cap in his hands. What she actually saw was Captain Morgan, doing a sort of spiritual impersonation of such a lad. His outer manner was as jaunty and brusque as ever, but that was the habit of a lifetime, a matter of bodily momentum that owed nothing to his spirit at that particular moment. It was the eyes that gave him away: wary, respectful, awkward.

"Miss O'Dee," he thundered quietly and strode directly to the porthole. He wiped a finger beneath it, tested it for wetness, and nodded with satisfaction. His manner now suggested he'd accomplished the main purpose of his visit and what followed was mere social obligation. "You're comfortable, I trust?" he asked as offhandedly as he could.

"Indeed and I'm not, Captain," she replied. "I am most uncomfortable at being favoured in this way. I'm here under false pretences and hardly like to ask why."

His eye scanned the bulkhead above, as if the answer might be written there as a kind of crib. "It distressed the men to see you standing there in the cold like that."

"Captain!" she said with weary asperity.

"And Mr Wheeler. It distressed him, too."

He loves me! The words popped suddenly into her mind, out of nowhere. All this while she'd thought only of her own feelings about him, mocking their shallowness — for how could they be anything other than shallow on so short and remote an acquaintance? She had shunned all examination of his, fearing they might turn out to be the usual and she'd only end up with a fight on her hands. But now the truth burst in upon her with all the force of a religious revelation: *He* loved *her!*

An enormous calm suddenly descended on her. He saw it, too — or, rather, he saw that some great change had come over her; so that when she said, "I think it distressed you most of all," he could think of no other reply than a simple "Yes."

She smiled. It was not one of those swift smiles that comes as easily as breathing, but a slow, profound smile that speaks of ecstasies too deep for words. She held out her hands toward him; he took them between his great paws, and for a moment they stared into each other's eyes, hardly able to believe it. He was no longer Captain; she a pauper no more; this was no ship; the storm was past or had never been. This was a moment outside that time and space in which society held sway, or the elements, or even life and death itself. Briefly they were touched with an intimation of immortality.

After that there was no need for words — which was where he at last parted company with that callow, remembered youth who had returned from the grave to lead him to this revelation. The youth would have babbled his surprise, would have overflowed with joy and promises — as once he had to Jenny Bright before she met the Goodwin Sands; the man just squeezed her hands, nodded once or twice, relinquished them unwillingly, and made again for the door.

"Frank," she murmured as his hand touched the knob.

He turned in delighted astonishment, overwhelmed at the intimacy. "Mmm?" It was the nearest thing to a word he could think of.

"Now I *do* have a fever!"

He laughed — and it was that laughter which signed his momentary release. "It's contagious," he assured her as he went out.

HILDA STARED UNHAPPILY at Miss Kernow. The earnest young woman reminded her of someone but she could not think whom. She said, "I find the entire business extremely distasteful," and turned her gaze to the street outside. "I cannot imagine why a supposedly loving Creator ever allowed it in the first place."

Miss Kernow cleared her throat delicately. "The science of zoology ..."

"Zoology!" Hilda exploded. "There you have it, indeed! Zoo-ology! As if *we* were mere creatures in a zoo! I shall have a thing or two to say on Judgement Day, I can promise you." She squared her shoulders and returned to her visitor, gathering her shawl about her more tightly yet. "What have we to do with zoo-ology? Are we made in God's image or that of the baboon?"

Miss Kernow dipped her head as if she were conceding the point. "But as to practical matters," she went on, "I mean, I presume you did warn her to expect some such event?"

For a second or two Hilda made no reply; then she said, more to herself than to the teacher, "Nobody ever warned *me*."

"I found her in the washroom, trying to pour cold

water inside herself, you know. Very cold. It could have brought on a hæmorrhage."

Hilda wrinkled her nose in disgust but said nothing.

"She was almost hysterical," the younger woman continued. "I gave her an assurance that it happens to every young girl at around her age. But I withheld the glad tidings that she may expect it to continue for the next quarter-century." She smiled wanly. "Sufficient unto the day, I thought."

Hilda no longer appeared to be listening. "I've been dreading this," she said. She rose and went back to the window, where she stared up and down the street as if some miraculous deliverance were momentarily expected. "Kathleen's innocence is such an ornament to this household."

"She has two older brothers, I believe?"

The question made Hilda realize who it was the young woman resembled. It was lightly put, almost inconsequential, and yet it could prick like a thorn. "Two," she replied guardedly. "Boys no more. Young men. With all *that* implies! I don't know when I last got the whole truth out of either of them." She turned in the bay window, a hind at bay. "Men are such furtive creatures, don't you find."

Yes! Miss Kernow even had the same smile as Daphne Dowty — knowing, superior, condescending. "Not that they have a monopoly in evasion," the teacher said. Her tone suggested she was offering the most abstract of philosophical comments but her smile made it quite clear that her target was more parochial. However, long experience at trying to cross swords with Daphne made Hilda wary of pitting herself against Miss Kernow, now.

It was absurd. How old was she? Twenty-two, perhaps? She'd be lucky to get a husband now. So why was she, Hilda Morgan, thirty-nine and mother of three, wife of the greatest captain in the Mercantile Marine — why was she deferring to this little chit of a thing? Deferring to? No, that was a bit strong. Entertaining the callow, bookish opinions of? That was more like it. Why was she entertaining such opinions? What could Miss Kernow know of life? Only what she'd read, or picked up in earnest, late-night discussions with others of her type — all second-hand stuff.

"Yes ... well ..." Miss Kernow rose, straightening the fingers of her left hand glove as if pulling an invisible ring onto each finger — exactly as Daphne did it. Hilda had a fleeting intimation that there are probably only two or three dozen human individualities, doled out at random; she rejected the thought at once, as being too uncomfortable to live with. We are what we strive to become. No matter what you were "born to be," you could become anything you wanted, simply by striving hard enough. Except men, of course. They could only struggle so far up the ladder to perfection; the Old Adam would always drag them back a rung or two. But for a woman the possibility was vast. "Yes," she said firmly. "Say not the struggle naught availeth!"

Miss Kernow smiled. Such a charming smile. It was a wonder some man hadn't snapped her up; if *she* were a man, she'd love to kiss such a creature. Hilda frowned at the thought; it was not quite the direction she had intended her mind to go. Meanwhile Miss Kernow was saying, "At the practical, everyday level, Mrs Morgan, I've advised Kathleen to tie a small bandage around her ankle when 'her friend' is visiting, and to find some unostentatious way of letting me or one of the other teachers see it."

Hilda nodded solemnly and rang the bell for one of the maids to show her visitor out. "I shall do all in my power to preserve her innocence, Miss Kernow," she said firmly, knowing that the woman's departure would now preclude any tedious discussion of the business. "Kathleen's virtue and purity is one of the ornaments of this household, the very jewel in our crown. I shall conserve it as if it were my own life, which, indeed, it is."

Miss Kernow was too nonplussed to make any reply to this. She bowed gravely and allowed herself to be shown out.

Hilda returned to the bay window and watched her emerge into the street. She walked a few yards and hesitated. Hilda shrank back into the dark of the room, knowing the woman was going to turn — which, indeed, she did. She stared back at the house, at the windows of the room where she had so lately sat, and shook her head before turning again and resuming her walk.

Was it pity, bewilderment, or admiration? Such an ambiguous gesture. She was so like Daphne! Or like Daphne had been at that age. A great warmth toward the young woman flooded through Hilda's body. She wanted to befriend her, talk to her, warn her … help her to avoid becoming what Daphne had become. She had a delightful vision in which the pair of them walked arm in arm over Highbury Fields on a hot and languorous summer day, as she and Daphne had done in that amazing summer of 'Sixty-six, when she was engaged to Francis and Daphne to Brian. The last summer of their innocence. The last truly happy period of her life, to be honest.

Now she wished she hadn't been quite so offhand with poor little Miss Kernow. She must write her a note … how much she'd enjoyed their little chat … tea, perhaps?

Kathleen entered at that moment. Was it a look of reproach in her eye? Hilda threw her arms wide. "Oh, my poor darling! My poor dove!"

Half the girl fell eagerly into that embrace; half permitted it with some diffidence — the girl and the woman, poised in a gawky balance. "I want to go back to school," she said.

"But you're ill, my pet," her mother objected.

"I'm not," she asserted and then softened it with, "not really, you know. I felt much worse yesterday." She gave a complicit smile. "And now I know why, of course."

Hilda frowned. How could she know? Miss Kernow? Could that woman have had the impudence and bad taste to *explain* the whole business to the girl? Provisional invitations to tea were firmly withdrawn.

"Emma says it's always worse before. She says she feels best of all when …" Kathleen felt her mother stiffen. She withdrew and looked at her in alarm. She had rarely seen such anger in her mother's face. Quickly she sought to appease her: "She was very kind to me. Kinder even than Miss Kernow." Praise hardly came higher; she hoped it was enough.

But her mother's face hardened yet further. "Go to your room, please," she said in a voice ominously quiet.

"What are you going to do to me?" the girl asked.

"Not you. You are the innocent in all this. I will not have you polluted. To your room!"

Kathleen stood her ground. "But what are you going to do? Emma? Is it something about Emma?"

"I shall not tell you again, miss."

"But Emma was only trying to be kind."

42

Her mother took one menacing step toward her and the girl fled. At the threshold she paused. The words formed in her mind: "If you punish Emma for this, I'll never forgive you," but the courage to say them deserted her at the last. She tried to convey the notion with a glance instead.

Five minutes later the housekeeper, Mrs Johnson, ushered — indeed thrust — an apprehensive Emma Harding into Hilda's presence. She sat in the bay window, a prim, dark monolith of righteous indignation. She motioned for the maid to stand before her, some six feet away, and then told Mrs Johnson that would be all. The housekeeper, who could not stoop to eavesdropping in front of the other servants, fled at once to the nether regions of the house — knowing that Nancy and Maria would glue an ear to the door and an eye to the keyhole. The mistress's moods were the weather of the house; to study their changes was as important to the servants as was the mariner's scrutiny of the clouds and winds.

"What have you been telling my daughter?" Hilda asked severely.

"Nothing, m'm." In the year she had been in this house Emma had never seen the mistress like this. Something warned her the moment she entered the room that, no matter what she might now say, she was for the chuck. An odd sort of calm descended on her — or was it a dread too large, too formless for her to apprehend all at once?

"Liar!" Hilda snapped.

Emma gaped at her. It *was* a dread too large and formless to grasp; it left her, for the moment, anæsthetized. She felt almost as if she were outside her own body, hovering somewhere, watching it all without the slightest feeling. She heard her voice say,

"D'you mean about the *flowers*, m'm?"

"Flowers?" It was a moment or two before Hilda recalled the euphemism, which had been common in her own youth. "Yes!" she snapped.

"I only told Miss Kathleen that I always felt worse the days before, m'm, and if I did wrong in that, then I'm truly sorry and will strive to mend my ways, for there was no wickedness intended, I assure you m'm."

Hilda sat there while the flood of practised insincerities poured over her. She felt the initiative drain away as the girl's utter submission, combined with vague notions of fair play and the ideal of the merciful Christian mistress, all tugged at her compassion. The trouble was, she'd always had a liking for young Emma. Such a *pretty* girl. She'd always felt a great sympathy for pretty girls, having been one herself and knowing what a nuisance it can be and the bothersome attentions it brought. Even her own son Lawrence, dragging the poor young maid into the doorway for a kiss last Christmas ...

But she was wandering again — losing the initiative. This time she must not dither. "You said more than that, I believe," she snapped.

Francis would be proud to hear her. He often said she lacked that extra bit of steel in her backbone. Talking of which, the steel in her corsets ... she shook the distraction angrily away and prompted the maid: "Well?"

Emma frowned. She was now quite certain she was going to be dismissed; the only negotiable item was her character. Surely Mrs Morgan wouldn't let her go without a character? "I truly can't remember saying more than what I just told you I done, m'm," she declared.

"Not that ... that ..." Hilda began an angry search for suitable euphemisms. "... that the arrival of 'your friend' was the happiest omen?"

"Omen?"

"Sign. Event. Occurrence. Did you not tell her it made you very happy?"

"No, m'm. Honest. I may have said it was a relief, but ..."

"Relief! Relief! Will you hark at the baggage! How dare you put such notions into the head of that innocent and pure young dove? Relief, indeed!"

Aghast, Emma now saw where her inept choice of words had led her. "But I never meant relief like that, m'm. Honest. I only meant relief from the discomfort and that, you know — the days before, like what I said was — you know ..." She lost her way in a many-branching delta of confusions.

"Well I'm sorry, Harding, but I simply don't believe you. Wouldn't it just tickle your degraded sense of humour to put such wicked thoughts, all in the guise of ..."

"Degraded?" Emma asked. The first hint of anger crept into her tone.

"Don't you dare interrupt me!" Hilda barked. "Do you dare question me?"

"Did you call me degraded?" Emma asked, now bold enough to square up to her formidable challenger.

"I said you have a degraded sense of humour," Hilda explained. Why did it now sound like a softening of the opinion? "Yes!" she snapped. "If you want it unadorned, I believe that anyone who tells an innocent young girl that 'flowers' spells relief is degraded. Anyway, I'm not here to bandy words with such a creature. I simply wish you to be out of this house by this evening."

The expected sentence was nonetheless a shock. Emma could only stand and stare.

"Surely you're not surprised?" Hilda pressed home her advantage.

It was a moment when anything could happen. Emma knew that if she went down on her knees, flung her arms about her mistress, sank her head in her lap, sobbed, begged to keep her place ... she knew Hilda Morgan well enough to be quite sure she'd capitulate. There'd be a tearful scene ... hugs ... she might even get a kiss on the brow; and a week later it would all be forgotten. She was a strange one, all right. Always trying to stir up feelings, touching you, giving your arm a reassuring squeeze over nothing. And you knew she couldn't help it; that's the way she was. Even now, with this terrible sentence just pronounced — a sentence to poverty and a genuine degradation if no character were forthcoming — even now, she could not find it in herself to hate the woman. Pity, yes. But how could you hate someone so trapped by her own feelings?

A mischievous imp urged her to do it. "Go on, gel!" it said. "You wouldn't feel a thing. It's the only power you've got over her — twist her heart! She'd be putty in your hands."

But the horror of becoming the sort of person who could obey such impulses restrained her. And behind it lay an even vaguer dread: that, though she might very easily bend Hilda Morgan to her will, there would, nonetheless, be some nameless emotional debt to discharge at some indeterminate point in the future. In the end the intimation of that formless but powerful obligation stopped her ears to all impish suggestions. "And my character, m'm?" she asked as meekly as she could.

"Character?" Hilda asked incredulously. "You may whistle for it!" Why had the girl's response left her so bitter and angry? What else had she expected? She was now, quite possibly, ruining the maid's life. No! She dismissed the thought out of hand. The wretched creature had brought it on herself. Never overlook that. She had brought it on herself.

Emma licked her lips. "And I'm due the month's wages, m'm."

"You may whistle for that, too."

The bonds of humility snapped. Emma stood up straight. "That's not fair!"

Hilda rose hastily, bringing herself to the same height as the maid. "As I said, I'm not going to bandy words. I want you gone by this evening."

"Gone? Where? Where shall I go? You know I can't go anywhere without money and a character."

Hilda brushed past her. "By this evening," she repeated.

Nancy and Maria just made it to the safety of the master's dressing room; they stared at each other in wide-eyed bewilderment and fanned their faces with spread-eagled hands.

Hilda went out onto the landing, leaving the door ajar behind her. She grasped the banister rail and stared down into the empty hall, which the long-case clock filled with its deep, imperturbable tick, tock, tick, tock … Such a comforting resonance it had; it had counted out the seconds in just those tones for as long as she could remember — for it had followed her here from her childhood home.

All those seconds! And you couldn't call even one of them back — what was the poem?

Never mind — Francis would be proud of her.

Why did she not feel better for knowing that?

Behind her, Emma simply stood and stared at that imperturbable back. She had just discovered how you could, after all, hate someone who was such a victim of her own feelings. "Right then," she said to herself. "You started it!"

S THE STORM TRACKED east the winds moved around to the north, settling finally into a great, howling monster on the starboard beam, now scant, now leading. Though *Pegasus* must be drawing ever-nearer its edge, there was no slackening in its fury. The glass, which had remained steady but low for the past thirty-six hours, while the eye of the storm had counter-moved more or less parallel to their course, now began relentlessly to fall. By the evening of that Tuesday, the second of their voyage, it stood as low as Morgan had ever seen it in thirty years at sea.

"Either she's turned north-east and is coming to get us or she's deepening," he said to Wheeler.

"... and still coming to get us," the First Officer added grimly. "I've never sailed faster with so little canvas. At this rate, we'll take the bare-mast riband for east-to-west."

Morgan grunted and returned to the chart. "I wish we could place more reliance on that log. We know how far west we've gone" — he drew an invisible circle on the Atlantic chart with the dividers, which were still set to his previous calculations — "but how far south, eh?"

The pair of them stared at the long New England shoreline, where the answer to that question could mean the difference between foundering today, running aground tomorrow, or missing the land by a whisker or a hundred miles and having to turn round and sail north again when the storm blew itself out. Neither said a word — or needed to.

At that moment an almighty wave caught them on the starboard quarter and hurled them half a mile, or so it seemed, toward the American shore before plucking them back again and dropping them into what felt like the very deeps of the mælstrom. The storm caught the crest of water as it rose over the decks and turned it to a kind of white shot — pellets of freezing ocean that bombarded the watch and stung like hornets even through oilcloth.

Both officers were thrown in a heap against the far wall of the chartroom, with a ferocity that finally made up Morgan's mind. "We must wear ship, Mr Wheeler," he commanded. "Set mizzen and mizzen-staysail and shiver the fore-trysail."

The First Officer hesitated the barest moment, as the unfamiliar manoeuvre quickly shaped itself in his mind. He frowned.

Morgan, who would normally have barked the order again at anyone who dared so much as hesitate, merely nodded and said, "I know. But I daren't face her arse into this sea."

"We've both watches on deck at the moment, sir. Shall I stand the port watch by to set head yards and fore-topsail?"

Morgan nodded, gave a severe little smile, and said, "Good man yourself."

"Aye aye, Cap'n!" He went out on deck to relay the order. Morgan followed in moments.

Grim though the situation was, Wheeler had time to reflect that his Captain's final words were more Irish than English, certainly not the sort of phrase one expected to hear from his lips — not before *this* voyage, anyway, he added to himself with a smile.

It was his last smile for a considerable time. The process of wearing ship — that is, of bringing her about until the wind is on the opposite side from wherever it was before — is, if not the trickiest, certainly the busiest of all nautical movements, even in a moderate breeze. In a storm, or great storm, it is not for the faint of heart to attempt. But at least on *Pegasus* every man could stay down on deck and pull with all his muscle instead of wasting his strength shinning up the ratlines into the yards and clinging on for dear life.

For the first few minutes all went well. The quartermaster put the helm hard down, and she slewed gratifyingly to port — with considerable assistance from the mizzen behind him. But as she got up into the wind, or "in irons," as the saying so accurately has it, she was taken aback and began to move as fast downwind to stern as she had previously, when running before it. Nothing, it seemed then, would make her come about that last few degrees, bringing the weather onto her port bow, where she would head into the waves and ride them out better.

Morgan then gave the order he had never thought to hear issue from his own lips — certainly not in such weather as this: "Counterbrace the fore-topsail. Set and close-reef the main-top!"

Not a man hesitated, though all were sure it was the last desperate throw in a life-or-death gamble with the laws of seamanship, a gamble that had already failed. *Pegasus* yawed and shuddered as the wind found its two new playthings. The masts groaned and shrieked while a merciless pressure built up. A great trembling seemed to possess the ship and to pass out into the storm-blackened waters all about her.

"She won't hold, Cap'n!" The quartermaster

struggled with all his might against the wheel.

The two officers tore their eyes from the canvas and sprang to help him. In the lurid, fitful light of the dying day they were like three creatures from the pit, devils with devilish faces and a strength born of devilish desperation.

At least they held her. If she wouldn't wear right round and come up on the starboard tack, at least she held her direction, head-up to the wind. How many miles leeway they sacrificed in the achievement was anybody's guess, but with the three-quarters of the Atlantic astern, that was hardly a present worry.

"Brace by the main-top," was Morgan's next command, and even he could hardly believe he was giving it, for it really was the last desperate gamble of the day, equivalent to saying, "If her head won't wear, tip her to starboard and see how she likes it!"

Incredibly, she liked it!

Before she'd developed even half a list to starboard she was back again, responding to the helm and coming up nicely on the starboard tack — except that her yards were now set at about the worst possible angle to the wind.

"Starboard your helm," Morgan cried and, leaving Wheeler and the quartermaster to manage as best they could, he ran to the rail and yelled, "Brace up all yards. Take in all fore-and-aft canvas."

"The cheek of the devil," they called it later when each nerve-rending second of that extraordinary act of seamanship was recounted in shanty and story in dockside taverns around the world. But it worked — as the singers and yarn-spinners were there to witness. *Pegasus* settled down to stay on the starboard tack until dawn, with the wind foul to port and the sea dead against her. Maybe she'd lose more leeway;

maybe she'd do no more than hold her station; maybe the wind would now take hold of her and sweep her inexorably into the storm's eye.

The dawn would tell.

But as she settled to her new course and the keel righted and the canvas filled, a great, spontaneous cheer went up from all hands. Old Morgan had done it again. He had tossed his contempt into the teeth of the gale ... and the gale had yielded to its master. They'd sail to hell and back with him now.

T HE RUN FROM TILBURY to Hamburg was considered a bit of a "bus-driver's job" among seafaring men. To be sure, they treated the German Ocean itself with the respect its mercurial moods and past ferocity demanded, but the business at either end — running up the Thames or the Elbe, berthing, discharging, and taking on new cargo — all this had to be managed with the proficiency of a bus setting down and taking up its passengers. The *Horsa*, registered at Lloyd's for 1,800 tons, was a typical case in point.

After no more than twelve hours in Tilbury, during which she discharged a cargo of small German steam engines and dried fish and took on a load of seasoned tropical timber and Kentish hops, she cast off and made half-steam ahead down the Thames on the thirty-hour crossing to Germany. Her hatches were still open, the derricks still deployed — and Lawrence Morgan was still on board, checking the mate's receipts and signing the bills of lading "for and on behalf of the captain."

"Late again, Mr Morgan," the mate said, sucking a tooth disparagingly and shaking his head as the vessel began to heave and roll beneath them.

Lawrence, who did it all on purpose, of course, merely smiled as he signed his last flourish. Then, gathering up the manifests, papers, and money in his battered old black bag, he ran up on deck, crying over his shoulder, "My mother always said there'd be days like this!"

A loud huzzah went up from the crew, who were just starting to timber the hatches. "This way, if you please, *Mister* Morgan, sir!" The bosun swept off his cap and gave an ironic bow, ushering Lawrence to the side, where the rope ladder still dangled precariously.

With all the agility of a reckless youth of eighteen (or, as he would say, "nineteen, jolly nearly!"), he bit on the handle of the bag, letting it swing between the ladder and his chest, and went down two ratlines at a time to the waterman's rickety little boat, which was trailing by a single rope. A moment later they were both rowing like demons to get out of the *Horsa's* wash. It was a well-practised routine by now.

So, too, was that wonderful moment when he rested oar and watched the mighty hull (as it seemed from down there on the river) draw out into the tiderace and start buffeting her way down to the sea. Old Harry Wicks, the waterman, gave his young companion the sort of pitying look that sober men give to drunkards. "Be thankful you'll sleep ashore tonight, sir," he said grimly. "There's a great storm a-coming or I've never tasted salt."

But Lawrence did not take his eyes off the boat. At that moment he could imagine nothing more splendid than to be aboard her, steaming into the teeth of a storm. He thought of Neil, his older brother, who was due to sail that evening from Hull to Rotterdam in the *Swallow*. Neil would probably give half his wage to jump into a waterman's boat and return to shore like this. Last time he'd been home, they'd hatched an absurd plot whereby Neil would pay himself off the *Swallow* and he, Lawrence, would give in his notice at Furnival's and then they'd be free to assume each other's names and occupations. It would work, too, except for one little fly in the ointment: Too many men on the Baltic knew "good old Cap'n Morgan"; word of their subterfuge would be bound to get out.

On the train from Tilbury back to London another strategy occurred to him. In a month or two he'd have worked long enough at Furnival's to ask for a salary; at the moment he was working "for experience only" — and, by his reckoning, earning between twenty and thirty quid a week for the firm, by the charters he wrote and all the other little dogsbody jobs he did, like the one today in Tilbury. Being the skinflints they were, they'd probably refuse. Then he'd have every reason to move on somewhere else — Runciman, perhaps, or Craven — anyone who had branch offices in Glasgow, Cardiff, Bristol … a million miles from Highbury. He'd offer to start in one of the provincial offices — which, with his London knowledge and experience, would seem very attractive to them. Then, when it was all arranged, Neil would take the position, calling himself Lawrence; while he, Lawrence, could sign on with a new tramp steamer under the name of Neil.

He was so delighted at his own ingenuity that, having dropped the papers and money at the office, he set off home, almost forgetting the last errand of his day — or the last official one, anyway. He had gone some way beyond the offices of John Pirie & Co before he remembered it. In fact, Albert Crane, the bookie's runner, who covered his tracks by selling evening papers as a sideline, had spotted Lawrence and was just getting ready to pass him his winnings when the young man punched himself on the forehead with alarming vigour and, turning on his heel, retreated the way he had come.

Pirie & Co's office was up on the first floor. Mr Knight, the clerk, looked to see who it was — though the beefy stamp of the young man's hobnail boots should have been signal enough by now — and said, "Go in." That was all he ever said, either "Go in," or "He's out." Never a smile, never another word. Lawrence sniffed and went directly into the sanctum.

Mr Heriot's desk, as usual, contained nothing but a copy of that day's *Times* — and, to be sure, Mr Heriot's elbows, which supported his hands, which supported his head in the seemingly onerous task of perusing the commercial columns. Mr Heriot did not look up.

"Please, sir, are you open for Singapore?" Lawrence asked diffidently.

Mr Heriot had a skull like eggshell; Lawrence supposed it might break very easily with one blow of a good fist.

"Hah!" Mr Heriot barked — and went on reading without looking up.

"Sir," Lawrence persisted, "I have a steamer that wants Singapore."

"Hmph!" Heriot's ears twitched.

"Five thousand tons. Ready Swansea twenty-fifth of March."

"Mmmm." It was the petulant sort of noise a dog makes when the weather cheats it of a walk.

Lawrence had a pleasant reverie in which his fist went crashing through the eggshell bone and made a satisfying pulp of the stubborn matter beneath it.

"Or two thousand tons, ready Cardiff on the twenty-eighth."

Heriot made no response at all to this. Lawrence waited a moment or two and then, with a silent bow, left the room.

In that brief scene everything he loathed about this trade — the trade his father had bound him to — had come welling to the surface: the hostility of those who should be cooperating in such simple matters of commerce, the rudeness, the contempt of men-of-little-power for those with even less. By God, he'd rather work the dirtiest tramp with the drunkenest, most foul-mouthed master to Archangel and back in January than put up with all this for another week!

Back in the street he almost bowled over a gentleman who was passing by; there was something familiar about him but in the confusion Lawrence could not place the man.

"Well well," exclaimed his near-victim with a jovial smile. "Just run across old Heriot, have we? But see here, there's no need to take it out on the populace, you know."

Lawrence recognized him then: Mr William Wright of Wright Bros & Co. He began to stammer his apologies, but the man cut him short with a breezy, "No harm done!" Then he gave a quizzical smile and, raising a finger toward the window of Heriot's office, asked lightly, "Much joy?"

"Not a sniff, sir. Are you, by any chance open for Singapore?"

"What have you got?"

Lawrence gave him the same two vessels, which they fixed on the spot at a rate pleasing to both. Wright said he was open for Azoff and the Danube, too (for it was really his brother who handled the Oriental trade) and Lawrence racked his photographic memory for Furnival's ships that wanted those destinations. In all, he fixed five vessels, there and then on the foot pavement outside Heriot's office. Then, while Wright continued on his way to the Baltic, in the old South Sea Bubble building, Lawrence returned to Furnival's to record his coup with William Wright.

Old Furnival was only half pleased; a few more like that and he couldn't possibly go on withholding his offer of a salary.

The trouble with me, Lawrence told himself as he went to collect his winnings off Albert Crane, the best impersonator of a newsvendor in Bishopsgate, *is that I'm just too bloody good at this trade.*

"You done it again, squire," Bert said as Lawrence drew near. "That's your second treble this month. Honest Jim's crying mercy — says you'll put him in Carey Street if you go on like this." The crisp, white fiver was neatly folded into *The Pink 'Un.* A peeler could be standing two feet away and not see it.

"May I live to see the day, Bert," Lawrence replied. "The gypsy said I'll see a hundred, anyway."

"With your luck and all!" Bert's eyes never stopped roving, this way and that, up and down the street — looking for the boys in blue, the boys with the bets, and a few, like Lawrence, returning for their winnings.

"There's seven bob on top of this, isn't there?" Lawrence added. "Keep it for tomorrow's stake."

"Oh, yeah." Bert grinned as if he'd hoped to get away with it.

Lawrence continued on toward Farringdon for the tram out to Highbury, on which he'd pick tomorrow's winners. It was too late to bank his winnings now. He'd have to hide them carefully; he was sure Mrs Johnson was nursing her suspicions. Ever since he'd offered Emma a couple of quid to let him touch her up. Emma must have ratted on him. Two quid was almost three months' earnings for her, so you couldn't blame her for boasting how she'd turned it down. But old Pruneface Johnson would have sniffed a rat at once. Half a crown was more the mark for a lad his age on a salary of nix-nihil per annum.

He slid the fiver from his jacket pocket down into the one inside his trouser belt and buried his face in *The Pink 'Un* while he waited for the tram. This had been his daily ritual even as a schoolboy, when all his wagers had been on paper only, betting against himself in a little pocketbook where he kept the tally. Lawrence the bookmaker had lost close on eighty-five quid by the end of the year, even though Lawrence the punter had never bet above five bob on any race — though, to be sure, a five-bob treble that comes up can be worth twenty quid or more on the third horse. Now, thanks to his early start in the game, Lawrence virtually carried the form book around in his head, only needing to refresh it each day to keep it in tip-top, bookie-milking condition. In the eight or nine months since last summer, when he started at Furnival's, he'd won nearly two hundred pounds — more than his chief clerk took home in a year.

He had to keep reminding himself of it: *Two hundred quid was a lot of spondulicks and don't you forget it, Lawrence, me old pal — or you'll go and do other rash things like offering two quid to the likes of Emma Harding.* But he couldn't help smiling every time he thought of it; she'd have been worth every penny. Pretty little thing. Perhaps she'd thought it over since then? Changed her mind, maybe. He shouldn't have sprung it on her.

His fancy began to reshape the incident the way it might have gone — until the reverie grew so hot and pleasurable he had to tear himself reluctantly from it and concentrate on tomorrow's card, instead. The tram was nearing the top of Cannonbury Road before he settled on Daddy's Girl in the two-thirty at Sydenham and Tomahawk in the four o'clock at Shelburne Park; two bob to win and five for a place. And another thirty-eight bob to him if they both came up. Every little helps, as the sailor said when he pissed off London Bridge at low tide.

When the tram drew near the halt at Highbury Circus, the conductor happened to be on the front platform, beside Lawrence and a couple of others who were waiting (at the wrong end) to alight — which was how Lawrence overheard him say to the driver, "Blimey, she's still there!"

"I see that," the other responded.

Incuriously Lawrence stared at the waiting line ahead to try and guess who they might mean ... and then blinked his eyes and stared again.

Talk of the devil, it was undoubtedly Emma Harding standing there! Waiting for him? Must be. Bad news at home? His heart missed a beat. Something had happened at home ... his mother ... or Kathleen. They were ... He deliberately did not pursue the notion. But why else would she be *still* there, in the conductor's own words? Obviously she was waiting for him. He was the only member of the family who ever used this tram.

Then he saw she had a battered cardboard suitcase and an old Gladstone bag at her feet, at which point the mystery passed beyond all practical guesswork. The driver gave the reins a sudden twitch, hauled at the brake, and the tram came groaning to a halt.

"Does this go to Whitechapel?" Emma shouted across the road to the driver.

The man started to direct her to the appropriate stop in the Ball's Pond Road but Lawrence cut across with, "Emma! What on earth are you doing here?" He leaped down in one bound and skipped across the carriageway to her, earning the curses of a draymaster, who had hoped to get by before the tram disgorged its passengers.

She stared at him in surprise. Then, to his acute embarrassment, she cried out, "Oh, Mr Lawrence!" and burst into tears.

T HE GREAT STORM, which was at that moment testing Cap'n Morgan's seamanship to the limit, and whose portents were soon to cause the waterman, Harry Wicks, to utter his dire forecast, had not even begun to stir the air over the Humber. A heavy, oily fog drifted upriver, clinging to the waters and turning the noonday brightness to a dreary amber twilight. The masts and funnels of the ships on the quay opposite *Swallow* were no longer visible, as they had been an hour earlier. The crew became uneasy, anxious, and Neil Morgan began to feel for himself what his father had so often said — that fog was the seaman's bitterest enemy.

This Humber fog did not stretch in a uniform cloud over the town of Hull, and its docks and ships; rather it drifted in patches, some thick enough to obscure your view of your own hand, others so meagre you could see clear across the decks.

Slim, the fat bosun, clapped a familiar hand on Neil's shoulder. "'Tis the ghosts of all the drowned seamen, matey," he said, "come to warn us not to put to sea."

He had timed his comment perfectly for at that moment the command came from the bridge, "Let go head rope. Quarter ahead."

There was a blast from the ship's hooter. The deck began to throb to the beat of the pistons below. A dark shape, vaguely remembered as the side of a warehouse on the quay, grew paler and vanished. It was the only landward sign that *Swallow* was moving at last.

Both watches were on deck for, like the *Horsa* in Tilbury — which Lawrence was at that moment clearing to sail — nothing was done in port that could not be done cheaper on the way down the estuary; wharves charged demurrage but the tideway was free.

"Right, lads! Let's get this …"

Another blast drowned the bosun's orders. Into its dying echo he called, "All ashore that's going ashore!" In a softer tone he added, "And if you can find it, let us know."

Men laughed reluctantly, not that they found it unfunny but the density of the fog worried them. Their only gauge of the ship's speed was the drift of what Slim had called "ghosts" along the deck toward the stern; and, since the breeze was off the sea, it made them appear to be going at a fair rate of knots. To compound matters, a ship in steam on the farther quay sounded her siren at that moment; the vapour magnified its intensity so that it seemed alarmingly close. They cursed *Swallow* for being a steamship; no vessel with sails could even think of putting to sea in a fog like this, with both wind and tide against her.

But the pilot knew the river well enough to keep them out of trouble. The "policeman" in the bow sang out his sightings of each chequered can buoy within moments of the pilot's prediction that it was coming up. All hands meanwhile settled to their tasks, some to clearing the decks of dunnage, others to timbering the hatches. Later came the tarpaulins, neatly tucked around the combings, "like a virgin's knickers," as Slim commented to Neil, who laughed hugely. The carpenter was hammering in the wedges as the policeman called out his final sighting, the white can buoy with cage and light, which marks the southern limit of the Humber estuary.

The men straightened their backs and made exaggerated noises of relief. "All right, all right," Slim cried. "Rogers and Willis, port and starboard lookouts. The rest of you, ten minutes for cocoa."

"And rum," Thomson, the leading seaman, added.

"Kind of you to offer, matey," Slim rejoined. "Come on, Mister, you and me's the only ones with any spirit left. We'll get the cocoa." His final survey challenged any man to add the explanation that he and Neil were also the only ones who had not bent their backs for the last hour. But their grins said it for them as they shuffled off to the forecastle. Slim and Neil turned back toward the galley kiddley.

"Cocoa for a hundred and fifty, chef!" the bosun called through the porthole as they passed.

The cook had it all ready for them, a steaming urn with quantities measured precisely for ten. "And the Vienna pastries?" Slim asked with a wink at Neil.

"Burnt them," the cook replied solemnly. "You'll have to go without today."

The *Swallow* made a sudden rolling heave as she passed beyond Spurn Head and met the German Ocean. Neil felt the first rumblings of nausea.

The young man's position as cadet aboard *Swallow* was ambiguous. He was not an officer, though that was his destiny. He called the officers "sir" and the men by name; the men called him Mister, and the bosun — or this particular bosun — sometimes called him matey. He did not engage in the purely manual tasks of the crew, such as battening down hatches, but he was supposed to learn the true skills of seamanship, from the handling of ropes to taking his turn at the helm.

All these tasks he had tried to learn on the *Orestes*, but things had gone wrong there in ways he still could not understand. His papa had said he might do better on a little tramp like *Swallow*. "She's nearer the water," he explained. And it was true, though Neil still couldn't see how that helped.

Swallow was not big enough to have her own quartermaster; everyone took a hand at the helm. Neil and young Freddy Bowles, an ordinary seaman on his first voyage, had their turn during the dog watches. During each voyage Neil would spend part of his time with the day men and part with each of the watches, port and starboard.

It had been interesting enough on his first voyage or two — so much so that he had begun to think his father's judgement was right and his own instincts were wrong. But already it was beginning to pall. The conviction was once again growing within him that, no matter how hard he *strove*, to use his mother's favourite word, to become a true seaman like his father, he would never do more than play the role. He might become the greatest actor in the world at it, but it would never be more than acting. A bit like Aunt Daphne; she always seemed to be acting her part in life. She always left you wondering what sort of person she'd really be if only she could break out of her present rôle.

"Getting thinner," Slim commented as they carried the urn between them to the forecastle. "I smell foul weather a-brewing." This last comment was added as they went within.

"What d'you call this, then?" asked Jakobsson, the Swede.

The siren's moan backed him up.

"Now if it's foul weather you want," Slim replied, filling a mug for Neil and then his own, "did I ever tell you of the time we sailed from Liverpool on the old *Maude*, a coaster bound for Avonmouth?"

He clearly had, but that didn't stop them settling to enjoy it again.

"She was sailing light, with just a few bales of cotton," he said, ushering Neil into the seat beside him. "You don't know that coast, I suppose, Mister? No. Wild Wales, they call it." He shivered. All hands dutifully shivered in sympathy. "Anyway, the moment we rounded the Skerries we hit a sou'wester like a fist." He set down his cup and drove his fist into his left palm. "Stopped us like that on every crest. Skerries to Holyhead took us four hours! The skipper, Cap'n Mann ..." His eyes roved among his hearers. "You knew old Grizzly Mann, didn't you, Dead-Eye?"

The sailor nodded and sucked wind through clenched teeth. "I knew *him* right enough! What a fate! What a fate for any man!"

"Why, what happened to him?" Neil asked.

"Ah, matey, hearken and it shall be made known unto ye! Old Grizzly was no sailor to go running for port in a storm, not even on a little coaster like the *Maude*. But he turned and ran into Holyhead that night, and no second thoughts." He sipped his cocoa with relish and shook his head at the memory.

"Howsomever, he couldn't abide it long, sitting in port doing nothing while our cargo of cotton rotted in the hold. And blow me down if, an hour later, he didn't ship anchor and put out again! Even the Irish boats were standing to their berths that night, but not old Grizzly. Talk about buffeting! I'll swear there were solid spars floating in every wave. You could hear them hammering into our bows like piledrivers. And poor old *Maude,* she chucked herself every way but turtle." He waited for the groans.

"Well, after four hours we could still see the breakwater light at Holyhead. I don't think we made a yard. And as for *steering* her, that was a joke. She saw more points of the compass that night than on all her other voyages put together. Grizzly cursed the helmsman but that was just his way. He knew he couldn't have done better hisself." He stared around to make sure he still had them with him.

"And then, around first light, six bells of the morning watch, a sort of haze fell down on top of the storm — thick as what this is now only howling with it. We lost sight of land at once, of course."

A shiver went round the forecastle; the present fog was bad enough in all conscience but to have it combine with a roaring gale was almost past imagining.

Slim went on: "Even old Grizzly beshat his breeches at that, but there was nothing we could do, only sail on by compass — one little spanker, that's all we dared show. And for three days we never got sight nor sniff of land. We had the ocean to ourselves, for there was no other fool who dared go out. And the weather never bettered itself once, nor the haze never lifted, neither. We could have been anywhere — off Wicklow Head or back in Liverpool — for all we knew. The log registered two knots, but what does that tell you when such a sea's running?"

He paused again to let the siren have its say.

"And what happened?" Neil asked, all agog by now. He had always loved the sea at second hand.

"What happened? What happened?" Slim asked dramatically. "Why we kept on piledriving into them seas, that's what happened. On the third night someone said he saw a light, but my opinion is it was the crest of a wave and the man was tired. But on the fourth day she lifted a bit and we got a fix at last. And d'you know where we were? Off Douglas Head, Isle of Man! 'Course, old Grizzly was like a dog with two pricks. 'Didn't I tell ye! Didn't I tell ye!' But *I* tell *ye* now, mateys — the haze came down again and the winds rose and that was the last we saw of land for another *seven days!*"

A groan of disbelief went up. "What? In the Irish Sea and never saw land for seven days? Tell it to the Horse Marines!"

"Seven days!" Slim insisted. "And when we did, it was Howth Head off Dublin Bay!"

Neil's eyes darted between the storyteller and his audience, wondering which could be right. The bosun was very convincing, and the crew, for all their naysaying, seemed more than half inclined to believe him still. Except for the Swede. "And then, I suppose, you lost sight of it again for *another* seven days!" he jeered.

Slim leaned across the table and jabbed him in the ribs. "Fifteen!" he gasped hoarsely. "And my, weren't we just desperate by then!" He turned to Neil and explained, "On a coaster, you understand, each hand brings his own grub. There's no stores. So you only bring enough for the voyage — and Liverpool to

Avonmouth is only three days. I tell you — we was chewing canvas and scraping for barnacles by then."

"Fifteen days!" Jakobsson echoed in disgust. "And where was it, eh? The Cape of Good Hope?"

"Sydney Heads," chimed in another.

"Labrador!" The ribald suggestions came thick and fast now.

Slim remained imperturbable until it subsided. "You're all wrong," he told them calmly. "You couldn't be more wrong. Our next sight of land, after twenty-eight days at sea, was ... the Bar Light on Liverpool River!"

"And still the storm raged," the Swede mocked, "and you couldn't get over the bar, and so you lost sight of land for another month, I suppose!"

Slim pointed at him as a teacher might point to the brightest boy in the class. "I could almost believe you was there, Swede," he said admiringly.

"But you must have been starving," Neil objected. "How did you manage?"

A hush fell. Slim looked all about them, checked there was no one at the door before he dared answer. "We started on the ship's cat, matey," he said in a sepulchral growl. "That was off the Isle of Man. A Manx cat, it was, so at least it died in home waters. And then" — he checked all around again, and the entire company leaned expectantly nearer him as his voice dropped to a conspiratorial whisper — "well, the fact is ... but don't you dare breathe a word of this to a living soul, not *ever* — I, yours truly, Slim Watson as ever lived, I was the *sole survivor* of that dreadful voyage."

A great roar of laughter went up and hands reached forward to punch Neil playfully with an ever-been-had grin.

"Come on mateys!" Slim roared above the merriment. "This ship won't sail herself. Port watch on deck — and you, too, Mister, if you please."

Of course, Neil didn't believe Slim's tale — not that he ate the *whole* crew. Still, even eating one or two was pretty bad. He doubted he'd have the courage to do such a thing, no matter how starved he was. It just showed — what he'd always told his father — he wasn't really cut out for the sea at all.

B Y FOUR BELLS of the middle watch, no one could any longer pretend that the roaring off the port beam was anything other than surf. Wheeler sent for Captain Morgan, who had gone to his cabin only three hours earlier, having been sleepless for nearly forty-eight before that. It speaks of the depths of the man's exhaustion that the pounding of that surf had not already roused him.

Within the minute the Captain was on deck again. No verbal report was needed. The roar to port was saying it all.

"You've dropped anchor?" he asked.

"Just before two bells, Cap'n."

"How many fathoms is she drawing?"

"More than twenty. The lead returns clean and scratched."

They were over rocks, then. Morgan asked grimly: "Is she dragging?"

"No sir. She seems to be holding. The sea anchor's slack and there's no sign of a tide."

"Then it's probably not Nova Scotia. Let's look at the chart. The question is, *which* chart!" He turned his face briefly skyward. "One star, that's all we ask." But the vault above remained as darkly impenetrable as ever.

"Better turn out the morning watch," he added as they spread the charts before them.

In the end they settled for somewhere off the coast of Maine — anywhere between Portsmouth and Isle au Haut. Whatever shore it was, the pounding they could hear not a mile away, was of a ferocity that would reduce *Pegasus* to matchwood. There was nothing they could do but sit it out and pray that the anchor held.

"Those tables in the forr'ard hold," Morgan said as they returned to the bridge. "Get the carpenter to have a look at them. See if he can cobble three or four rafts out of them."

Wheeler went to relay the command. When he returned, Morgan added, as if there had been no interruption, "We haven't boats enough to save all passengers, let alone all hands."

It was a sombre note on which to await the dawn.

When it came at last it proved the harbinger of bad tidings. The First Mate, McLennan, whose watch was about to stand down, reported to the bridge that the seaman in the chains said he thought she was dragging her anchor. Morgan ran forr'ard to see for himself. He gripped the cable where it passed through the hawse pipe ... and the last remnant of hope died within him. The cable was as taut as a violin string. He could almost *hear* the scratching, grinding sound of the anchor as it slithered over the rocky bed of the sea — not evenly but in fits and starts. He could certainly feel the telltale vibration in the anchor chain itself.

"Is all the chain paid out?" he asked.

"Aye, Cap'n."

He formulated his plan as he ran back to the bridge,

calling both mates and the bosun as he went.

"We're going to cut and run for it," he told them, "though we've no room to put up canvas and go about. I'm going to turn her on her anchor chain. Feehan, take two men and file a nick in the link at the hawse mouth, inside. McLennan, take the whole port watch and bend the stern rope to the anchor chain just outside the hawse pipe. The after breast, too, if you have time. Strain them up hard. Jump to it now!"

When they had gone he told Wheeler to take the starboard watch and prepare to set the storm trysail and mizzen-top — and then to set them without waiting for a command as soon as they felt the wind large on her port quarter.

The port watch got the stern rope bent to the anchor chain in less than five minutes — finishing just as Feehan's gang managed to weaken the link in the hawse pipe to the point where two or three sharp blows with a maul would snap it. Both reported to the bridge simultaneously. Morgan gripped the port rail and listened to the roar of the surf. It was beyond doubt much closer now. He guessed they had lost half the open water between *Pegasus* and the breakers since he had come on deck.

"Sir, the anchor's holding again!" A breathless seaman reported directly to the bridge.

It seemed like a gift from the gods. If she could only hold station until daylight, their chances of surviving these present perils would be a hundred times better. He sent Feehan back to the cable locker, to stand by, ready to break that link. He sent the port watch to relieve the by now exhausted men with Wheeler, who had been on deck since midnight after disrupted watches for several days; he told them to find what shelter they could but to stand by to set canvas if the link snapped or if she started to drag her anchor again. And then came the worst time of all — the time when he could do nothing but stand and wait for the dawn, which, if this were, indeed, the coast of Maine, should be around three bells of the morning watch.

Three hours to go!

Three hours in which every nerve would be racked between the state of the weakened anchor chain and the unremitting roar of the surf. Three hours in which his command was useless — for what orders could he issue beyond, "Stand by!"? And hope. And pray.

Three hours in which he would somehow have to restrain himself from going aft to the second-class cabins — to one particular second-class cabin — and helping its occupant to save her own life.

At last he could bear it no longer. He sent the bosun to relieve Wheeler, whom he called to the bridge.

"I'm going to rouse the passengers," he said.

"You, sir?" The First Officer was taken aback — and too tired not to blurt out his surprise.

"It will alert them as to how grave our situation is," Morgan explained. The words were so confident he even convinced himself of his intentions. "Also I trust it will have a calming effect."

"Even the steerage passengers, sir?" Wheeler asked, as if that had really been the cause of his amazement.

"I'll tell them not to come on deck," Morgan assured him. He went forr'ard to alert the steerage first.

Poor bastards! he thought as he stood in the men's dormitory, wrinkling his nose against the intolerable fug that had built up down there ever since they had been forced to plug the ventilators. It was hard to say which was worse — the men's or the women's. He was doubly glad now that he'd got Miss O'Dee out of here when he did.

"There is no question of abandoning ship," he assured them. "But we are anchored too close inshore for our health. As soon as it's daylight and we can see what we're doing — which will be in about two hours' time — we're going to weigh anchor and make for deeper waters where we can continue to ride out this storm in comfort." He laid an ironic stress upon the phrase, which brought a startled laugh or two from his sleep-sodden hearers. "However, for as long as we *are* so close inshore, it's a matter of common prudence for you to get up, get dressed, and, like the rest of the crew, stand by."

Grudgingly they obeyed, filling the air with their complaints.

When he got back on deck he detailed one of the seamen to batten the door and guard it. Then, bent double against the wind and spray, he went aft to the other passengers, whom he mustered in the second-class dining room — all except Miss O'Dee, who was still officially held to be in some kind of quarantine. He told them more or less the same tale and left them in more or less the identical state of anxious reassurance.

"And what about the wee colleen?" a jovial Londoner asked when it seemed that the Captain was going directly back on deck.

Inwardly blessing the man for taking the bait so well, Morgan thanked him gravely and said it was hard to remember everyone and everything at a time like this.

Teresa was up and dressed; indeed, she had not taken off more than her dress and bodice for the past five days. Morgan found her sitting at the foot of her bunk, writing her journal. Her missal lay open on the blankets, its pages pinned down by a rosary.

"I know we are near our end, Frank," she said as soon as he entered. Her voice was calm, her manner composed.

His heart turned over at the mere sight of her. "We're near the end of our voyage, my dear." He made it a jovial correction. "Near the American coast, that is. Too near for my liking." And he went on to explain his plan — this time without either glossing or gilding the truth. "If all goes well, we'll be fifty miles away by nightfall," he concluded brightly.

"And if all does not go well?" she asked.

"Then I want you to get into the lifeboat, the last lifeboat on the starboard side — or whichever side is nearest the shore. If it capsizes in the waves …"

"I'll go in whichever boat you go in," she told him.

"I'll have to stay aboard until the last. You know that."

She smiled stubbornly.

"No!" he commanded. "You'll do as I tell you now."

Her smile did not waver.

"I'll have you carried into that boat in irons," he threatened.

The ink on her journal had dried by now. She laid it down and came to him. No woman's lips had ever felt so soft and warm, nor her body so firm and … and what? There was a kind of desperation in the way Teresa clung to him.

"How much longer have we?" she asked.

"I must go back on deck." He felt like a traitor as he raised his hands to pull her arms down from about his neck.

"How long?"

"About two hours."

She gave a startled little jump and then began pressing her lips to his neck in a rapid succession of kisses, hot and urgent. Morgan, who had quite forgotten what it was like to have a woman do that to him, almost yielded to her unspoken invitation. But, with superhuman effort, he disengaged himself at last and retreated to the door. "It's …" he stammered. "We're … everything's going to be all right."

The look of reproach in her eyes harried him all the way back to the bridge.

After several eternities dawn came at last, and with it a scene of desolation that struck dismay into every heart. The unknown shore was half a mile off the port beam, running almost due north — south at that point. To the north they could see it curl round in a more northeasterly direction; its southern end, however, was lost in squally rain and the dark of the storm.

"There's a stretch of coast south of Portsmouth looks like that, Cap'n," Wheeler said. "Shall I fetch the chart?"

Morgan nodded, but with little enthusiasm. "Not that it matters much. There's no getting nearer, no matter *what* coast that is." His practised eye was scanning the line of the surf, up and down, down and up, seeking any irregularity that might spell hope.

When Wheeler returned Morgan passed him the spyglass. "What d'you make of that bit there? Look dead ashore and then south a point or two."

"Got it." The First Officer confirmed. He watched several mighty rollers break before he added, "Well, it'd take three or four of them to smash us to bits. Any *one* would do the job along the rest of the line!"

"Mark it," the Captain told him.

He did better than that, for he found a place on the chart where two shelves of rocks parted in a vee — which would cause just such a weakening in the power of the surf. And better still, the narrowest part of the vee was obscured by the speckled texture that, on a marine chart, denotes sand or fine shingle.

There was a sudden, sickening thud, deep in the bowels of the ship. Both men thought at first that she had struck a rock, though the leadsman had been continually reporting depths of twenty fathoms and more. Still, there were such things as pinnacles.

Then Morgan realized what it was. *Pegasus*, held fast on her anchor, felt solid and heavy; her timbers creaked at the assault of each giant swell. No longer was it so; now she felt skittish and light, tossing freely at each movement of the ocean. "That link has snapped of its own accord!" he cried.

He ran to the back of the bridge but the bosun, also guessing what had happened, was already preparing to set the storm sail and the mizzen-top. Wheeler was calling all hands on deck — for the umpteenth time that voyage, it seemed. Morgan returned to the chart. His heart was pounding and every muscle was tense; it amazed him to feel how the tiredness simply drained away in seconds. He felt like a new man, fresh from a sleep around the clock. Quicker almost than thought itself, he formed a reserve plan if his attempt to cut and run failed. "Stand by to set every last stitch of canvas we carry, Mr Wheeler," he barked.

"Aye aye, sir!" Both men were suddenly in their element.

"Starboard your helm, Mr Quartermaster. Full turn."

"Aye aye, sir!"

Orders and responses came crowding on each other's heels. It took an amazing time for the liberated *Pegasus* to drift downwind to the point where her stern rope took up the slack — so much so that Morgan even began to wonder if the chain hadn't snapped at the anchor itself rather than at the hawse pipe. But at last they felt the check as stern rope and anchor chain stretched into a single, taut cable.

This was the most critical moment of all in a plan that was, in itself, a string of desperate expedients. The wind was nor'easterly, oblique to the coastline; the waves came from due east, running dead onshore. So far, *Pegasus* had been held at anchor, facing somewhere between the two, with the wind to port and the sea to starboard. Now that she was no longer held by the bow, the wind should nudge her round, swinging her on her stern rope until she came broadside-on to the waves. By then the wind would be fair and large behind her, still on her port quarter. Morgan's plan was to sever the stern rope with an axe at some point during that swing-around, roughly when she was pointing south east. At that angle she should be able to sail steadily before the wind, on storm sails alone, quickly putting the miles between herself and that treacherous coast. It all depended on catching the right moment.

In fact, she never swung at all; it all went wrong from the start. Though the wind was generally nor'easterly, it became capricious as it neared the coast, gusting anywhere from northerly to due west. A gust from the north would have spun her in half the time; one from the west would send her tripping over her own stern rope, which was running the full length of the port side to the remnant of the anchor chain ahead.

The gust — and a fierce one at that — came from the west. *Pegasus* immediately keeled over her own stern line, turning broadside on to the seas. Even that would not have been fatal if it had happened *between* two waves. Unfortunately, at the very instant when she was keeled over, a mighty swell got beneath her and lifted her twenty feet or more toward the skies. The whole crew prayed for the anchor to lose its grip and start to drag once more, leaving them still tethered and able to give it another go.

Too late the bosun released the stern capstan, hoping to pay out a little slack. The rope parted with a mighty crack, came lashing sternward with a vicious whistle, and whipped the man's head clean off, leaving the rest of the watch miraculously untouched.

For a moment nobody moved, nobody screamed, nobody even breathed. It was done so suddenly, and now so eerily calm again. The rope lay on the deck, so limp and inanimate you could not believe it capable of anything so lethal and terrifying. Only the bosun's headless corpse, pouring blood in diminishing gushes, bore witness to what had, indeed, taken place.

Morgan was first to recover. In fact, it was the splash made by the severed head as it plunged into the sea about a cable's length off her stern that broke the spell of horror for him and alerted him to their present danger. "We'll go for the gap, Mr Wheeler." There was twenty years of command in his voice.

"We've no time to come about, sir," the First Officer replied.

"No. We'll run her aground backwards. Set all her foresail first with yards braced back."

While the officer ran to carry out these commands, Morgan turned to the port watch, where McLellan had assumed command, and shouted, "Counterbrace the mizzen-main. Set and counterbrace mizzen-t'gallant."

Pegasus, now at complete liberty, responded to the wind with alacrity — too much so, to start with. "I can't hold her, Cap'n," cried the quartermaster.

Morgan ran to share the wheel with him. "We'll have the foresails to help in a jiffy," he gasped. "See that gap in the breakers — three points off the stern? Just off the port capstan?" He was laughing suddenly. Free! He had never felt so wild and free.

"Got her!" the man grunted.

Morgan took a grip on himself, though he was still elated. "Port your helm and bring her through that, Mr Rogers. And steer as you never steered before. If the charts are right and the tide with us, we have no more than twice her beam to slip her through."

"A camel!" the man grumbled. The foresails, well braced aback, were helping to push her bows to starboard now, considerably easing the wheel. "A camel through a needle's eye."

"If any man afloat can do it, Mr Rogers, that man is you. I'm staking the lives of all aboard on that!" As he turned to go forr'ard he added, "I'll give you what help I can with the sails. We'll put up all the canvas we can."

Abe Rogers understood then that he was to take her through the gap and run her straight at the shore without any further command, using his experience and judgement alone.

Frank's sense of elation persisted. He was in paradise. He forgot the cargo, the passengers, the crew — even Teresa. They were all going to die, himself among them. By no stretch of the imagination could this slender vessel, built for speed, be brought over reefs like that, in such mountainous seas, to the unknown shore beyond. And yet he would do it! He would cheat Death. He would bring them all through to safety. This was no mere hope, elevated to a certainty; it was certainty itself, elevated as much again, to something beyond even the most powerful conviction.

There on his own deck he was the centre of the universe. He surveyed it and saw it was good.

Three sails were now set on the foremast — the split fore course and the lower half of the split main. Since the wind was ahead of the yard they were all braced back and pressing tight to the mast, billowing out in a graceful curve to each side. The mast groaned and screamed in protest, for, in the ordinary way of things, the entire vessel should be carrying no canvas at all in such a gale, apart from a single storm sail at the mizzen.

"Think she'll take any more, Cap'n?" Wheeler asked dubiously.

Morgan laughed again. "Set the same three sails on the mainmast," he roared. "We'll show these Yankee farmers! We'll plough a furrow from here to Chicago, if we can!"

The leadsman, who had raced aft the moment he saw what way they were taking her in, now sang out his soundings as fast as he made them: "By the deep, fifteen! ... By the deep, twelve! ..." But all Morgan listened for was those first three words: *By the deep*. At seven fathoms, where the strip of red bunting tied to the line first showed above water, the call would change to, *By the mark ...!* and they would be in danger, for the chart showed the channel between the rocks (if it were, indeed, the chart for this coast at all) to be nowhere less than eight fathoms deep.

"By the deep, nine! And sand!"

Sand? Morgan started at the news. That didn't square with the chart, which showed bare rock all the way in to two hundred yards from high-water.

Wheeler, thinking along the same lines, shouted, "This storm could bring sand from anywhere, Cap'n."

Even down from the beach! Morgan thought, but he kept it to himself.

"By the deep, eight! And sand!"

Morgan returned to the bridge and picked up his megaphone. "Mr Mate!" He shouted aft. "Dowse all flame between decks. Muster the second-class passengers below — *all* the second-class — and brace them against an after bulkhead." He repeated the instruction to the sailor on watch by the steerage companionway up forr'ard.

"By the mark, seven! And sand!"

Morgan turned and stared at the gap between the two lines of breakers, which was now only a couple of lengths ahead. *Pegasus* seemed to be facing square on to it, and bang to the centreline. There was nothing for it but to pray. As if to emphasize the thought the main topsail filled at that moment and the sudden extra thrust pitched her down at the stern, threatening to drown the poor leadsman — and certainly making his next sounding pointless. He swung his lead again. "By the deep, eight!" he cried — adding, when he had the lead back aboard, "And hard!"

But matters were now too perilous for anyone to feel much relief. *Pegasus* was now less than half a length from the gap. Huge ocean rollers were rearing and breaking on either side, dwarfing her as they reared and mocking her graceful fragility as they fell in a tumultuous thunder and, like horses at the flag, set off on their suicidal gallop toward extinction on the distant shore. The channel of relative calm between them — which was no calm at all, save by comparison with that churning white frenzy on either hand — was precariously narrow.

She was now making fifteen knots on a following sea. This effectively veered the wind a point or two behind her, especially when a great bank of swell got under her and pushed her hard toward land. The opposite was the case when the swell overtook them, leaving them wallowing down its backward face. It was imposible to trim sail quick enough to meet these huge but fleeting changes in the wind's apparent direction and intensity. The sail set to take advantage of a fierce blast from almost dead behind could, when the strength and quarter apparently changed, throw out her helm and set her straight for the rocks. Only superhuman efforts by the quartermaster were keeping her out of such peril.

"By the mark, seven!" the leadsman called. Frank held his breath until the next cry came: "And sand!"

It was not worth the risk, he decided. Better shed a couple of knots and hold her line better. "Take in all foresails!" he bellowed. "Brace up all main yards."

"And a half, six!"

The die was cast now. It didn't really matter what the leadsman called, they had no choice but to run aground as high up the beach as possible.

"And sand!"

"Leadsman! Clear the deck!" he boomed.

Her masts were bound to snap when she struck. He wanted the decks as clear as possible by then. "All hands forr'ard!" he added.

Like slipped greyhounds they ran, needing no second bidding. A moment later only the bosun's body was left, lying where it had fallen among the ropes on the poop deck.

And a moment after that a little knot of second-class passengers emerged on deck and peered about, blinking in what, to them, was a too-bright day.

"Get below you dogs!" Morgan thundered at them.

Grapeshot could not have cleared the decks quicker. "I'll shoot the next man who shows his face," Morgan added as they almost fell over each other to get back down the companionway.

The quartermaster chuckled, despite the seriousness of the moment.

"Jump when she runs aground, Mr Rogers," Morgan warned him.

"I'll stay with her to the last, sir," the man replied. "And as for the masts, they're as likely to fall overboard as on deck. There's no place more venturesome than any other. You go up forr'ard with the rest, sir. No point both of us risking it."

Frank ignored the offer. "Ever run a ship aground before?" he asked.

"That I did, Cap'n. Twice. But never astern. I put the *Enterprise* ashore in the Scillies. She lost a hatch, carrying grain from Azoff. And I ran the *Laura*, a steam collier from Cardiff, ashore off Singapore."

"Oh, I remember her, the *Laura*. She took years to break up, didn't she. Often used to pass her. So that was your handiwork, eh!"

Both men stared ahead — which was really astern. Both found it hard to believe they were engaging in such a trivial and mundane conversation at a time like this.

"I was only practising for this one, Cap'n." Rogers laughed.

He laughed! Morgan understood then that he was not alone in this universe of his; it held other immortals, too.

Nearer and nearer came the shore; they could even make out the different high-water marks of jetsam and seaweed, threading along the strand like half a dozen incompetent stabs at making a line. It seemed impossible *Pegasus* could still be drawing water beneath her keel. Yet on they sailed.

The swell in the narrow channel began to rear and break, its boiling foam at last uniting the galloping white walls on either side. Surely now it was only a matter of moments?

At that very instant, to his horror, Frank saw the door to the *other* second-class companionway open to frame a bewildered Miss O'Dee.

"Teresa!" he cried — in a tone that could hardly have been more different from the one he had just deployed on her fellow passengers. "Go back for the love of Christ!" Then, forgetting himself entirely, he threw the megaphone aside and leaped toward the companionway down to the afterdeck.

It proved a far greater leap than he expected for *Pegasus* ran aground at that very moment. He went flying through the air and would have dashed out his brains on the afterdeck if he had not landed against a pile of netting, placed in readiness for helping the passengers abandon ship. Even so it left him stunned, so that when he came to it was to find the mainmast splintered and dangling at the royal stay and the foremast snapped right off and lying across the bridge.

"Mr Rogers!" he shouted, rising uncertainly to his feet.

There was no reply.

He stared at the bridge.

He turned and stared at the opening where he had last seen Teresa. "Miss O'Dee?" he called.

There, too, he received no reply.

Distracted half out of his mind he stared at the bridge, and back at the opening, paralyzed with indecision.

G IN WORKS WONDERS on babies of all ages. A single stiff snorter in the private bar of the City Arms, Highbury Corner, soon took the red out of Emma's eyes and put it back where it belonged, on her cheeks. It also loosened her tongue to the point where she could explain, without too much embarrassment, the precise reason for her dismissal. Lawrence sat facing her, his eyes like brass buttons, wondering if he was actually hearing the words. But the thought immediately struck him with its banality and he asked himself why, indeed, Emma should *not* explain such things to him in such a matter-of-fact way. They were both adults now — at least, they were both working for a living, even if he wasn't quite being paid for it yet.

His own tot of rum couldn't entirely explain the warm glow that now suffused his body. He felt privileged to be trusted with such feminine mysteries by young Emma. He must show himself worthy of the trust. "It must be jolly beastly," he said solemnly. "We chaps don't know the half of it, do we."

His interest took her by surprise; for a moment she could only nod and smile, blinking rapidly.

Alarmed at her silence, he blurted out, "I expect you wish you were a chap at times like that." Lord, what a fool he felt! Whither had his aplomb fled all of a sudden? If the chaps in the City could see him now! Cheeky, suave young Morgan stammering out gibberish with one of his mother's maids!

She grinned slyly. "Why? Ever wish you was a gel, then?"

"Not when *that* can happen."

"Forget that! Other times. What about other times?"

She had an extraordinary ability to change the mood between them within the space of two or three words. Her first posing of the question had been arch — not really expecting a serious reply. Now, suddenly, she was more philosophical. Her change of tone permitted him a moment of silence. He took advantage of it to stare at her, apparently in abstraction.

She was an attractive young thing, yet he could not decide what made her so. Her face was round and moonish and her nose like a butter bean covered in freckles, which spilled out onto her cheeks. They were not well-behaved freckles, either — not small, neat, and delicately placed — but large blotches that coalesced like brown water drying on parchment. And the ginger of her hair was almost too bright to be real. And yet she had the most captivating greeny-blue eyes he'd ever seen — and beautiful cheekbones that he just ached to reach out and touch.

What would it be like, he wondered, to inhabit that body and look out at the world through those lovely eyes set in that unpromising and yet somehow beautiful face? It couldn't be bad, he decided; certainly he had never seen Emma when she was not being cheerful and vivacious.

"Never thought of it before," he answered. "But meeting you — well, it's bound to make a fellow think."

"Oh, does it!"

She was slipping back into her former archness. Anxious to prevent that, he said quickly, "I mean, you're usually so … you know. I can't tell you what a shock it was to see you in tears out there. You're always so merry and bright. You're a real ray of sunshine in our house, Emma. Honestly you are."

"Ah … well." She stared into her glass, half raised it to her lips and set it down again. "I don't know what I'm going to do now."

"Where's your home. You're from London, aren't you?"

She stared pityingly at him, hinting that people like him could never understand.

"Not a hope?" he asked.

"I wouldn't put the shame of it on them."

"But you've been *unfairly* dismissed."

She laughed bleakly. "Aren't they all!"

He took another sip. "You're not drinking."

She nodded absently but left the glass untouched.

"Well," he went on, "knowing my mother, she'll never go back on her decision. And knowing you, you wouldn't return, not if she went down on bended knee."

She stared at him in mild amazement. "You *do* know me, don't you! And you're right — I wouldn't." The spirit deserted her again. "But that doesn't put a roof over my head tonight."

"No brothers or sisters?"

"Same thing."

"Kind auntie and uncle?"

She closed her eyes wearily.

Lawrence thought of his own kind auntie and uncle, by courtesy, Aunt Daphne and Uncle Brian. They'd certainly give her a skipper for the night, a heap of blankets on the scullery floor. But his spirit rose in angry rejection of the very idea. Anyway, Aunt Daphne would never let him forget it. She'd be making what Mama always called "those little corkscrew remarks of hers" for years to come about the night Lawrence played Sir Galahad.

His thoughts strayed to the fiver tucked inside his belt; a monstrous scheme popped into his head, fully formed, and made his scalp prickle.

"You all right, Master Lawrence?" she asked anxiously.

He drew a deep breath and babbled, "I don't suppose you'd allow … no!"

"What? I'm not in a position to refuse much, am I?"

He licked his lips nervously and wished he knew some trick to calm his suddenly pounding heart. "Well, it just so happens … I mean, I had a bit of luck on a horse at Kempton today." He scrabbled for the banknote and plonked it on the table before her. She stared at it in apparent horror. He reached over and straightened it out, just to fill the silence.

An amused barman watched the transaction; he nudged the barmaid and nodded at the young couple by the window. "Disgustin'," she commented, taking the situation in at once with a practised, if jaundiced, eye.

"I mean, it's not as if it were *my* money," Lawrence explained eagerly. "Not like something I earned fair and square. Just a flutter and a lucky win."

His nervousness distressed him greatly; he could not help thinking how calm and collected his father would be in circumstances like this.

Emma was mesmerized at the sight of so much money — as much as she would earn in half a year. She wet her lips. "What'd I have to do for it?" she asked warily.

"Nothing," he assured her, assuring himself it was, indeed, true. Just to get her inside the gilded cage —

that had been as far as his dreams had reached. He hadn't thought of any specific quid pro quo — or, to be more honest, he had not dared let it cross his mind as yet.

"Only I seem to recall a previous offer," she pointed out. She had recovered something of her scattered wits by now and was smiling again, rather provocatively, he thought.

She took up her tot of gin and placed it on the note, laying a kind of provisional claim to it, which she could now abandon or pursue at leisure.

He realized he had been waiting for some such change in her. In the same moment it also struck him he could not simply give her the fiver and have done with it — which had been his first, rather thoughtless impulse. If she took it, her very acceptance would create "a situation" of some kind between them. That was why he had been waiting for her to claim it; he wanted her to have the initiative. His heart was calm again now but its earlier riot still worried him; it showed him how raw and untutored his emotions were. And some instinct told him that, for all her outward girlishness, she had a maturity in these affairs that he still lacked. He trusted her to get it right — not absolutely, but far more than he trusted himself at that moment.

She leaned back in her chair and, smiling lazily, added, "Or have you forgotten it? Two quid for a kiss and a bit beyond!"

"Don't!" He shook his head vehemently. "It's one of those ghastly, ghastly moments I wish I could take back. It makes me cringe with shame."

His reply astonished her out of her playful mood. "But why?" she asked, slightly petulant. "I was flattered. It buttered me up all week."

"Well, you shouldn't have been."

"'Ere! Was that winnings on a horse, too?" The thought appeared to intrigue her.

He nodded glumly.

"D'you bet often?"

"Every day."

"Blimey! And d'you win much?"

"Mostly." He dipped his head toward the fiver. "Not as much as that, mind. That was a lucky treble that came up."

"I'll say! You should come and talk to my dad. He can lose a tanner a day. It's a mug's game, he says, but he still goes on punting."

"It's a mug's game if you don't follow form. Takes me an hour every day." He patted *The Pink 'Un*, which was folded in his pocket.

The barmaid, who had found half a dozen good reasons for flitting through the private bar since her colleague had drawn her attention to the young couple, reported back, "She's copped it with her glass but she ain't pocketed it yet. Sly little bugger, he must be!"

"Jealous?" He reached down and gave her garter a surreptitious twang.

"It'd take more'n a fiver to get me," she assured him acidly, pinching the back of his hand smartly.

Emma whistled silently. "Still — a fiver for an hour's work each day!" With enormous reluctance she picked it up, folded it twice, and passed it back to him. "I could never pay you back," she said. "Take me half a year to earn that much. Lend us five bob instead. I mean, I stand a chance there."

"What can you do with five bob?" he asked glumly, refusing the note for the moment.

"Get a week's board and lodging."

"And then?"

She shrugged.

"I know a man in the City who can give fake characters for servants," he told her. He didn't, actually, but he was sure Albert Crane, the bookie's runner, would.

"How much?" she asked at once.

"Not much. What have you got saved?"

"Nothing," she admitted ruefully. "I just blew it out on this dress. D'you like it?" She straightened herself up and breathed in, giving him plenty to see and like.

"She's going for more, sensible gel," the barmaid reported.

A rush of thoughts and sensations went to Lawrence's head. *Why not!* he exhorted himself angrily. *D'you think such chances are going to come your way every day of the week?* "Listen!" He swallowed hard and spoke out before the leaping of his heart could paralyze him again. "I don't want you to go back into service. I don't want you to get a fake character."

She stared deep into his eyes and saw she had won. She had formed no strategy and there had been moments when she believed she had thrown the whole game away; but now she saw she had been right simply to follow her instinct. Even so, the strength of the young man's passion awed her more than somewhat, and little alarms began to sound, telling her she was beginning something whose end she could not even glimpse. She knew its purpose, well enough — to revenge herself on that hateful mistress; but purpose and end might be poles apart. She drew another deep breath and cast the die. "What do you want, then?"

"I don't know. Does it matter yet? Let's think about it. I just want to … be able to go on seeing you. To talk to you. I've never known a girl I can talk with so easily as you."

"You mean about … your sister and such like?"

"Everything. I think you and me could just be … tremendous friends."

"Well, I'm a good girl," she told him solemnly. "There won't be any of *that*. You know what I mean."

He inhaled deeply and said, "Not for money, anyway." Delicately he tweaked the note out of her grasp.

Her freckles turned bright scarlet. "Oh, Master Lawrence! I never meant …" she stammered into silence.

Meanwhile he pulled out all the change he had and, without counting it — though it was certainly more than five shillings — took her hand in his and pressed the coins into her palm. "We'll work something out later. One thing at a time, eh? Let's go and find you some digs. At least you'll be spared the park bench tonight."

"Well?" the barman asked when his colleague returned, looking puzzled.

"She's playing a very deep game, that one," she replied, unable to hide her disappointment. "That's all I can say."

KATHLEEN CHOSE HER MOMENT carefully. Her mother was writing a letter to her father, a sacred and almost daily ritual that consumed at least an hour. She always wrote in her bedroom, lying half up on the counterpane with a rug over her limbs and using the breakfast table for support. Anyway, it meant that the front of the house was not guarded.

She rescued a pair of old envelopes out of the waste paper basket and told Mrs Johnson she was just popping down to catch the fourth collection — oh, and she'd give George a little extra walk, too. If she took George, the family's sort-of golden retriever, she could go into the village without a chaperone — even though he'd do nothing more threatening than lick a stranger to death.

She put on her warmest gloves and her new fur hat and let herself quietly out. She knew what an appalling risk she was taking but she didn't care. Not that she had any very clear idea what she was going to do once she got down to Highbury Corner, beyond asking policemen and tram conductors and the ticket clerk at the station if they'd seen Emma Harding. At least she wasn't difficult to describe.

And if they had seen her, what then? She shrugged the thought away angrily. At least it was better than sitting at home like a jellyfish, kicking herself for lacking the courage to speak out when it mattered. If her mother made a fuss about this unauthorized expedition, she decided, she'd just run away from home. She'd cut off her hair, put on a shirt and breeches, and run away to sea as a cabin boy, like Harriet the Hoyden in *Girl Before the Mast,* which Miss Kernow had confiscated from Deirdre Vine. As long as she could remember, Kathleen had always wanted to run away to sea.

But now, walking down Highbury New Park, she had to tear herself away from this, the happiest of all her daydreams, in order to rekindle her anger at what had happened today — though "what had happened today" was still rather bewildering to her. Until now she'd only become aware of herself at moments of petty crisis, like falling and cutting her knee or being put on bread and water and getting terribly hungry. In between such moments her selfhood had more or less vanished into the background.

She tried to explain it to Miss Kernow this morning — how when she fell and cut her knee she hadn't gone crying indoors but had just run the garden tap over her leg until the bleeding stopped; that's all she was trying to do this morning. Miss Kernow seemed to have it all confused with vague talk of "psychic guilt" or some such nonsense. Kathleen had no patience with schoolfriends who whimpered at every little hurt, whether of "psychic guilt" or actual physical pain. Her father always said the only thing to do with pain was to ignore it, and she agreed.

Except that now there were pains of a different kind, pains you couldn't just ignore because you needed someone else's permission to send them away — like the pain of letting poor Emma down so badly today. If only she'd had the courage to tell her mother what had crossed her mind at the time, how different it would be now!

"If you do anything bad to Emma because of this, I'll never speak to you again!" There! What would it have cost to say those few words? Bread and water. All right, but her mother would also have taken the threat seriously. She might have ticked Emma off but she'd never have booted her out like that.

Kathleen closed her eyes and stamped her feet angrily. George looked up and whimpered. "Not you," she assured him. "You wouldn't harm a ... yeurk! Now look what you've done to my glove!"

She arrived at Highbury Corner and stared around, at a loss what to do next. A policeman's head suddenly appeared level with hers, almost resting on her right shoulder as he leaned over her from behind. "The pillar box is over there, young lady," he said jovially. Then, seeing the letters from close to, he added, "But I wouldn't go posting them, if I was you. What did you bring them out for?"

She looked at the letters and, casting her eyes heavenward, gave out an exaggerated "Tsk-oh!" long and drawn out. It was not her usual gesture at all but a good imitation of what most of the girls in her class would have done.

"Picked up the wrong ones, eh?" he asked sympathetically, squinting to read the name and directions on the envelopes. "You Cap'n Morgan's daughter then?" he added. "Miss Kathleen, isn't it? I know your mother. We're both in the Operatic." He rose to his full height and she saw he was a sergeant. "Yes," he added. "I recognize you now. You came to our *Parsifal* last November, if I'm not mistaken."

She smiled brightly at him though inside she felt as disgusted as could be. Just her luck! She couldn't meet any old policeman; she had to run across Sergeant Corby, one of the finest baritones in the Operatic Society — who, of course, would be bound to let it drop that he'd met her.

Actually — she thought rapidly — if she offered to take the afternoon post down a couple of days this week, her mother would assume the meeting had

94

occurred on one of those occasions. Her smile became more genuine. "Then you must be Sergeant Corby," she said, holding out her hand. "How do you do? My mother says you have one of the finest voices she's ever heard."

"Amateur voices," he said, shaking her hand with some diffidence. She was surprised to see that her compliment had embarrassed him.

"Amateur *or* professional," she assured him.

"Come come, young lady!" He was more embarrassed still.

She took a chance on it. "Actually, I also came out to see if one of our maids was here. She left us to work somewhere else today but she went without saying goodbye and I wanted to give her a little memento."

Who did she sound like? Where did these light, delicate, perfectly formed little phrases come from, so trippingly off the tongue? Then she had it: her Aunt Daphne, of course.

The Sergeant frowned. "Not under a cloud, I hope?"

Kathleen-cum-Daphne gave him an admiring smile, much as to say, "You see and understand everything!" She sighed. "There was" — what would Aunt Daphne call it? — "a discord of souls, yes. She's seventeen, I think, a little taller than me, with bright red hair and freckles. She'd have carried a bag."

"Or two," the Sergeant confirmed. She knew from his eyes, the moment she'd mentioned Emma's hair, that he had seen her. "She was stood over there by the tram stop about an hour ago," he said.

"Ah." Kathleen slumped in disappointment. "So she'll have gone by now."

The man held up a finger and smiled. "I noticed her first on my way up Holloway Road — about an hour ago, like I said. And I noticed her there not fifteen minutes ago, on my way back."

"So she wasn't waiting for a tram?"

He shook his head. "For someone getting off the tram. And he came, too. They went straight inside that pub there." He pointed to the City Arms.

"Ah." She smiled gratefully at him, wondering why he would be hanging around the area all that time. "I'll just wait here then."

"I'll go in and chase her out, if you like," he offered.

"No, no — please!" She was aghast at the image it conjured up.

However, at that moment, she got the shock of her life to glance across at the pub and see Emma leaving on the arm of her own brother Lawrence. Fortunately, Sergeant Corby was staring away up the road at that moment — as he had done, casually, from time to time during their conversation. She had an intimation that he had only stopped to talk with her to give himself an excuse to go on loitering there.

The suspicion hardened when he suddenly stiffened and said in an altogether brisker tone, "Anyway, I must be pressing on. No rest for the wicked, eh?"

Only after he'd gone did she think of saying, "Not while you're around, I'm sure, Sergeant!" It would have rounded off her Aunt Daphne impersonation nicely. She was just going to call out to Lawrence when she saw the pair of them vanish round the corner into Canonbury Road. She had to wait a while until a safe moment came for crossing, so she was only just in time to see them turning into Goldsmith's Place. There were no other pedestrians on that side of the road so, feeling rather visible, she crossed to the tram stop and mingled among the crowd waiting there. As she turned she saw Lawrence and Emma standing half way up the front steps to a house on the left of the street, about five doors down. A hand-lettered card in the window read: ROOM TO LET. Even as Kathleen spotted it a woman stood up on a chair and took it down. Lawrence held out a hand to Emma. She shook it warmly and then stooped to give him a quick peck on the forehead before she turned and bolted indoors.

Kathleen's heart leaped with joy. They were lovers! Secret lovers! They had been in love for months and now he was "doing the decent thing by her" — a phrase she had once heard Uncle Brian use. And what had Aunt Daphne replied? "Very, very often, I imagine!" Well, it didn't make complete sense, but oh, what a weight off her conscience! Good old Lawrence!

She gave the family whistle, which her father said was the cry of the hoopoe. Respectable people turned and stared at her askance but what did she care? She'd never see them again. And anyway, today was the day when she'd just grown up, and grown-ups could do what they liked.

Lawrence turned and sought her out. What a glorious smile he had! What a wonderful bro he was to have! Built like a rock. The Rock of Gibraltar. Depend on him always. "What brings you down here?" he asked.

"Oh, Larry, it's so dreadful! Mama has booted her out — Emma. She kicked her out without notice or wages or anything."

He could keep a secret, too! Looking into those frank, pale-brown eyes you'd never suspect for one moment that he already knew all about it. "Hold your horses," he said, taking an obstreperous George from her. "Start from the beginning. The mater's given poor Emma the order of the boot? Is that it?"

"Yes. And I don't know what she's going to do. She's got no money and no character. What can she do? I came down to see if I could find her. Oh, do help me look for her."

He hesitated a moment and then fell in with her suggestion. Twice they went round the Circus, peering in at all the café windows, asking likely people if they'd seen a girl with bright red hair and a gladstone bag. "She'll be all right," Lawrence said comfortingly when at last they abandoned the futile search. "Tell you what, Little Face. I'll get her parents' address off Ma Johnson and pop round and see her tomorrow. I'll bet she's gone there. And I'll make up at least her wages out of my own pocket."

"How can you? I thought Furnival's aren't paying you yet."

He winked. "Bit of luck with the gee-gees. Not a word at home about that, though, eh?"

"D'you know the cause of it all?" she asked out of the blue. "Why Mama booted her out?"

He blushed but recovered quickly. "Water under the bridge, eh?"

It occurred to her that Lawrence could teach her more about growing up than anyone — more than Aunt Daphne, whose amused aloofness from all life's battles had always seemed to Kathleen to be wonderfully grown-up — more, too, than all her earnest talks with Miss Kernow, important though they were. But Larry had a whole repertoire of useful tricks for stopping conversations and preventing people from finding things out — which was what "growing up" seemed to be mainly about.

Like just now: murmuring "water under the bridge, eh?" and staring off into the distance with an all-knowing little smile. What did it mean? Nothing. It was one of those marvellously empty phrases. But when he spoke it, with such confidence, it just convinced you he had an entire handful of trumps.

"What'll her parents think when you just turn up like that?" she pressed, realizing that her best chance to get things out of him (like the fact that he bet on horses — which she could well believe) was now, before he had time to think and prepare.

"Dunno." They turned off the main thoroughfare into Highbury New Park. "Don't really care much, either."

She took his arm on the less-crowded footpath. "They might think you're in love with her or something."

The sudden tension in his arm belied the lightness of his guffaw. "Good heavens!" he exclaimed.

"You're not in love with her, are you?" she continued.

More of his cleverness. He turned and faced her solemnly. "Of course I am, Little Face. And how cunning of you to sniff it out. Please, please don't breathe a word of it, though."

"Larry!" She gave him a soft punch and pretended to accept his making a jest of it.

That was another way of being grown up: When people accused you of something, admit it so facetiously they'd feel foolish for speaking out.

All these things she stored away in her mind, feeling quite certain that each would have its day.

THE LANTERN CAST a fitful light as Frank Morgan made his way along the bottommost decks to the after hold. Every now and then he paused to lift an inspection hatch and peer down into the bilges. So far he hadn't found a single sprung timber — for, even though this was not the part of the ship that had run aground, the snapping of the masts might well have done some damage down here. He knew, however, that the likelihood of finding a leak increased the nearer he drew to the stern. Even so, he had already seen enough to be sure that any such breach must be small; the amount of water in the bilge, though considerable, was no more than you'd expect after a week of such storms as *Pegasus* had endured.

Judging by the way she'd yawed and rolled at high tide, during the operation to get the passengers and crew ashore, she wasn't held very firmly in the sands. This was the period of neap tides, so, though the storm would have added a foot or two of surge, today's highest mark would still be the best part of a fathom lower than high water during the spring tides, which would be on them in about two weeks' time. In other words, if her timbers weren't too badly sprung, there was a good chance she'd float again. That was why he had remained behind, the sole hand on board — to prevent *Pegasus* from turning into "salvors' meat." For anyone may claim salvage rights on an abandoned vessel.

In the after hold he discovered that her cargo of cheap furniture had turned into a cargo of even cheaper matchwood. He spent a good while clearing its shards from the deck before he could lift the two aft inspection hatches and peer down into the bilges.

Sherry casks of export ale stirred lazily in the tar-reeking water, but there was no sign of a leak there, either. He noted the waterline and, leaving the hatches open, made his way back amidships. Half a dozen hands on the pumps tomorrow and she'd be dry as the American Navy. Perhaps Wheeler would have arranged a tow by then; it would be no works outing to try sailing by her own canvas alone, with just the mizzenmast and main courses left to her.

Being the thorough man he was, he went forr'ard to carry out a similar inspection of the bilges there — only to discover that she had shipped rather more water than he had supposed. *Pegasus* was down by the head, of course, so the water level in the fore hold would be high, anyway. But he arrived to find there was no need to open the inspection hatches; the cargo deck itself was awash with some three inches of water at its deepest part.

On his way back up to the open deck he decided not to get her pumped out after all — assuming she didn't ship more water overnight. It would be no bad thing, he reflected, to have her a bit heavy and sluggish to handle; a half-dismasted vessel with a rigged rudder, floating three feet above her plimsoll line, could be blown all over the ocean. He gathered an armful of matchwood on his way.

One item remained to be checked: the four lines he had secured to ground anchors ashore, two from her bows, two from her stern. *Four* lines! He'd seen how the men smiled with disgust and gritted their teeth when the orders came down to secure the third ... and then the fourth. Never mind that they'd been five days at sea with hardly any sleep, that their muscles shrieked for respite now they were safely aground, that they could hardly keep their eyes open — old

Cap'n Morgan never yielded an inch of his principles; he would certainly never use one line where two would do, nor two where four were better.

He stood on deck in the last glimmer of dusk and stared at the three shoreward lights they had set, red at the ends of the two outermost hawsers and white at the watchman's hut, which was higher up the beach. He gave an all's well with his lantern. There was an answer from the hut. He returned his attention to *Pegasus* and noted with satisfaction that smoke still curled from the galley stovepipe. He dropped his bundle by the galley kiddley and went round the farther side to check the stern ropes. The twilight was now so deep that he could see only the first few feet before their graceful curves were swallowed in the gloom. The three lanterns ashore were now the only visible sign that there was land there at all.

The storm had abated considerably during the day and was now a mere half-gale; but the seas were still running high. The breakers came roaring in over the rocky shelves on either side. It had the curious effect of sapping the strength of the unbroken rollers, which lagged behind in the deeper channel between them — the channel through which, by luck and good seamanship, he had brought *Pegasus* aground. The effect was that the spent rollers were already sizzling back down the strand, even as the laggard swell arrived, undercutting it as it tried to break near the ship. As a result she lay in a seething cauldron of white water, assaulted more by sound than fury.

Remembering the scene as daylight had greeted them — for the fading of that same day had now swallowed it completely — he marvelled yet again at the narrowness of their escape. A cable's length more to port or starboard and they'd surely have been pounded to splinters. Now, for the first time that day — with every passenger and all surviving hands safely ashore, and her timbers seemingly tight, and the tempest dying — he felt secure enough to go down on his knees and thank Almighty God for their deliverance. He added a prayer for the souls of the bosun and quartermaster, whose remains were now in a mortuary ashore. He rose and stared shoreward into the dark.

And how was *she* faring there, he wondered? Doubled up head-to-tail with four others in some hospitable Maine homestead? Or quartered in some community assembly room, an impromptu re-creation of the hell of the female steerage dormitory? He remembered her pleas to be allowed to stay aboard with him, and the look of reproach she had given him when he had ordered her to the port mustering station. Lord, but he'd give his sea legs just to have her here now. He decided he'd sleep in her bunk tonight — just to torment himself the more.

You'll forget her, a voice promised inside his head.

A sudden, violent anger seized him — not at the unlikelihood of such an event but at its very certainty. He *would* forget her, just as he had forgotten Jenny Bright in every sense that mattered. Of course, he remembered her name, her looks, her smile, the sound of her voice; he even remembered that once upon a time she had filled every waking hour; whether she was in the forefront of his mind or not, she had still been *there*, consuming his day, consuming him. But the quality of that passion, its texture and its power, had died beyond recall — until Teresa came along.

Frying bacon! Suddenly he could smell bacon, frying in the pan. A hallucination? Was he tired enough for that? The wind eddied round him and the aroma vanished. He shook the illusion from his exhausted brain and returned to the bitter-sweet of his contemplation.

Teresa! At first she had merely awakened the echoes of that earlier love, reminded him of all he had scoured from his soul, sacrificed, and buried, merely to survive. Then she had taught him he had not scoured well enough. How swiftly those long-cauterized emotions had revived; how speedily they had transferred from the dead past to the all-too-living, breathing, vibrant present. *You will forget her*, the demons whispered — and every particle of him rose in outrage that it was true, that he would, if he were wise, endure his long death a second time.

Bacon again! And was it eggs, too, frying in butter? A sudden cramp bent him double round his hunger. When it passed, he straightened himself gingerly and stared out into the dark, toward the watchman's white light, the source, surely, of this present torture. Actually, he reflected, it was torture only because he could not tear himself away from the stern, where he stood nearest to her, and go fry his own eggs and bacon.

If he were wise he would lock her cabin door against himself tonight, cast the key overboard, and sleep in his own virtuous bed.

Two bells rang softly on the moaning wind. Had the bosun …? No, of course not. The hair prickled on his scalp, for he was as superstitious as any man who has spent thirty years at sea; he knew what play the ghosts of long-drowned sailors made of grounded ships. He held the lantern high and strode amidships, stamping his seaboots to recruit his courage.

On a calm night Teresa's laughter would have

carried to the shore. "Cot you! Cot you!" she cried, throwing her arms about his neck and bathing his face in kisses.

If there was ever a moment when common sinner turned into uncommon criminal, that was it. He resisted her embrace for a second or two, trying desperately to summon the anger he knew he ought to feel — and then he yielded. It was more than the mere withdrawal of his opposition; it was a whole-hearted endorsement of her rebellion, a blood bond in mutiny against his own command, both of the *Pegasus* and, even more vitally, of himself.

"Come and see," she urged, her eyes dancing in the soft light of the galley lamp. And, picking up a tray, all covered in silver service, she led the way round the bridge to the officers' wardroom. "You may bring your firing with you," she added as they passed the heap he had dumped on the deck.

Half bewildered still, but wholly delighted, he did as she told him and followed her below. The wardroom table was set for royalty, with silver everywhere, two candelabra ablaze with light, white and red wines decanted ... there was even a pink rose — of silk, to be sure — in a narrow silver vial between the two place settings. "Don't be getting your hopes up now," she warned. "I've only two courses but didn't it look mean with just knife, fork, and spoon. I'd have baked some soda bread had I time, but that's not too stale."

He dropped the firing by the upright stove and turned to relieve her of the tray. He laid it on the sideboard and held his arms wide for her to come in.

"'Twill go cold," she warned, huddling herself happily into his arms.

"You're the chance of a new life to me," he murmured, grazing her red curls with his lips. "Oh

God, I'm lost! I'm lost for loving you."

"Frank?" she murmured into his neck.

"Mmm?"

"We are going to live, aren't we? I mean, the danger's past?"

"We'll live forever," he promised her, "you and I." The second question he left hanging on the air.

FRANK LEANED FORWARD and opened the door of the stove. He'd had no proper sleep for nights; in all that time he'd lived with the near-certainty of death, not only for himself but for all the hundred-odd souls in his care; yet with God's help he'd brought them safely through it at the last. By rights he ought now to collapse in grateful exhaustion and sleep until the crack of doom — or at least until Wheeler returned tomorrow with whatever science he'd gleaned from the local fisherfolk. Instead he felt bright and mellow, stretched out on the rug, half-up on his elbow and cradling a brandy in his hand. The soft glow of the fire, which was now their only light, made a line of dark gold down Teresa's profile. He wondered if he would ever be able to look at her without this turmoil of his innards. "Tell me something of yourself," he said.

"Oh God, that'll be done in a hack," she replied. "What's to tell? I'm from Philipstown in the King's County, which is famous for nothing except a reformatory for the bad boys. My daddy, God rest his soul, was a cabinetmaker, and a good one. And my mammy, Lord 'a mercy — well, she was just my mammy. She passed on to her rest on St Stephen's Day last."

"How did she die?"

"She just wasted. Sure there wasn't a pick on her bones when we buried her. The man said 'twas like lifting the coffin of a child."

"And your father? Is he long gone from you?"

"Six months before the mammy, but he drowned. I don't know which is worse, sudden death or lingering." She smiled, not wanting a sadness she had mastered to come between them now. "I'll tell you the worst death, Frank. 'Tis the death that comes up and threatens ye and then goes away again. Aren't we after meeting *that* death often enough, those days that went by!"

" 'Cowards die many times before their deaths'." He quoted Brian Dowty's lines from last year's Drama Society production — an untimely reminder of life in Highbury, which made him uneasy.

" 'The valiant never taste of death but once'," she capped him.

"You've had a good education," he commented.

"Stop! My father and the Bard ..." She shook her head at the impossibility of conveying the depths of such an obsession. "But I did have a good education, too. There was a widow woman, Mrs de Quincey of Derrin, who took a liking to me when I went with my father once to deliver some chairs he'd made. She's a Protestant but a dacent sort, fair dues to her. And she took me in and trained me up as her lady's maid, but I ended up more companion to her than anything. And you never saw the library like that one had — her husband's it was, of course. And now 'tis her son's."

A slight frown creased her forehead at this last mention.

"Are you a great reading man, Frank?" she asked, looking up at his one shelf of books. "The Bible, *The*

Whole Duty of Man, Griffin's Law of the Sea, The Anatomy of Melancholy ... sure you've all you need for a wet Sunday!"

He laughed. She could not possibly be reading the titles at such a distance and in this dim light. Where else had she pried? In his journal? No, he could feel the key to it in his pocket now, for it was one of those fancy books complete with its own hasp and lock — which, come to think of it, any child with a good pin could pick. If she had, she'd know the truth about him. Not that he'd lied to her; he'd simply failed to correct a misapprehension.

It was on the tip of his tongue to blurt out the truth now, to trade happiness for honesty and hope she'd forgive him enough to love him still. After all, if he could love her so desperately, knowing it was a sin, knowing he'd roast in hell through all eternity for it, then why should she not do the same?

But one look at her in the gentle firelight, her face all eager to see his response to her teasing, and he knew he couldn't risk it. He felt a brief intimation of the earthly torments he'd have to endure, long before he started on those of eternity — the lying, the prevarication, the terror of discovery, the shame of facing her when he was at last unmasked, as he did not doubt he would be in the fullness of time.

"I bought them all before I knew you," he pointed out, stretching forth his hand to caress her cheek.

She shivered and inclined her head to trap it in the fold of her neck.

"Could you not have stayed with Mrs de Quincey?" he asked. "After your mother's death?"

She shook her head but said nothing.

"Did you fall out of sorts with her?"

"The son. I'd liefer not talk of it." He made to remove his hand but she trapped it more firmly and said, "No!"

"Come and lean against me, then," he said, reaching his other arm behind and pulling a chest toward him, where he could rest against its side.

When she'd settled in his arms she leaned her head against his shoulder. "Talking of the terrors of those days that went past, d'you know the worst of it? The one thought that camped in my ear, day and night?"

Every little movement of her body sent intoxicating draughts of warm air up out of her clothing. He remembered Napoleon's signal to Josephine: "Home next week. Do not bath!"

"Do you?" she repeated.

He drew a deep breath and replied, "I'll tell you mine. Let's see if they're the same. I lived in mortal terror that Death would take me before I'd had the chance to … to *know* you."

"Yes!" She breathed rather than spoke the word as she craned her lips up to his. "Oh, Frank! Go on now, my darling man. My whole body's on fire with welcomes."

Hating himself, loving the moment, he loosened her bodice and slipped his hands inside, feeling for her breasts.

She shuddered in surrender when he held them.

"I'd forgotten." His voice quivered. "A woman's body. The wonder of a woman's body. It is the most glorious thing in all the world."

She lifted her arms up around his head to pull him hard against her. She marvelled at the strangeness of it all, at the strange touch of a man's hands where no man's hands had ever touched before. Yet strangest of all was the feeling that none of this was new to her; it was like some ancient lore, long forgotten, but now, at last, dimly returning, bringing with it all the warmth and wonder of a forgotten childhood ... another life ...

A S THEY BEGAN THE second slow circuit of Highbury Fields, Lawrence dared to take Emma by the arm — a gentle but proprietorial gesture. Or so Kathleen chose to interpret it as she sat in Aunt Daphne's window, watching the pair of them through Uncle Brian's telescope. At least it was an advance on last Sunday, when they had not touched at all — not while they were in the public gaze, anyway.

To Lawrence, however, it was less of a proprietorial gesture than one of amazement. He couldn't recall what they'd talked about last week. Nonsense of some kind — the verbal equivalent of those silly little notes schoolchildren love to pass around the form: BILLY THINKS SUSAN'S HAIR IS LUVELY! TEE HEE! The reason he couldn't remember was he'd been obsessed with but a single thought that afternoon. It was only seven days ago, too, and how things had changed meanwhile!

The thought that consumed him last week was how to suggest to her that he should find a pretty little apartment somewhere in Holloway or Islington, far enough away to be anonymous, near enough to reach on foot; and there she could lead the wonderful life of idleness that all servant girls dream about, while he could visit her daily and enjoy those melting moments all slave-men dream of (and all men, he now realized, are slaves in that department, even to the most servile of servant girls). "Just popping out for a walk, Mama — shan't be long!" He had practised the right degree of nonchalance in his mind until he had it off perfectly. He had also practised how to put the notion to Emma. He had a stammering way of doing it, and a cheeky-cheerful way, and a soulful way, and a lordly-and-masterly way. Never had he been more thoroughly prepared for any contingency. And all last Sunday he had waited his chance to trot out at least one of them. And what had happened? Nothing! They had simply strolled round and round on the dog-dirtied grass, talking scribble — almost relishing their ability to be childish once again.

And now, this Sunday, everything had changed. Now such an arrangement was the last thing he wanted to suggest. Not that he'd gone off her — quite the reverse; but the very thought of forming such a shallow, mercenary alliance with her now made him cringe with shame. The difference may be summed up in two daydreams he had, with Emma at the centre of each. In the week leading up to last Sunday's non-proposition, he had pictured her in that dainty apartment, which was all turkey carpets and silks and divans and a bearskin rug, slowly removing her garments and permitting him to adore each revelation with his eyes and hands and lips; he had nearly driven himself demented with it. The second daydream belonged to the past seven days. Gone was the bearskin rug, the silks, and all the trappings of his incandescent desires. In their place was padded leather, uncut moquette, antimacassars, and all the ornaments of domestic bliss. She no longer removed her clothing but rather permitted him to add to it with jewelled lockets, pendants of ivory and gold, and a diamond tiara to outshine even her shining hair. *I adore what I adorn*, he wrote, thinking to knock it up into a sort of poem for her, *And adorn what I adore!* But then it seemed such a complete and well-rounded thought, in itself, that there was nothing to add.

His taking of her arm now was part of that same adoration. His adoring fingers adorned her adorable arm. "It's a miracle," he told her happily.

"What is?" she asked, raising her eyebrows and smiling in what she hoped was an encouraging manner. If he didn't come out with something soon — something to the point, that is — she'd have to start taking the initiative herself, which was the last thing she wanted.

"Your arm."

"Ohmigawd," she replied wearily.

"No, listen! It's not just your arm, it's all of you. I mean ... how long were you with us? A year? Eighteen months?"

"Best part of," she said, now more wary than weary. "Why?"

"Well, there we were, all that time, you and me, living under the same roof, and I hardly ever thought about you at all. Of course, when I saw you — I mean when you were actually in my sights ..." He withdrew his hand for a moment to aim an imaginary rifle at her. "Pow! Didn't my heart just race at the thought of kissing you! But no more so than with any one of a dozen pretty girls, to be honest. I mean, I hardly ever thought about you in between times. But now ... I mean I just kick myself now at what a clod I was."

"Was you?"

"*Were* you. If you're serious about wanting to talk properly, say were you."

"Were you? How?"

"Not to have realized how utterly different you are from all those other ... I mean, from *any* other girl. How unique and wonderful you are."

"Am I? Me?" She gulped. His sudden leap from childish nothings to what sounded like the confession of a lifetime left her breathless and bewildered.

"To me it's a miracle that you're there, in the world, that you exist, that I've had the good fortune to meet you." He took her arm again. "I have to touch you just to be sure it's not a dream. A wonderful dream that'll leave me shattered when I wake up."

"Blimey!" She stopped in her tracks and, laying a hand to her breast, fought a little to breathe. "Why this all of a sudden?"

"Oh, it's not all of a sudden, Emma, my darling. It's taken an eternity — all this week. Each day has seemed like a hundred years. You've transformed the world for me, you know. I think about you all the time." None of these were from the phrases he'd practised but now he was off and running nothing could stem the flow. "When I go to sleep at night I carry your image with me into the dark. When I wake in the morning, your smile is there to put the dawn to shame. You're everywhere, all about me, all the day. And when I come home, when I get off the tram, I cross the road at once and peer into Goldsmith's Place but I daren't put a foot into it."

She laughed, half with delight, half with embarrassment. "Why ever not? You ain't half silly!"

"I know, I know. Only bear with me, Emma, my dear. I'm so sick in love with you I don't know what to do. Just humour me, eh?"

"Why can't you put a foot in Goldsmith's Place? It just sounds daft."

"I just look at the paving stones and say to myself, *'She* has trodden here!' The bits of grass between them and the dandelions at the foot of the walls — they seem so *green!* And I say, 'That's because *she* has passed this way!' The very air seems to cage the magic of your presence there. Honestly, before I saw you today, I was petrified."

"Garn!" she mocked. She was by now even more embarrassed at his outpouring of passion.

"It's true. I couldn't even hold my hands still enough to pull on my gloves. Did I go to church today? I must have, but I can't remember a thing. I live like an automaton except when I'm with you. But you've no idea how frightening you are to me."

"Silly!" was all she could say. Much to her annoyance she felt tears sprouting behind her eyelids.

"You are! I mean, just to touch your arm like this, is almost as much as I can bear. This" — he gave her elbow a squeeze — "is the most precious *stuff* in the entire universe to me. I'd give my life a thousand times rather than have it suffer the slightest scratch. Just to be able to touch you is like the most wonderful dream I ever had — you know, the kind you know is a dream even when you're dreaming it, so you're desperate not to wake up and you already feel the sharpness of the loss." Artlessly he added, "I daren't even *think* about the rest of you."

"Oh!" she exclaimed on three wounded notes, currying humour to vanquish her sadness.

He was so intoxicated with confession by now that he rushed on: "I did, of course. Last week, that's all I could think of. I wanted to rent an apartment for you — I could afford it, you know — and, and just keep you there, and, and visit you, and ..." The hæmorrhage fell to a trickle and swiftly petered out.

Suddenly she felt more miserable than ever before in her life — and she was not one to whom misery came easily. Lawrence's absurd outburst — not just this final confession but the entire pouring out of his feelings for her — left her so far behind him that she felt deserted, desolate, barren of any worthwhile thought or emotion.

"Now you'll never talk to me again," he concluded miserably.

"Listen!" She stopped abruptly and pulled him to face her, gripping him by his arms and holding him away from her. *What are you doing?* she asked herself. Nothing was going the way she had planned it at all. The whole point of aiming at Lawrence was — apart from the fact that he was *there* — the whole point was that she had no feelings for him either way, neither love nor hate, nor their milder cousins, like and dislike. Nothing at all. The idea was to ensnare him, make such a fool of him that his mama would come to her on bended knee. And after that? Well, she hadn't thought too much about after that; it had all been hatched in the sting of the moment, anyway. But none of it would work if she started getting *feelings* about him. However hazy her scheme, it had to allow her to walk away from him at any moment.

"What?" he asked when she said nothing.

He ought to look like a silly little puppy, she thought. That was what the plan had called for. Instead, he looked ... all right. The intensity of his gaze sent a small shiver through her. "I can't feel as deep as what you do," she said, surprising herself even more than him. "D'you see? I like a good time. I like a laugh. I can't go in for all that ... stuff."

"I know." He swallowed hard. "I shouldn't have said any of it."

"Of course you should! That's what I'm telling you." She hung on her own words every bit as avidly as he, for she, too, had no idea what would come out next. "It's being honest, innit. That's what I'm being with you, too, though Gawd knows why. I mean, what have we got in common?"

"Not much. But it doesn't seem to matter, does it."

She smiled wanly. It was true. "That couple's moved off," she said. "We could go and sit down if you want."

Glad to be moving again he resumed his grip on her elbow and walked with tiny skips at her side. "If you don't mind me leaping up every ten words. I feel so restless after getting all that off my chest. Oh, Emma! You've transformed the world for me!"

"All right!" She laughed at his impetuousness as she sat down.

He thought the way she pulled her skirts beneath her and gave her bustle a little chuck to one side was one of the divinest things ever. "I love you," he said, gazing down at her. "That's what I've been trying to say all day."

She felt an impulse to say she'd never have guessed it, but he was just a little too serious to make it kindly. She had an intimation of many future exchanges between them, exchanges in which his emotional strength would defeat her in just such petty ways. And so he would progress with her, from one insignificant victory to another until the power of his feelings had won what her feebler sentiments could not defend — in other words, everything, for, when all was said and done, she saw little in herself that was worth defending.

"I wish *I* did," she said.

"What? Love me?" He sat beside her, preparing for

an orgy of comfort — telling her she was not to worry, it would come, just give it a chance, he had enough to last them both ...

She cut across all that with her next words, a surprisingly bitter bark: "No — *me!* I wish I could see one small bit of what you see in me, Lawrence."

"That's the first time you've called me that."

She stared deep into his eyes, not taking him up on the point. "How honest can we be?" she asked herself aloud.

"Utterly, absolutely!" he assured her.

"I wonder."

"Try."

Kathleen, who had raced up to the attic when her brother and Emma sat down, was disgusted to find that the thick bole of the plane tree obscured them from there, too. She was sure they were kissing behind its shelter, even though it obscured them only from the Dowtys' house and a few of its neighbours; that was why they'd been strolling around waiting for that particular bench to become vacant, of course, so that Aunt Daphne and Uncle Brian wouldn't spot them at it. Now she'd have to put on her boots and leggings and her coat and muffler and take George out for yet another little walk. "Grr!" she snarled.

The dog leaped up hopefully.

"How *can* they sit out there in this cold, Georgy Porgy?" she asked. "If that's what love does for you, I'm never going to fall for it!"

Aunt Daphne came in at that moment and from the supercilious smile on her face, Kathleen just knew she knew everything. She'd probably been down in the drawing room, spying with her opera glasses. "Aren't you, dear?" she asked lightly. "If mere curiosity can drive you out into that same cold, just think what a monstrous horseshoe Cupid is even now slipping into his boxing glove for you!"

"I thought he fired darts," Kathleen complained.

The smile did not waver. "Most women suffer the same delusion, darling. It's all part of his cunning, you see. He's a pugilist, not an archer. Knocking us out is his game. I'll walk with you, if you like. I had no idea all this was going on. Isn't it exciting!" She took the girl's arm before she could think of refusing.

"I can't seem to love myself much," Emma was meanwhile saying. "When you go on about me like what you was doing, I can't think you mean me. It doesn't sound like me. I just stand there, thinking to myself, *E's gone and got the wrong gel. This can't be me.* That's all I think about it." She reached out a hand and touched his arm hesitantly. "D'you know what I mean? I'm a very common, ordinary gel, that's what. Nothing special."

He drew breath to protest his love again and then, catching the suspicion in her eye, reined himself back. "I know." He nodded uncomfortably, like a horse champing to be off. "I know it's stupid, really. I mean, I *do* feel all those things for you, and I *do* think about you all the time, but — you said be honest — well, if I'm honest, I must admit there's one small bit of common sense left in me that says it's all too much and I'll come down to earth with a bump one day ... and all the things that all the sensible people in the world *always* say to those who are head over heels in love."

She was about to respond to this when a further thought struck him. "Actually, common sense tells me even more than that. It tells me I'm not doing *you* any good by painting you all in gold and sepia ..."

"That's what I mean! Gawd, if only I could talk the

words like what you can. It don't do me no favours if you …"

"I mean, if I could be just a little *less* in love with you, then I might find there's an even *more* wonderful girl waiting to be discovered in you. I don't mean wonderful-wonderful but *real*-wonderful. The *real* Emma Harding. To be honest, I don't know you at all, so how can I be in love with you! But to be even more honest, I want to know you better than anyone else on earth — so that's how I *can* be in love with you. Because I want to know you like no man ever knew a woman before." He swallowed heavily. "Is that better?"

Suddenly she could not stop the tears from flowing. She did not exactly cry. In fact, she felt curiously happy, happier than she could remember in a long while, as the water brimmed over her eyelids and the whole world shuddered to pieces behind an ocean of hot salt.

"See!" Kathleen whispered excitedly to Aunt Daphne, hidden in the bushes some sixty paces away. "I *said* they were kissing!"

"Bread and cheese and kisses," Daphne murmured. "Bachelors' fare."

THE STORM BLEW itself out during that third week of March. Over the same period the tides approached their spring flood, at the height of which Captain Morgan had decided to refloat *Pegasus* — or at least to try. The peak would occur on the twenty-second of the month, which was, coincidentally, the day on which Kathleen and her Aunt Daphne snooped on the lovers in Highbury Fields.

By then, Frank and Teresa had been lovers, in a more profound sense of the word, for ten blissful days.

During all that time Wheeler was the only other person who knew she was still on board. The rest of the passengers had dispersed overland at once, either to Boston, their intended port of arrival, or directly to their final destinations, which ranged from California to Newfoundland. A skeleton crew remained against the day when *Pegasus* would refloat; they had come aboard briefly to jury-rig a rudder of sorts but otherwise lodged ashore, many of them in the town jail. The remaining hands had either been paid off or had joined other Shaw & Eggar vessels that happened to be in eastern coastal ports at that time. In such confusion, it was understandable that people would be more interested in their own arrangements than in the fate of yet another surplus female from the oul' country — even "a fate worse than death," as the saying had it. Teresa herself had, of course, kept well out of sight during the repairs to the rudder.

To Frank it seemed a fate as far removed from death as could be imagined. Time and again he told Teresa she had transformed his life. And Wheeler himself had commented to her — well out of Morgan's hearing, to be sure — that he'd never seen the Cap'n so altered.

"D'you know," Frank said to her on the night before they were to try to refloat the ship, "there has never been a week in my life when I literally had nothing to do but sit tight and wait."

"Ten days," she corrected him.

"Ten centuries! It's been timeless. But you know what I mean? Of course, I've known times when promised cargoes failed to arrive and we had to scrape around. That was idleness of a kind but it wasn't doing *nothing.*"

"Nothing, is it!" She eyed him askance. "Is *nothing* what we're after doing?"

He sighed at the impossibility of conveying feelings and discoveries that still overwhelmed him. "What I mean, I suppose, is that I've never had a week — very well, ten days — that I could simply devote to ... to my ... to our ..."

"To love." She settled herself in his embrace.

"To love," he murmured. "Even now it's hard just to say it: I love you." He spoke the words with an experimental lilt. "It makes me ashamed of all the years I ... what's the word? Why don't I have the words for this kind of thing? All the years in which that ... *faculty* within me, the faculty for loving ... all the years in which I allowed it to wither. I actually watched it happen and thought *good!* I thought all it did was get in the way." After a pause he added, "And I thought it was dead, too. Finally dead. But ..." He chuckled contentedly. "Apparently not."

"Your wife ...?" she suggested hesitantly.

"Oh yes. I loved her — once upon a time. In fact, that's what frightens me now." He hugged her more tightly. "The memory of all that. The longing that was never ... the slow killing of ..." He gave up trying to plumb the awfulness of those depths and started a new, more hopeful tack. "But I'll tell you what's different this time. You! You're going to make it different."

"Tell me about it." She sat up, not leaving his arms but shedding her languor. "Even if it scalds your heart, I want to know."

She leaned her head gently against his shoulder, to remove the direct challenge of her gaze. All she heard was the breath rushing in and out of his nostrils.

"Unless you think I have no right," she offered.

"No, no. Of course you do." After a reluctant pause he added, "I want to tell you. But it's not easy. These aren't easy matters to talk about. But you know when I touch you ... like this?"

"Ooh!" she responded with her customary delight.

"Just so!" He withdrew his hand again. "Now that is something she never does. Did, I mean. She never said *ooh!* like that." He hesitated.

"But?" she prompted.

He mimed Hilda's brand of distaste and, feeling the most wretched traitor, said, in her tones, "Really, Francis! Is that *all* you ever think about?"

Teresa closed her eyes and shook her head.

"Imagine what that does to a man," he added. "You begin to doubt yourself. There's no one you can talk to about it."

"Oh?" It appeared to surprise her. "Don't men ...?"

"Not quite in that way. In fact, not at all in that way. Until I met you, I've been more than half ready to believe I'm some species of monster." He smiled and craned his neck to peer into her eyes. "I'm not, am I?"

"Ah, well now!" She chuckled and settled herself fully back into his caress. "You might be and you mightn't. And if you are, then so am I. How can anyone ever know? Nobody talks about it. So how can we ...?"

"Oh, really?" Now he seemed surprised. "Don't women ...?"

"Not quite in that way." She laughed, knowing she was echoing his words. "In fact, as the man says, not at-all-at-all in that way."

"But you do discuss it? Women do?"

"Sure we do and we don't."

"How?"

"Lord!" she replied. "It's a fence you'd lepp over any way but straight. Aren't there ten ways to skin a cat?"

"Oh, are there," he commented glumly.

"Well, I might be walking down the street with Mary Feehan, say — she was my best friend at home, so she was — and I might whisper in her ear, 'Mother of God, would you ever look at the muscles on that fella!' if he was working with his shirt all open in the heat of summer. And she'd know what I was thinking, well enough. But I'd never say it, nor she'd never ask, neither. But we could go on talking about him like that till it rained fresh oysters."

"But you'd never actually ...?"

"There was once," she interrupted as a memory suddenly returned. "After Bridey Hoey got married last year. She married Tommy O'Gorman, a great snail of a man altogether, but he had money. His family owned the sawmills at Ballycumber ..."

"And?" he interjected, knowing her capacity for rambling.

"Oh yes. Well, didn't they have a honeymoon in Dublin — Friday to Monday. And when she came back, Mary and me asked her what like it was. 'Oh, Laawd!' says she," — Teresa spoke in tones of pretentious civility — "'Tis fiercely exaggereeaated altogether.' But she must have gone some way up the mountain, for she's after having a fine little boy last month." She pecked him a quick kiss. "And what ails *your* hands, me darlin' Frank? They seemed quite promising a minute ago."

"I want to talk."

She was about to make a facetious reply when his seriousness broke through her mood. "About us?" She swallowed audibly.

"Yes. The future. I said these ten days have been like ... something outside time altogether, but come tomorrow and it's back to this year of grace, eighteen seventy-five, and the world and its ways. We've — as you put it — 'been up the mountain' so many times that we must expect ..."

"Around Christmas," she interrupted.

"Ah. So you've thought of it."

"Before I loosened one single button. Oh Lord, but that sounds so calculating! I don't mean that. I mean, it crossed my mind and I dismissed it in the one moment." She raised her head and pressed warm lips to his bearded neck. "Oh Frank, you could cast me out tomorrow and I'd bear your child with all the love and pride in the world. God, I love you so much!"

For a moment he was too choked to reply. Then, easing her a little out of his embrace, he said, "May I walk on deck a while? Alone."

"Alone?" she echoed, slightly resentful.

"I have ... ghosts to lay."

It was at once too cosmic and too vague to allow a direct reply. She rose and released him with a smile. "I'll turn in, so," she said.

"Don't fall asleep now," he warned her from the door.

It was a full moon, almost directly overhead. He picked his way forr'ard, past the galley kiddley, where the glow of the banked-down fire gleamed briefly on the pans she had scoured. Someone would notice that in Boston, he realized. They'd know Cap'n Morgan would never have done such a thing.

What was he to do now? How to get out of this mess?

He stood among the chains and gazed out over the silvered tranquility all about. It had snowed heavily in the dying throes of the storm, so the whole world was now either pristine white or jet black; only the sea, with its shimmering translucence, offered him something in between.

It was what he now sought, he realized: something in between. An in-between kind of marriage. Wasn't it what he already had? No! In fact, he had no marriage at all. Try and make the courts believe that! Try and make *Hilda* believe it, even. She had everything she wanted, just the way she wanted it: a husband who wasn't there to "bother her" most of the time, and who'd been so emasculated by her fastidious disapproval that his "botherations" had almost ceased, anyway; a fine pair of sons who were settling well into their chosen professions; a bright daughter who was biddable, good looking, and modest; a home to be proud of; and a circle of friends as wide and diverse as any could wish for; and, to be sure, a more-than-generous allowance. Try convincing Hilda that such a marriage was a mere charade!

"Why?" he suddenly cried, raising his eyes toward the chill skies.

A myriad twinkling stars ignored him.

The question startled him. It had come suddenly and from nowhere, not pausing to form itself in his mind before it erupted. He realized then that he had not actually thought of God for years. Well ... in a way he'd thought of Him. He'd said his prayers every night, of course, conducted services at sea every Sunday, married the occasional couple, committed the occasional body to the deep, but he had not ... what was the word?

With a sardonic smile he realized the word was *bothered*. He had not bothered God for years. And now, suddenly, God had bothered him!

"Why?" he repeated aloud.

Was it a test? Had these ten days of Paradise been granted him merely to show him what he had lost, or never found, with Hilda? Was he now expected to play the Archangel Michael to himself and Teresa, casting them outside its gates and locking it against them for ever?

"Why?"

Or was Teresa a reward? "Well done, thou good and faithful servant!" He had, indeed, been a good and faithful servant. The chances he'd had to go astray — and never taken one of them! Such fidelity deserved recognition. And what better reward could anyone ask than to be given a second chance?

"Second chance, indeed!" he said morosely to God. "The first was no chance at all. I asked for bread and You gave me a stone. Why?"

So this new life with Teresa ... no, this *possible* new life with Teresa would be like his first real chance in life. God must know that. God knew everything. He knew their paths were going to cross. He knew they'd fall in love. He knew they'd "eat of the Tree of Knowledge." (Why was there no word for it half as beautiful as the act itself?) If she was quickened now with child, He knew it was going to happen *even before they met!* And yet He still allowed them to meet, He still allowed it all to happen. He could have stopped it at any moment — He was all-powerful, wasn't He? — yet He hadn't intervened.

"Why?"

A thought almost too great for his mind to contain suddenly occurred to him: *No matter what I decide, God already knows it! If I sever all connection with her, He knew I'd make that decision, even before He allowed us to meet. And if, on the other hand, I decide to marry her —*

God alone knows how, but ...

He chuckled at the unintended significance of the words. God did, indeed, know how, and had always known how.

So what it boiled down to was this: He, Frank Morgan, could decide any way he liked and it would be God's will, at least in part. For if a person, or a God, has power to stop something He *knows* beyond doubt will happen and yet does nothing to prevent it, how can He later claim He didn't will it to happen? Especially if He did everything to *make* it happen — allowing two perfect strangers to meets like that.

There was some flaw in the reasoning somewhere, but he couldn't see it.

"Why else?" he asked aloud.

A myriad twinkling stars ignored him.

She was tucked up in bed, lying on her back with her eyes closed, when he at last returned. He stood there awhile, knowing she was only pretending to sleep, willing her to look up at him and smile. If there had been any last lingering trace of doubt in his mind, about how to resolve this impossible dilemma, the sight of her lying there was enough to resolve it. She was surely the most beautiful woman who ever lived. The candle's glow bathed her face in its warm radiance and his heart vaulted with pleasure at the thought that she was now his, just as surely as he was now hers.

He knelt at the side of the bed.

"Jesus, Mary, and Joseph!" she said mildly, still not opening her eyes. "I forgot to say my prayers."

"Sssh!" He slipped a hand between the sheets and found her naked.

She gave a little scream and jumped a foot, skewing her torso beyond his easy reach. "Oh God, it's cold here, too," she complained, straightening herself up again, preferring his icy touch as the lesser torment.

"Sorry." He pulled his hands back to the edge of the bed, still keeping them under the covers to warm up. "I didn't realize how cold it was out there."

"Did you swim or what?"

"I floundered," he told her. "Will you marry me?"

Tears brimmed in her eyes. She blinked and they rolled down her cheeks.

"Yes?" he prompted.

"Darling Frank!" She sniffed glutinously. "Do you ever doubt it? Hold me. Don't mind if you're pure ice, just hold me."

His hands were merely cool now but her body felt like an oven. "Your chest is all breasts," he murmured in wonder.

"Get in!" she urged. "By all the holy ... be quick!"

He raced out of his clothes, scattering them to the four corners of the cabin, and slipped in beside her. He half turned to blow out the candle but she put a hand to his shoulder and said, "No!"

Her insistence surprised him.

"I'm not ashamed of us. We need no cloak of darkness for this joy."

He bridged her body with his knees and elbows, making a protective arch of himself above her. She was like a small furnace beneath him, writhing and giving out little sighs of happiness. Their loving was a piece of magic that never lost its wonder; nothing, it seemed, would ever make it dim. When he felt the warmth of her belly engulf him, the sensation was as bewitching as always. And she taught him *how* to love her, too. With sighs and little expressions of joy she encouraged him in the ways that pleased her. And when this or that did nothing to increase her pleasure, her tender, silent patience nudged him elsewhere.

Afterward, when they had recovered their breath and their heartbeats fell to a mere racing pitch, he said, "Would you prefer us to set up home on this side of the Atlantic, then?"

"D'you mean it?" she asked incredulously.

"It's for you to decide," he assured her.

"Lord love you, Frank, my angel!" She flung herself upon him and smothered his face with kisses. "There's nothing goes on in my head you don't know about and understand, or so I'll swear."

"Why d'you say that?"

"Will you hark at him! Didn't you know what did be going through my mind at just that instant? There was I, thinking to meself, if he asks me to set up house in London, how will I tell him?"

"Ah, yes."

"And there was you, thinking to yourself, the last place on God's earth she'd want to be living is where me and Hilda once set up home."

"House," he corrected her. "I never truly had a home with her."

"Whisht now!" The quick hail of her kisses dwindled to a gentle rain. "Don't be thinking you need blackguard her memory just to please me. Sure, the happier you were with her, the greater's the compliment to me!"

"I'll say not another word, then. So it's agreed? We'll set up home here?"

"Near New Haven?" she suggested. "Between there and New York?"

"Or Boston, perhaps. I call there more often than New York or anywhere else. Why?"

"My brother Ignatius and his wife Concepta live near New Haven, Connect-i-cut." Playfully she pronounced every syllable, smiling to show she knew it wasn't done, really. "He'd be company when you're at sea."

"Whatever you wish," he said. "But if I were only two days in Boston or New York, I'd spend a lot of it on the trains."

"Sure, we'll lepp that ditch when we see it," she said, slithering off him and settling at his side. "Why wouldn't I sail with you? Lots of wives do."

"Not while they're having babies," he said. "Can you imagine giving birth in that last great storm?"

She gave a little shiver of pleasure against him. "Having babies!" she echoed. "Lord, I can't wait. I wish I was eight months gone. I wish it was over and done with. I wish this next year could pass just like that!" She gave a light puff, as if blowing out a candle. "I'd love to be holding him in my arms this minute, the milky little thing! Don't they smell only gorgeous! I held Bridey O'Gorman's in my arms just before ... incidentally — Tommy O'Gorman was born plain Gorman, did you know. He acquired the 'O" in mysterious circumstances just before his marriage. Did I tell you that?"

"How would I know?" he asked with a laugh.

"God, you're right, Frank. I do talk too much, don't I. You talk instead! Tell me about your boys — and Kathy, is it? What sort of a colleen is she?"

"I told you about them already. Aren't you tired? We've got a long ..."

"Tired? I'm on fire! You set me all on fire! Poor Bridey may think it 'fiercely exaggereeaated,' but for meself I think you could write ten million books in praise of it without a whit of exaggeration. I could go at it all night. Aren't I only awful! But couldn't you?"

130

He groaned. "You should have met me twenty years ago."

"Pretend I did, then!"

She began moving her hands over his protesting body, recruiting his animal spirits for a new assault upon his will and better judgement.

L AWRENCE LAY FLAT out on the threadbare carpet, where he was most comfortable, looking up at Emma, who was sitting on the even more threadbare sofa, where she was least uncomfortable. With one half of his mind he was thinking she was still the sweetest and most adorable creature ever, but the other half had to admit that her life story (which she was unreeling at his request and at some length) made just about the most boring tale he'd ever heard.

It was now April, almost the end of April, in fact — a full month since they had unwittingly made such a thrilling spectacle for Kathleen and Aunt Daphne in Highbury Fields. In the intervening weeks he had, by sheer force of will, achieved an impossible amalgamation of his two earlier daydreams. He had rented a flat and installed her there with an allowance of thirty shillings a week, which, his friends assured him, was about the going rate for "a bit of fluff of one's own." They thought him no end of a dog for starting so early and he said nothing to enlighten them as to what was really going on.

In fact, if he had tried to describe it, he would have failed, for he had no clear idea himself. All he knew with certainty was that he was embarked upon one of the most exciting adventures he was ever likely to experience. All those wan poets who mooned around in their garrets, catching consumption and bewailing the fact that their beloved was as a closed book to them, a baffling, unknowable divinity who walked in ethereal mystery ... and so forth. They just went the wrong way about it, that was all. He, Lawrence Morgan, was going to show them!

At least, that had been his idea in the beginning. Unfortunately, the goal seemed as elusive to him in the prosaic, everyday world as, in verse, it seemed to them. He took to reading all the great love poems in the language and was sickened to realize that his entire being leaped up in agreement with their despair. "Beloved" was, indeed, just another way of saying "utterly and absolutely mysterious ... an enigma beyond all comprehending."

How, for instance, could he lie here now, listening to her distressingly detailed recall of some tedious and long-done family argument in Whitechapel, knowing what a bore she was, and yet adoring her to distraction, not wanting her to pause for breath even? How could he still bless that quirk of fortune which had thrown them together? If that wasn't a mystery worthy of any poet's pen, he was a Dutchman.

"Are you listening at all?" Emma asked.

"I should jolly well think so," he assured her.

"What did I just say?"

He was glad she hadn't asked what she'd said a minute ago; her most recent words were still ringing in his ears. "About your brother, telling your father he'd made five bob his first day up the markets."

She gave a sigh of despair for she honestly did not see how she could make her tale more boring than she already had. When he'd first started on this "I want to know you as well as you know yourself" nonsense, he'd been so persuasive that he'd actually set her to it with some enthusiasm. But, as the minutes ticked by and she listened to herself, her old conviction returned — that she was nothing but a rather dull, dim-witted young girl from a dirt-common family, and that her only redeeming feature was that she could usually manage to forget the fact and enjoy quite a happy life.

He sat up, full of concern for her. "Does it make you unhappy, my darling?" he asked solicitously. "Raking back over all these things?"

"Bored!" she exploded. "It bores me silly. All I want is to have a good time, enjoy life before it snuffs me out. Why can't we have a good time instead of all this ... slop?"

"What d'you call having a good time?"

"You know." She smiled archly but with little hope. "I mean ... we got this room, haven't we. Everyone thinks we're doing it anyway. We're being hanged for a sheep and we've not even tooken the lamb yet! You should see her next door." She raised her voice and shouted at the wall. "I'll bet she's got her ears glued to a tumbler right this minute!" In a more normal tone she added dourly, "Unless she's gawn to sleep, that is — which I wouldn't blame her for doing."

At that moment the springs of the bed in the apartment above began to creak in an unmistakable rhythm.

"See!" She smiled at Lawrence. "Everyone's at it! Sunday afternoon ... the nippers are all at Sunday School." She sniffed and added, "except the one they're making now."

He laughed with delight. "You see how much you know! How wise you really are. Why d'you always run yourself down so? You know so much about *life!*

A thought like that would never occur to me in a million years. And to you it's so obvious!"

"Oh Gawd!" she told the potted plant he'd brought her. "Now I've started him off again."

"Started me off on what?"

She stared at him with a blank kind of fatalism, as a horse might face a twenty-foot wall in a jumping contest; unlike any horse, however, she attempted the impossible. "I know just what you'll do now. You'll come at me with all your words, telling me I don't know the half of how wonderful I really am, and ..."

"You don't!" He was delighted that at last she seemed to understand.

"Stop it, Lawrence! The reason I don't is because I'm not. I'm *ordinary*. Ordinary, ordinary, ordinary! I'm so ordinary I fall asleep just thinking about me. Whatever you dream you've found in me ... I mean it just isn't there! It's a ... a ... what's that word?"

"Wonder?"

"Yes! *No!* The bleeding opposite. What you see in a desert."

"Mirage. But it's not. It is there."

"It fucking isn't!" She faced the wall again. "Got that did you, gel? It fucking isn't! I said it."

He frowned. Her language distressed him but he knew she was trying to pick a quarrel, so he forced himself to smile instead.

She settled grumpily in the nook of the sofa and went on, "Anyway, it isn't true — about them upstairs. They haven't got no nippers to send to Sunday School. 'Tisn't even their lodgings, it's his mum's, only she fell under a horse two months ago and broke her back. She's in hospital down Gray's Inn Road."

"And he brings his floozies here and ..."

"No!" she interrupted him. Her tone and eyebrows signalled that the truth was even more amazing than that. "That's his *wife* with him up there! Disgusting, I call it. He brings her here every Sunday and they do it on his mum's bed."

Superficially Lawrence thought it disgusting, too. But, to his surprise, he caught a whiff of understanding somewhere in his mind, saw a flash of it as it darted through the shadows where, he was beginning to suspect, all genuine discoveries about life and people came from.

"What's up with you?" she asked accusingly.

"I don't know. What you just said ... I felt a sort of ..." He shrugged.

"Don't you think it's disgusting? On his mother's bed? In her own sheets?"

"I don't know. Perhaps it's something he has to do."

"Has to?" she asked scornfully. "I'd like to know how you work that out. You mean there's a law or something? Is there a copper standing by the bed, saying 'You got another five minutes, my lad!'?"

He rose and sat on the sofa, a foot or two away from her. Staring down at the carpet he had just quitted — almost as if he were speaking to a former self — he mused, "Perhaps it's his only way of leaving home. My Aunt Daphne once said a lot of men never leave home, really. Even if they marry and rent a new house, they bring their mother along with them" — he tapped his forehead — "in here, I mean. Not in the flesh but in here."

To her horror Emma remembered that her own mother had once made the identical comment about her father. She stared venomously at Lawrence, hating him for his ability to strike chords inside her that she would prefer to remain unstruck. He was going to end up changing her completely, and at moments like this she felt powerless to stop him. Because there was, in fact, a certain awful fascination in discovering these things about yourself — thoughts and fancies that were there all the time but you never knew it. Even so, given the choice, she'd rather go on living from moment to moment, grabbing what fun she could and not thinking too much about herself and the future and things like that. If only *he* would allow her that choice!

Before she could stop herself she said, "Here! Is that what you'd like? Do me in *your* mum's bed?"

He drew back his hand to strike her ... realized with horror what he was about to do ... and let it drop limply back to his side. "Yes," he admitted after a vehement pause. "Not really, you know. I mean, if it came to it, I wouldn't. But when you said that about *them*" — he jerked his head toward the ceiling — "I did sort of, you know, understand."

In the ensuing silence there was nothing to do but sit and listen to the rhythmic song of the springs above. It was absolutely even, with a mechanical regularity that hardly seemed human.

"It can't be much cop for her," Emma commented. She observed Lawrence closely, hoping he hadn't noticed the tremor in her voice, for the sounds from above — and the thoughts they evoked — were disturbing her somewhat.

"Why?" he asked, knowing it was a silly question but being unable to think of anything else. A curious paralysis seemed to have come over him. His limbs felt weak, as if his blood had dropped to only half strength.

"Like a bleeding machine," she said.

He remembered a vulgar song from his schooldays, about just such a machine: *Round and round went the bloody great wheel* ... He shook his head angrily and felt sick of himself.

"Give us a kiss," she said.

He turned to her in surprise — and was even more surprised at what he saw. Usually when she said something like that she had a coy smile on her lips but now her face was pale and drawn; her jaw shivered — indeed, her whole head seemed affected by a small tremor. "Please?"

Instead of moving to a more comfortable position near her, he leaned across the gap and tried to reach her with outstretched lips. The result was that he toppled against her, almost falling with his head in her lap. But it released whatever spasm had held her. Now she pounced on him with exaggerated glee and, twisting him as he fell, pinned his head on her thigh and held him there where she could stare down at him and pretend he was at her mercy. "Now, Mister Clever-Dick!" she exclaimed.

"Now what?" He smiled and abandoned the struggle to sit up again.

"This!" She lowered her head and raised her thigh, bringing their lips together — but at right angles to each other. In a series of rapid, tender kisses she worked her lips across his, left to right and back again. She had bad breath but he relished it because it was hers; funnily enough, her mouth, when he pushed his tongue gently inside it, tasted sweet and warm. Just another of her many enigmas.

He relished, too, the nearness of her body, the pressure of her bosom on his cheek, the way the back of his head fitted so perfectly in the depression between her thighs. It felt very grown-up to be so near those exciting and dangerous parts of her — and even more grown-up to be paying no apparent heed to the fact, treating it like the most normal and everyday occurrence.

She released him at last and lowered her thigh, cuddling his head tight against her belly, in the depths of which he could hear liquid rumblings.

"I wish I'd never started this," she said in an oddly happy tone.

He was about to ask what when there was a marked change in the rhythm of the creaking from above; instead of two or three firm but moderate creaks each second the interval stretched out to more than a second between each and they acquired an almost desperate force. Five ... six ... seven, Lawrence counted, and then came the faintest sound of a male, "Aah!" There was no sound from the female at all.

"Poor woman," Emma commented.

"Have you ever done it?" he blurted out.

"No," she replied at once. "You?"

"No," he said.

There was a silence during which neither of them breathed. Then he said, "If you make a pot of tea, I'll toast the crumpets. Then I'll have to go."

"All right," she said, giving him a quick, almost sisterly kiss before she lifted his head away. "Why not?"

He took his leave half an hour later and sauntered homeward along Upper Street. *It wouldn't have done,* he assured himself. *It wouldn't have been right at all. She thinks she's ready for it but she's not.*

He caught sight of himself in a tailor's shop window full of cheap reach-me-down suits, which offered a flattering comparison with his own reflection.

All the same, he'd have the lapels just a shade narrower on his next, he thought. *She's definitely not ready for it,* he told one of the suits.

Over his shoulder — or the shoulder of his reflection — he was surprised to see ... surely not? But yes, on turning round he saw it was, indeed, his sister and Aunt Daphne. "I say, hello!" he called out to them. "Out for a stroll? Pretty cold, what?"

As he crossed the road to join them, the last verse of that awful schooldays song popped into his mind. He had been fighting off its crudities ever since it had first come crawling out of the slime of juvenilia in the unswept angles of his soul. Now two whole lines recurred before he rang down the curtain on it:

> *This is a case of the biter bit —*
> *There was no way of stopping it ...*

A T HIGHBURY CIRCUS, by an agreement reached before Lawrence had emerged from The Nest (as Daphne had dubbed it, in her best sepulchral voice), Kathleen suddenly "remembered" she was wanted urgently at home — leaving Lawrence to squire his aunt across the Fields.

"It won't do, young man," she said bluntly as soon as the girl had gone.

Lawrence felt his stomach fall away inside him. "What's that, Aunt?" he asked lightly.

"You know very well. This business with Emma Harding."

"How ... I mean ..." he stammered. "You *know* about it?"

"My dear young Lawrence! Do you seriously suppose you can wander around this tiny patch of green for an hour on a Sunday afternoon — where at least a dozen of our friends reside — and *not* have it noticed?"

"Oh." He took rapid stock of the situation and brightened. She knew about the walks on Highbury Fields but not about the rooms in Upper Street. "You're right, of course, Aunt Daphne, as always. 'S'matter of fact, I've chucked her."

"Really?" The tone was polite but not very interested.

"Well, as you can see, we haven't been strolling about here this afternoon. I chucked her, as I said."

"I don't understand what you saw in her in the first place. She is quite excessively plain and ..."

"Oh come!" he protested. "I can't allow that. I mean everyone to his opinion, I grant you, but it's in the eye of the beholder, what?"

"It's a singularly odd eye you must have, then." She smiled sweetly. "But ... if you've 'chucked' her ... no harm done, eh?"

"Actually ..." He scratched his head diffidently and gave an engaging smile. "Don't breathe a word to Kathy but Emma chucked me, if you must know."

For the first time his aunt's interest seemed to quicken. "Oh?" she said on a steeply ascending note. "How rash of her. Did she give you any reason?"

Now he wished he hadn't started this hare. He'd only done so to add conviction to his story. To round it off and bury it. But now it was up and running he had no choice but to run with it and steer it as far from danger as possible. He knew Aunt Daphne well enough to realize that, if he strayed too wide of the truth, she'd be onto it like a fox terrier. And once she

140

owned the line on a lie she'd not rest till she'd harried it all the way to earth. "Er, she said she's just a boring, empty-headed girl from a dirt-common family ... not good enough for me. Such rot!"

"I see. And what did you say to that?"

Lawrence came to a halt; they were now about a half way up the asphalt path. "Oh, I tried to make her see that she wasn't, at least not to me. I mean, education isn't the sole measure of a person, is it?"

"No," Daphne allowed. "There's also breeding and taste and gentility. But ..." Her tone wandered fastidiously. "I shouldn't have thought — on the face of it, mind you, and not knowing the young person terribly well — I shouldn't have thought her scores in those departments ..."

"What about simple goodness?" Lawrence asked pugnaciously. "And what about the sort of person a person could have been if only they'd been given a chance in life?"

"Ah!" Her solemnly mocking tone suggested that she could *just* remember having been so quixotic once herself, but oh, so long ago. "Yes, of course — what about them?"

Of those six words the first three were a soothing foil to the final three, which came at him like a rapier.

"Well," he said, turning the thrust over the arm. "It's all water under the bridge now."

"Lawrence," she said, putting just enough edge into the word to make him realize that unless he told her a lot more than he had done so far, she'd start getting blunt with him. Such understandings between people — expressed in the merest intonation of a single word — usually take a lifetime to establish; but with Daphne Dowty a week was enough. Lawrence, having known her all his life, was now almost certain she already knew everything. She'd probably even followed him to Emma's rooms in Upper Street. Or perhaps she only suspected something was afoot and was now fishing for more. Any direct challenge on his part would be fatal; she'd have the whole truth out, flayed and dissected, in seconds. His best hope of avoiding such a fate now was to give her enough to chew on. At least he could continue talking about the whole affair in the past tense, still; for one of the good features about Aunt Daphne's rather oblique character was that she'd withhold any blunt, direct questions as long as she felt she was getting somewhere.

"May I be utterly frank, Aunt?" He took her arm and resumed their stroll.

"Oh dear!" she sighed, and then surveyed him with an amused, speculative eye. "How you've matured since starting to work in the City! Or is it the Dramatic Society at work? Don't I remember a line like that in the play you did before Christmas? Do you *have* to be *utterly* frank, dear? Can't you just give it me in little hints?" The smile turned steely as she concluded, "I'm quite good at them, you know."

Lawrence drew a physical deep breath before taking a metaphorical plunge. "I am ... I mean I *was* entirely to blame. When I came home from the City — that day she got the boot — I mean, I just felt so sorry for her ..."

"Yes, about that, by the way ..." Daphne decided to feed him some of what Kathleen had told her — without, of course, revealing her source. Also, she saw a chance to kill one or two other birds with the same stone. "It so happens I walked through the Circus about forty minutes before your tram drew up — to see Mrs Drew, as a matter of fact. D'you know her? She lives down Upper Street — just beyond where you met Kathleen and me just now."

He admitted he did not know the lady.

"Such a tragedy! She fell under a horse shortly after that. She's in hospital still. Her son is in the Choral Society."

"Mrs Drew ...?" Lawrence made a lightning decision to reserve a bit of ground ... just in case. "It does vaguely ring a bell. Anyway?"

"Yes, anyway, I saw your Miss Emma Harding waiting for a tram there at the top of Cannonbury Road, almost opposite ... what's the name of that little street? It escapes me for the moment."

"Ah ... Compton Mews, was it?" He suggested the next street down from Goldsmith's Place.

"Something like that. Anyway, she let two or three go by — which did make me wonder what tram she was, in fact, waiting for. You don't suppose she could have been waiting for the one that eventually brought you?"

"Oh, of course she was."

His admission startled her but she was swift to recover her place. "Really? How extraordinary! Did she have any reason to suppose you'd go to some heroic length to help her in her straits?"

It struck him as quite extraordinary that he had never questioned Emma's motives in waiting there. Now, having to speak almost without thought, he decided to put the worst possible construction on her actions — knowing that Aunt Daphne never questioned anything scurrilous. "She wanted to try and snare me in some way — get her revenge on the mater through me, and all that, don't you know."

"Snare you?" It wasn't a real question, just the first thing that came into her head to give her time to think.

But Lawrence was onto it. "In a rather *obvious* way, I should have thought, Aunt Daphne." His tone suggested that his aunt's naïveté amazed him.

"My, my, Lawrence," she said calmly. "You do rather take one's breath away at times." She did not, however pause in her energetic stroll up the hill. "So you foiled her, did you? Got her to chuck you! How clever!"

"If only ..." He hesitated.

"What, dear?"

"That's what I meant when I said could I be utterly frank. You see, I rather fell for her. That's the amazing thing. I'm so full of her, I think about nothing else, and there's no one I can talk to about it. So I wondered if I could talk to you, Aunt Daphne? There's no one else."

"Such a testimonial! Oh dear, well, I did ask for it, I suppose. It serves me jolly well right."

They had reached the front door of her house by now.

"Come in," she suggested eagerly. "We'll have oodles and oodles of crumpets by the fire. Just what a growing ... young man — I must stop saying *boy*, mustn't I! Yes — just what a growing young man needs, eh?"

"Oh ... yes ... jolly, what!" Lawrence replied wanly. He did not, of course, intend telling his aunt anything like the whole truth — just enough to enable her to help him see his way forward.

SIR HECTOR SHAW, founder and senior partner in the Shaw & Eggar Line, came to New York in person, early that May. His first business there was to summon Frank to the company's offices in West Forty-Second Street, by Pier 82. An old seadog himself, he had started before the mast in the 'thirties and worked his way up to master, and then owner, by superb seamanship and innate ruthlessness — qualities he saw in the young (to him) Morgan.

Frank, knowing the Old Man had an unrivalled nose for information, was afraid that news of his "marriage" might have somehow leaped all the intervening parties and landed at the rim of Sir Hector's ear; if so, this interview would be the parting of the ways between himself and Shaw & Eggar. It was with some misgiving, therefore, that he marched down the slope at the end of the street toward the company's offices — not that any who saw him would have guessed it. There were many in that area who knew him, of course, if only by sight — sailors and longshoremen. To them he seemed as ever, Cap'n Morgan, the whispering volcano — walking tall, stiff as a mainmast of steel, and radiating that kind of contained menace which commanded respect, if only out of self-interest.

Frank himself was more acutely aware of his reputation and the effect it had on those around him than ever before. The contrast between his ironclad exterior and the turmoil within made sure of that. He could still hardly believe he had actually gone through with the marriage. From time to time he would remember the scene as if it were a particularly vivid dream, or a monstrous, far-fetched yarn told under slack canvas, waiting for a breeze. Still less could he believe that her brother and his wife in New Haven had accepted and acquiesced in his reasons for keeping the marriage quiet: "When Hilda died I took a solemn vow I'd never marry again. I've told every man and dog who ever sailed under me that my only wife is the sea. That's my reputation, my power of command. If it ever gets out that a girl half my age fluttered an eyelash and made me her slave, I'm for the breakers. No, if I'm to sail under different colours, I need time to get new papers ..." And so on.

And they had swallowed it!

What a frightening glimpse of power that had given him — which was curious, because it was the same power as he exercised daily, whether at sea or at home, and it had never disturbed him before. He was so accustomed to being obeyed that he no longer questioned the cause; he simply knew in his bones that he was the sort of man whose orders were carried out. There seemed to be a kind of instinct in people, a need for leadership, that made them obey him.

And what was *his* need? Whose call would he obey? Not Sir Hector's. Not any man's, nor any woman's either — not even Teresa's, in the end.

Death, perhaps? That had certainly been true in his younger days. Then he needed to look Death in the eyes almost daily, touch its shrouds, smell its chill breath — and cheat it of its victory, one more time. In all the universe there was no thrill to equal that.

But somehow, on the night he ran *Pegasus* aground, that phase of his life had come to an end. Now he courted thrills — by which he meant dangers — of a less physical kind: exposure, ruin, disgrace. Like three captious jesters, they spiced his waking with their jeers at the safe, respectable world; like three unctuous courtiers, they flattered his retiring with their cries of "One more day, Cap'n!" and "You've done it again!"

What would Sir Hector say if he knew the sort of man who now paused and smiled to himself at that august threshold!

He tapped respectfully on the chairman's door.

"Come in!" It was a familiar and forbidding bark; his spirit fell.

He entered to find the Old Man standing half way between his desk and the door, waiting to shake his hand. That had never happened before.

Face to face at last, Frank felt in reverse all the feelings he inspired in others. Sir Hector, though all of eighty years old, still stood six foot two, still shook your hand with a grip that made pythons sound friendly. His huge, craggy forehead sprouted a more luxuriant growth of eyebrow than ever — twin thickets from beneath which he ambushed you with eyes that could cut diamonds. "Good of you to come so quickly, Morgan," he said. "You're looking well. You've made a good recovery."

"Complete, I think, sir. I hope you had a fair crossing?"

A faint smile creased the leather face. "Fairer than yours! Do sit down." He waited for Frank to obey and then crossed the room to a plan chest beside the door, saying, "Stay where you are," over his shoulder.

"I won't beat about all seven seas," he added as he returned. "Tell me what you think of her." And he unfurled a large roll of blue paper — so large, indeed, that Frank had to hold it at arm's length to make out its contents. It was a drawing in white ink of a steamship — but what a ship! He counted five decks above the waterline. His eye sought among the details in the box in the lower-right corner: 7,500 tons!

And … yes, it said there, right enough: Shaw & Eggar Steamship Line.

Steamship Line?

His head shot up. He found Sir Hector was staring at him intently.

"Yes," the Old Man said quietly. "It had to come."

"But our largest steamship is the *Ariadne* — and she's only just over two and a half thousand tons."

Sir Hector nodded. "And yet I believe the day is not far off when even that leviathan will seem very small beer."

"Well, sir." Frank waved a dismissive hand over the plan. "Thank the Lord, canvas and sheet will see me out!"

"I want you for her master."

Frank was so astonished he could think of nothing to say except what had been on his mind just before the Old Man dropped his bombshell: "Why is it drawn in white ink on coloured paper?"

Sir Hector crossed to the window and, after a moment's contained silence, burst out laughing. "Eggar and I took bets on what you'd say to the proposal. Now we've both lost. I don't know, Morgan. You're a law unto yourself. What the hell does the colour of the drawing matter?"

"I'm sorry, sir. I was taken aback."

"Let's hope you've not forgotten how to come about!"

"What did *you* bet my reply would be, sir — if I may make so bold?"

"I said you'd say no, of course."

"Ah. And Mr Eggar?"

"He said you'd say absolutely not."

Frank pondered the subtle difference between the two, knowing well that the wily Old Man had deliberately found some way of introducing the bet — which he was almost sure had never taken place at all. But Sir Hector would be equally sure that his partner's "absolutely not" would annoy Frank and make the response that much less likely. And now the next port of call — a plain "no" — was also tainted, with Sir Hector's prediction nailed to its flagstaff. The old bastard knew how he'd hate it to be thought he was so predictable. Very well, he'd show them! "Why *is* it in white ink?" he asked.

"Ship me green!" Sir Hector roared. "It's some newfangled *thing* they have in the office. It's not a drawing, it's a copy, a print. Is there anything else you'd like to know?" He waved his hand with largesse around the office, inviting questions on any fancy that entered Frank's head.

Slowly Frank rolled up the drawing. "I accept, sir," he said. "I needn't tell you how keenly aware I am of the offer you've ..."

"Aye aye!" Sir Hector interrupted. "You've earned it. You'd already earned it before this last voyage, but the way you managed to save *Pegasus*, for the loss of only two hands ..."

"Two of the best, sir."

The other conceded the point with a dip of his head. "And saved every last passenger. You've proved yourself the best man by far."

They did not discuss the financial side of the new arrangement until they met for dinner the following evening. The salary alone, at £1100, was a hundred more than he earned in total at present, including his share of the profits on each voyage. His share of the profits on the new vessel would easily top six hundred and might even double his salary. And, as if that were not enough, he was also to receive shares in

Shaw & Eggar when they were publicly floated in the autumn. "I can't put an exact figure on it until the underwriters have had their say," Sir Hector told him. "But we intend to give you three and a half percent of the new company."

Frank made a hopeless sort of gesture. "I'm speechless, sir. I honestly don't know what to say."

"Say nothing then. One day you may own a much greater share than that — and one of the things you'll learn is that a shipping line, great or small, lives or dies by the quality of its captains. And a line that has good ones and does nothing to acknowledge it deserves to sink without trace. It's naked self-interest, that's all."

In a rare gesture of intimacy he took his pipe from his mouth and dug Frank in the ribs with its stem. "It's not just that you're a damn fine seaman, Morgan, you're also a damn fine man. Straight as the Greenwich meridian. You'll never let the old firm down. That's the beam end of the matter."

NEIL RETURNED FROM Genoa aboard the *Swallow* with a cargo of wine, olive oil, and raw cork. It was the second Saturday in June. They tied up at the Surrey Commercial Dock shortly after noon and he was clear to go ashore by four. Land had never felt so good beneath him; London had never looked better. He was lucky with the trams and his train so it was no more than twenty to five when he stepped into Highbury New Park and began counting the paces to their front door. He walked with self-conscious stiffness, determined not to show the rolling gait of the sailor.

He'd only been gone three months yet the trees seemed taller — and the houses, paradoxically, smaller. Perhaps it was the bushing out of everything, all the new green leaves, obscuring the façades and pushing them more into the background. He thought of Lawrence, walking up and down this street twice each day on his way to Furnival's ... lucky young tyke! Then he tried not to think of Lawrence, to accept that his own destiny was the sea.

Lawrence knew from *Lloyd's List* that *Swallow* was due in that day, so the fatted calf was well killed and roasted by the time he docked; indeed, it had taken all Lawrence's powers of persuasion to stop his mother from going down to Rotherhithe and standing on the quayside to welcome her son in. Every five minutes throughout the afternoon she went to the window and peered anxiously down the street. Twice she caught Lawrence trying to slope off (to Emma, of course, though she did not know that) and gaffed him back with an angry cry.

"You're not to ramble off," she told him when he was safely back indoors for the second time. "Mooning around the shop windows in Upper Street when your brother's due home at any minute!" She picked imaginary lint off his lapels and smoothed creases that weren't there.

"He's only been gone since March," Lawrence objected. "Anyone would imagine he's been away years."

She gave him an impulsive but rather perfunctory kiss. "You're just jealous." Then she thought about it and added, "Actually, we *haven't* heard the Song of the Sea from you for quite a few weeks, have we. Are you learning to accept it more now?"

He shrugged. "I suppose I must be." Through a slant opening of the drawing room door he saw his sister smile. She was leafing through Aunt Daphne's photograph album, which she had borrowed last week; was she smiling at one of the photographs — or at what he had just said? There had been a spate of knowing smiles from her lately. She was altogether too sharp and bright for his comfort.

"I got some strawberries in specially," his mother said. "The first this year. Wildly extravagant but I don't see that your father could object."

"He never does," Lawrence pointed out unkindly. "I've never heard him once question any household expenditure. Why d'you say such things?"

"If he heard you taking that tone with me, you'd soon feel the rough side of his tongue. I forbid it."

It wouldn't stop him from agreeing with me, though, Lawrence thought. He smiled his most charming smile and apologized; and she felt her heart melt — against her will — and wished there were some way of forbidding that, too.

Afternoon tea was always at four sharp, so the rumblings of hunger were almost audible by the time Neil's knock went echoing through the house. He never rang the bell nowadays; he said his life already had too many bells in it for his liking.

Hilda came running downstairs as the maid walked up from the basement. The girl thought she was about to get a drubbing for not moving faster, but all the missus said was, "All right, Walker, I'll see to it."

Walker, who had replaced Emma Harding, marvelled; she had never known the missus answer the door before. As she returned to the servants' hall she heard the ecstasies of welcome from above: "Darling! You're late! How wonderful to have you home! We thought you'd be here ages ago! Let me look at you. When d'you have to sail again?"

As the maid continued her descent she realized it wasn't so much the money she envied posh people for, it was their love, the way they could show it. She herself hadn't seen her own mum for three months, just like those two up there; but what would they say to each other now if she went home? "Oh, it's you!" and, "'Lo, Mum." It wasn't that they didn't love each other, they just couldn't show it. With a sigh she returned to *The Perils of Leah* and waited for the summons to carry up the tea.

"You've grown," Hilda said accusingly, trying to straighten the creases under his arms. "This jacket fitted when you left. Was it a good voyage? You know *Pegasus* was caught in the Great Storm?"

"I saw an item in the *List*. Could I just go and wash my hands, d'you think?"

Kathleen tugged at his sleeve for her welcome-home kiss. "Guess what Father's been given!"

"I'll tell him that if you don't mind, miss!" her mother snapped.

Neil left them to it and took the stairs to the bathroom three at a time. "Hallo Beast," he said as he passed Lawrence on the way.

"Hallo Beast."

They exchanged playful punches.

During tea Hilda told him the splendid news of his father's appointment to the "flagship" of the rapidly expanding Shaw & Eggar Steamship Line. "Seven and a half thousand tons!" she exclaimed, and then laughed as she added, "You'll never guess what dear little Walker said when I told the servants about it. She said, 'Seven and a half thousand tons! How ever does it stay afloat, ma'am!' Isn't that sweet?"

"What's she called?" Neil asked.

"Walker. I said."

"No! The ship!"

"Oh … they haven't decided. Your father wanted her named Hilda, bless him, but they insist on something classical."

"Hilda of Troy?" Kathleen's suggestion was greeted with withering stares. "Sorry, I'm sure," she muttered and returned to her strawberries.

Neil picked up an earlier thread. "Did you say Walker? What happened to little Harding?"

"We don't mention her any more," his mother told him.

"Really?" he asked with interest.

"Most decidedly not!" She closed the subject firmly.

Kathleen was careful to look at both of them before she casually let her gaze settle on Lawrence. He was just as casually picking his nails — in a way that he knew infuriated his mother.

"Don't do that, dear," she said in a jaded tone.

As soon as tea was over Lawrence said he was going to pop out for a minute.

"Where?" Kathleen asked, a fraction of a second ahead of her mother.

"What's it to you?" he replied. Then, thinking better of it, "To Aunt Daphne, actually. I'll return that album if you wish."

She said she might do it herself later.

Hilda left them, saying she had letters to write.

The moment the front door had closed behind Lawrence, Kathleen grabbed Neil's arm. "Come on, quick! Get your hat and cane and come with me. I'll explain as we go." And she dashed off to get her own hat and parasol.

"Just popping round to Aunt Daphne's," she called out to her mother. "Neil says he wants a breath of air, too."

"Don't be late for dinner," was her only reply.

"That's a relief," Neil said as they set off down the road. "I thought she'd be eager to hear all about my wonderful time at sea — and ask me things she could put in her next letter to Papa. Is he home, by the way? I saw they're refitting *Pegasus*. He did jolly well to save her."

"He came back last week," she replied, "but he went to Belfast the very next day. Thet's where they're building the *Hilda of Troy*."

"That's not funny, you know." He laughed. "Anyway, why are we taking this walk? What's all the mystery?"

She half lowered her parasol, collapsing it enough to aim it like a rifle. "Bang!" she said.

He followed her aim as she put it up again. "The Beast!" he said. "Shall we catch up with him?"

He took a stride or two before she caught his jacket and pulled him back. "No, you'll spoil it."

"Spoil what?"

"You'll see."

When they reached the Circus, Neil said, "What's he going that way for? I thought he said Aunt Daphne's."

"You'll see," she promised again. She made him wait until Lawrence had disappeared into Upper Street. "We must be careful. I think he's beginning to suspect I know something."

"Funny," Neil told her. "I was just beginning to suspect the opposite! Anyway, I'm not sure it's ethical to be spying on our brother like this. How would you bally well like it?"

"Hah!" she snorted. "I'm spied on all the time. I can't put a foot out of doors without saying where I'm going or having a maid to chaperone me."

"You're growing up, that's why. Anyway, it's different for females."

"Who chaperones the maids, then? And who'll chaperone the chaperones of the maids, eh?"

He did not think the question worthy of reply. "Talking of maids," he went on as they, too, started down Upper Street, "what was all that about little Emma Harding? Blot her copybook, did she?" He took her arm to create the sort of intimacy in which she might blurt it out.

She blurted it out, all right! "Oh," she said airily, "I started my monthly periods, you know, and Emma tried to comfort me by saying that for many girls it was the happiest week of the month and Mama chose to misinterpret that and gave her the boot."

She was delighted to feel his arm go rigid at her side.

For Neil it suddenly seemed the whole day had changed tempo and even colour. Details in the scene — cracks in the paving stones, piles of dog dirt — suddenly assumed a supernatural reality and he thought he could hear windy, echoing chords of unearthly harmonies. "I say, Kathy!" he exclaimed.

"What?" she asked with provocative indifference.

"Well! I mean to say!"

"It's perfectly natural," she said crossly.

After a pause he said, "I suppose so. All the same. Bally private, what?"

She jerked his elbow, bringing him to a sudden halt. "Watch the Beast!"

Neil was just in time to see his brother, who was a furlong or so ahead of them, fish out a key and open a door. "Eh?" he exclaimed.

"Now," she said, "you know the Beast as well as anyone — what d'you suppose that's all about?"

He stared at her, then back down the street, then at her again. He shook his head. "Is he running a little shop on the side, or something?"

To be sure, he was well aware of the most likely explanation, but he could hardly trot that out to his little sister! However, she now more or less confirmed it by replying, "*Something* on the side, anyway."

He stared at her in horror. "You've changed, Kathy! What has been going on these last few months?" He turned and took a pace or two back the way they had come. "I'm not sure I like any of this." Then he took a pace toward her again and stared deep into her eyes. "Why are you showing me this? And *half*-telling me? What's your game?"

Even at the time he realized the question was something of a landmark in their relations with each other. He knew she was secretive and devious, of course — like all the females he'd ever met; but this was the first time he'd allowed she could be devious in a grown-up manner. It was no childish prank she was playing. She did not bite her lip and grin like a naughty schoolgirl — though she was still quite capable of behaving like that in more appropriate circumstances. She was a woman, thwarted of a secret, and it pained her as much as it would a female twice her age.

He suddenly felt a sharp compassion for her. He remembered his recent humiliations at sea — that feeling of not-belonging, of being excluded by people who did not even pay you the compliment of *intending* it. To help her, he took a great leap in the dark — for even if he was wrong, it would loosen her tongue and give her a chance to parade her grown-up knowledge. "This isn't in any way connected with ... what we were talking about a moment ago, is it? A certain young serving wench?"

She showed the child who still dwelled within her then by throwing her arms around him and giggling in glee. "Clever! Clever old Neil!"

"Oh yes," he replied scornfully. "Drop a hint weighing a ton and clever old Neil can always hear it fall!"

But from that point on the matter became extremely delicate; hints were weighed in fractions of an ounce. "I'll tell you one thing," he said, taking her arm firmly and leading her away up the street toward the Circus and Highbury Fields. "I'm certainly not staying to spy on him now!"

When they were safely on the Fields, and out of sight of Upper Street, he went on, "So, what it amounts to is that Mama booted poor little Emma out. And she's taken lodgings in Upper Street ... presumably found some living-out position ... and the Beast calls on her from time to time. It's rash of him, I must say. I'll find some chance to have a word in his ear before I sail again."

"He calls on her from day to day," she said evenly.

"Worse and worse! Oh calamity!" He parodied the sort of melodrama he used to write for the three of them to perform as children. "But don't worry your dear little head about it any more, Little Face, eh?"

"He pays her rent," she continued stolidly.

His eyes raked the cloudless skies. "I think you must have fallen under a misapprehension there, little one. Unless Furnival's have started paying him a salary at last."

"He doesn't work for Furnival's any more. He's

been elected to the Baltic and he's now a clerk with Turnbull and Trotter. Five guineas a month."

"Good for him." Neil contained his surprise and stuck to the point. "But he couldn't do much on five guineas a month."

"He doesn't have to. He bets on horse races. And he wins a lot more often than he loses. Between five and ten guineas a week, in fact."

"How d'you know all this?" he asked in despair of outflanking her.

"He keeps it all in a little book, in the second drawer down in his room."

"All this about Emma, you mean?"

"No. All his bets. He takes *The Pink 'Un* every day, you know, and puts it in the waste paper basket by the tram stop. He's saved more than three hundred pounds already."

Neil stopped and stared at her. "You're making this up, surely!"

"Not a word of it. I'm sure he keeps a book about Emma, too. In the bottom drawer, but I can't pick that lock and I've tried every key in the house on it."

"Kathy!" Now his horror had a focus. "D'you spy on us all?"

She grinned and said "Of course not!" in such a way that he couldn't be sure. "I would, though," she added, "if you started having secrets like that from me. I don't think we should ever have secrets from each other, do you? I think we should always tell each other everything. What harm would there be if I knew what was going on with the Beast and Emma?"

He chose not to answer that. "I only hope you don't go rooting through my drawers," he said. "If I ever catch you, I'll break your arm. Are we actually going to Aunt Daphne's? You forgot the album after all."

"I want to keep it another week," she replied. "We can call and tell her so. And if, sometime during this hol, you could ..."

"Not hols any more, Little Face," he reminded her. "It's called shore leave nowadays, don't you know."

"Anyway, if you could pump her a little sometime, about the Beast and Emma, you know ..."

"Good heavens! Is she in on it too? How far do the ripples spread?"

Kathleen explained how Aunt Daphne's involvement had come about. It left her brother wishing he were just a year or two older. He'd certainly put a flea in his aunt's ear about the shameless way she had involved his little sister in these distressing affairs.

"Only," Kathleen went on, "I'm sure he told her something that day I left him to escort her home. And she's gone tight as a limpet ever since then."

Notwithstanding her belief that siblings should nurse no secrets, she felt it unnecessary to explain why she wanted to keep the album another week. It contained a long-ago photograph of her father, posed at a dinner given for the master and crew of his first vessel, the one that had gone down on the Goodwins. It dated from the days when people had to hold a pose for about three hours or something ridiculous, so they used to fix their gaze on something they'd find easy to maintain. And her father had chosen to stare at a rather pretty young girl sitting at the master's right. And the pretty young girl had chosen to stare back at him. And the pretty young girl wasn't the Hilda Watson he had later married!

Now couple that with the fact that Aunt Daphne always wrote the names of the subjects on the back of each photograph, and then copied the list in white ink underneath before sticking it in — but not with this photo! Uniquely it carried no *dramatis personæ* underneath. Now *there* was an intriguing mystery!

There must be *some* way of softening that glue — and of sticking the photograph back in its place without Aunt Daphne ever noticing it.

L AWRENCE LAY ON his bed smoking a cheroot from a packet he'd been given by a Dutch captain whose vessel he had placed very profitably. He wasn't enjoying the taste but he admired the picture he formed in his own mind: languid, serene, a young man in control of his world and at peace with himself. He hadn't kicked his shoes off, either. His mother would flay him alive.

"All right, give us one," Neil muttered, as if his brother had been pressing cheroots on him at every other word.

"I thought you said you didn't like them."

"They're all right once in a while. Russian cigarettes are phenomenal. They've got paper tubes."

"I know. Several chaps on the Baltic smoke them."

"Yes, congratters on that, by the way. A member, eh! You must be the youngest ever."

"I suppose I am," Lawrence replied, as if the thought had never occurred to him. "They couldn't keep me out, see. I made too many good deals." He sighed. "That's going to be my trouble in life — I'm just so bloody good at everything I turn my hand to. Ow!" He rubbed his arm where Neil had punched him. "I was going to give you one," he complained as he offered the asked-for cheroot, making it seem that his brother had punched him for being so slow about it. "Never mind your Russian cigarettes, what are the Russian girls like? I imagine them all mysterious and dark-eyed and they've got forests under their arms and their bush goes right up to their navels. Is that right?"

Neil laughed between puffs to get his cheroot well alight. "They give a fellow a bally good jig, I can promise you that." He leaned back, making the wicker chair creak alarmingly.

"You two boys!" their mother called from the landing below, "don't stay up talking all night now. I want to go to the early service tomorrow so we can meet your father off the train."

"Aye aye, Mater!" Lawrence cried.

Neil said quietly, "The old man is sure to like that! Remember the day she took us all to Southampton to welcome him ashore?"

"And no smoking in the bedrooms!" she added.

Lawrence blew a large, slow ring and pushed a smaller, faster one through it. "Of course not," he called back.

In the bedroom next door, Kathleen froze and prayed that her mother wouldn't come up to see her. She had just managed to lift the photo and the room was full of steam. Hastily she scribbled down a list of names off the back of the card, not just that of Billy Bright and his daughter Jenny (or she could be a niece), but everyone — because you never knew. And that was how she discovered that the man in half-shadow at the end of the back row was Uncle Brian. It was hard to believe it but at least it explained why the photo was in Aunt Daphne's album. But it still didn't explain why this was the only photo in the album in which the sitters were not named in white ink underneath.

As her mother's footfall died away, she relaxed, but not completely. There was still the business of the good-night kiss. She put the photo back on its old glue marks and then, noticing that it didn't quite line with its neighbour (a matter in which Aunt Daphne was always so careful), she pushed it slightly upward. A fine line of glue showed along the bottom, which she wiped carefully away with wet hair-curling papers. Then, this being Saturday night, she put the rest of the papers in her hair. She had chosen this night on purpose, so that the papers she used on the album would cause no comment in the morning. One could never be too careful.

"What *are* Russian girls like?" Lawrence asked. "God, if I went to sea, I'd get to know all the girls in the world. Is it true about Chinese girls, by the way? Oh, of course, you wouldn't know yet."

"Talking of girls ..." Neil tried to blow a ring out through the open window but a sudden breeze came from nowhere and worried it to tatters. "What was all that about little Emma Harding? I'm sorry to see her gone, she was always so cheerful about the place. This new one, whats-er-name ... Walker? Sleep-Walker, it should be. She goes about as if her thoughts are miles away — which they probably are."

Lawrence gave a terse account of Emma's dismissal.

"How do you know all this?" Neil asked, imagining he was tightening the noose, for surely his brother's only source could have been Emma herself.

"Kathy told me — unabashed. She's going to be a Modern Girl, I fear. I blame that Cornishwoman who teaches her. They've never been properly tamed, you know — the Cornish. They still wreck boats."

Neil had an image of a prize fish vanishing in a dart of silver among the black troughs of waves — his brother, who would never take the proffered bait. "I wonder what became of little Emma?" he mused over the creaking of his chair. "She left without a character, I imagine — from what Mama said?"

"One can get characters very easily. Half the characters in London are counterfeits."

"You know all about it, do you?"

"There's a business card in a window in Cheapside, just round the corner from Turnbull and Trotter: *Characters supplied from Members of the Peerage, Clergymen, Justices of Peace, et cetera. Guaranteed genuine.* Give us a quid and I'd buy you five sheets of the Lord Mayor's personal notepaper. Or any law lord's, if that's what you'd prefer."

"Ph-h-hew!" Neil exhaled a long ribbon of surprise, which hung blue in the window; the gaslight from the street cast it as a brown shadow on the wall. Lawrence always seemed to *know* things; he was never at a loss.

"The Thames on its dirtiest day is cleaner by far than the city it divides," Lawrence added.

"You still don't take to life ashore, then?"

He shook his head. "Nor ever shall. What about you?"

Neil shrugged. "I got on better this voyage. I mean I managed better. I can *do* the work, all right, but I still don't take to it. I sometimes think I don't understand *people* very well." He tried another smoke ring, with better success this time. "D'you remember that mad idea we had last year — swap places? D'you think we could pull it off now?"

"Why now? I mean, what's different about now?"

"Well ... the old man's been shot up into the stratosphere. While he was tramping around the world there was always a chance he'd run across 'my'

164

— i.e. *your* — ship if we did swap."

"Or drop in at Turnbull and Trotter."

"Quite. But now he'll be simply *nailed* to the Atlantic crossing. Liver-pool—New York, New York—Liverpool, twenty times a year!"

Lawrence chuckled. "Just a glorified bus driver. He'd never get to Valparaiso or Shanghai or Bombay ... ah, the romance of names!"

"Or Cheapside and Leadenhall Street and Threadneedle Street ... the romance of names, indeed!"

Lawrence shot him a pitying glance. "You'd be fed up in two months."

"Well, I don't suppose you'd find life afloat all it's cracked up to be, either."

After a ruminative pause Lawrence said, in a more serious tone, "Actually, you know ..." and then fell silent again.

"What?"

"I was only going to say, the old man seemed somehow ... *different* when he came ashore this time."

"In what way?"

"Hard to put the old finger on it, as the whore said to the cabin boy. You know how he used to say, 'Race you to Aunt Daphne's!' on Highbury Fields?"

"Lord, that's going back a bit!"

"Well, he said it this time. He won, too — but only because I was so flabbergasted he got twenty yards start on me. And he was ... I don't know ... cheerful! This promotion has done wonders for his spirit."

"Well!" There was a hint of polite disbelief in the exclamation.

"I almost get the feeling that if we put it to him, man to man, you know ..."

"Save your breath," Neil interrupted. "He couldn't change that much."

"Well" — Lawrence abandoned the attempt to persude him — "see what you think yourself. I just got the feeling that if we both went to him and said something like, 'See here, Papa, we've both stuck it a year and we've had a jolly good stab at it, and we haven't disgraced ourselves — or you — but nothing will change our minds. We'd each prefer to be in the other's shoes ...' well, I don't think he'd do the old Vesuvius impersonation like he used to. But don't take my word for it — see what you think tomorrow."

Neil pondered on ways to get back to the subject of Emma — knowing how his failure would disgust Kathleen — but could think of none.

Clever little Beast!

T HE TRAIN WAS on time; it must have realized who it was carrying, as Lawrence muttered to his sister. Their father had been known to bawl out the driver and fireman for arriving only five minutes late. They saw him at once, leaping from the first-class carriages, which were half way down the train, and setting off for the barrier with a jaunty stride. Of course, he was not expecting his family to be there; when he saw them, he checked himself and adopted his more customary nautical roll. But his sprightly gait had regsitered with Neil, who gave his brother a concessionary nod that was more than slightly surprised.

"I thought we'd all go to the zoo, dear," Hilda explained before he was really within easy earshot. "The zoo!" she repeated when he frowned. "Euston's half way. It seemed silly to fetch you all the way back to Highbury and then ..."

He smiled and stemmed her flow with a quick kiss — on her mouth, which surprised her, for she was plainly offering him her cheek, as usual. He hadn't kissed her on the mouth since ... she couldn't recall. She used to hate it.

He, meanwhile, was exchanging bluff, manly handshakes and shoulder squeezes with his two sons before turning to his darling Kathleen. She stood there, half wanting him to pick her up and hug her and swing her around as he used to and half dreading that he might demolish her dignity by doing so. He compromised, grasping both her hands and swinging her in a circle, as in the schottische. "My, my! You've grown even in this last month."

The admiration in his gaze was balm to her. Men of power, men who wield command as if it were their birthright, develop a certain glint in their eyes, which a woman is quick to notice, even quicker than other men. Admiration in such eyes carries a special thrill that a hundred lesser men together could not match; and when that singular man is also the woman's father, there is no pleasure quite like it in all the world.

Hilda noticed the flush in her daughter's cheek and was annoyed at her lack of self-control. "Your bonnet is crooked," she said, knocking it awry and then jerking it straight with a sharp tug that elicited a vulgar "Ow!"

"The zoo on a Sunday morning?" Frank asked. "I thought it was members only on Sunday mornings."

"I've still got the fellowship Uncle Brian gave me for my birthday last year," Lawrence explained. "Apparently he renewed it without telling me." He lifted the corner of his card from his breast pocket and tucked it back again.

Only a year ago, Hilda thought, he would have pulled it all the way out and shown it to Francis. *Two* years ago, Francis would have taken it from the boy's pocket and satisfied himself that all was in order. But he was no longer a boy — that was it. She had the first intimation that these three were catching up and would one day overtake them. One day, she and Francis would be the children, and Lawrence or Neil or Kathleen would be pulling things out of their bags or pockets to make sure they weren't getting in a muddle. She smiled at the thought. That day was a long way off yet.

"Well!" Frank punched a fist into his palm. "A cab? Or shall we walk there? A nice stroll through the park, eh?" He stretched a hand to Kathleen and offered the crook of his other arm to Hilda. "I've been stuck on that wretched train since four this morning."

"I owe you an apology," Neil murmured as he fell in beside his brother. "What a transformation!"

"Shall we chance it?"

"Let's see. Don't say anything yet."

Over the next half mile or so, between Euston Arch and Park Square, they fell progressively behind the other three, who were impelled by their father's perennial eagerness to arrive somewhere, or anywhere. "Catch up!" he bawled when they reached Great Portland Street.

"All sail set," Lawrence commented. It was an appropriate image since both mother and daughter had their parasols open and there was a good following breeze. "We'd better step out, though — they're waiting for us."

"He won't be setting much sail in future," Neil pointed out. "I'm surprised he's so sanguine about it. He always said he'd never give up sail for steam."

"Is it very different? It must be."

"The sea is the sea, whether you're sailing, steaming, or adrift. And there's good and bad in steamships ... no different from sail."

Lawrence chuckled. "D'you realize you're already beginning to talk of it with a certain nostalgia."

Neil saw his chance. "What about you? Isn't there *anything* you'll miss about the landlubberly life? Nothing at all? I can't believe that."

Lawrence heard the humorous innuendo in his brother's tone. "You mean girls," he said. "God, I'll have one in every port."

With the tip of his cane Neil fastidiously pushed a lump of dried dog turd into the gutter. "You wouldn't, you know."

"Think not?" Lawrence gave a brave laugh, as if to say "try and stop me"!

"You know you wouldn't. They cost a bally fortune, if they're any good."

"All right. I'd have a *wife* in every port. I'd be loving and faithful and sincere to them all — does that suit you better?"

"Loving and faithful and sincere to who?" Kathleen asked, for they had just come within range of her sharp ears.

"To *whom*," her mother corrected.

"All my wives," Lawrence told her vaguely.

"He's going to turn Mussulman," Neil put in swiftly — not wanting to broach the subject of Lawrence as a seafaring man just yet.

"Such a text for the sabbath!" Hilda said. "Why can't you discuss some improving topic."

"Sorry, Mama," Lawrence replied earnestly. "You're right, though. The subject of *wives* could not possibly be considered an *improving* topic."

Hilda turned to Frank, confident she could leave this piece of impertinence to his anger; to her surprise, he just smiled and shook his head, as people do at the incorrigibility of youth. "I regret having called you young brats to catch up," was all he said.

His two sons smiled awkwardly, having no means of coping with him in this rare, mellow mood. He saw it and was dismayed, though he was old and wise enough not to show it. Again and again these past few months he had seen — in other people's eyes, in their hesitation, in their baffled silence — glimpses of a Frank Morgan who was as dead to him as the dodo.

Only Wheeler had been able to adapt; but then Wheeler *knew*.

Lawrence, though his Fellowship of the Royal Zoölogical Society was available to one and all at the drop of a mere guinea or two, felt he should make some gesture to justify it. "The cassowary," he announced before the kiwi cage, "so called because at the mere sight of a casserole it will run a hundred miles without even pausing for breath."

Two fellow Fellows within earshot glowered at him.

"Steady now, my boy," Frank warned, doing his best not to smile.

Lawrence gave the sedate old gentlemen a contrite bow. "Come," he said soberly, herding his family away, "I must show you our latest acquisition in the finches cage — the double-breasted backchat."

Once round the corner, by the entrance to the ape house, they exploded with laughter. Fortunately, the Fellows there were in a lighter humour, being heartily engaged in a face-pulling competition with the orang-outang. A few minutes later the ad hoc judging committee gave Lawrence the palm, a judgment confirmed by the creature himself, who spat a hearty and evil-smelling quid on his cheek.

"I've seen them in the forests in Sumatra," Frank said as they wandered on toward the snakes. "They're very shy there."

Neil saw his sister frown. "What's the matter?" he asked, seeking some cause in the nearest cage.

"I've just realized … I mean, we come here three or four times a year and we see all these animals all neatly separated in their cages and we start thinking this is where they *belong*. But they don't, do they. When Papa said that, about seeing them in Sumatra, I suddenly realized they actually belong in the forests, and not just in ones or twos but by the hundreds."

"By the thousands," Frank told her.

She rounded on Neil. "Oh, you are *lucky!* To be able to travel and see all these things. That's what I'm going to do — travel."

Neil put an arm round her. "Cut off your hair and sign on aboard *Swallow* as cabin boy. I'll keep an eye on you."

Lawrence, with a wary eye on his father, said, "Sign on aboard the *Hilda of Troy* and Papa can keep an eye on you."

"Now that's quite enough of this frivolity," Hilda said sharply. "Cut off her hair, indeed! Francis, say something to them."

"Enough!" Frank said, reasserting something of his old self. It felt rusty.

They sauntered on into the snake house where their varying interests broke them into two groups again; Frank, who would rather have been with his sons by the crocodiles, felt obliged to stay with the ladies near the python, whose cold silken skin they loved to touch and stroke.

"I'm surprised Mama went into the ape house," Lawrence said. "D'you remember that time a vervet monkey started tossing himself off and she tried to distract our attention — 'Oh look over here, children!' — only to find her parasol pointing at a great bull chimp shagging the arse off one of his harem!"

"Yes!" Neil chuckled. "And all the Fellows staring at her in horror! Trust you to remember exactly what sort of monkey it was."

"I often used to think of that little chap. Felt quite sorry for him. No mate of his own. Forced to watch that brute of a chimp at it day and night. Knowing he could do it with so much more grace and charm."

Neil smiled and patted his arm consolingly. "Fellow sufferers, eh."

"Happy days!" The reply held a grand ambiguity.

"Ah! A sufferer no more, then? Is that it?"

Lawrence hesitated, poised between flippancy and seriousness. "I'll tell you later," he said. "Perhaps you can help."

Kathleen was glad her brothers had drifted away. She had devised a splendid way to test her father's response to the name of Jenny Bright — without even hinting that she herself even knew of the young lady's existence. She took her chance now. "Last month we came here with Miss Kernow," she said, "and the llama was sick all over Jenny Seabright's sketchbook. Miss Kernow said the llama was an art critic."

There was a distinct twitch in her father's arm, the moment she mentioned the name — which she was rather proud of having invented; it didn't sound like a made-up name at all.

"The Seabrights, dear?" her mother asked. "Where do they live?"

"They don't, as a matter of fact. Not any more. They were in a hôtel …"

"*An* hôtel."

"An hôtel. They were only waiting for a passage to India."

She made no further mention of the name — but then she didn't need to. It had entirely served its purpose.

THEY STAYED ONLY an hour or so at the zoo and then took a cab home, arriving in time for lunch — or luncheon, as Hilda insisted. Afterwards the two young men went out for a stroll on Highbury Fields; their sister came with them. She was at last returning Aunt Daphne's photograph album.

"I can hardly believe the change in the old man," Neil said as they reached the edge of the green.

"Commodore of the line," Lawrence pointed out. "Perhaps everyone changes when they get what they've worked for all their lives. Actually, that's a funny phrase, isn't it — 'worked for all one's life'? I can't imagine working for anything, I mean any one single thing, all my life, can you?"

"Very easily," Neil assured him.

"Me too," Kathleen chipped in.

"What's even more surprising, in a way," Neil went on, "is his reluctance to talk about the Great Storm. I mean, think of all the other hairy escapes he's had. They were our bedtime stories almost. But this one … nothing! The biggest storm in our lifetime. I'll bet they're still talking about it on the Baltic."

Lawrence chuckled. "Not half as much as they are at Lloyd's." A sudden thought struck him. "Perhaps this time he really came face-to-face with death. I mean, think of it! Trying to run a ship aground backwards down a narrow channel between two great shoals of rock in a hurricane! That's not face-to-face with death, it's nose-to-nose. Who knows what that does to a man? We can't imagine it. What goes through your mind at a time like that?"

"They say a drowning man sees all his life pass before him," Kathleen said, looking up, first at one, then the other.

"Whatever it was," Neil replied to Lawrence over her head, "you may be sure *we'll* never know."

They came to a fork in the path, the right branch of which led up to Aunt Daphne's. "I'll go on my own from here," Kathleen said, holding out a hand for the album, which Lawrence had been carrying for her.

He passed it over with a rueful smile. "I never did get a look at it," he commented. "Anything of interest?"

"Not really. See you at Evensong." She took a pace or two and then thought better of it. "Actually, there was just one." She opened the book and showed them the photograph of their father as a young seaman staring at the girl she now knew to be called Jenny Bright.

"God, that's a long time ago!" Lawrence exclaimed.

"*Is* it him?" Neil asked, moving the book to a position where the leaf shadows no longer dappled it. "It is, too. Who's the fair young maid?"

"No names under it," Lawrence commented. "That's unlike Aunt D. Ask her." He snapped the book shut and passed it back to his sister.

"D'you think I should?" she asked, biting her lip.

"No harm in it." He grinned. "Why? D'you think there's a shameful secret hidden there? The old man's first true love?"

"He does look rather smitten."

They laughed at her romantic ideas. "I'll bet he was smitten a dozen more times before he settled for Mama," Lawrence assured her.

"Just like you, eh?" She laughed and dashed away up the path, her hair streaming out behind her.

"Yes, like you, eh?" Neil echoed when they were alone.

They strolled on beneath the trees toward the sun and open space on the west of the green. Lawrence stared after their sister, who was now walking sedately across the road to the Dowtys' house. "I wonder does she know anything?" he mused.

Neil heaved a sigh.

Lawrence turned to him. "What's up with you?"

"What a family we are! Secrets, secrets everywhere. And loyalties, too. I don't know. I think I'm the only one who doesn't have secrets. What a dullard you must all think me!"

"But didn't you know that?" Lawrence asked disingenuously. "It's what we've always said about you. Beast!" he cried as Neil gave him a short jab in the kidneys. "Shall we stop and smoke a cheroot?"

"You're hitting these things rather hard," Neil commented as he puffed his own alight. "You never used to smoke so much. It'll be the bottle next."

"Don't!" Lawrence shuddered. "You don't know what you're saying."

Neil watched the smoke drift lazily away, bright blue against the warm, dark shadow beneath the trees. "Tell me then," he said. "Isn't that what this stroll is for?"

175

"I'm in the most bloody awful mess, Neil. That's what. And it's all my own fault." Then, hardly pausing to draw breath, he scampered through the events following Emma's dismissal and his setting her up in rooms.

"Have you shagged her yet?" Neil asked brutally.

"No."

"You bloody fool! It's what she expected. How d'you imagine *she* feels?"

"I know all that. I mean we do talk about it a lot."

"Talk! What good is talk?"

"I just wanted ... I don't know ... something different. That's what I wanted to explain to you."

"How can you afford all this, by the way?" Neil suddenly remembered he wasn't supposed to know about Lawrence's gambling.

"Oh ..." His brother waved a hand vaguely at the grass and sky. "Bit of luck in the office sweepstake."

"How much?"

Lawrence thought rapidly. "Forty guineas."

Neil gave a whistle, then a chuckle. "So the Beast has forty guineas rattling in his pocket and the first thing he thinks of is a bit of fluff! Well, that's no surprise. But why don't you want to slip between the sheets with her?"

Lawrence exhaled a long, weary column of smoke. "That's what's so hard to explain. I *do* want to slip between the sheets with her — of course I do. But there's something more than that. Something about really getting to know her. I mean ... don't you think it's extraordinary? We grow up surrounded by females — mother, nannies, aunts, sister, sister's chums, maidservants — and yet we have no idea what they're really like, have we? There's no real closeness, like there is with another fellow."

"For the simple reason it's not even possible."
Neil's tone made it clear that although he was trying
very sympathetically he simply could not understand
his brother's dilemma.

"But it *is* possible. I had a glimpse of it those first
few days with Emma. And she saw it too. The
possibility of a real ... I don't know ... a real meeting
of mind and spirit. And that's what I want to try and
establish before our sordid bodies get in on the act."

"The act?" Neil echoed with a laugh. "That's the
point, old Beast. The Act is the only one possible
between men and women. What you're seeking is a
chimæra. She's got more sense than you."

"But she saw it," Lawrence insisted. "She saw it
and it frightened her. I saw it and it ... delighted me.
More than delighted. It was like ... oh, haven't *you*
ever been in love?"

"Ah! Is that what you think it is?"

"I'm not going to talk if all you can be is flippant."

"I'm not being flippant. I'm just talking common
sense. Look — women are put into this world for a
purpose — to have babies and look after homes and
keep civilization from going to the dogs. Or the
horses. Or the sweepstakes." He stooped low and
peered into his brother's eyes, forcing an unwilling
laugh from his lips.

"I know all that," Lawrence said tetchily.

"Well, you don't seem to act on it. The point is, it
would be a pretty dull world if that was the beginning
and end of it. So Providence has also arranged for
them to have beautiful faces and the most glorious
bodies — I mean, don't you agree that the female
body, unadorned, is the best argument you know for
the existence of a wise and loving Creator? And He's
also given them stubbornness, bloody-mindedness,

ungovernable passions, incomprehensible emotions, and bags of what we can only lump together under the name of *mystery*. I agree with you there, all down the line — they are an absolute bloody mystery."

"I know." Lawrence scratched two vertical and two horizontal lines in the gravel. He put a cross in the central square thus formed. "I tell myself all that. But it doesn't help. I keep remembering that glimpse of ... something else."

Neil put a nought in a corner. "And where's the difficulty? She won't go near it again?"

"That sort of thing. I mean, I've tried every way I can to *really* get to know her. But there's always this ..." He mimed a wall in front of him and added a cross next to his brother's nought. "And now she's started tippling on the sly."

"Can't blame her." Neil put his nought to stop the third cross in the row. "All she wants is a jolly good shag. You've got all the right equipment — and you won't oblige!"

Lawrence put a cross in the corner where the two noughts could otherwise have intersected. "I found an empty port bottle. She said one of the neighbours left it when she wanted to borrow vinegar. The thing is, I think I've ruined her life now."

"That's going it a bit strong, don't you think?" Neil put his nought at the diagonal corner. "Ruined her life? Why not buy her a 'genuine' reference from the Archbishop of Canterbury and let her go back where she belongs — in service somewhere? Driving the young masters mad with flashes of tit and bum."

Lawrence looked up sharply. "Really?" he said.

Neil grinned. "Don't tell me she never had that effect on you! Why else d'you think I ran away to sea?"

"Be serious!" He returned to the puzzle of the noughts and crosses.

"Well, I've had my daydreams about her in my time. Not to mention the wetter variety. Hell, she'd find *me* willing enough!"

Lawrence wiped out their scratchings with his boot. "No one can win now," he said, staring across the green to the Dowtys'. "Are we going to wait for our dear little sister or what?"

Kathleen thanked her Aunt Daphne for the loan of the album. Yes, she had found it *extremely* interesting. Indeed, they *were* funny fashions in those days. And it *was* amazing how you could recognize people when they were only nine or ten even though they were now in their … well, much older.

Daphne laughed merrily. "Much, much older," she agreed. "One day I'll tell you what it was like living in the Ark."

Kathleen accepted the invitation to stay to tea as if it were the last thing she had anticipated.

"Did your brothers not want to come and see their ancient aunt?" Daphne asked as she handed Brian the cup to pass to her.

So she had been watching from her window.

"I think they intend calling round after Evensong." Kathleen made a note to tell the boys to do so now. "Actually …" She put a note of intrigue into her voice and then glanced uncertainly at her Uncle Brian.

"Oh, *he* knows," Aunt Daphne assured her, though the wave of her hand implied it didn't really matter one way or the other. "Do tell!"

"I think Larry is telling Neil all about *her* at this very moment."

Daphne did a refined little buttock jig on the sofa. "Oh, I should so love to be a little chirping cricket in the grass at times! What d'you think they're saying? Men are so incomprehensible."

"I don't know. But Neil is so ... I mean, he's such a ... well, you know. He's *Neil*. He's bound to dish out the most disastrous advice." She bit her lip and then remembered not to. It was so schoolgirlish. All very well in front of her brothers, but not with real grown-ups like Aunt Daphne and Uncle Brian. "I've been wondering if I shouldn't call on her myself?"

Aunt Daphne made a movement that could only be described as "shrinking from the touch of her own clothing." She stared dubiously at the girl. "D'you think that's wise, dear? You know our motto. Never become involved!"

Kathleen relished the seed cake a while. "You haven't seen her. I saw her sitting on a bench at the station the other day. She didn't see me, but oh, she looked the picture of misery. Couldn't *you* write her a character? Then she could escape."

"Perhaps she doesn't wish to escape, dear. Or perhaps she'll find her own method. I don't think your mother and I would remain friends if I were to do that. Apart from which, it would be a lie."

"Well, let her work here for a week or two. Then it wouldn't be a lie. And she's jolly good with the housework, you know."

Aunt Daphne smiled sweetly and said that people must be allowed to go to perdition in their own way.

Uncle Brian stared at his courtesy niece in amazement. "So macchiavellian," he murmured. "And so young! What hope is there for the world?"

Daphne laughed. "The world, my dear, is a man's world — as we all know. Which is another way of saying that we women must tend it, care for it, mend it, iron it, and generally sponge it clean — without in any way interfering with the uses to which men choose to put it." She turned to Kathleen for support. "Would you call that macchiavellian, dear? I wouldn't."

"Who gives it away to the rag and bone man when it's worn out?" he asked.

She turned back to him with a smile of triumph. "Who says there *is* a rag and bone man — in this particular case? Perhaps we have to go on using it for ever and ever!"

The badinage had become too refined for Kathleen to follow, or wish to follow. "I just lie awake in bed sometimes worrying about her. She was always so cheerful around the house. I hate to think of her like that — first losing her place because Mama chose to misinterpret something she said to me, then having to live in misery because Lawrence is such a fool about her."

Daphne, realizing that the discussion could get rather too near the knuckle, started riffling idly through the pages of the album, which was still on the couch at her side. "Margate Pier," she murmured. "Remember Margate Pier?"

He nodded and smiled.

"The Panorama in Leicester Square! I'd forgotten. And the Sunday School treat on Hampstead Heath ... d'you remember Madge what-was-her-name who ate gallons of winkles and was sick!"

"Hood. Madge Hood."

"That's right — fancy you remembering little Madge Hood! She had that *vast* baby, which you said should be entered in the prize pumpkin contest."

"One of us said it, anyway," he agreed.

Kathleen followed the banter with her eyes, wondering what they were trying to avoid. Then it struck her that her aunt had suddenly gone silent.

"What's wrong?" she asked nervously. "Have I got jam on it or something? I was most careful."

Daphne slowly raised her eyes until they stared levelly into hers. "On the contrary," she replied with a knowing little smile. "You've improved it — and without saying a word! Look, darling, the famous *Hiawatha* dinner, with you trying to hide your black eye." She turned again to the girl. "It always annoyed me that this photo didn't line up with the others. And you've done it for me! Clever girl!" Her gaze remained quite level as she repeated the words. "Clever girl!"

HILDA LAY IN BED pretending to sleep, though she doubted it would come easily that night — if, indeed, it came at all. So much was going on that confused her, things of which she was only dimly aware. Lawrence was up to something, she was sure of it — skulking off twice like that on the very day his brother was due home after months at sea. Saying he just wanted to look in the shop windows! Something smutty, no doubt. It always was when men got that sly look in their eyes.

There was probably one of those ... *houses* ... somewhere in the district. She must find out and put a stop to it. Who could tell her? Reverend Calthrop, perhaps. No, it would embarrass him dreadfully. Daphne. Yes, she could ask Daphne to ask Brian to find out.

Or leave well alone?

If men were subject to those disgusting urges — and everyone seemed to agree they were, especially young men — perhaps it was just as well. Lightning conductors, her mother had always called them. "If men couldn't resort to such places, decent women like you and me couldn't even go out in broad daylight, let alone at night." That's what Mother always said. (She must remember to send her that jam. And she'd promised a couple of jars to Daphne, too.)

She stretched her feet into the cooler corners of the bed, making all her muscles tense and then letting them go suddenly, to increase the feeling of relaxation even if the reality of it eluded her. She wondered why she was still consciously pretending to be asleep, exaggerating the depth and regularity of her breathing and making those little lip-smacking noises as she settled into a new position. She even wondered why she had pretended to fall asleep before Francis came back from his dressing room. He had shown no inclination for that sort of thing since ... well, since his return after the Great Storm.

An involuntary sigh escaped her.

"Hilda?" Frank whispered. "Is something the matter? Can't you sleep?"

She drew a deep breath and said, "Only shallowly. Fits and starts." After a pause she added, "You?"

"I keep thinking of improvements — things I must remember to tell the architects." He turned on his back and stretched himself vigorously enough to make the whole bed shake.

Some imp of mischief impelled her to tickle him but she plucked her hands back just in time and lay upon them very firmly. The shock of what she had almost done left her heart racing. She was so flustered, indeed, that she missed his next words, so that he had to repeat them.

"I said there is one other thing ... something else on my mind."

"What, dear?" She hoped it would prove to be Lawrence; she wanted to talk to him about the boy but she didn't want to be the one to start it off.

"I think I ought to get my hand in — with a steamship, you know. Any steamship. The new leviathan will be launched next March, followed by a couple of months fitting out in Belfast Lough. Then trials in June. So the earliest we can start in service will be ... thirteen months from now. So I'm going to ask for command of a steamship in the American trade. Not regular, you understand, but if I can make a crossing once every couple of months — five or six between now and ..."

"But Shaw and Eggar haven't got anything even half the size of ... oh, what *can* we call it? I'm not going to call it the *Hilda of Troy* — and I wish you'd speak to Lawrence about that."

"They can charter a big one for me. Why not call it the *New Leviathan?*"

"I did. Daphne said it sounds like some dreadful socialist newspaper."

He chuckled. "So it does."

She turned on her side to face him, letting her eyes roam with possessive satisfaction over his craggy profile. "You've changed, Francis. You'd never have laughed at one of Daphne's little jokes before — certainly not if it was about one of your precious ships."

"Anno Domini," he said mildly. Then, half turning to her, he added in a slightly teasing tone, "The famous hush of life — for which you've been praying ever since we married."

"I have not!" she protested. Her heart was suddenly pounding in her throat.

"It's all right, Hilda. Truly, it's all right." He

reached across the gap between them and gave her shoulder a comforting squeeze.

He was going to pull his hand away but she reached up and clamped it there. "What's all right? I wish I knew what you're talking about."

"You know very well what I'm talking about. 'Can't you ever think of anything else?' That's what I'm talking about. 'It should be perfectly possible for you to express your love and respect for me without doing *that!*' That's what I'm talking about."

"I never said such things."

He made no reply.

"I mean, I never said them in that way," she added. "Not in that tone."

He squeezed her shoulder again. "It no longer matters, my dear. That's what I was trying to tell you. You had the correct view of the matter all along — as in so many other departments of our marriage. You were right."

Again he started to remove his hand and again she clamped it tight; she *almost* wished he'd start to caress her as he used to. "Surely ..." She faltered.

"What?"

"Well ... I mean, there's surely something in between? You don't have to rush from one extreme to the other?"

"Extreme?"

"Tskoh! Now it's *you* who knows perfectly well what *I'm* talking about. I mean going from the extreme of mauling me about every single night to the extreme of never so much as touching me."

She felt his grip tighten on her shoulder; his anger was strangely thrilling. Then, to her disappointment, he relaxed and, with a light laugh, edged himself to her side. There, propping himself on both elbows, he reached his lips across a gap that still seemed a mile wide to her and kissed her warmly on the brow. "Every single night!" he chided.

Despite his good humour he found it sobering — and not a little saddening — to remember the nights he had lain in this very bed after being repulsed by one of those icy remarks. "Can't you think of anything else?" had been the mildest of them. He remembered himself lying there, consumed with rage and plotting orgies of revenge in the brothels of every seaport he'd ever visit in future. He had never carried them out, of course. Fear of God, fear of the clap, and, in an odd sort of way, his abiding love for Hilda, always deterred him at the last. But the anger had been real enough, and deep, too. Yet, though he could remember it now, he could no longer feel it. Some of life's threads connecting this Frank Morgan with that former self had parted.

"Oh!" She flung herself away from him, to the very edge of the bed.

"What's the matter now?" he asked, making no attempt to follow her there.

"Oh nothing!" she snapped. "Go to sleep, do. Now you've woken me up thoroughly, you'll sleep well contented, I'm sure."

He knew better than to try arguing with her in that mood.

And she just lay there seething. There was so much more she could have said but she did not trust her voice. She was too close to tears. Even now, in her silence, they threatened to overwhelm her.

She fought them with all her might; and at last she won. But it was an odd sort of war that brought no peace in its wake.

ON THE MORNING OF Christmas Day, 1885, in a private residence with the quaint name of *Pegasus*, in the Connecticut township of Fife (pop. 850; alt. 62ft), Anthony Francis Morgan was born. Within the hour Doctor Hebble was able to announce that the mother was coming along fine, but it was the following day before the same confident announcement could be made concerning the father. The baby himself had made his own announcement within a few seconds of achieving his independence in a bright, cold world.

Frank had worn himself to a wraith with worry over Teresa and her lying in; Doctor Hebble had even considered certifying him as temporarily insane, just to get him out of the way, but Teresa's brother, Ignatius O'Dee, had got a little poteen down his throat and more-or-less kidnapped him into a long, sobering walk through the snow, to the Tomlinson Bridge and back. As they came within a quarter of a mile of the house, the business was clearly — *loudly and clearly* — over.

Frank covered the distance in no time, went charging up the stairs like a hundred of bricks, brushed past a startled Jemima, the female help, and Mistress Knox the midwife — and a wearily tolerant doctor — and halted breathless at the just-tidied bedside.

"Twenty minutes ago," Teresa said happily as she passed the bundle of swaddling up to him. "A boy."

He had as much hair as an ape and the wizened face of an old pixie; his eyes wandered like an idiot's and when they fixed briefly on his father, that entire bundle of raw desires gave out one great howl of anguish and started yet again to bawl the house down. But to Frank he was still the second most precious thing in the universe. "The finest twenty-minute-old I ever did see," he said as he handed the boy back to be pacified. "But he obviously knows what side his bread is buttered on." He bent and kissed her on the brow, murmuring for her ears alone, "I love you, and I'm more proud of you than I'd ever believe possible."

She smiled and blinked back her tears. The baby went on crying.

"Was it hard?" he asked.

"I had a little laudanum. Lord knows what it'd've been like else! It was like ..." She glanced around and said, "I'll tell you later. Are you sober again?"

"I was never anything else. What, did they tell you I was drunk?"

"Not drunk but hearty. Anyway, go out and make up for it now. Sure, haven't you earned it. You're far more kill't than me. Look at you! I'm fine."

He smiled ruefully. "Kill't is the word for it. I couldn't stir from the house."

"What's that?" Ignatius shouted from the door. "Here's me face! If you like it, I'll show you the rest." And without waiting for leave he pushed himself in past the midwife, who was just packing up the last of her things. "There now, Doctor," he said as he chose a broken-handled cup from the dressing table; he tipped out the hair grips it held and poured a good measure from his hipflask. "The finest moonshine this side of Tennessee, though I say it meself."

Doctor Hebble considered the colour and texture of the liquor before he took a sip.

"Ah take a good fill of the mouth now!" Ignatius chided, winking at his sister and Frank. "Sure a ship never sailed in a teaspoon."

The doctor relished the sip, tossed back the rest, and held out his cup for more. "And a bird never flew on one wing — I know!"

Ignatius laughed as he replenished the measure. "And some have trouble flying on only two!"

The doctor glanced toward Mistress Knox and then lowered his voice to say, "Put me down for a dozen."

"I'll have to talk to the man I get it from." Ignatius gave a further wink. Then he turned to the bed. "Well, colleen! Is that another fine Fenian you've given the world?" He clapped Frank on the shoulder and roared with laughter.

"By God," Frank growled, "if you weren't carrying such precious cargo ..."

"Lord, wouldn't I forget me own head if it wasn't held on with six-inch nails!" He protruded his hip toward his brother-in-law. "Feel in that pocket there. I have a glass brought up for you."

"A glass and a half!" Frank exclaimed as he extracted a large tumbler.

"And I have its brother." He proved it. "But on second thoughts we'll fill up below." He dropped into his imitation of a born American. "We got us a whole passel o' see-gars to *dis*tribute."

But Frank shook his head ruefully. "Tomorrow," he said. "All I want now is to sleep."

"Is it a girl?" came the inquiry from beyond the door.

"Father Hines!" Teresa called out. "Come away in. You're very welcome. But it's a boy, I have to tell you."

"Ah well, 'tis the will o' God, sure." He radiated a rueful but sportsmanlike acceptance of his Church's defeat in the matter of the child's sex. A girl would have been brought up in the faith of her mother. "I

189

dare say the giving out of *sons* is a habit He has on the day that's in it. A Merry Christmas, Mistress Knox, I didn't see you there. Ah, and you, too, Doctor." He took the glass Ignatius proffered without a word. *"Sláinte!"*

He savoured the mouthful, smacked his lips, and placed the tumbler on the bedside table before settling like some great farmyard animal on his knees. One of his socks had a huge, undarned hole at the heel, which Mistress Knox pointed out with silent glee to the doctor. "We may still say a decade of the rosary," he told Teresa. "And pray for the soul of the poor wee fellow."

Frank, feeling it would be awkward to stand there and yet take no part, followed the doctor and midwife out. He was just bidding them farewell and thanking them yet again when Ignatius came out on the landing and hissed, "Where the hell are you going? Do you want to lose that boy to the Holy Mother Church?"

Frank frowned at him in bewilderment.

"Sure that crafty fellow will have him baptized before your back is turned. Go in now and pacify the babby — or he'll use the tears for holy water."

There was, indeed, a suspiciously wet area on the baby's brow when Frank lifted him up — but what could he say or do about it? Better to be baptized into two churches than none at all. This time the child allowed himself to be comforted by his father's embrace; his crying petered out in a shivery little sigh of exhaustion. Frank had forgotten how unbelievably tiny their hands were. He offered his son a hooked finger, which he at once gripped with an amazing strength. "Haul away, Joe!" he murmured, turning his back on the praying couple and walking slowly off to the farther end of the bedroom.

It no longer felt like a new start, not even on "the day that was in it," as Father Hines put it. He had long since ceased to be Frank Morgan, husband of Hilda, father of Neil, Lawrence, and Kathleen, stealing a second chance in life; he became a completely different Frank Morgan once he arrived on this side of the Atlantic. Technically, he knew, he was still guilty of bigamy, but it no longer felt like that, either. He stared down at his son and tried out the word *bastard*. It carried no emotional charge at all, no fear, no guilt, no incipient pity. He might as well have said, "Timbuctoo," for all the difference it made.

They came to the end of their decade, Father Hines gabbling away like an auctioneer taking bids on Anthony's soul: *"Perjesuchristudominumnostrum ... Amen!"* He kissed a strip of coloured cloth and tucked it away with his left hand while reaching for his half-consumed glass of poteen with his right. "A man needs some fortifying against the blast this day," he asserted.

Ignatius returned with a new tumbler for himself. He winked at Frank. "You'll be staying for a morsel of Christmas dinner, Father," he announced.

"Thank you, no. I'm invited to the Hennessys."

"Ah come on now, Father. Just a round of roast beef that'd shlip down your throat the way you wouldn't even know it? And roast potatoes and gravy the way the missis can make it? And colcannon like you haven't tasted it since we left Ireland? And a slice-een of the plum pudding with maybe a sixpence in it for luck? And a glass of port to help seal it once it's down? Now where's the harm in that?"

"Well now ..." The priest tried to make his hesitation seem due to politeness rather than appetite.

Ignatius had no pity. "Sure the Hennessys have nothing on their table but that oul' rooster that's woken you up ten minutes too soon those five years that went past — which I know for a fact. You'll want a good lining to drop that bag of sinew and bone into, I can tell you."

Father Hines drew out his watch, stuffed it back with a sigh, and said, "Well, maybe just something in the hand now."

"Good man yourself, Father!" Frank clapped him on the back and ushered him out. At the door he turned and blew a kiss to Teresa. "Will I bring you something? I mean shall I?"

She shook her head. "I'll just lie here and play with my Christmas present."

"Well, Father," Ignatius was saying, "will we turn this Welshman into an Irishman yet?"

Lord, Frank thought. *If the Morgans of Highbury New Park could see and hear me now!* He almost laughed aloud when another voice within him added, "Never mind them! If *Frank Morgan* himself could see and hear you now!"

I T WAS A YEAR to the day since Emma Harding had been dismissed — the tenth of March, 1886. Kathleen, now "rising seventeen," as she liked to put it, though she would not pass that milestone until June, had to look twice in her diary before she could believe it. A year! A whole year gone by, and what had happened? Nothing!

Lawrence was *still* on the Baltic in London; Neil, *still* on the *Swallow,* divided his time between the *real* Baltic and various home ports; and she herself *still* had not plucked up the courage to knock on Emma Harding's door — which was, of course, *still* in Upper Street! Talk about the art of still life!

To be quite precise, it wasn't so much lack of courage that detained her as the influence of Aunt Daphne, who said that since everyone in the world was headed for perdition, the least a civilized person could do was to allow others to choose their own way to get there. Apart from which, it was more fun just to sit back and observe the mess that other people made — "Like sauntering along in a carriage, all wrapped up in a nice warm fur, and looking out at the poor people scurrying past in the rain," she explained.

However, it was a waning influence on a Kathleen who was visibly growing in stature and assurance; and if ever there was a day to widen the breach, this anniversary was surely it.

"Well, that's *that!*" she cried, folding her old and new diaries into each other at the page headed *10 March*. "If I don't go and see her today, I'm a coward and a hypocrite and I shan't ever deserve a husband."

Then, shutting out all echoes of Aunt Daphne's voice, telling her that the highest form of life was that of the observer, she drew on her hat and gloves and went downstairs. "I'm just popping out for some bias binding," she told her mother as she flung her cape about her shoulders.

"Mrs Johnson got some yesterday, dear." Hilda came out holding a new roll of it in her hand.

Damn!

"I need it in white, actually."

"Oh but I have white — yards of it." Her mother returned to her boudoir.

"Half-inch?" Kathleen called hopefully after her. "Or inch, preferably."

"What on earth for?" Her mother returned empty handed.

Kathleen almost screamed. "I'm taking up a hem on that white summer dress and there's a bit that's frayed and I want to bridge over it."

Hilda smiled indulgently. "And you're going to buy yards of it just for that? Why not simply sew two together for the few inches where you need it?"

Kathleen gave up trying to elaborate her argument. "Well, anyway, I'm all dressed now. And I could do with a bit of fresh air. And so could George. And I thought I might meet Lawrence off the tram."

George put his nose outside and slunk back to his nice warm hearthrug. He was getting old and rheumy.

Home life was becoming intolerable, she thought as she set off alone on her errand of ... what? Mercy? Inquisitiveness? Meddlesomeness?

Better not to ask. Just do it.

The rain had eased off but a cold wind had followed it, seeming to fall out of the northeastern sky; there could even be snow tonight. The lamplighter was out fifteen minutes early, bicycling from lamp to lamp, hooking the valve levers down with his long pole. He was so skilled he could do it one-handed without actually stopping — though there was half a second or so when a snail could easily overtake him.

There was a drunken man lying on the foot pavement about fifty yards ahead of her. Two respectable gentlemen stepped carefully over him without a pause in their conversation. She remembered a day at the zoo, long ago. They were standing by the aquarium tank, the one with the shoals of fry; most of the little fishes darted this way and that in amazing unison but there were one or two that never went with the crowd. She had asked her father why and he had said they were the future leaders. "Or trouble-makers," Aunt Daphne had put in. Then she, Kathleen, had pointed to a few who were lying on the bottom, apparently dead, and asked, "And are they the drunkards?" Everyone had laughed, of course, because they saw the connection. But her mother, who hadn't wanted her to be thinking of drunkenness — or death — on such a lovely day, told her, "No, they are the fishy philosophers, dear." After that the Dowtys and the Morgans never referred to drunkards, they always called them "fishy philosophers."

She stared into the unseeing eyes of this particular "fishy philosopher" as she drew near. What could possibly be happening inside such a fuddled and damaged mind, she wondered? Certainly no philosophy! The lamplighter passed at that moment and the lamp above them burst into orange brilliance. "Jesus saves!" the drunkard cried, rising on one elbow. "Long before I heard!"

Kathleen was several paces past the man before she realized it was a fragment of a revivalist hymn: *He called me long before I heard.*

Did it have any meaning for her? Reverend Calthrop said that life was full of little buried sermons. God strews our path in life with signs and auguries which it is our duty to seek out and heed. But how? Was this a sign to her to believe? But she already was a believer. To renew her faith? But she did that every Sunday. Was this a call to something beyond the ordinary, then? After all, the words were: "He *called* me long before I heard." Was this what people spoke of as "a religious calling"? She hoped not. Could it come upon one in so strange a guise? She sought uncomfortably within herself and heard no echoes of such a call.

In any case, she reflected as she crossed the road by the railway station, would God destroy that poor creature's life just so that he could lie there on this particular afternoon and issue her Call? Ah, but perhaps the man had destroyed his own life! No, that wouldn't do, because even before that man was born, God already knew he was going to end up a hopeless drunkard. So perhaps He'd just used him for one good purpose. And now it was up to her. Perhaps if she became a nun or something like that, or married a missionary and worked herself to death in a fever hospital, it would save that drunkard's soul from everlasting damnation. He could stand up on Judgement Day and point to the exemplary and sacrificial life of Kathleen Morgan and proclaim, "But for me and my drunkenness, ten thousand savage souls would never have known Thy saving light, O Lord!"

She felt a glow of satisfaction. Even if she didn't go to such heroic extremes but just led an exemplary life, she could still help save that poor fellow's soul. Didn't Reverend Calthrop also say that the petty heroism of daily piety and good example was ten times harder than the grand heroism of the martyrs?

The cold wind at her back nudged her forward to the encounter she was dreading; it was far more comfortable to think of grand, sonorous things like piety and the Will of God than the small practicalities of Emma Harding's future. Anyway, how could she think of the girl's future when she didn't even know what the present was like? Try and think about piety, instead.

She looked at the house numbers. Only twenty to go. Did piety mean absolute submission and obedience to one's parents? That certainly was hard!

Think of Emma Harding, then. She hadn't even decided how to begin.

"I just happened to see you using the latchkey here the other day ..."

"I saw you coming out of the library and when I went in your ticket was still on the desk. I couldn't believe you were living so close!"

"Lawrence told me all about it." God no!

"I saw Lawrence one day and followed him."

She reached the door and felt her soles start glueing themselves to the flagstone. *Don't stop!* she urged herself and dragged one foot after another through the front door — which was on the latch — and up the stairs. The same act of sheer willpower impelled her feet along the faded linoleum of the first-floor landing. There was no card stuck to the door and no name beside it; just an ornate 2 in gold paint whose gloss had since cracked.

Kathleen drew a deep breath and knocked three times: *rat tat-tat!*

There was a stirring within and then Emma's voice: "Who is it?"

Kathleen answered but no sound came out of her throat. She could no longer count her individual heartbeats. She cleared her larynx and tried again but by then Emma was opening the door anyway. "Well!" she exclaimed with a light, unsurprised laugh. "You've taken your time, I must say!"

She stepped aside and ushered Kathleen within. She drifted in and looked about her in bewilderment. "What d'you mean?"

"Come off it! Don't tell me you haven't known about all this until now. I've seen you! Walking up and down the street, trying to catch sight of me reflected in the shop windows, following Larry here.

You knew what was going on from the start." She laughed pleasantly enough and Kathleen could detect neither bitterness nor annoyance in her voice. "Cup of tea? Or something stronger? It's as cold as charity out there. Port or sherry?" She poured herself a good measure of port.

A world of new possibilities suddenly opened before Kathleen. "A small glass of sherry, please," she said. "If you can spare it."

Emma chuckled and echoed the words. "Spare it! Throw your cape on the foot of the bed. There's nowhere else."

"D'you sleep and eat and ... do everything all in this one room?" Kathleen asked. All her anxiety had vanished now and she could have kicked herself for not having called months ago, when the possibility first crossed her mind.

"What d'you mean by 'do everything'?" Emma passed her a smallish tot of sherry. "Is that what you've come to find out? If so, I can tell you — you're in for a few surprises."

Kathleen sipped her drink and pulled a face.

Emma laughed. "It's what they call an acquired taste. Did your mother send you here?"

"Heavens no!" Kathleen almost spilled her glass. "She knows nothing about it."

"Oh yes she does!" Emma was grimly positive, and then, in a more reflective tone, she added, "Mind you, she only discovered it last week. Saw me coming out the butcher's and dodged me here. She's a better dodger than you or your Aunt Daphne, I can tell you. Anyway, that's why I thought she might have sent you. I don't think she knows about me and Larry yet."

Kathleen took another sip and found it not quite so

nauseating as the first, though she still didn't like it. "But she never said a word to me."

Emma lost her slightly bantering attitude. "No," she said seriously. "I can believe that. You never talk to each other in your family, do you."

"What d'you mean? We talk all the time."

"Yes, but never *about* nothing — I mean, anything. Has Larry told you about me?"

Kathleen shook her head.

"And have you told him you know?"

Another shake of the head.

"Nor dropped a hint to your mother?"

"I told Neil. Why do you laugh?"

"Don't talk to me about Neil! He came round here — last summer it was — and again before Christmas — thinking if Larry had already cut the cake, another slice wouldn't be missed. But I don't think he'll come sniffing round here again somehow!" She spoke these last words with a fierce satisfaction, took a gulp of port, and breathed out its fire.

"I see." Kathleen put her glass down carefully.

It crossed her mind that Emma was in the first stages of the sort of alcoholic degradation that would ultimately land her in the gutter, shouting fragments of truths that no longer added up to any sort of Truth at all. It must begin in precisely this way — with the mind no longer able to distinguish between important things, like who knew what and who spoke to whom about it, and trivial things, like who got an extra slice of Christmas cake.

She stared about her. "Actually, it's two rooms opened out into one," she said brightly. "And you keep it spotless."

"For a drunkard, you mean?"

Kathleen blushed.

"I'm not a drunkard, Kathy. All right if I call you Kathy? It seems silly to call your brother Larry and go on ..."

"Please do. I'd be very glad if you do."

Emma stared hard at her and then said, "Blimey! I think you mean it."

"I do."

Emma reached across and took away her sherry. "I'll make you a cup of tea," she said, knocking the glass down in one gulp. "In fact, I'll make us both a cup of tea." She downed the rest of her port in the same fashion and went to the "kitchen," which was, in fact, a large cubby hole at the far end of the room. "I'm not a drunkard," she repeated as she filled the kettle. "I'm just an ordinary heavy drinker, see?"

"Of course," Kathleen assured her. "I never for one moment thought of you as a drunkard. Were you ... er, a heavy drinker when you were with us?"

"Never touched the stuff." She came back and resumed her seat, waiting for the kettle to boil. "But it does fill out the day."

"Yes, what d'you *do* all day now?"

Emma stared at her in a quandary. "I don't know, Kathy. I don't know about you at all."

"I should think you know more about me than I know about you. Servants always do, don't they."

"I mean about life. You know? Men and women and ... girls who live in apartments with an allowance from an obliging gentleman ... you know?"

Kathleen fought an urge to say something suave to show she knew it all; instead, she played for time. "*Does* Larry pay you an allowance?" she asked gaily. "Out of his winnings on horses, I suppose."

Emma closed her eyes briefly and shook her head. "So you don't know nothing. Oh dear-oh-dear ..."

"I know he bets on horses — and usually wins."

The singing of the kettle deepened. Emma rose to catch it as it boiled. "Well, I'm not going to be the one to tell you."

Kathleen pondered this fresh puzzle while the welcoming sounds and aromas of the tea-making ritual came from the kitchen. "If you've known all this time," she called out, "about me, I mean — about me knowing about you and Larry — does he also know?"

Emma returned with a tray on which it was all set out — marie biscuits, caraway cake, dainty cups, a sugar bowl with silver lazy tongs, and a milk jug with a lace doily to cover it. "I keep it ready for Larry," she explained. "He's a lover of the domestic scene." She shot a significant glance at her visitor and added, "And that's all he's a lover of, too."

"And of the sea," Kathleen reminded her.

"Oh yes. The sea. To be sure. One fine day!"

"Does he know about me?"

Emma shook her head in mild amazement. "Doesn't it make you feel ashamed, Kathy — having to ask me such a question? See what I mean about your family — never talking to each other and that?"

Kathleen wriggled uncomfortably. "I thought he was a lover of you, too," she said.

"Milk?" Emma asked.

When she had poured the tea and set it in front of Kathleen, she said, "Why did you come here, Kathy?"

Now it was Kathleen's turn for mild amazement. "Don't you know what day it is?"

Puzzlement turned to understanding in the other's countenance. "Blimey!" she exclaimed. "So it is!" She stared about her at the now familiar furnishings, the oleograph prints, the plaster stag's antlers over the door. "A whole bleeding year, eh!" She shivered.

"I came to see if I could help at all," Kathleen added.

"I've got to get out," Emma went on. "Otherwise this could go on for ever."

"What?" Kathleen asked eagerly. "What *is* going on?"

"Nothing! That's the whole point." She emptied her cup and stared into it as if there might be an answer in the tealeaves.

Kathleen took a bite of cake and chewed thoughtfully. "Tell me about it," she suggested at length. "I mean, I know how ignorant I am but I still may be able to help. You never know."

Emma rose, went to the sideboard, took out the port bottle, looked at it ... and put it back. "Start now," she said with a wan smile. She reseated herself, drew a deep breath, and said, "Very well. I'll tell you everything. Some of it won't mean much to you now, but it will one day. More tea?"

"You shouldn't say 'more.' It implies that *you* think your visitor may already have had sufficient. You should just say, 'Some tea?' as if it were their first." She held out her cup and smiled. "Yes, please!"

Emma laughed as she refilled it. "Well, well, Kathy! How old are you?"

"Almost seventeen."

"I think I might quite like to know you in a couple of years from now. Your heart's in the right place, as they say. Anyway — are you ready for the story of my life? The most boring tale ever laid before an ungrateful public? I don't know what it is about you Morgans but I always seem to end up doing this!"

Kathleen wriggled with pleasure and settled herself for a nice long listen.

SHE WAS FAR AND away the grandest vessel of her day. They called her the *Pride of Liverpool* since she would ply exclusively between that port and Manhattan. The books of record will tell you she drew 7,500 tons, that she carried 203 first and 82 second-class passengers (and no third or steerage); also that her working speed was 14 knots, thanks to her three-stage compound engines. They duly note that she was the first liner to have electrical illumination throughout, the first to have forced ventilation in individual cabins and staterooms, and the first to have twin screws rotating counter to each other — which was a revolution in comfort in itself, since it made ordinary conversation possible without either party sounding as if he or she were shivering half to death. But what no book of record — no mere photograph, even — can convey is the sheer opulence of the vessel as turned out by the craftsmen of Harland & Wolff.

Imagine a vast country mansion built to his own glory by some vast North Country plutocrat — a man who does not mind the promiscuous mingling of half a dozen ornamental styles, from Ancient Doric to Rococo — a man who insists that his architect must fill every last square inch with decoration of some kind or he will accuse the poor fellow of selling him short — a man who can live with a day-long, night-long Hallelujah Chorus of scarlet, white, gold, and silver, of Spanish mahogany and crimson leather, of burr walnut and Carrara marble, of stained glass, cut glass, etched glass, and bühl, of swags, garlands, cartouches, and crests ... imagine such a noble pile lifted bodily and squeezed between the steel decks and watertight bulkheads of an ocean liner and you have the beginnings of an inkling of the impression the *Pride of Liverpool* made on all who saw her.

Even on the day of her launching, Wednesday the 31st of March, 1886, when the plasterers and gilders had barely started on the dolphins and tritons, the naiads and mermaids who were to be the only permanent inhabitants of the first-class dining saloon ... even then it left Hilda and the two youngest Morgans speechless with amazement. Being the Captain's family — or all of it that was available for the occasion — they were privileged to go aboard after the launching and make a tour of her spectacular interior.

"Do you two ladies want to see the engine rooms?" Frank asked in a tone expecting the answer no. "All the first class staterooms are amidships, forr'ard of the grand staircase, and the cabins aft of it. The stewardesses are fully aft; waiters and stewards all forr'ard. Second class is all on the deck below this. Lawrence and I could meet you there in about twenty minutes?"

And so it was agreed.

Lawrence turned at once to the incomplete bulkhead that would give them access to the stokehold and engine rooms, but Frank lingered awhile, staring after the two women.

"She's growing, isn't she," Lawrence commented. "She's simply shot up these last few months."

"Taller than her father," Frank answered ruefully. "She's changed in other ways, too."

The women disappeared into one of the staterooms. The men turned and made for the companionways that led into the bowels of the ship.

"Doesn't it frighten you, sir?" Lawrence asked. "To

stand in the middle of something as vast as this and know that in a few months' time you'll be up there on the bridge, steering it across the ocean?"

His father gave a brief, dry laugh. "I'd sooner be doing it under poles and canvas, if that's what you're asking. But I know full well there's no future in the old ways. And the sea, vast as it is, has never found room for sentiment. Haven't *you* noticed other changes in your sister?"

Lawrence tilted his head noncommittally. "Oh … well, she's grown a bit more serious. A lot more. But not in the way I thought she might. I always imagined she'd be a sort of bluestocking. I felt sure there'd be arguments between you about … I don't know, going to university or something."

"Good heavens!" Frank turned and stared at his son. "D'you think I'd have been against it?"

Lawrence almost risked replying that he certainly would have been against it a year or two ago; instead, he pursued his original thought. "But she's the one who's changed. I don't think she knows what she wants to do now — except not get married, of course."

"Why 'of course'? Has she told you she doesn't want to?"

There were two decks where the only way down was by ladder, which made conversation difficult. Fortunately the electric light had been installed almost everywhere, so they could see their way clearly. Lawrence noted that his father already knew the location of every switch. On an impulse he said, "How many rivets on the watertight door we've just come through?"

"Twenty-two by seven," Frank replied at once. "A hundred and fifty-four."

His son laughed in joking despair. "You always make us feel inadequate."

"Nonsense, sir!" Frank boomed — then clapped him on the back. "It was all done to encourage you."

Though he welcomed the new intimacy he seemed to be developing with his younger son, he knew the boy well enough — and was a a shrewd enough judge of men in general — not to be too impressed by it. Lawrence had always been swift to exploit *any* change in the world immediately around him. He went on: "Getting back to Kathleen a moment ... this not wanting to marry — I take it that's just one of her phases?"

"Probably," Lawrence agreed. "Up until last month I'd have blamed Miss Kernow's influence — the very picture of the independent woman. But now she's gone and got herself engaged! We'll see if Kathy changes her tune, too."

The huge compound engines were already installed, of course; indeed, the *Pride of Liverpool* had practically been constructed around them. But the pipework and condensers and all the ancillary equipment was yet to be fitted. The two men stood there a moment, awestruck, admiring its simplicity.

"It's more impressive now, in my opinion," Frank said, "than when all the pipes and valves are joined up. They're like fetters that hold it in check."

It struck Lawrence that his father was looking for a "romance of steam" to replace the one of sail; but since nothing in their past dealings with each other would allow either steam or sail to possess any vestige of "romance," he had no way of expressing the notion. All he could say was, "Yes."

When they turned to retrace their steps Frank revived their earlier topic for the third time. "I know it's a bit of an awkward thing to ask you, my boy, but your comment about Kathleen not wishing to marry — especially when you throw in, 'of course' — has worried me. It wouldn't have anything to do with ... I mean, d'you know whether your mother has told her the facts of life? They must seem pretty shocking to some girls, I'd imagine. D'you think it could be that?"

"Facts of life, Papa?" Lawrence almost managed a straight face.

An earlier Papa reasserted himself. "Don't trifle with me, sir! You know what I mean."

Greatly daring, Lawrence gave his father's arm a manly squeeze. "I was only pointing out in my hamfisted way, that nobody told *me* the 'facts of life'!"

It amazed Frank to see how boldly his son tested the new limits of his tolerance; Neil would be far more circumspect. It reminded him of Wheeler, somehow. Perhaps — the idea merely flitted past his consciousness — perhaps Lawrence was the one who ought to have gone to sea? "It's different for boys," he said curtly. "We pick that sort of thing up as we go along."

"I think girls do, too. I've seen them sniggering together in playgrounds. I always assumed that's what's going on."

Frank recalled Hilda's ignorance on their wedding night, then her horrified disbelief and his own careless anger at her. "It's not right," he muttered.

Lawrence found the resulting silence even more awkward than the idea of prolonging this extraordinary conversation. "D'you mean you think it's better to try and keep women in total innocence, sir?" he asked diffidently.

"No, dammit! I think they should be told. And boys. Properly. It's the only way to avoid ..." An exasperated sigh completed the sentence.

He became aware that Lawrence was no longer at his side; he turned and saw him standing two or three paces behind, his expression a perfect study of indecision. "Did I say something?" he asked his son.

Lawrence, who was happy to gamble only when it was onto a near certainty, now took the least happy gamble of his life. "It might have saved me a lot of ... I don't know," he said flatly.

"What?" Frank was at once alert. "Trouble?"

Lawrence was already beginning to wish he hadn't spoken out at all. "Not in the conventional sense," he replied. "In fact, everything *but* that. I don't know if you remember Emma Harding, one of the maids."

They climbed the two ladders but, instead of joining the ladies in the second class, as promised, Frank led his son out onto the promenade deck. It was easier to lean against the rail and talk to the dockyard and the sea. "Emma Harding," he echoed. "The one who was so impertinent to your mother?"

Lawrence shrugged. "There are two sides to every conflict." He explained briefly what had happened, making it seem that it was Kathleen's sense of the injustice done to Emma that had moved him, in a weak moment after winning the office sweepstake, to put Emma in temporary lodgings in Goldsmith's Place, with the promise to help her in some more permanent way. "And then I found myself getting rather fond of her, d'you see?" His brief smile begged a little tolerance.

"I begin to, I fear. Is she still in those 'temporary' lodgings?"

"I've been keeping her in an apartment in Upper Street for the past ..."

"Where?" Frank roared. "My God, you took a risk!"

"It had to be within walking distance, so I could use small errands as an excuse for seeing her."

His father began to laugh as the shock wore off. "Well," he said, "so she's made a man of you, eh?" He glanced over his shoulder. "Between you and me, my boy, there's no real harm done. I know it doesn't measure to the highest ideals you learned in Sunday School, but, by the lights of the real world, no one's going to be too hard on you."

"But it isn't like that," the young man started to explain.

Frank went on regardless: "When you first said you were in some kind of trouble, I thought you meant with one of our friends' daughters! Now that would be quite a different kettle of fish. But Emma Harding — a dismissed servant without a character ... well!" The expansive gesture of his hands was almost an act of blessing.

"But I haven't touched her," Lawrence insisted. "Not in that way. We haven't gone to bed together."

"Good heavens!" Frank stared at his son, whose face was an impassive profile, lit mainly from below by the lights on the wharf. "And you've been paying the rent all these months? That won't do. High time you read the riot act to her, my boy. That's not the arrangement, eh! Quid pro quo!"

Lawrence gave up the attempt to explain. "I suppose so," he said, as if he were now determined to take his father's advice. "Yes, decidedly."

Frank glanced at him quizzically. "D'you go and see her often? I still can't quite believe your recklessness. You might as well have taken a room for her in the guest house at the bottom of Highbury New Park!"

"I see her every day, in fact."

"But what d'you *do* — if not the obvious?"

"Talk. I didn't think it possible I'd ever get to know a girl as well as I know her — and yet I still feel I hardly know her at all."

"Not in the biblical sense!" Frank laughed alone.

"I mean, we're not brought up just to be *friends* with women, are we."

When the words were out, when he heard their echo on the air, he expected his father's reply to be quite heated: What did he suppose his parents' association was, then, if not true friendship? That sort of thing. But his father held his peace. Lawrence looked at him, staring impassively into the dark of the shipyard. The next words slipped out unexpectedly: "I'd give my life for Emma, you know. But I'd give it as a friend."

His father nodded — and went on staring into the nothingness.

Lawrence felt he must now explain his outburst. "I think, if we did ... what everyone obviously suspects us of doing ... well, I think it would spoil what we have. And what we have is like nothing else I've ever felt, or heard of, or read of. It's like ... nothing else."

"I know." His father spoke to the gathering night. "Pay no heed to what I said, Lawrence. I've no cause to tell you anything. You do what you think is right. If this feels right to you, do it. And damn the rest of us! Go and see to the ladies now. I'll join you in a few minutes."

And without a glance at his son he strode off toward the bow. Lawrence watched until the darkness swallowed him.

A MOMENT AFTER THE two women went into the stateroom Hilda returned to the open doorway and stared back up the corridor; Lawrence and Frank were just stepping over the unfinished portion of the watertight bulkhead, deep in conversation. Kathleen joined her mother as her father and brother disappeared below. "What?" she asked.

"I was just thinking how Lawrence has changed lately," Hilda said. "Haven't you noticed?"

"In what way?" The girl peered into her mother's eyes, fishing for clues.

"Well, for one thing, he doesn't grumble about not going to sea any more. We used to get that for breakfast, lunch, and supper."

"Perhaps he's just lulling your suspicions," she suggested lightheartedly. "And secretly he's getting ready to do a bolt."

"Is he?" Hilda asked in alarm.

Kathleen sighed heavily. "It was a joke, Mama, dear. Of course he isn't."

"Then why did you say he'd be lulling *my* suspicions — as if *you* were already party to whatever's going on?"

Kathleen walked disgustedly back into the stateroom. "If I'm now going to be picked up on every little word, I shan't talk at all."

Her mother pursued her. "But it's the little words that give away our inner thoughts, my dear. *Is* he planning to bolt?"

"He may be, for all I know — but it would be as great a surprise to me as it would be to you. There! Is that clear now?"

"Well, there's no need to snap, I'm sure. You behave as if it's not a mother's duty to worry about such things."

"I'm sorry. I didn't mean to imply that." Kathleen ran her hand over the carved panelling, which was in place but not yet polished. The frame of the bed was already fitted and she saw that the panels in its head formed part of the general scheme. Instead of a porthole there was a large, square window whose engraved and frosted glazing carried the same motifs as the panelling. Parquet blocks for the floor lay in counted piles beside the blocks of bitumen in which they would be laid. "It's going to be luxurious beyond description," she murmured. "Could we sail on her maiden voyage, d'you think?"

"They wouldn't give us a stateroom like this," her mother warned.

"But we'd still travel first class. We'd eat in that sumptuous saloon. Why do they call it a saloon? It sounds so common. It's really a banqueting hall. And you'd be the hostess at the captain's table — just think! There'd be princesses and lords and great opera singers. And you'd be the queen bee!"

Hilda savoured the pleasant fantasy awhile before she applied the cold douche of realism. "Your father has always had strong ideas about wives travelling at sea."

"On those dangerous old sailing ships, yes. And with reason, wouldn't you say? But surely this is different?"

Hilda shook her head. "It has nothing to do with safety, dear." She chuckled. "In fact, it's more to do with his bigamy than anything."

"What?" Kathleen stared at her aghast.

The chuckle became a merry laugh. "Haven't you

ever heard him say that? Perhaps he wouldn't consider it a suitable joke for your ears. He says he has *two* wives — me and the ocean."

Kathleen pulled a face. "Not a very flattering comparison."

"Oh, I don't know." Hilda, now in a rare, skittish mood, took her daughter's arm and led her to the next stateroom. "Rather an agreeable life for a man, I'd say. Two wives. One moody and unreliable and cold, the other constant and steadfast and … and uplifting. Not a bad life at all."

Kathleen was swift to take her up. "Oh, I grant that. All the same, I think you're a bit hard on yourself. Moody and unreliable … yes. But cold?"

Hilda gave her a token smack on the bottom — and then, reverting at once to her usual self, said, "Have you left off your corsets?"

Kathleen gave her long hair a shake. "Obviously, if you have to *feel* me to discover it, I don't need them."

"But it's not decent to go out without corsets. Suppose there had been an accident to the train and we'd all been taken to hospital — what would the nurses there have thought to find you half naked?"

The girl glanced wearily at the ceiling and made no reply.

"You're not going in for all this rational dress and pre-Raphaelite nonsense, are you?" Hilda asked anxiously.

"Miss Kernow hasn't worn corsets for two years, Mama. She says they constrict our lungs and cause pockets of stale air to fester and become tubercular. They confine our livers and intestines and give rise to any number of gastric disorders …"

"Well I hope she ends her catalogue there!" Hilda said anxiously.

"They also prevent us from enjoying life to the full."

Her mother shivered. "This obsession with enjoyment! There's very little to enjoy in life, I may tell you. Especially for a woman."

Kathleen thought of adding: "... who wears corsets," but thought better of it just in time. Her only outward response was a sigh.

Hilda became aware that the mood between them had been far more pleasant only a moment earlier; she sought for the vanished thread and then remembered: Francis's joke about his bigamous marriage to the ocean. "These staterooms are all the same," she complained. "Let's go and look at the first-class cabins, shall we?"

Kathleen regretted the change of subject and mood, too. As they walked back down the corridor she said, "There are places where men are allowed to have two wives — and more. I often wonder what the poor ignorant savages in Africa think when we tell them they must have only one wife — and then we tell them that the Bible is the Word of God and it's full of holy men and prophets and things, who all had lots of wives. When did God suddenly change His mind? Anyway, I thought God *couldn't* change His mind."

Hilda stopped and stood still for a moment. "You're quite right, my dear," she said in surprise. "D'you know, that has never occurred to me before now. Aren't you clever!"

Her daughter shrugged. "Not really. It was Reverend Handy who pointed it out to me at the missionary supper last January. He said he found it very hard to explain. I mean, we're absolutely convinced that monogamy is the Will of God, aren't we. But all those Old Testament kings and prophets — God's Chosen

People, after all — they were equally convinced that bigamy ... no, what's the opposite of monogamy?"

"Polygamy."

"Yes, they were equally convinced it was God's Will, weren't they."

"Well, it's all very confusing," Hilda said dismissively. "I'm only glad it's been decided at long last. I'll accept monogamy if that's what everybody seems to want."

The first-class cabins had painted panelling and ornate brass bedsteads. The floors were of oak and the areas to be left rough — to stop the rugs from sliding — were already marked out with a finely chiselled groove.

"Look," Hilda said, "there's an electric switch beside each bed, and a connection for a lamp."

"They had them in the staterooms, too," Kathleen replied. "They were actually part of the panelling."

"Just think! No reaching out of bed to turn down the lamp, no smoky ceilings, no wicks to trim, and no stench of hot lamp oil for hours after lights-out!"

The implications of her mother's concluding words on the subject of monogamy were only now filtering through Kathleen's consciousness; they hardly suggested a profound personal commitment to the idea. "If you'd lived in Biblical times," she said, "d'you think you'd have gone along with the swim then, too?"

Hilda peered out of the porthole but saw only random points of light in the darkness. "A lot of those women actually urged their husbands to take another wife," she pointed out. "They even chose them. I can see certain advantages in it."

"For instance?" Kathleen was amazed at this sudden turn in the conversation; until now she'd have sworn that her mother would take the strictly modern legal and religious view of the matter.

One wife — a rather coarse-minded or frivolous type — to cater for the husband's baser needs; another — the born-manager type — to run the household; and another — the ethereal type — to be a true spiritual partner, encouraging his interest in art and the nobler aspects of life ... Hilda's mind ran pleasurably along such lines for a moment until she realized she could hardly put it in those terms to her young daughter. "Those Old Testament wives," she said, "they were women like us, I'm sure, with the same needs for a home, a family ... security ..."

"Love."

"Yes, all those things. And I'm sure they found them in abundance in their system. And I'm equally sure it wouldn't be beyond the wit of women today to find them, too."

Kathleen noted that her mother had avoided answering the specific question as to the advantages of the ancient system.

They found that all the first class cabins were identical, too. They strolled on then toward the stern, past the incomplete bulkhead where the men had stepped from the decorated quarters to those that were strictly utilitarian. Kathleen ducked her head through the gap and marvelled that such differences could exist cheek by jowl with only one thin wall of riveted steel between them.

"Miss Kernow says there's a tribe in the Himalayas where the women have several husbands each," she said. "I quite like the sound of that. As soon as you got bored with one of your husbands you could bid him adieu and move on to the next."

"Where did you say?" Hilda asked. She had only

half heard her daughter's words, having returned to the pleasurable notion of having different wives for every function.

"The Himalayas."

"Very remote," Hilda said. "That must explain it."

Kathleen couldn't see how, but the vision stirred up by her teacher's information was too pleasant to relinquish. "One of them would be a captain in the cavalry," she said. "Terribly handsome and manly, always going off on manoeuvres and bush wars and coming back with beautiful scars and exotic presents for me. And another would be frightfully nice and dependable, softly spoken and ... you know, comfortable. What the Germans call *gemütlich*. And the third would be old and wise, rather stern, but always right; you could ask him anything and his judgement would be just and profound."

Hilda, highly amused at her daughter's daydream, said, "Only three?"

Kathleen gave her a slightly naughty smile and answered, "You're right. There'd have to be a fourth, wouldn't there." She took her mother's arm and fell in step with her. "A bit of a howling cad. A wastrel. A gambler. And a bit of a baby, too, who'd get into all sorts of scrapes and come home licking his wounds and want you to mother him. And the only thing you could be absolutely sure about was that he'd *always* let you down. Perfidy would be his middle name."

"Good heavens!" her mother exclaimed. "It sounds as if you know him already — and as if you'd like him best of all."

"I know!" Kathleen stooped forward and let her shoulders slump in a theatrically glum fashion. "That's why I'm never going to marry. I'd be sure to fall for a man like that."

The stewardesses' cabins, being much simpler than anything intended for the passengers, were all but finished. The bunks, two to a cabin, were in plain mahogany, less than three feet wide. The lockers, drawers, and washstand were made up in a single unit, also of mahogany, and fixed to two walls. The porthole was painted and lacked the brass rings that adorned those in the first class cabins. The floor was of pitch pine, covered with a carpet of rough cord.

The moment Kathleen entered, something within her said, "Yes!" It was a true epiphany, her own encounter on the road to Damascus. The amazement came after; at the time it seemed the most normal decision of her life.

The lower bunk was already furnished with a mattress. She flung herself upon it and lay there, examining her new realm. She looked at the locker and imagined her uniform hanging there. Her gaze moved on toward the washstand, and she imagined getting up in five minutes and washing herself there before going on duty. And then the drawers. The two at the bottom would be hers, and in them she'd keep the letters she'd be posting home at the next port of call — letters filled with accounts of the wonders she'd seen ... Rio de Janeiro, the Gold Coast, the Spice Islands, the shores of far Cathay, the Hanging Gardens of Babylon ...

And the other girl in the bunk above ...

The hair rose on the back of her neck as she realized she already knew who that other girl was ... had to be ... could *only* be.

Of course! How *stupid* not to have thought of it months ago!

KATHLEEN STARED AT Emma in exasperation. "But don't you see?" she urged, "it's the perfect way out of all your difficulties. And you should see those cabins, Emma! They're like ... oh, I don't know — beautiful little *nests*. Lord but I'd give my eye teeth to be a stewardess on the *Pride of Liverpool*. And there's you, free as a bird, and you won't take the chance when it's handed you on a silver salver, practically!" She put the character, which she had spent hours forging last night, onto Emma's lap again.

Again the girl put it back on the whatnot. "No thank you," she said primly.

"But why not? Give me one good reason."

"'Cos I get sick on a row boat on the pond in Victoria Park."

"That's no reason at all. Nelson got seasick on every voyage. Anyway, these big liners don't get tossed around like small sailing boats. And it's not as if you're years at sea and then months off when you lose your sea legs."

"What is it, then? Not that I'm interested, mind you." She glanced at the sideboard, where the port and gin was kept, then at the clock. Five minutes more. This time tomorrow it would be ten; the next day, fifteen. "Weaning," Lawrence called it. She'd been very good so far.

"It's six days to cross, then forty-eight hours to turn round — and you get thirty-six of them off — then six days back ... two more days tied up, again with thirty-six hours off. That's not long enough to lose your sea legs. So you'll be sick the first two days and then ... never again."

"It's more days off than I got in service," Emma allowed. Even so, her tone was still dismissive of the whole project. "What d'you say the pay was?"

"Ten shillings a voyage!" Kathleen tried to make it sound huge. "And that's all found, including your uniform. "And they say the tips are easily double that. Mr McGann, who's going to be the purser when she sails — which Papa says is the second most important officer on board — he told me that stewardesses easily get fifty pounds a year. And good ones, who get big tips, get more than a hundred.

Emma sniffed. She wondered precisely what the girls had to do to get big tips like that, but she said nothing of it to Kathleen. Unfortunately, it left her with no other strong argument against high earnings. A deep-rooted desire never to have more than a few miles between her and London was hardly a logical riposte. "I'm not qualified," she said flatly.

"Of course you are!" Kathleen said angrily. "Most of it is upstairs-maid's work — which you can do in your sleep. The rest of it is the easier bits of being a lady's maid — sponging clothes and emergency repairs. And don't tell me you can't do that, because I've seen you. Also you know things most of the other stewardesses won't."

"Such as?" Emma sneered. "How to hold your liquor?"

"First aid, for instance. And life-saving in the water."

Emma stared at her in astonishment. "How d'you know about that? I never even told Larry about that."

"Never mind. I know a lot about you. I know you're worth ten times what you give yourself credit for being. You could be ... you could be really *somebody*, Emma, if only you made a little effort. And this is your big chance. Don't be such a wet little goose — sitting there and bleating about seasickness and your general unworthiness!"

Emma felt a lump rising into her throat. One minute to go. "You're going to argue me into it, aren't you," she said glumly.

"If I can. I'd horsewhip you into it if I thought it would work!"

"How *did* you know about my learning first aid and that?"

Kathleen sighed, as if it were really too obvious. "Because Mr Lejeune of the Royal Humane Society also happens to be a member of the Operatic and Choral Society and ..."

"Don't tell me! Bleeding Aunt Daphne again, I know! Blimey, it'd be worth running away to sea just to get beyond the reach of her long nose."

Kathleen laughed. "Oh, you'd never do that — unless it was one of the seas on the moon. So at least you'll think about it, eh?" She pushed the forged character back toward the girl's elbow.

A cunning look stole over Emma's face. "You said you'd give your eye teeth to be able to do it, eh?"

"I should jolly well say so!"

"All right. I'll go if you come with me."

Kathleen laughed. "That's just a way of getting out of it. You know you're asking the impossible."

"Why?"

"Well, for one thing, it's my father's ship. He'd have an apoplexy if I even suggested such a thing."

"There's other ships. I should think there's hundreds of ships with stewardesses. Just 'cos you saw a nice little nest on this *Pride of Liverpool* it don't mean we can't sail on no other. Go on — I'm serious. Either we both go or I don't go at all."

She glanced at the clock and saw that for the last minute she could have been drinking. She was just about to sprint to the sideboard when a powerful sense of revulsion filled her. *Don't you ever look at yourself?* her conscience asked. *You're pathetic!*

The strange thing was, her conscience could have spoken the same judgement any day during the past six months or more; the only difference now was that she had a new standard of comparison, a genuine alternative to what she had allowed herself to become — or at least the first alternative she could even think of taking seriously.

"The poison's working already," she commented balefully, more to herself than to Kathleen.

"What poison?" Kathleen asked.

"What you poured in my ear, my love!"

The girl smiled ruefully. "And what d'you call what you poured in mine?"

Emma stared at her a moment and then broke out laughing. Kathleen resisted briefly and then joined her. In that moment of merry sisterhood everything seemed possible.

I T WAS THE END of April before Kathleen finally managed to persuade Emma that it really was impossible for the daughter of Captain Morgan to become a stewardess, too. By then Emma had seen so many photographs of the *Pride of Liverpool* and read so many glowing accounts of her opulence in the newspapers — not to mention equally lavish descriptions of the rival liners then being built for the Inman, the Cunard, and the Peninsular and Oriental lines — that it was well nigh impossible for her to resist the siren call to become a small cog in that wondrous new machine of the age.

Oddly enough it was a stray remark of Kathleen's that finally tipped the balance. "Just think!" she said in one of her panegyrics, "you'll be able to boast you were lady's maid to half the aristocracy of Europe, not to mention royalties and actresses and opera divas. And even if one or two of them are absolute *cows*, the longest you'll ever have to endure them at any one time is less than a week."

Whenever Emma thought of those words she laughed. She remembered when she was a little girl of thirteen, just before she was sent into service, Annie Davis, one of the big girls in her street who was a fancy lady up the West End, had come home for a day off. How envious she had made Emma feel — dressed like a queen and dishing out pennies to all the admiring little girls and boys around her. And Annie had boasted of entertaining lords and generals and members of parliament and bishops and all sorts of people with their names in the papers. Handsome young nobodies she dismissed out of hand; but the rich and powerful made her feel exalted, too.

And now Emma was shrewd enough to recognize that the thrill she felt at the prospect of being a temporary lady's maid to the grandest women in the world was identical to Annie's pride in *her* glittering clientèle! Even so, it did nothing to diminish the allure of the job for her. And so it was that on the morning of the last Friday in April she sat in the offices of the Shaw & Eggar Line in Liverpool, holding in a slightly trembling hand her First Aid Certificate, her Life Saver's Seal of Merit, her birth certificate, her brand new passport, and her record of smallpox inoculation. The trembling hand might have been partially explained away as the result of her total abstinence over the past three weeks; but mainly it was due to the final and most important document among that sheaf — a glowing character signed by one "Kathleen Dowty" of 6 (or was it 8 ... or even 9?) Highbury Crescent, London N.

The applicants were being scrutinized by Mr Abel McGann, Purser, and Mrs Maude Glover, Chief Stewardess of the *Pride of Liverpool*. Were such august personages chosen mainly for their appearance, Emma found herself wondering? Or did the work impose upon them the facial lineaments their positions required? Mr McGann's eyes, for instance, were both sympathetic and piercing; here, you thought, was a man who would understand the foibles and weaknesses of the pampered upper classes without ever once being deceived by the knaves and scoundrels among them. Had he always been such a man, or had bitter experience moulded him? And, turning to Mrs Glover, what of those grim lines that bracketed her trap-like mouth? Did Sir Hector Shaw once see her in a crowd and decide she was exactly what he wished his chief stewardess to look like? Or had they grown there, bit by bit, as she dished out her daily reprimands to the girls in her charge? Either way, Emma had no doubt the reprimands would be daily — and by the dozen.

However, her qualifications were impressive enough to get her over this first hurdle. The only sticky moment came when Mr McGann held up her character and said, "Mrs Kathleen Dowty ... I see she lives in the Highbury area. She is surely related in some way to the Dowtys of the shipping line?"

"Miss Dowty," Emma corrected him. "I believe she is, sir. I believe her cousin is a Mr Brian Dowty who lives farther up the Crescent."

"Ah well, enough said!" The purser put down the sheet of paper and patted it reassuringly.

"I'm only surprised you didn't apply to the Dowty Line in that case," Mrs Glover snapped.

"Oh, I shall if I don't secure this position, ma'am," Emma replied. "But my father always said I could lose nothing by aiming at the highest first."

That was a laugh, she thought. The highest thing her father ever aimed at was to piss on all the other doorknockers in the street when he had a skinful.

The purser beamed at her and even Mrs Glover seemed taken with her reply. They gave her a warrant for the Belfast ferry that night and told her to report aboard the *Pride of Liverpool* at midday tomorrow for two weeks' training at the dockside, to be followed by another two weeks at sea while the vessel ran her trials.

"Please understand, Miss Harding," the chief stewardess snapped, "you will be one of twenty-five girls selected for this training — of whom only twenty will be finally employed. So you are not to suppose you may now rest on your laurels!"

"A girl of very high calibre, Mrs G.," commented Mr McGann when Emma had gone. "I'm very impressed that she has taken her first aid certificate and a medal in lifesaving."

"We shall see," the woman replied grimly. To her mind there was something just a little too *mature* about Miss Emma Harding.

A S LAWRENCE SET OFF to visit Emma that first Saturday morning in June his heart was hammering against his ribs and he had to stop every now and then to catch his breath. This was going to be the most momentous day of his life. He had decided at long last that his association with Emma should take the form that all the world had long assumed it to have taken from the start. He would finally make a woman of her — and, incidentally, a man of himself.

He had lain awake most of last night, blowing hot and cold on the decision, but now the die was finally cast. What a brutal catechism he had endured!

Was his decision based on his brother's sneers and his father's incomprehension that the situation could be anything other than that of man and mistress?

No, for if that were the case, he would have succumbed long ago, when those influences were at their strongest. Indeed, his father's attitude had, in the end, become highly ambiguous; it had almost seemed that he admired his son more for his nobility of sentiment than he had previously scorned him for being so understanding of Emma's coyness (as he then saw it). And Neil, too, had changed his tune. Indeed, having spent a little time getting to know Emma last Christmas, he had pronounced her "a lady of no mean character!" So, no, his decision had nothing to do with pressure from those quarters.

Was it simple lust on his part, then?

No. Lust came into it, of course — or, to give it a more gracious name, natural desire. What could be more natural than to desire a female in whom youth, beauty, and availability were combined in such perfection. Not to mention a strong and frequently expressed desire of equal strength on her part! But he had desired her far more avidly at the beginning, when he literally had to imagine that his hands were cuffed and chained so as to keep them to himself. So it was more than mere desire.

Was it another kind of lust, then — the lust of the powerful male to exert his will on the subordinate and dependent female?

No. Because he had long ago freed her of any sense of obligation she might harbour toward him merely because he paid her an allowance. Not that she had accepted it at once, but she had, finally, he believed, come round to his way of seeing it. Again and again he had assured her that only when she felt perfectly free — free even to leave him, if that were her wish — could he even think of putting their association on a more intimate footing. Several times lately he had tested her in this, saying, "If you wanted to leave me, leave these rooms, go away and make a life of your own, you would do so without hesitation, wouldn't you? You don't feel any obligation to me now?" At first, of course, she had protested she would never be able to repay all his kindness and concern for her. But slowly he had convinced her that he had already derived far more spiritual satisfaction from their association than money could possibly buy; and then, only last week, she had finally yielded and assured him that she felt free enough to leave with an easy conscience.

It was, he now realized, all he had been waiting to hear. The consummation of their friendship would now be the pleasurable union of two free and equal bodies. That, indeed, was the answer to the final question of his overnight catechism: Why, then, do you now so ardently desire what you have heretofore shunned with such fervour? Because, in a sentence, Emma had at last freed herself of him! The difference in their class mattered not a jot. Her continuing financial dependence on him was of not the slightest account. Her former servitude in his parents' house was consigned to history. She had discovered her own perfect freedom and, in doing so, had liberated him from the fetters of his own conscience. Now that same free conscience assured him he could love her in the fullest sense of that most beautiful word.

Love! He hardly dared speak its name until now, for fear of tainting it with the petty tyrannies that she, not he, took to be part of her dependence on him. Love! He was surely the most sublimely happy young man in the world on this fine June morning! To know he was in love with the most adorable girl who ever lived ... to know simultaneously that their love could be celebrated with the most profound embrace a couple can achieve, instead of waiting through those agonizing months and years of abstinence that sour the conventional courtship ... why, probably no more than half a dozen men in all the world could assert so joyous a claim at this very hour.

Love!

Emma Harding! I love you Emma Harding. You are the sweetest, most delightful, most perfect girl who ever lived. I revere you from the topmost hair of your adorable head to the uttermost tip of your dainty toes. Your body no longer fills me with fear. Your soft breasts now beg the touch of my fingers, which yearn to comply. I am fevered with my longing to pierce you with this arrow of my desire and lose self and my senses in your belly ...

Love!

"Love?" he called out at her door, half ashamed, half proud of the uncontrollable shiver in his voice.

When he inserted the brass key in the lock of her door, it was so powerful a symbolism he almost spent himself then and there.

"Emma, love?" he repeated, annoyed at her lack of response to the word.

There was a commotion in the hall below, running feet, someone out of breath, gasping his name. Indeed, she was so breathless it required the sight of her to confirm what his hearing alone had rejected — that it was, indeed, his sister Kathleen.

How she escaped even one of the half dozen deaths he devised for her as she came to him from the stairhead — never mind all of them — was a wonder in itself. The speed with which his anger superseded his desire was another. "Of all the days to choose!" he screamed at her.

"Have you been inside yet?" she gasped.

"How dare you!"

"Have you?"

"It's none of your business. Anyway, where did you get to? You've been gone an hour or more. Mama was asking everywhere for you ..." His voice tailed off when he realized she was holding out an envelope. All it said was, *For Larry* — in Emma's distinctively bold hand.

It was still sealed, but she showed him briefly another that had been opened: *Miss Kathleen Morgan, Poste Restante, Highgate PO*. It was cancelled from Liverpool Central with yesterday's date.

"Liverpool?" he said in bewilderment as his fingers, almost of their own accord, reached for the one addressed to him.

WITH A HEART FULL of forebodings Lawrence took the letter from his sister's trembling fingers. "What d'you know about this?" he asked, giving a mistrustful nod at the opened letter in her other hand. "Have you been meddling in what doesn't concern you?"

"Read it." She offered him the letter Emma had written to her, too. "And this, too, if you like."

He turned from her and went to the window, praying, *Please God, let it all be a jape got up by those two. Let Emma be hiding behind these curtains.* In fact, the curtains were neither high nor wide enough to conceal a child. He put a thumbnail to the envelope and ripped it open.

Dear Larry,

If Kathy gives this you it'll mean I got the job which she'll tell you all about, it's stewardess on your papa's new ship the Pride of Liverpool. First thing off, of course, is you'll go blaming her, but you'll end up blaming yourself which is the right thing to do. Blame me too, for I never should ought to of agreed.

When I waited for you to get off of the tram that day it wasn't what I said, about you being so kind and good. I didn't even know you then I was beside myself with fury at your mama for giving me the boot so unjustly and I thought I'll make her pay through you her darling son. Don't ask me how! I was beside myself like I say. And then of course I go and fall in love with you proper! Typical me!!

I been in love with you ever since and love you now. I write this in a boarding house in

Union Place waiting for my interview and tears in my eyes thinking of leaving you. First off, I didn't know nothing about love, not like what I know it now. I thought it was slap and tickle, and cuddling and that. I read in those books from the Library about deeper love but I never understood it, I thought it was just the way they carry on people in books. But now I do know, because I love you deeper just like that. If I had those books by me now I could copy out the bits to tell you.

Anyway, the worst of it is you remember what I always told you about me? You remember me going on and on about being so common and ordinary and not worth you bothering? How true! The worst of it is the more deep I loved you the more I seen it was true. I am no good for you my darling Larry. What life could we have together? You would end up ashamed of me for being so common. And so as I loved you deeper and deeper I saw more and more it was impossible between us. Believe me, but for the drink which helped me forget I'd of gone long afore now. You are a man of class and education and you should of seen it even more clearer than what I done, that's why I say blame yourself not Kathy. All she done was save me from Demon Drink and show me the prison door wasn't barred.

You know where I am now so you can play the fool and follow me but it won't do no good. My mind is made up. I will always love you but I will always know it won't do no good.

Your ever-loving
Emma.

He lifted the letter to his face and sniffed at it. *Emma!* He felt too numb even to weep. Anyway, Kathy was there. He stared at her and saw a stranger. The door behind her was still open. "Prison door!" he said in anguish. "She called it her prison door!"

"Larry? I'm sorry." She wanted to throw her arms around him and hug him and do all she could to comfort him.

"I've got to get out of here." He lurched past her, but at the door something held him back and he could not go one step beyond the threshold.

He closed the door and went to the sideboard in search of a drink; the first bottle he pulled out was unopened. A bottle of port — unopened!

Kathleen saw how closely he examined the seal. "She bought it three weeks ago," she told him.

He nodded and gave her a brief smile to show he understood what she was actually trying to tell him.

"You know I'm to blame for her going, Larry. Does she tell you that? I expect not."

He shook his head.

"I am. It was my idea. It came to me on the day of the launching. The moment I saw those cabins for the stewardesses I thought at once of her. Do you have any idea how desperate she was?"

He broke the seal and offered her a tot, which she declined. He poured himself a modest measure, and then doubled it, shooting her a guilty look.

She risked saying, "It's a sight I'm used to by now."

He took a gulp and breathed out the fumes with relish. "She told me you knew but she never said you'd actually been here."

She sat down on the arm of the sofa. "Only in the last couple of months. But I knew long before that. In fact, even when she was in Goldsmith's Place."

He closed his eyes, as if in pain. "Why did you never say?"

She shrugged. "What would have been the point?"

"You could've told her not to be so stupid!" He handed her the letter.

"Are you quite sure?" she asked, even as she started to read.

He watched her intently but she made no response, either by word or gesture, until she had finished.

There was a lump in her throat but she swallowed on it and said as she handed him the letter back, "I wouldn't, you know. I wouldn't have told her not to be such a fool."

"You think she's doing the right thing?" he asked incredulously.

Kathleen was about to utter a decisive yes when some imp made her ask, "D'you think *I* could go off and join her — become a stewardess, too?"

"Don't be absurd!" he exclaimed crossly.

Now the implications of her question began to dawn on her. "Why not?" she asked, and her tone was no longer so playful.

"Because you're ... I mean ..." The implications were dawning on him, too.

"Yes," she said coldly. "All right for *common* girls, isn't it!"

He came and sat on the sofa beside her, letting the tumbler of port dangle perilously between his knees.

"It is still how you think of her, isn't it," she said more gently. "No one could blame you."

For some time he made no reply. Then he said bleakly, "I'm certainly not staying here now. With her gone, there's nothing to hold me ashore."

When she had digested this she said, "Ships that pass in the night!"

"God but you're hard," he told her. "There's a hardness in you ... well, you get if from Papa, of course."

Kathleen made no reply. She rose and began going through the chest of drawers and wardrobe. "Nothing left," she commented. "Not a stitch. Just a few scraps of food. How long is the rent paid?"

He shook his head, as if he thought she had asked a different question.

"Oh, come on, Lawrence!" she snapped. "Don't go to pieces now! I'll miss her, too. I've grown very fond of her. She was such a ..." The exact word eluded her.

"Anything but a sister-in-law!" he sneered.

"On the contrary!" she said angrily. "I'd be far more ready to accept her as a sister-in-law than you would as a wife."

"But I thought ..." The glass fell from his fingers; it didn't break but a red pool began to spread across the linoleum. He ignored it. "You said you wouldn't have stopped her bolting."

She brought a cloth from the sink and wiped the spill with vigorous, angry circles. "Not because I thought she'd make an unsuitable wife," she explained, "but because I know you'd make an unsuitable husband."

"How dare you!"

She spoke over her shoulder as she returned to the sink. "What did you intend doing here today, then?" she asked coldly. "Put your hand on your heart and tell me you were going to propose marriage."

She watched him closely, to be sure of catching the subtlest hesitation. He did not disappoint her.

His eyes could no longer meet hers. Staring at his boots he said, "All right. The thought of marrying her never even crossed my mind — until this." He patted the letter in his pocket. "But now I will." He gave a single ironic laugh. "I told Papa I'd give my life for her, but I never thought it'd be ..."

"You told Papa? You mean ... about Emma and everything?"

He nodded.

"And what did he say?"

"Nothing. He told me it was my affair."

"Just like that? I mean in so many words? He didn't talk about it at all?"

Lawrence began cleaning one set of fingernails with the other. She slapped his hands and told him to stop it. "It's a jolly awkward subject to discuss with one's sister, you know," he muttered.

"You needn't worry," she told him impatiently. "I'm no longer the little innocent I was on the day Emma got the boot." *Or even*, she thought wryly, *on the day when I misunderstood Emma's remarks about slices of Christmas cake!* But she said nothing as to that.

"Was it Emma who told you?" he asked

"Never you mind. Yes it was, if you must know. She also told me you'd been a perfect gentleman to her. Did you tell Papa that, too?"

Lawrence chuckled.

That was the moment when Kathleen realized he was in earnest about going away to sea. The decision had liberated him enough to be able to laugh — because it made a meeting with Emma possible again. More than a meeting — a life.

"He didn't believe it," Lawrence replied. "He leaped to the same conclusion as everyone else — including you, I imagine?"

She shook her head and resumed her perch on the arm of the sofa; it was easier to talk with him side by side. "I knew nothing of these matters until Emma explained the facts of her particular case. What did Papa say when you told him it wasn't so?"

"I thought he'd say the same as Neil. I told Neil about it last year and he said I should ..." He swallowed and scrabbled for words with his hands.

"Make a kept woman of her," Kathleen said. So that would explain why Neil had come round "looking for a slice of a cake that had already been cut"!

"Quite."

"And didn't he? Papa, I mean — say the same as Neil?"

Lawrence still felt awkward to be discussing such matters with his younger sister. "To start with. But then ... I don't know ... he just went about completely and told me to do whatever I thought was right. Ignore the conventional ... you know, whatever anyone else might say — ignore it and stick to my own guns. Then he wandered away on his own. It was that day in Belfast, when we were looking over the *Pride of Liverpool*. I suppose he had a lot on his mind and couldn't be bothered with something so trivial."

It didn't sound like the father she knew, but she could think of no better explanation. She recalled her earlier question. "How long *is* the rent paid?"

He pulled a face. "I just paid the whole quarter. Four quid down the drain!"

"Let me move in!" she said impulsively.

"Move in?" he asked in surprise.

"Well, not to live, but you know what I mean. Just to say it's mine."

"You're extraordinary! What'll you do here?"

"I don't know. Give little tea parties for the other girls at school. Smoke gaspers. Write letters to Emma. She can come and visit me here on liberty. You know she'll get thirty-six hours' liberty every six days when the *Pride of Liverpool* is in service? But, of course, you'll be on your way to New South Wales by then, won't you."

"Every six days?" he repeated guardedly.

"Every sixteen days on *this* side of the Atlantic, actually." She explained the arrangement in detail. "Of course, if you went to sea with Papa's blessing, he could probably haul in a few sheets and get you on a Cunard boat — or even another Shaw & Eggar."

He stared up at her. "You didn't *plan* all this from the beginning, did you, Kathy? It's beginning to sound like it."

She rose and went to sit opposite, laughing and telling him not to be so silly. But the moment she was seated she became serious again. "What about this idea of me becoming a stewardess, too?" she asked. "You know Emma would have gone weeks ago, except she tried to make it conditional on my running away and joining her. Of course, I told her it was out of the question and she finally accepted it. But now I don't know. I've thought about it a lot since and every time I turn it over in my mind it seems just a little bit less absurd. And now ..." She shrugged and gazed at him hopefully.

"Now?" he repeated.

"Now it's just a question of doing it with their blessing or without it. I'd far rather do it with, of course. But how?"

He smiled wanly. "You could soften them up a bit first. Tell them you want to be a barmaid or a chorus girl down at the Gaiety."

"Ha ha! I'll do it somehow. Just you see!"

THE NORTHERN END of the great Landing Stage in Liverpool, the largest structure of its kind in the world and now completely rebuilt after the recent disastrous fire, was to be the regular bay for the *Pride of Liverpool*. She affirmed her claim to it when, on the morning of Monday the second of August, 1886, she steamed away on her triumphant maiden voyage — the one that, on the return trip, ensured her the Blue Riband for the next two years. The band played "Britons, to Sea!" and "Rule Britannia!" for all they were worth, the bunting stirred in the listless summer breeze, and the whole city of Liverpool turned out to watch her slip gracefully away. She was not the largest steamship ever built (Brunel's *Great Eastern*, launched some twenty years earlier at almost 19,000 gross registered tons, still towered over all comers for sheer size); but the *Pride of Liverpool* was far and away the most modern and luxurious and the city was duly honoured to have been chosen as the home port for such a vessel.

On the bridge Cap'n Morgan was doing his best not to live up to his reputation. He smiled thinly at the ladies, Lady Shaw and the Hon. Mrs Eggar and their several acolytes, who wandered about twittering at each new wonder and getting in the way. The owners' party were, in fact, going only as far as Queenstown, where they were to disembark and proceed to Lord Charleville's estate in King's County for the Glorious Twelfth. Until then, the officers on the bridge would just have to put up with them. Normally, of course, the *Pride of Liverpool* wouldn't be calling at Queenstown at all since she had no steerage accommodation.

"Gangways?" he queried.

"All clear and stowed, sir," Wheeler responded.

"Let go aft."

They were sailing on a rising tide.

"Let go aft ..." The order was repeated all the way to the stern.

"Quarter speed ahead."

The telegraph jangled. The decks seemed to come subtly alive though there was no detectable vibration. Frank's eyes met Sir Hector's and received an approving nod. "Let go forr'ard!"

It was a command whose utterance he would never forget — the moment when the great liner cut her umbilical ties with the land and began what all aboard hoped would be her long and distinguished career. He handed over command to the pilot, who now controlled her navigation until they reached open water, and crossed the bridge to the landward side, where he gazed down at the ceremony he had just inaugurated. When the great jute hawser went sliding across the stage and fell with a slap against her steel bows, a mighty cheer went up, uniting the crowds ashore and the souls on board for the final time. From now on, give or take the odd nudge from a tug, the *Pride of Liverpool* was on her own.

Down in Sir Hector's stateroom Emma heard the roar of the engines, felt the deck begin to hum beneath her feet, and dashed to the window for just one peep. And, of course, it was the very moment Mrs Glover chose to glance in to see that none of her charges was slacking. "Harding, on report," she snapped and was gone.

Too late, Emma dashed back to the wardrobe and continued unpacking Lady Shaw's unending selection of gowns and day dresses.

Just her luck! Cissie Williams even smoked in her cabin and was never caught. Joan Bolton dropped her drawers with the Eyetie waiter in the life-jacket store every evening and got away with it. And as for Mavis Hopkinson ... but why go on? The only one who got caught was Harding. Dirty fingernails, button missing, hair not tucked into cap ... and now looking out of window while supposed to be unpacking dresses. "What a wicked gel I is, to be sure," she said gaily. Since she had pulled the wool over Captain Morgan's eyes yesterday, nothing could mar her happiness for long.

But it had been a sticky moment.

"Don't I know you?" says he with a funny, twisted sort of smile.

"No sir. I don't think so, sir."

"I feel sure I do, Miss Harding. You're from London, I can hear. Have you ever been in the Highbury district?"

"Oh yes, sir. I was at a house in Goldsmith's Place. The sausage man."

Prepared for everything — Mrs Glover's motto. Something to thank the old battleaxe for!

"Ah, that must be it, then. I knew I'd seen you before. I never forget a face!"

She hoped her eyes had been twin pools of admiration for his manly superiority; it would help him not to question his amazingly wonderful million horsepower memory in any future moment of doubt.

And now she could go on report daily for all the dent it made in her happiness. For this was surely one of the best jobs going in the whole kingdom, for a woman. The envy of the other girls in her lodgings in Union Place when she first heard she'd been picked for training was proof enough of that. Anyway, what did "report" mean? A finger-wagging from nice Mr McGann. And no liberty in port if you were up more than three times in a voyage. Not that "liberty" was the word for it, anyway. You were only allowed to stay with the Christian Girls' Guild, where Mrs Glover put up, and you had to book in and out with her in fours and say where you were going and why and how long — and always back before ten. Some liberty!

She held one of Lady Shaw's silk evening gowns to her and did an impromptu waltz, admiring herself in the glass. To her horror, she saw Mrs Glover standing in the doorway once again, staring at her. To her amazement, the woman left her without a word of reprimand.

Up on the bridge Sir Hector leaned confidentially close to Frank and murmured, "Brace the main yards to the port tack, after yards to starboard! Port and starboard the helm!"

"Ah, yes!" Frank's eyes twinkled. "It was a different ocean, sir."

"Port two degrees," said the pilot.

The quartermaster repeated the command and turned the wheel a spoke or two. By now they were nearing the northern tip of the great Burbo Bank; over the next four miles they would swing in a long arc to port, which would bring them to open water at last.

"A different ocean," Frank repeated.

To Sir Hector there seemed a surprising lack of nostalgia in his tone.

"You appear to have taken well enough to steam, Morgan, I must say."

Frank smiled. "In a way, Sir Hector, it's a more manly trade. Under canvas you had to woo the sea.

You had to cajole it and flatter it and pretend to go along with its moods if you wanted to get your way with it — you had to be like a woman when she wants to impose her will on a man."

"And now?" Sir Hector was enjoying the comparison, especially because he knew his wife was eavesdropping on their conversation.

"The sea boot's on the other foot. And the sea's a woman at last. Respect her, of course — and never underestimate her strength, her fickleness, her malevolence, if that's her mood. But while we've coals in our bowels, we're no longer at her mercy. We have fifteen thousand horses down there that owe nothing to her."

Lady Shaw's nostrils flared in contempt. She considered him a thoroughly odious little man. Yet, even as she turned her back upon him, she could not but acknowledge that there was something fatally attractive about him, too. When his eyes rested on her, and seemed to look right into her ... there was a decided *frisson* of something in response to it. On a future voyage ... perhaps with Sir Hector not there ...? The taming of such a brute would be ... piquant.

She gathered her court and they went below to attend that morning's concert in the saloon. "Are you coming, Shaw?" she asked coldly.

"Those cat-gut scrapers?" he replied without turning round.

They picked up the buoy off Formby Bank, and then the Formby Float, which caused them to make a little semicircular detour to pass it on the south.

"Has she drifted off her moorings?" Frank asked the pilot.

He replied that mud had shifted off the Little Burbos; it was always changing out here. If it didn't shift back naturally this week, they'd have to start dredging.

The *Pride of Liverpool* resumed her long, lazy arc to port.

"When you retire, Morgan," Sir Hector said, clapping him on the back, "we'll get one of these ocean sailing yachts and just sail the seven seas for the sheer pleasure of it. Sail until the chippie puts his stitch in our nostrils, eh? Leave all these bloody women behind!"

Frank replied that by then he might well be glad of the opportunity. He caught sight of Wheeler, pinching his lips gravely to avoid smiling. "Number One!" he barked. "Prepare to drop the pilot!"

They dropped him at the Bell Beacon and then, keeping the North-West Lightship three or four miles to port, they set course west-by-south for The Skerries and Holyhead.

"Burn the funnels off her on your way home," Sir Hector told Frank as they disembarked in Ireland. "Not that we're in the ocean-racing business, mind! I hope we never stoop to anything so vulgar. But that Blue Riband belongs to the *Pride of Liverpool* by right, d'you see! So be sure you get it for her, eh!"

S HE DOCKED AT Pier 82, at the foot of West Forty-Second Street, the following Monday at ten in the morning — a week almost to the hour after leaving Liverpool; but it was the five days and two hours from Queenstown that gave them hope of the Blue Riband on their return voyage. As a mark of the company's pleasure and gratitude, Captain Morgan granted an amnesty to all whose liberty had been curtailed for misdemeanours during the voyage. He did not know it at the time, of course, but it was an act of clemency whose consequence upon his own life was profound.

Emma, who had expected to spend her first visit to New York with her nose pressed against one of the windows whose enticements were, in part, responsible for her confinement aboard, now found herself at liberty with the other stewardesses, much to Mrs Glover's annoyance. Joan Bolton had been a stewardess before, on the *Servia* and the *Hamlet*, and knew her way round the city — and, or so she believed, around life in general.

"Now the best place for a cheap slap-up meal," she said as they stepped upon solid land, "is the Park Avenue Oyster House in front of the Grand Central Depot. That's on Park and Forty-Second." Her insistence on the local idiom, like saying *dee-poh* and *on* such-and-such a street greatly impressed the other girls. One of them wanted to know if it was far from there to the Christian Girls' Guild. For a moment she pretended not to know what that was; then, with a tinkling laugh, she replied, "Oh, the Fallen Angels! No, it's very near — on East Forty-Seventh, in fact."

So, as soon as they had left their bags in at the CGG, which was, indeed, in East Forty-Seventh Street, six of them set off with Mrs Glover's grudging blessing for a "whizz-bang blow-out" at the Park Avenue Oyster House. At first they walked six abreast, arm in arm, but as they approached the intersection with Forty-Second Street, which seemed to be one of the main east-west thoroughfares, the press of the crowds forced them into threes, then, finally, pairs. Emma found herself arm-in-arm with Joan.

"We can slip away from these ninnies after the meal," Joan told her. "They won't dare split on us. I know the best place to pick up a dashing macquereau for the evening."

"And Antonio?" Emma asked, not liking the sound of this plan at all.

"Who?" Joan asked. "Oh, him! He's all right for the voyage. Not much to choose from on the *Pride of Liverpool*, is there! But here there's men with real style. Only make sure they don't get you to lie down. If you do it standing up, you're safe."

"Is that what you've come ashore for?" Emma asked, scandalized.

"Why not? The men all do. Only they have to pay for it. We get paid *for*."

Emma felt sick. She just wanted to turn and run by now. "You mean ... do it ... for money?" she asked, colour rising to her cheeks.

"No!" Joan was angrily scornful. "But you can get a dance, a visit to the theatre, a slap-up supper, all the drink you can hold, and a hansom or a jitney back to the Fallen Angels. And presents, too. That's where this came from." She passed her elegant fingers through the feather boa she was wearing. Then, clutching Emma's arm again with a gushing bonhomie, she said, "Stick by me, kid, and I'll show you the ropes. Have no fear."

In a daze of apprehension Emma allowed herself to be hastened the last block to the Oyster House. Joan must still have felt unsure of her for, just before they caught up with the other four, she said, "You don't know what pleasure is until you've done it with a macquereau you've never met before and are never going to set eyes on again. Come on, Emma! Men have been doing it for thousands of years. We're just catching up, that's all. Cotton on!"

To lull the woman's suspicions, Emma pretended to "cotton on." But even as she smiled and chatted, and tried not to blush at certain remarks Joan made about the oysters they were wolfing down, she was desperately casting around for some excuse to make good her escape. They had just started on the clam chowder when she overheard one of the waiters telling a lady at the next table that there wasn't one and she'd have to go over to Grand Central. It seemed heaven-sent.

She waited until near the end of the meal, for it really was very good, and then asked the same question as the lady — getting, of course, the same answer. She told the others she didn't want any sorbet and she'd meet them outside in ten minutes; she paid for her own meal as she left.

From their table there was a clear view across Forty-Second Street to the tower that bore the legend NEW YORK & HARLEM R.R. So she had no choice but to cross the road and go inside — by which time, indeed, she was ready to use the "sweet pea garden," as the waiter had called it. She was just crossing the concourse when she heard a familiar voice asking a passing conductor, "Does that train call at New Haven?"

FROM THE UNION DEPOT in New Haven it was a pleasant ride out past Fort Wooster to Fife, just over a mile beyond the town line — especially on an early August evening, and even more especially if you are the captain of the finest liner in the world, about to relax for an entire day and night in the bosom of an adoring family before setting out on a voyage that will surely secure the most coveted trophy in the business. Frank stretched himself luxuriously in the gig and puffed a contented "seegar," as the shop by Grand Central had spelled it. The danger — or, as he saw it, excitement — of exposure and disgrace was such a common companion to him by now that he hardly noticed its presence any longer. The days when he had to stop himself from looking over his shoulder every time someone this side of the Atlantic called Teresa "Mrs Morgan" were long since gone.

Teresa, who had not truly expected him to arrive until the following day, was overjoyed to see him at the gate; she came skipping down the path, tearing off her pinafore and patting her hair and smoothing her blouse and shucking off her house shoes to run the faster. She almost bowled him over in the deluge of her welcome.

"I planned dinner for tomorrow night," she complained as soon as she had her breath back. "I felt sure you'd come tomorrow."

He put his arm round her and walked her back to the house, leaving Noah, the help, to bring his bags.

"Aren't you going to pay the man?" she asked.

"He'll collect me tomorrow. I have to leave at three, I'm afraid."

"Oh," she said bleakly.

"I don't really want much to eat," he added. "We had a sort of celebration banquet last night and …" He patted his stomach gingerly.

"It doesn't stop you smoking cigars, I see. Oh dear, I wanted to ask Ignatius and Concepta over, and Father Hines. Can't you stay until evening?"

They went indoors, where Jemima, the nursemaid, was holding the seven-month-old Anthony Francis ready for a spell of doting admiration. Transferred to his father's arms, he lay there a moment gazing uncertainly up into his eyes; then he noticed the mutton-chop whiskers and gave one of them a delighted tug, accompanied by an equally joyous laugh. Frank pulled a sorrowful face and pretended to cry. The baby's face creased in sympathy and soon real tears flowed down his cheeks, with sounds to match.

"Serve me right," Frank said as he handed the boy back to his nurse.

"Can't you?" Teresa repeated as soon as they were at peace again.

"Come here." He held out his arms. "Let me just hold you."

For a long minute there was no need for words.

"Oh Frank," she murmured as they broke their kiss, "let's go to bed now?"

He shivered and held her even more tightly. The sound of Noah dumping his bags, coupled with the still only half pacified baby, was answer enough to her question. "We'll never be as alone again as we were that week on *Pegasus*," he replied gloomily.

"Next time I'll come to New York," she said — and was astonished to feel how tense he suddenly became. "No?" she asked.

He shook his head and hugged her to him with an odd sort of desperation.

Such a strange man!

"Why not?" she asked.

"I can't really explain it. Just take it from me. New York, to me, is shipping. Everyone I know is in shipping. We talk of nothing else all the time. We breathe shipping. We eat it ... we dream it. But those few days with you aboard *Pegasus* were a revelation to me. Their memory is precious for so many things — among them the discovery that there is *another* life, nothing to do with gross registered tonnage and horsepower and bushels of coal and bills of lading ... and the latest from Big Nellie's in Sydney." He held her briefly at arm's length and peered deep into her eyes. "I don't want you to get caught up in all that. You are my refuge from it all — you, this house, little Tony. You are all so special and dear to me because you are *not* part of that other world."

"All right! All right!" She buried herself again in his darling embrace and let the notion wither. "It was only an idea."

"Not a very bright one. Besides, it's considered to be bad luck."

"Yes, yes! I said all right!" Then she kissed him again and said she was sorry. "To be honest with you, Frank, I'm annoyed with meself, so I am, for not having a dinner ready for tonight."

He took her hand and led her out to the back porch where they sat on the swing seat and watched the sun fall among thin wreaths of purple-gray cloud. "I don't want banquets and fatted calves," he told her. "There shouldn't be any special celebrations each time I come home ... except ..." He brushed her left breast gently with his knuckles.

She licked her lips and, eyeing him with merry daring, said, "Can't you ever think of anything else?"

He made a pistol of his hand and shot her through the temple.

"I'll be here again on the twenty-fifth, and again on the tenth of September, and *again* on the twenty-sixth … and so on. Every sixteen days — at least, that looks like being our timetable for the rest of this year. I'm really just a bus-driver from now on. Don't you see?"

She sighed. "Yes … I suppose so."

EMMA ARRIVED BACK at Liverpool to find letters awaiting her from both Lawrence and Kathleen. The *Pride of Liverpool* had made the crossing in five days, twenty-two hours, easily beating the previous record of six days, five hours set by the *Berlin*. They docked at eleven o'clock on the night of Monday the sixteenth. Some passengers caught night sleepers to London but most stayed on to disembark at their leisure the following day. Emma was not free until early afternoon on that Tuesday — but she was in luck at the station and just managed to catch the London train.

She was in even more luck with her liberty. In winning the Blue Riband the *Pride of Liverpool* had consumed over two thousand tons of coal, some ten percent more than Shaw & Eggar had planned for a regular trip; Frank had almost literally obeyed his instructions to "burn the funnels off her." But he had also demonstrated that, by cutting her speed back from nineteen to seventeen and a half knots, she could maintain an eight-day schedule quite easily, and without consuming more than her estimated eighteen hundred tons of coal per voyage. In the normal run of things, therefore, she would not have docked before Wednesday, ready to sail again on the Friday. And now the company had decided to adhere to that sailing date, because it would give them time to strip her engines and inspect them for damage — without giving rise to unfortunate rumours. So Emma found herself with almost three clear days in London; not to mention five pounds in wages and tips in her purse.

She settled in the railway carriage and took out the two letters to read again. They were brief, to say the least — and couched in amusingly similar terms. They baldly stated the fact of their meeting at the apartment in Upper Street on the day after she had vamoosed — without even hinting at what passed between them. They each partially excused their silence by adding that there was now so much to talk about — though, again, with no hint of what that might be. Kathleen said that Lawrence had given her the run of the apartment until the end of the quarter, so she, Emma, was welcome to stay there; Lawrence said the apartment was hers for as long as she needed it; each said they would be at Euston Station to meet her train if she would telegraph them poste restante at Highbury post office from the *Pride of Liverpool*.

She hadn't, of course, telegraphed from the ship. A fine time she'd have had, explaining why she was informing the old man's son and daughter, not about *his* arrival — which she just might have managed to explain away — but about hers! Instead she had telegraphed from an office on the way, which was why she had almost missed the train.

She scanned the letters again and smiled to herself, wondering if the two young Morgans would run across each other in Highbury post office, or would the surprise come at Euston? She did not know that an even bigger surprise awaited all three of them, for, in dallying at the telegraph office in Liverpool, she had failed to see Cap'n Morgan himself getting into the first class carriage, some two coaches nearer the head of the train than hers.

It is one of the curiosities of London's topography that, while the walk or carriage ride from Chalk Farm at the foot of Hampstead Hill to Euston seems more or less flat, the train journey over the same terrain is a fairly precipitous downhill run. The Liverpool train came into the terminus preceded by the usual screeching of brakes and showering of sparks. Kathleen, who had met Lawrence at the post office — and refused to yield to him the sole right to greet Emma off this train — pressed her hands tight over her ears and watched the torture machine intently for the slightest sign of an abatement.

She was therefore the first to see her father poke his head out of the window and look up and down for a porter. Fortunately, the seeking of a porter is a task so fraught with doubt that a man so engaged is quite likely to miss such lesser sights as the unexpected presence of his own son and daughter, also upon the platform.

Kathleen spun around, turning her back to him, and edged away until she was standing behind a trolley piled high with luggage. "It's Papa!" she exclaimed tersely to her brother.

"Where?" he asked; then, "Damnation! He's gone and spotted me."

"I'll keep behind this thing," she told him. "Don't look at me, you fool! Pretend you came to meet him — congratters on the Blue Riband and all that. I'll head

Emma off and take her to the apartment after you've gone. We'll wait for you there."

"Aaargh!" Lawrence cried under his breath, even as his face split in the broadest smile of welcome for their father. "Papa!" He stepped forward to greet him as if that had always been his intention. "Congratulations! You must be cockahoop!"

"You might have nabbed a porter while you were waiting," Frank grumbled. "You know how they vanish as soon as a train arrives."

Kathleen, standing not five yards from them, but well concealed by the luggage trolley, saw Emma walking down the platform toward them. She waved to catch her attention — and succeeded in the same instant that the girl caught sight of the two men. She turned around and walked back down the platform, apparently seeking a dropped ticket. Not until the men had found a porter and gone did she resume her progress toward the barrier.

"That was a narrow squeak," she exclaimed as she drew near Kathleen.

"Let's give them a minute or two," the girl replied. "Just to be sure they got a cab. Well! Let's have a look at you. That's a pretty bonnet. American?"

She was intrigued to see that Emma blushed at the mention of it. "Got your sea legs?" she added.

That, seemingly, was an easier one to answer. She said it was now the *land* that couldn't seem to stay still.

When they were sure the men had gone, they took a tram up to the Angel, then another through Islington to Upper Street. It being a hot August day, they rode on the top deck, in the open; all the way Emma gushed about the splendours of the *Pride of Liverpool*, the joys of life as a stewardess, the fabulous time she'd had in New York ... though on this last marvel she faltered and — when they were finally in the apartment — told the truth.

"It was awful, Kathy. There's this stewardess called Joan Bolton. When she's on duty, butter wouldn't melt in her mouth, but as soon as she's off ... well!"

"What d'you mean — well?" It interested Kathleen to see how much of her London accent Emma had lost.

"You know — taking up with men. Macquereaus she calls them. Anyway, she promised to arrange one for me. So I slid out of it — I thought — by vanishing into the railway station to go to the ladies. Incidentally, I saw your dad there. The Cap'n! He was asking for the train to ..."

"Did he recognize you?" Kathleen asked eagerly. "On the ship, I mean."

"Half and half. I told him I was with the pork butcher in Goldsmith's Place, so he thinks he must have seen me around and about these parts."

"That's funny. Because Larry went and ..."

" Anyway," Emma insisted, "Joan and the other girls came over to the station, too — because I'd started them off by saying I needed to go. So then I couldn't get away from her. And he was *awful*, this macquereau she got me as companion for the evening."

"Ugly?"

"Oh no — quite a good-looker. But he couldn't keep his hands off me. I was fighting him all evening. He said he likes a challenge so he'll meet me next time I'm there."

Kathleen writhed with pleasure to hear at safe second hand these steamy details of Emma's exciting and dangerous life. "And will you?"

"I will not! Bella Mooney says she takes the train to

a place called Newburg up the Hudson River and goes for walks in the woods, which are really what we'd call forests here. She says it'll be the fall soon and it's breathtaking then. So that's what I'm going to do do next time."

Kathleen took a leap in the dark. "No nice bonnets from her, I'll bet."

Emma stared at her in surprise and then laughed. "You'll do," she said. "Oh Kathy! I wish I'd dug my heels in and insisted you'd come with us. It'd be so much fun with you!" And to her surprise Kathleen did not immediately pour scorn on the idea and tell her how impossible it was.

"Actually," Kathleen said. "I may be going to America anyway. There's a choir from some tabernacle or something in Chicago who are over here in London at the moment. Mr Fiorelli, you know — the tenor with the Operatic Society — he arranged it all. They're giving their farewell concert this Saturday, here in Highbury, and they've invited us to visit them in December, to sing the *Messiah* with them, which they always do at Christmas. Wouldn't it be fun if you were there at the same time, and we could meet!" She bit her lip and, with a naughty smile, asked, "Would you get *me* a macquereau?"

"A hundred!" Emma promised gaily. "They're like flies round bad meat in New York. Are you really going?"

"It depends on Papa, of course, but Mama's sure he'll say yes."

They wrote a note to tell Lawrence they'd gone for a stroll up in Highbury Fields, but, just as they were closing the apartment door behind them, they heard him come dashing in from the street, leaping up the stairs, three at a time.

"Thank heavens!" He almost bowled them over. "Have you just got here?"

"No, we were on our way out for a stroll," his sister told him.

"Oh." He had eyes only for Emma, of course — who also seemed unable to take hers off him.

"Well," Kathleen said shrewdly, "I think I know what you're trying to say."

"You're a true brick!" He smiled gratefully at her. "D'you mind awfully?"

"Would it matter if I did? What shall I tell them at home?"

"Oh ... say I'm ornithologizing down at Hackney Marshes. I haven't used that one for a long time. Come back here after supper if they'll let you."

"I'll see you tomorrow," she told Emma. Then, with a sideways nod toward her brother, "Try and earn a ribbon for that bonnet!"

"Ha ha!" Emma responded uncomfortably.

Lawrence followed her to the stairhead and called down after her, "Thanks, Little Face! I'll do something for you one day."

"Oh, you will!" she assured him heavily.

Emma had meanwhile reopened the door and gone back inside. She was just unpinning her bonnet when he joined her. "We could go for that stroll instead, if you like," he said.

She dropped the bonnet on the table and eyed the sideboard.

"There's still *half* a bottle of port," he added drily.

Her jaw dropped. "Kathy?"

He shook his head and patted his breastbone.

"Good." She grinned. "Me? I've not touched a drop for ... oh, two months. Time was, I could have told you to the nearest hour."

"Did you mean what you wrote? About being in love with me?"

"And also what I said about it being no good for either of us. Have a drink if you want. It doesn't bother me any longer."

"The thing is, Emma ..." He took a step toward her and then paused awkwardly. "I love you, too. I can't get you out of my mind. That's what I was coming here to tell you that Saturday morning."

"I'll take my clothes off if you like," she offered.

"What?" He stared at her aghast.

"I mean, I'll be your missie if you wish — and there's no other man in all the world I'd say those words to. But if you have any thoughts about wedding bells and me ... forget them."

He was about to reply when it struck him that he could use her offer to achieve his own much more limited ambition — at least in the immediate term. Smiling he went to her, took her in his arms, and kissed her passionately, massaging her lips with his and playing a delicious game with their tongues among her teeth.

She resisted him at first; he could feel the tension in her everywhere their bodies touched. But then she yielded and surrendered herself, almost limp, into his embrace. And when at last he took his lips from hers the time for words had gone. Dumbly, shivering with her need for him, she took a pace back toward the bed, grasping his hand and pulling him after her.

But he held his ground and said, "No!"

"I do want you," she replied in a voice she barely recognized as her own.

He closed his eyes against the enticement of her beauty. "I want you, too."

"Well then."

He turned his back on her and stared at the window. "Listen," he said. "If you want war, you may have it. But I'll tell you now it's a war I shall win. And the victor's trophy will be your hand in marriage. And I won't go to bed with you until we *are* married. So make up your mind to it now. We can have a long agony or a short one. You decide."

She came to him and wrapped her arms about him from behind. "Don't," she pleaded, laying her head against his backbone.

"Don't what?"

"Fight me. Because you'll only go and win."

He went tense at once. "Are you accepting my proposal?"

"I'm telling you to withdraw it. Marriage between you and me would just never work."

HILDA REMOVED A comb and watched a long hank of her ash blonde hair slowly uncurl itself. Briefly it caressed her shoulder and then, like the unfurling of a lightly clenched hand, came gently to rest on the curve of her upper arm. She withdrew another comb, and another, and in the space of a minute was transformed from a respectable Highbury lady to ... what? She moved the lamp a little and considered herself in the looking glass. Light from the two bedside tables behind shone through her disordered hair, giving her a halo of frozen lightning, all in gold. A mænad? What did they call them in those pictures in the Academy last summer? Wild, tender, luscious, energetic young women with tambourines and leopard skins. Wood nymphs? Or was it hetærai? Or bacchantes? So many names they had! What did they *do,* anyway — never mind how they spelled themselves. What were they *for?* Lurking and dancing in olive groves and wild places all day.

Come to that, what was she for? Lurking in Highbury all day but most certainly not dancing!

Bringing up children. But that was over and done with, almost. Get Kathleen married off in the next year or two and that would be that; she'd be someone else's problem then. Boys could fend for themselves.

And wives?

The house looked after itself — at least, it did with Mrs Johnson here.

Francis looked after himself — at least, he now had a vast floating hôtel of his own to look after him.

Could a life of whist afternoons, opera and drama evenings, and the occasional day for the missionaries be all that she was now *for?*

Francis's dressing room door opened. For a moment he stood there, staring at her in amazement. "Hilda?" he said.

"I hope so — or you've some explaining to do, my lad!" she swept up her hair in a single tail and reached for the ribbon.

"No!" He crossed the room swiftly and picked up her brush and comb. "Remember I used to do this?"

She remembered.

"How long ago?" he mused.

She remembered that, too, but didn't tell him. "D'you ever wonder why we go on?" she asked.

His hand froze in mid-stroke. "Why we go on?" He swallowed heavily. "You and me, d'you mean?"

She was staring at the curtains, as if they were not there and she could see a million miles beyond the stars. "Yes," she murmured. "What's it *for* now? Once

259

we've done our duty by the race, begot our children and reared them to the best of our ability ... what's left?"

"Ah, I see your drift." He resumed his combing. She closed her eyes and luxuriated in it. "Well, for me there's a ship to run, passengers to ..."

"Yes, but for me?"

He rested his hands on her shoulders and pulled her lightly to him. The handle of the brush was sharp against her collarbone but she didn't complain for once. "Are you feeling under-employed, my dear?" he asked.

"Distinctly."

"Why don't you start a private school, then? You and Daphne. You know she's always talked about it."

"Talk! Daphne's always *talked* about everything. I think half Kathleen's discontent comes from all Daphne's talking — and the other half from Miss Kernow." A flush of heat prickled her skin. She opened a few buttons of her nightdress and flapped it to cool herself.

His combing became suddenly mechanical, a mere dog paddle. She glanced in the mirror and saw him staring down at her. She became aware that he could see into her décolleté. At any other time she would have clasped her nightdress to her and become all annoyed and flustered, but now some streak of mischief made her ignore the impulse. She closed her eyes once more and resettled herself against him.

A moment later she felt against her spine the indisputable evidence of his excitement. That was too much.

"Oh Francis!" she said in disgust, standing up and sweeping her hair into a single tail which she angrily tied with the ribbon. As she went to the bed she reminded herself he had almost promised that all that distasteful business between them was over. The hush of life, and so forth. "Don't remind yourself, remind *him*," a voice said in her skull. She tried to think of the words but couldn't. She tried to think why she had reacted with such distaste, and once again found she couldn't.

Francis had dowsed the dressing-table lamp and was now standing at the window, peering out through a slit in the curtains. "The days are drawing in," he murmured. "Last time I was home it was still light at this hour."

"Don't catch cold," she said ritually.

"Cold," he repeated. A few moments later he sighed and turned from the window. When he walked toward the bed all sign of his excitement had gone.

She stared bleakly at her toes beneath the counterpane; another flush of heat passed over her but this time she merely endured it.

"What was that about Kathleen being discontented?" he asked as he climbed in beside her.

She lay flat on her back and pulled the tail of her hair round onto her breast. "Just one of her phases, I expect."

What beautiful hands she still had, he thought. Indeed, she herself was beautiful still, with those deep, dreamy, pale green eyes which — in the days of their courtship, at least — had seemed to promise endless nights of connubial bliss. It was still hard for him to believe that a woman of such beauty, with such take-me eyes, could have proved so cold in marriage. "What particular form does this 'phase' assume?" he asked.

"She wants to *work!*"

For a moment the word made no connections in his mind; then one or two remote possibilities began to suggest themselves. "Help with the missionaries, you mean?"

"No. Paid work!"

"Ship me green! D'you mean ... be a nurse? Or teach?" He brightened at that. "If you and Daphne started your school, perhaps ..."

"Nursing." Hilda's tone was slightly surprised. "I didn't think of that! Now why not?" She rose on one elbow and turned to him, her eyes glowing with all the excitement he wished she had shown as a wife. "The thing is, you see, she has taken this insane notion into her head that she wants to be a stewardess. On a liner like the *Pride of Liverpool*. Actually, she wants to go to sea. That's her real ambition. And all she could think of was being a stewardess. But you have doctors and nurses, too, on those big liners, don't you. Why couldn't she be the nurse? Honorary, of course."

Every rational cell in his brain cried *No!* of course. But his viscera said it was just the tightening of the screw he needed. The thrill that went with his fear of discovery had waned.

"Nurse?" he repeated dubiously, to hide his excitement.

"Yes." Hilda was now quite excited at the idea. "Unpaid, as I say. Oh *why* didn't I think of it before? I was just so stunned at the thought of her becoming a stewardess. Not that we'd have allowed it — but that she should even have wanted it. But there's no stigma attached to nursing. I know they have to do disgusting things, but it's only until they marry a doctor, isn't it. After all, Mary Abercrombie was a nurse until she married the doctor, and I'm sure no one meeting her socially now even thinks of all the disgusting things she had to do as a nurse." She reached up and kissed him briefly. "Francis, you are the world's cleverest man, you know."

She does it without even thinking, he told himself as he watched her settle on her back once more. All the same, he could produce no immediate argument against the idea that Kathleen might take up nursing on an Atlantic liner.

"On an Atlantic liner!" he mused.

"Of course!"

He laughed. "Sorry! Thinking aloud. I was telling myself she could hardly go on the *Pride of Liverpool* or any other Shaw & Eggar vessel. People would either make her life hell, to work off old scores against me, or they'd let her get away with murder, thinking they were ingratiating themselves with me. It would be bad for her. Bad for me. Bad for the line. Bad all round ..." He felt like a ship making heavy leeway on a scant wind, desperately spreading canvas. "And she could hardly go with Cunard or P & O — not on the North Atlantic, anyway. The same sort of arguments would apply there."

"Ah, I see what you mean. My goodness, Francis, you do think quickly! I can see why you're such a splendid captain. What you're saying is, she could go as a nurse on the run to the Cape or the Orient? Perhaps she'd nab her doctor on the first run! They're usually young, aren't they? Just qualified and looking for a bit of travel before they settle down. It would be ideal for her. And if she couldn't do it in sixty days, she's not our daughter."

"Well, we'll see," he said uneasily as he reached to turn off the lamp on his side. "It needs a bit of thought."

He settled himself on his back and waited for her to put out the light on her side, too. But she just lay there, toying with her hair and staring dreamily at the ceiling.

"Of course," she said after a while, "she'll have to do a bit of training in London first. At Bart's or somewhere. Doctor Abercrombie went to Bart's didn't he? Perhaps he could pull a string or two and get her in there. Mary told me they're terribly strict. She was gated a whole week for the unspeakable sin of buttoning up her gloves as she was crossing the quadrangle. So I think we need have no fears there."

"She seems to wander around here freely enough," he pointed out.

"Yes, but Highbury's a village, dear. She couldn't walk ten yards without being under the eye of one or other of our friends. But London's different." After another pause she said, "But that would have to be after America."

"Eh?"

"Oh, I didn't tell you. The most exciting news of all. There's been so much!" And she went on to explain about the visit of the whatsit tabernacle choir from Chicago and their concert on Saturday — such a pity he'd miss them — and their invitation for the Highbury Mixed Choir to join them in Chicago, two weeks before Christmas, to sing the *Messiah*. "Kathleen will have to come too, if I'm going," she said. "She might meet some nice young man on the voyage and then we'd hear no more about being a nurse. Anyway, I don't know how long the training is, but she can hardly commence until the new year. And who knows *what* she'll want to do by then! But won't it be exciting, Francis! You must be in New York at least once while we're over there. And I've looked it up on the map. It's only a stonesthrow to Chicago."

"It sounds *wonderful*," he said. Then, aware that his tone was rather *too* enthusiastic, he moderated it. "Yes, er, quite splendid. How will you be crossing — or are you each making your own way?"

"Well, that was the first idea — because, of course, half the choir is connected with shipping in one way or another, and could go for nothing. But obviously we can't allow that, or how would we practise? So old Furnival got us a charter on the Baltic, to Halifax, and then we go on by train, and we'll see Niagara on the way, and we might be able to go by steamer a bit, on the last of the Great Lakes. Chicago's on that one, you know."

"Is it?" he asked with a theatrical show of interest. She punched him playfully.

"Well!" He relaxed again. "That sounds ... splendid. Aren't you going to put out your light?"

"Can't bear the sight of me, eh?" she teased, glad that she had managed these appalling hurdles so brilliantly. Just one more to go.

He rose, leaned over, and kissed her briefly on the forehead.

At last she turned and put out her light. "And on the way back," she said, as if it were the merest, dreamiest little postscript, "I thought Kathleen and I might try out this new luxury liner everyone's talking about."

PART TWO

New Haven

IT WAS A BITTER cold night for the first watch; by five bells the deck hands were finding every excuse to hang around the engine-room and stoke-hold kiddleys, merely to be able to remember where their fingers and toes were. To first-class passengers, however, like Hilda and Kathleen, that same hour — ten-thirty of an evening — brought an overpowering need to escape from the stuffiness of the salon and breathe welcoming draughts of frosty air on the open end of the promenade deck. The evening in question was that of Friday, the twenty-sixth of November; they were almost exactly half-way over the Atlantic, an ocean whose moods they had known by proxy all their lives; only now were they experiencing it at first hand — from the frost-rimed deck of the *SS Champlain*.

The mood of the ocean at that particular moment seemed benign — one could not add "on the surface," however, for that was precisely where it was least amiable, being freckled with small ice floes as far as the eye could see. They gleamed under an almost full moon, which, at that hour, was almost at its zenith in a cloudless sky.

For a long while mother and daughter gazed over that scene of perfect tranquillity. Then Kathleen shivered and said that silk mantillas and stout woollen capes were no proof against the frost; she'd slip below and get their furs and muffs. She had hardly left the deck when Walter Grandison appeared. Now forty-two, a year older than Hilda, he had lately inherited the Grandison Line, built up by his father from "one leaky bathtub" in the 'thirties. Lawrence said there were bets at the Baltic on the survival of the Grandison Line. However, he had surprised everyone by proving himself even better at the business than his late father — though his style could not have been more different."

Hilda was in two minds about the man's "style." There were those who criticized Francis and herself for insisting that the boys should work for their livings when, as captain of vessels like the *Eldorado*, the *Pegasus*, and now the *Pride of Liverpool*, he could certainly have afforded to let them live like gentlemen. But she only had to think of *gentlemen* like Walter Grandison to know they had been right. All the same, she had to admit he was devilish handsome in his rakish way. He was, into the bargain, a beautiful tenor and splendid company if you were in a light-hearted mood.

In fact, she realized with something of a shock, she had now known him more than twenty-five years, for they had first danced together at her fifteenth birthday party and she had had something of a "pash" on him for a year or two after that.

"Dear Hilda!" he called out from the door of the smoking lounge. "I went into the saloon just now and wondered why it was so dim. Now I see — its chief illumination is out here on deck. All alone?"

The words in her mind were, *I don't remember giving permission for you to call me Hilda!* The words she actually spoke were, "Kathleen's just slipped below to get our furs."

"Ah!" The merely technical absence of a chaperone made it possible for him to join her at the rail, and even to slip his own astrakhan around her shoulders, murmuring, "Poor girl, you must be frozen." He was particularly fussy how it draped, which involved many rearrangements — which, in turn, involved what, in other circumstances, could only be called hugs and squeezes.

"Well now," he said when he had wrung every last hug out of the situation, "do I stand downwind because of my cigar, or do I throw it away and stand upwind to shelter you?"

"Oh, don't throw it away," she said. "I don't mind the aroma of a good cigar. And, knowing you, you wouldn't smoke anything else!"

"Ah ha!" he said as he placed his elbow a bare inch from hers on the rail. "But *do* you know me? That's the question."

"I was just thinking — it's more than twenty … I was just thinking how long it was since I first danced with you on my fifteenth birthday. I don't suppose you even remember."

"Remember?" The echo was cavernous. "I went in mortal terror of you for years. I suppose I may safely confess it now. And yet *even* now, you know …" His rising voice petered out in a sigh.

"What?" she asked with a mildly embarrassed laugh. "What d'you mean, terror?" Where was Kathleen? She wasn't sure she welcomed such a frank conversation with Walter Grandison.

"Literally. Didn't you ever realize? I *worshipped* you, Hilda. I thought you were an angel. But still …" His tone switched from lugubrious to brisk in those two words. "Long time ago now, what? Good for a laugh, though. But wouldn't it be splendid if one could feel as passionately — and as *purely* — about anything, anything at all, as one felt in those days! Are you a little warmer now?"

"Much, thank you, Mister Grandison. It is a beautiful coat." Kathleen, please hurry!

He puffed at his cigar. "Of course, you know why you get cold so easily? Because you've kept your figure. Think of the other little girls around your age who were at that dance. No names, no pack drill, but at least three that I can recall are here on the *Champlain* with us." The ship obligingly listed to port as it swerved to avoid an ice floe. It allowed him to add, "I believe one of them has just moved over to this side. Did you feel how the ship leaned over?"

"Really, Mr Grandison!" She laughed. "I'm not sure you should be saying such things to me."

"Nor am I," he agreed solemnly. "And yet I feel that *someone* should."

Kathleen! she thought. *Can't you hear this scream in my mind?*

At that moment Kathleen was far too absorbed to play tricks with telepathy. She had come down to the cabin to catch Dilkins, their stewardess, standing in front of the mirror and holding one of her, Kathleen's, dresses against her slight frame. The look of frozen horror on her face suggested that the punishment for such an offence was a keelhauling at the very least.

Kathleen laughed and said, "I wish I could say keep it, for it suits you far better than it does me. But I'm afraid I shall need it when we get to Chicago."

The girl remained frozen, but now it was in astonishment at her own luck.

"D'you want to try it on?" Kathleen suggested.

"Oh no, Miss!" The spell was broken. "I couldn't!" She hung it back in the wardrobe before the temptation overwhelmed her. "I don't know what I was thinking of in the first place. Don't tell Miss Stokes, please?"

"As if I would!" Kathleen went to the other wardrobe and took out the furs.

"I know you wouldn't mean to, Miss, but you

might just think it a joke. *She* wouldn't though."

"What would happen then?"

"I'd be on report and I'd probably get no liberty in Halifax." She fanned her face as girls do at a narrow escape. Halifax was where the charter party would transfer to the railway, to go overland to Chicago.

"Is it a hard life?" Kathleen asked. She threw off her cape and sat at the dressing table. For want of something to do she picked up a brush and comb and began to make minor — and pointless — rearrangements to her coiffeur.

"Shall I do that?" Dilkins asked. "I'm very good at hair — or so I'm told."

"I should go back on deck." Kathleen handed her the implements. "Is it a hard life, being a stewardess?"

"I've known harder ashore, Miss Morgan. And I've known easier ashore, too. It's like parlourmaid and lady's maid in one, see. The hours are very long at sea. Up at six every morning and into bed when we're not wanted any more. But there's good liberty allowed in port by way of compensation. And of course the pay is about four times what even a lady's maid would get."

"You'd never go back to domestic work ashore then?"

She smiled drily, "Not even for a husband, Miss. He'd have to bring home enough to keep a tweeny at least. And a cook. I can't abide cooking."

"Oh, I do *envy* you," Kathleen exclaimed. "It's my ambition, you know, to be a stewardess like you."

Dilkins nearly dropped the brush in her amazement. "You!" she exclaimed.

"I know. That's what everyone says. I don't know what your accommodation's like here but ever since I saw the cabins for stewardesses on the *Pride of*

Liverpool I've envied them. In fact, one of the maids who used to work for us, a girl called Emma Harding, I suggested to …"

"Oh, I know her!" the other exclaimed. "Of course, we all get to know each other quite well on the North Atlantic runs, because we all stop at the Christian Girls when we get liberty in New York. I met her there … oh, September, I think. Nice girl."

"Yes, isn't she. I put her up to going as a stewardess."

"She never said … can I take this comb out and brush this bit properly?"

"I really ought to go back up on deck." Kathleen pulled a face as she loosened the comb in question.

"She never said she used to work for the great Cap'n Morgan himself," she went on.

"No, I don't suppose she would. Actually, she left our employment under a bit of a cloud. It was all a misunderstanding, but she's still *persona non grata* at our house, so don't ever say anything. My mother would be furious. But I kept in touch with her."

"And put her up to it? Well, well!"

"We're good friends, actually, despite the differences and all that. I wanted to run away and be a stewardess with her. Not on the *Pride of Liverpool*, of course. I don't suppose there's a vessel in all the world where *I* could hide?"

The hopeful little rise in those final words caused Dilkins to reply, "Not one you'd *want* to go on, anyway, Miss."

"So now the general idea is for me to become a nurse and go to sea that way. What d'you think of that?"

"Well … it's more your class of work," Dilkins conceded. "I'd have to say that, to be honest."

"But you don't think much of it."

"It's a bit lonely, that's all. It's a bit like being a governess ashore. Know what I mean? You're neither servant nor mistress — and you're not all that much better paid, either. Well, you *are* better paid but you don't get no tips. People don't feel it's nice to tip you, see."

"Lonely." Kathleen nodded glumly. "It's what I thought. There isn't a nurse on this voyage, is there."

"Miss Stokes has a certificate for it. They say one ship she was on the sawbones was so tiddly *she* took off a sailor's leg herself. Never turned a hair." She came back to Kathleen's predicament. "Still, in your case, Miss ... I mean, if nursing's the only thing on offer ..."

"And there's no ship I could hide away on ..."

"Not under your own name, anyway."

Kathleen pricked up her ears at that. "What d'you mean?"

Dilkins shrugged and her tone indicated how far-fetched she felt the idea was. "You could get false papers, change your hair ... but no. The way you speak would give you away." She shook her head and dismissed it.

"Wha' if oi spowke loike vis?" Kathleen asked merrily.

The stewardess laughed. "Good enough for a turn at the Old Alhambra, Miss, but that's about all." She completed Kathleen's coiffeur and proudly lanced it with the comb. "There!"

"Ah me!" Kathleen sighed. "Nursing it'll have to be. And now I really must go back on deck. I only hope my mother's had the sense to go back inside and wait for me."

Like a hoyden she raced for the promenade deck, clutching the two fur coats to her. She was just about to push open the swing doors — the upper halves of which were glazed — when she saw that her mother was still there, now with a man's overcoat draped over her shoulders, and that the man himself was leaning against the rails beside her. A moment later she recognized him as Walter Grandison, whom she did not like at all. While she hesitated she saw him apparently putting his arm about her mother's shoulders. A moment later he withdrew it and she realized he had merely been adjusting the overcoat. Had it been any other man she would have thought no more about it, but Grandison had a certain lordly, proprietorial way of doing such things that made her hesitate still further.

Then, on the spur of the moment, she raced up one more companionway and emerged on the boat deck. A quick glance about her showed it to be deserted, except for a seaman sheltering in the lee of the funnel. He straightened when he saw her but soon returned to the warmth of his lair. She put on her own fur and laid the other on a stack of deck chairs beside the deserted quoits court. Then, apparently aimlessly, she strolled to the rail and stared out to sea. Every moral fibre within her shouted her shame, but she stood there nonetheless and eavesdropped.

"What is that strange noise?" her mother asked. "I've been hearing it on and off all evening."

"Growlers, they call it," he replied. "Ice floes rubbing together. If we hadn't such a good moon, we'd be down to five knots." After a brief silence he added, "It's a world of its own, isn't it, a voyage like this. One can almost forget there's a whole continent out there ahead of us."

Her mother made no comment.

"It's often a godsend to a howling cad like me."

Her mother laughed.

"Oh, I know what you're thinking, Hilda," he said at once.

Hilda! He actually called her Hilda!

"You think I'm hoping to turn you into one more scalp on my trophy pole. Well, I'd never dream of doing such a thing. You're the only woman in my whole life of whom I can honestly say I feel absolute respect. I won't say 'nothing but respect,' mind you. But whatever other feelings I may entertain for you, they pale into insignificance beside that respect. You are a woman without peer. I esteem you above all the rest. And I would rather experience five minutes' true companionship of the mind with you than five hours or five *days* of the tawdry dalliance I find with ... so many others ... too many others."

"Oh," Hilda said.

You would have had to know her very well, better even than Walter Grandison thought he did, to catch that faintest hint of disappointment in her voice. You would, indeed, have had to know her as intimately as her own daughter did.

F EW HOSTS IN ALL the world can be as persuasive as the variety that springs in such abundance from the soil of North America. An English hostess can gush, "Oh but you *must* call in on us next time you're down in the country," and you know straight away from her inflection that she'd throw a fit if you were unwise enough to take her up on it. But when the leader of one of the finest amateur choirs in America tells you (you, collectively, that is — the Highbury Operatic and Choral Society of London,

England) that you are one of the best visiting choirs they have ever heard, you naturally glow with pride.

And when she adds it's such a pity that only a few thousand people in and around Chicago got to hear you, you begin to think, *Why yes, it is, too!* — even though you were formerly delighted at the size of your several audiences.

And when she goes on to say that her own choir has a long-standing invitation to sing in Boston on New Year's Day and it would be so splendid if you could join forces for the occasion and she's sure the Bostonians would be only too delighted and it surely wouldn't throw people's schedules out too far ... well, even the merest hints of objections that might arise in your mind sound at once churlish and discordant.

And when she hammers home the final nail by pointing out that the gate receipts from the three performances you've already given will easily cover all the expenses, what possible argument is left?

"After all," as Hilda pointed out to Kathleen, "if we give our secular concert on New Year's Day, and perform the *Messiah* the day after, which is the Sunday, we can spend the Monday seeing Boston, go to New York on the Tuesday ... the *Pride of Liverpool* doesn't dock until Wednesday — so we can meet your father as arranged — spend Thursday in New York with him and sail on the Friday. It all works out perfectly and it won't cost us a penny. And best of all — that hound Walter Grandison won't be coming. He's become a perfect pest since we arrived."

Kathleen couldn't imagine why she had added that final bit since she had appeared to enjoy the man's company greatly until now. However, she agreed that it was, indeed, splendid, but she had her own reasons for that. The leader of the Chicago choir, a Mrs Eunice Burgoyne, was a handsome fireball of a woman who, since her widowhood about five years ago, had taken her late husband's Seltzer-water business, which had been phut-phutting along nicely for a couple of generations, and turned it into one of the leading manufacturers of sodas and pops in the country. They said of her that she could organize a plate of spaghetti into a fishing net by word of command alone. Of more immediate interest to Kathleen, however, was Carleton, or Chuck, Burgoyne, the eighteen-year-old son and heir to the family business. Handsome of face, fair of hair, and bashful in disposition, he had quite stolen her heart away. She was sure he reciprocated her interest, but was far too shy to reveal it. However, though he had no singing voice at all, as his mother's squire, he would naturally be coming to Boston; and on the train, on those interminable American journeys, who knew what might happen?

What happened — the best of what happened — was that they played brag and whist under Mrs Burgoyne's ever-vigilant eye. Not even just the pair of them, either; there were always four at least, including a hateful girl from Winnetka, called Millicent Trotter, who flirted outrageously with Chuck and was, indeed, the chief reason for his mother's caution. Even worse, Chuck seemed flattered by her utterly vapid attentions and played up to her for all he was worth. He managed to cast the occasional glance in Kathleen's direction, too — a glance that implied he would so much rather be rid of this yapping little puppy and engage himself in some serious discourse with her instead. But for that she would have given him up as a lost cause.

Once Kathleen made the excuse of needing some air; at the door of the car she turned and lifted an inquiring eyebrow at him, only to be met with a barely perceptible shake of the head and an even subtler tilt in the direction of his mother. She tried it again later in the day, only to be met with the same response. But this time Mrs Burgoyne must have seen it, for that night she invited the Morgans to join her at dinner in the restaurant car. When it was over Hilda gave out a great sigh of relief and said to Kathleen, "Now I know just what a dishcloth feels like when a pair of very strong hands has squeezed it dry. I always thought Lady Shaw was in a class of her own at that sort of interrogation but Mrs Burgoyne has her beat into a cocked hat. Still, it's all in a good cause — I hope."

Kathleen was not so naïve as to ask what she meant by that; nor did she question it when her mother made a rapid detour to the stores in New York, between the Pennsylvania and Grand Central depots. There she bought her daughter a new corset, one with a firmer and more positive action on the bust. She also opened the secret compartment in her jewelry box — whose existence even the inquisitive Kathleen had never discovered — and showed her how to apply the faintest and most discreet touch of jeweller's rouge to her cheeks and how to make her eyes larger and darker with belladonna.

Mrs Burgoyne must have been at work, too. The train to Boston had barely reached Fordham before Chuck was suggesting that the air in the car was oppressive, and now it was his eyebrow that rose in an inquiring lilt, directed at Kathleen — who received a simultaneous kick under the table from Hilda.

"Yes, for a fact ...," Miss Trotter began, but before

she could say another syllable Mrs Burgoyne said, "No, you don't, Millie. Two weeks I've been waiting to hear all about your first semester at college and I guess now's as good a time as any."

It was ten below, outside, so they stayed in the corridor and stared out through Jack Frost's picture gallery at the rapidly passing scene. Chuck pointed out the Jesuit College and the cottage where Edgar Allen Poe once lived. That led to a fairly morbid conversation, which concluded with the information that if they were on the other side of the car they could now see Woodlawn Cemetery. Kathleen began to wonder what on earth they were doing out here and what she could possibly say to retrieve the situation.

The last thing she intended to say was, "I expect you'd much rather be out here with Miss Trotter?" — but those were the words, the awful, flesh-crawling words she heard fall from her lips into the silence between them.

To her amazement, the question seemed to unlock something in him. For the first time he smiled at her and the lines of strain in his features vanished.

"Do you now?" he asked confidently. "What would make you suppose a thing like that?"

"Well ..." Kathleen gulped. "She's very ..."

No acceptable word occurred to her.

He laughed. "Isn't she, though! I couldn't have put it better myself."

"You seem to like it, though," Kathleen — in for a penny, in for a pound — pointed out.

"Well, I've known Millie Trotter since we were seven. She makes a set like that at all the fellows. One day, one of them is going to ..." He hesitated.

"What?"

"Oh, teach her a lesson. A girl like Millie is easy to get on with. She's good fun but no real challenge." He tapped his brow in case Kathleen should misunderstand the sort of challenge he had in mind. "But if you think I'd rather be standing out here swapping joke insults with her than sharing your company, Miss Morgan, you've never been more wrong in your life — if you'll forgive me for saying so."

"Oh." Kathleen swallowed hard again and wished she weren't so tongue-tied with him. Why couldn't she just treat him like Lawrence or Neil or one of their friends? She wished he wouldn't admire her figure quite so blatantly — and then, when their eyes met and he looked away quickly, she wished he'd never stop admiring her figure, no matter how blatant he was about it.

It was no good. She just felt too confused and stupid. "I think I'd like to go back and sit down again," she said, hating herself.

"Of course," he said amiably — but made not the slightest move to escort her there. "Your father's quite a legend, it seems," he went on. "Mom stopped off in New York and made some inquiries — as only she knows how. You must admire him a lot."

"Oh, I do," she assured him. "But your mother's quite a legend, too, isn't she? You must admire her just as much, Mr Burgoyne. Few women could do what she has done."

He looked surprised. "D'you really believe that? I think there must be hundreds ... if not thousands. But how many of them get the chance?"

"Ah." She wondered if there was anything she might say without his immediately putting her on the wrong foot. "If you put it that way ..."

"What about you? If you don't object to my asking,

that is. Wouldn't you like to *do* something in the world?"

Kathleen closed her eyes. Every cautionary instinct she possessed warned her against it but she could already feel her will on its irrevocable downward slide toward confession. Suppressing the shrieks of protest that rang through her mind, she told him of her ambition to go to sea, also about Emma Harding (though nothing, of course, about Lawrence's part in her life), and of her conversation with Betty Dilkins on the *Champlain* coming over. "I suppose," she concluded, "that, being an American, you think I should forget nursing and become a stewardess. You think we're all the most dreadful snobs."

"I used to," he replied, "until I went to Boston. You just wait! As to what I think you should do, I think you should do just whatever *you* want. If I were in your shoes, I certainly wouldn't hesitate."

"You'd choose stewardess?"

"Sure. Say — I'll come and be steward. Would you like that?"

"Yes!" Her eyes shone, and then she pouted. "You don't really mean it."

He shook his head. "I can't. We boys aren't free to decide these things, you know — not the way you girls are. I'll tell you what, though." He leaned confidentially nearer her, just an inch or two, but enough. "Make sure you're on the New York run. I'm going to Yale next fall. I'll point it out to you when we get into New Haven. It's right downtown. We could meet there or in New York every time you get liberty. Joking apart, Miss Morgan, there's nothing I'd like better in all the world."

After that their relations, whatever one might call them, moved into smoother waters. Her gauche tendencies and his shyness seemed to evaporate, though the excitement of sharing each other's company persisted. In Boston, after church, he was permitted to take her across the snowbound Common to see the State House and the statues of Daniel Webster and Horace Mann. Also the replica of the Beacon Monument to the success of the Revolution. "Only a century ago," he said as they stared up at it. "I guess we'd have been spitting fire at each other in those days. And now … it's hard to associate oneself with all that bitterness."

On their way back he took her arm for the first time. He did it in a way she came to think of as characteristic of the Burgoynes: in easy silence. Only when he held her firmly did he ask if she minded.

"I guess not," she replied, which made him laugh.

Then, serious again, he told her he hoped she would take that stewardess position and come often to New York. "The world is going to seem pretty flat after you've gone," he confessed.

"For me, too," she told him.

"You," he went on, "seem to carry some kind of a charge, like electricity or something. The air around you is special. It has a vibrant quality … no, *you* have a vibrant quality I've never encountered in any other person, ever before. Somehow you're ten times more *real* than anyone else. I think about you all the time, Miss Morgan."

"Me too," she confessed shyly. "About you, I mean. And it's exactly the way you describe it. Everything's very *real* around you."

"I guess we must be in love, then," he said solemnly.

"I've guessed that ever since I saw you," she replied. "D'you think we could call each other Chuck and Kathleen? Or Kathy? I prefer Kathy."

They went behind a tree, which, in that white downtown wilderness, gave only the most token shelter from prying eyes, and kissed. For both of them it was like no other kiss they had ever experienced — in party games and snatched embraces at balls and dinners. Her innards fell away inside her so rapidly she only just managed to catch herself before she buckled at the knees; and he, who had wondered for years why poets and novelists made such a song and dance about it, suddenly understood.

"Oh, Kathy!" he murmured when at last, reluctantly, they broke contact.

"Oh Chuck!" She flung her arms around his neck and pulled his lips to hers again — and wriggled her body against his, and marvelled at the powerful sensations it released in her. Where had they been hiding all this time?

The two concerts were as great a success as anyone might have hoped, despite the threat of Fenian disturbances once it became known that a choir from London was to share the platform. Three men held up placards calling for Home Rule, but that was all.

There was no further chance for kissing on the journey back to New York, but they stood in the corridor for long stretches of the two hundred-and-thirty-four-mile journey while their mothers smiled and told each other how sweet it was and alas it would probably never come to anything but then one never knew and wouldn't it be nice if perhaps ... And the upshot was that Kathleen received an invitation to visit the Burgoyne household again some time in the spring.

Hilda wondered whether, as mother (and thus chaperone), she was automatically included in the invitation — so much so that it would be considered crass to say it in so many words. Then Mrs Burgoyne said, "It will do her the world of good, too. I think it's so important for girls to find their own feet and make a few practice flights from the nest before they leave it for good, don't you, Mrs Morgan?"

Hilda replied that it was certainly a point of view. "Of course, her father will have the final word," she added.

"Of course," Mrs Burgoyne agreed, but with a merry, conspiratorial smile that said, *as long as he agrees with us!*

The curious thing was that when they got off at Grand Central, she could almost swear she saw Francis himself, walking up one of the neighbouring platforms in rather a hurry. "Saw" is too definite a word for it. She thought she glimpsed him. But a moment later a nearby engine let out a great blast of steam, which enveloped them all so that they had to stand still and allow it to clear. When it did so, he was nowhere to be seen.

"Of course, it couldn't have been him," she said to Mrs Burgoyne. "My husband, that is. I thought I saw my husband walking up that platform" — she now saw its arch bore the legend NEW YORK AND NEW HAVEN R R — "before that cloud of steam. But it couldn't have been. The *Pride of Liverpool* won't dock before tomorrow."

"Pity," Mrs Burgoyne commented. "We could have asked him then and there." She had doubts about this Mrs Morgan's strength of character, or at least her perseverance; she had also decided that, of all the girls in whom her son had shown an interest, no matter how faint, Miss Morgan was far and away the most suitable.

In fact, Kathleen and the young man himself joined them at that moment, just in time to overhear her last remark.

"Ask who what?" Kathleen said.

"Ask what of whom?" Hilda corrected her. But, not wishing to answer the question, she sought to divert her daughter with a most graphic account of having seen her father — to such good effect that the girl, squired as ever by Chuck, raced away to the New Haven platform, quite convinced she would find him there. However, before she'd got even half way up the train it drew out of the station.

"Now we'll never know," she said.

But there she was wrong.

T HE NEXT SURPRISE was to call at the Shaw & Eggar office, only to see the *Pride of Liverpool* already towering over the pier. The chief clerk explained that she had made another swift run across the Atlantic, helped by the winds, and had tied up just a couple of hours ago, almost a day ahead of her schedule. He had not seen the Captain and felt sure he was still aboard.

But he wasn't.

"D'you suppose that really was him we saw at the station?" Kathleen asked.

Her mother was still dismissive of the idea. It had been an illusion. Quite common. Good heavens, the number of times she'd stood on railway platforms, waiting to meet Papa or one of the boys off a train, and seen a *dozen* copies of them before the original appeared. She shouldn't have said anything about it.

He was sure to be found at whatever hôtel he usually stayed at in New York.

"You wait here," she concluded briskly, "in case he returns. Find out from the head stewardess which is to be our suite. And I'll pop back ashore and make some inquiries."

A minute or so later Kathleen felt the world begin to collapse about her, for there, busy assisting Walter Grandison to settle in his stateroom, was Emma Harding. It had been arranged between them that she would report sick with all the symptoms of appendicitis, which would, of course, mysteriously clear up in time for her to catch the *next* sailing.

So, when Grandison made a beeline for the bar, Kathleen went to his stateroom to discover what had gone wrong with their plans.

"I couldn't go through with it," Emma said at once.

"Oh you … ninny! Why not?"

"It wasn't me. Nothing to do with me. Only Joan Bolton *says* she's got appendicitis, too."

Kathleen clenched her fists and stamped a foot in vexation. "Oh! Wouldn't it happen just on this trip! Couldn't you have talked to her and persuaded her to have it next time? You obviously don't think she's telling the truth."

Emma was slightly surprised at this show of worldly *qui vive* in someone she'd always considered rather green. "Personally," she said, "I've got my suspicions. But I'll say nothing as to that." She curved her hand through the air in front of her belly and winked.

"Lord!" Kathleen's wide eyes signalled a mixture of dismay and fascination.

"They're suspicious enough about her. They'd never wear two of us going off like that. Anyway, I don't want to be tarred with *that* brush, thank you!"

"No, indeed," Kathleen agreed fervently. "But now you'll have to disguise yourself somehow. Couldn't you have toothache?"

"Toothache?" Emma asked in bewilderment.

"Yes. Stuff a wad of cotton wool in your cheek and wrap half your face in a kerchief. Or get pink eye. Wear an eye patch. Why not both?"

Emma sighed. "Toothache, maybe," she said hesitantly.

"That ginger hair is the real difficulty. You couldn't colour it darker?"

"It's got a lot darker since when I was at Highbury New Park. Also I'm quite a bit taller and" — she breathed in and threw out her chest — "bigger."

"You mean you're just going to do nothing? Take a chance on it?"

She nodded. "It's often the best way, love. I've seen Cissie Williams walk down this corridor with a fag in her hand, straight past old Ma Glover. And nobody smokes down here, not even if his name's Rothschild."

Kathleen's expression was dubious.

Emma added, "Eye patches and kerchiefs, I think they're just a way of saying look at me!"

"But what if it still doesn't work? What if my mother challenges you?"

"Try it." She grinned.

Smiling, too, Kathleen sat down in a lordly way, grossly parodying her mother, and inspected her friend through imaginary lorgnettes. "Haven't I seen you somewhere before, gel? What's your name?"

"Harding, Mrs Morgan," Emma replied blithely. "Emma Harding."

"I knew it!" Bewildered, Kathleen found it hard to stay in character. "You worked for us in London."

Emma's expression was a perfect mixture of amusement and alarm. "Begging your pardon, ma'am, but I don't believe I did. Perhaps …"

"But you did! As if I would ever forget it! I dismissed you without a character in March, getting on for two years ago."

"Ah!" Now relief and amusement mingled to perfection. "That's my cousin Emma. Emma *Harding!*" She stressed the name as if it were different from the one she had just given. "Oh no, Mrs Morgan — I'd be grateful not to be confused with *her!*" Mild surprise took over. "But fancy! I never knew *you* were … I mean, I've sailed on the *Pride of Liverpool* under Captain Morgan's command ever since her maiden voyage and I never thought it was the same Morgan, if you see what I mean. Well, well! Would there be anything else you might require, madam?"

Kathleen had to hand it to her; the performance was pretty seamless. And, like Cissie Williams and her cigarette, if done with enough panache, it might carry the day. As a rearguard volley she asked, "What are you going to say became of that other Emma, then?"

The girl grinned. "Never explain nothing if not asked."

"Yes, but suppose she does ask?"

Emma shook her head and sucked a draught of air through a tiny "o" of her lips. "We don't talk about her in the family these days, Mrs Morgan …" She broke off. "But where is your mum, anyway?"

"Oh, well, after we got to New York … we came from Boston, by the way … Oh, and I *must* tell you! Guess what?" She bit her lip and promised marvels with her eyes. "You'll never guess. I'm in love!" Unable to contain her excitement, she stood up and clasped her hands behind her, swaying like an awkward child who has just reeled off a jolly good entry for a recitation prize.

"I'm sorry to hear it," Emma said lugubriously. "It's not something I'd wish on a dog."

"Oh, *Emma!*" Kathleen skipped to her side and gave her a hug. "You old curmudgeon. You know you don't mean it and you're pleased as Punch — or you will be when I tell you about him ..."

While she was talking, Mrs Glover happened to walk past the open door. The sight of an unknown young lady hugging one of her stewardesses so startled her that she walked a few paces on in disbelief before she stopped and turned round. "Who are you?" she asked as she stood in the doorway. Her peremptory tone had a skilfully provisional character, ready to turn servile at the drop of the right words.

Kathleen dropped exactly the right words: "I'm Captain Morgan's daughter, Kathleen. And you must be Mrs Glover. How d'you do. My father has often spoken of you, and very highly, too." She was desperately trying to think of some reasonable explanation as to why she should have been hugging this presumably unknown stewardess. Then she remembered: *Never explain nothing if not asked.*

It worked, too. Her enormous self-assurance made it almost impossible for Mrs Glover to pose the obvious question without at least a tinge of impertinence. And anyway, the Head Stewardess wanted to unravel much more of this mystery before she risked that. Instead she curtseyed and said it was kind of Miss Morgan to say so, and could she get the stewardess to show her to her stateroom? She turned to Emma and added, "And you, Miss Harding, were supposed to go on liberty as soon as you'd arranged Mr Grandison's things for him."

Emma curtseyed, too, and said, "Yes, Mrs Glover," — again, Kathleen noticed, offering no explanation for anything.

Mrs Glover watched them closely all the way to the Morgans' stateroom.

"Can you get away now?" Emma asked under her breath, in case the old bag was just outside the door.

Kathleen nodded tightly. "I'll think of something. I want to tell you all about Chuck, the boy I'm in love with."

Emma put a finger to her lips and said aloud, "Well, if you're quite sure that's all, Miss Morgan, I'll be going." *Sotto voce* she added, "See you at the Christian Girls' Guild. If you're not there by six, I'll know you can't come. East Forty-Seventh between Park and Lexington. Big grey building. Bye!"

Kathleen hung around a while, hoping Mrs Glover would come to the suite. She had just devised a wonderful explanation for the strange scene the woman had witnessed and, like any true storyteller, couldn't wait to blurt it out. But Mrs Glover's curiosity burned with a slower, surer fuze and she had decided to stay well clear of the Captain's daughter for the present.

Eventually Kathleen wrote her mother a note saying she'd heard from one of the crew that Papa often met old shipmates at the Park Avenue Oyster House. (In fact, she had noticed the name as they climbed into their hansom outside Grand Central.) So she was going there in the hope of catching him before he vanished with one of them for the evening.

As she walked up Park Avenue, counting off the streets to Forty-Seventh, she once again envied Emma the freedom she enjoyed. The thinking behind it remained a mystery to her. Why should the difference in class be so important? What did she, Kathleen, risk in going out unchaperoned like this, that Emma could face with impunity? It made no sense at all.

Her envy was doubled when Emma showed her the sweet little room — or cubicle, really — that she enjoyed for only a dollar a night, including supper and breakfast at the Guild's hostel. Then they went down to the visitors' lounge, which was deserted at that hour of the day, and continued their interrupted tête-à-tête.

Emma listened patiently while Kathleen told her all about Chuck and what an amazingly wonderful, superhuman man he was. "So — that's the end of all your dreams of nursing at sea, eh," she said when the torrent abated. But to her surprise, Kathleen hesitated. "No?" she added.

"Chuck says I should do what *I* want in life. If I want to be a stewardess, then that's what I should be, even if I have to wait until I'm twenty-one and they can't stop me."

For the first time since his name had been mentioned, Chuck began to interest Emma. "Would he wait for you? That long, I mean?"

"It's only two years," Kathleen pointed out. "And a bit. Anyway, we're not engaged, at least, not formally, or not in that way. He's an extraordinary boy, you know."

"Well, I did sort of twig that!"

"No! I mean ... well, he's not like boys I know in England. Perhaps all American boys are like that? He didn't talk to me like ... he didn't treat me as if I was ... you know how in England, if you say something clever or get the answer to some puzzle before a man does, you know how they seem to pat you on the head or behave as if it was a fluke or something? They always act as if they know best and you should listen to what they tell you …" She noticed a faraway look in Emma's eyes and asked what she was thinking.

"Larry's not like that," Emma admitted reluctantly. "But go on, I know what you mean."

"Yes, that's right." Kathleen's tone revealed that the comparison had not struck her before. "I kept wondering who he reminded me of. Anyway, Chuck's like that. Even more than Larry, in fact. He's the first boy I ever met who behaved as if my ideas are just as good as his. And my feelings, too."

"Blimey, you *are* hooked," Emma said dourly. "Just like me. Hooked, lined, and sinkered."

Kathleen laughed. "Why d'you say it like that?"

"Because I'll tell you why," Emma said, not sharing her good humour. "There's a lot to be said for the other kind of man. At least you know where you are with him."

"Yes — one foot still in the nursery!"

"Only in his opinion. But you can say to yourself, 'Right, my lad, if that's your game, I can play it ten times better than you. You treat me like a pretty little girl and I'll *heap* you with my prettiness! I'll torment you with my girlish tricks until you're putty in my hands!' All right, I'm exaggerating. No one can win all the time. Men can turn back into granite when they really want to. But most of the time they settle for the easy life. They let you win. So you still win more than you lose. And you keep yourself — your real self, I mean — a secret from them."

Kathleen stared at her in distaste. "What an awful vision, Emma."

The girl grinned and relaxed. "Not really, love. It's just the way things are. But boys like Larry — and

294

your Chuck, by the sound of him — they're ten times more trouble. Because you've got nowhere to hide from them, see? They keep asking you what you think — and they really want to *know*. When they ask your opinion, it isn't just to pat you on your pretty little head and tell you ten thousand ways you're wrong. Half the time they tell you you're right, and before you know where you are, you're having to live by it. We're not brought up to cope with that. We're brought up to weasel our way with them."

Kathleen sighed. "Perhaps you're right. But I like it, anyway." Then she laughed as a new idea struck her. "I was just thinking about all this — in a way — walking up Park Avenue. I was envying the way you can go about the world completely unchaperoned whereas I, as soon as I set foot outside our own village in Highbury, can never be alone."

"Well, surely you know why that is?"

"Just let me finish. The joke is, there's you, free as a lark, and what you really want is a man to dish out the orders so you can weasel your way around them. And here's me, cribb'd, cabinn'd, and confin'd, and all I want is a man who'll treat me like an absolute equal — which Chuck does. We can't both be right."

Emma lost interest in the topic at that. "You can't be all that cribb'd, cabinn'd, and confin'd, either," she remarked. "How did you get away?"

Kathleen told her of the note she'd left for her mother.

Emma was intrigued. "Why did you pick that particular oyster house?" she asked. She remembered telling Larry about it but she didn't think she'd told Kathy, too.

"I just happened to see it as we came out of Grand Central. Funnily enough, my mother thought she saw my father just before that. Just after we got off the train … why are you looking like that?"

Emma drew breath to speak and then said no, it was nothing, not really.

Kathleen, of course, wouldn't let it go at that. "Come on," she urged. "Something crossed your mind."

Reluctantly Emma related what had happened to her in August the previous year.

"And that was also the New Haven platform — or track?" Kathleen asked.

"I didn't see him actually go down to the track," Emma admitted. "He just asked if that was the train to New Haven. That's all I heard."

"Could he have said *from* New Haven?"

Emma shrugged. "Could be. I never thought anything more about it."

"Probably one of his old shipmates," Kathleen said. "Either he was going out there to stay with him, or meeting him off the train. Wasn't the *Pegasus* shipwrecked somewhere there? Lord, I forgot to ask in Boston."

After a pause, Emma gave a naughty smile and said, "Or …"

"What?"

"You know what they say about sailors."

Kathleen, trying not to smile, said she didn't think that funny — or possible.

Emma said, "I asked one of the officers once, just teasing, like. And d'you know what he said? He said, 'Heavens above, girl, don't you think *one* of you lot in just *one* port is trouble enough?' And I couldn't say I disagreed."

"Especially if that one spends all her time … what was it? *Heaping* him with her prettiness and *weaseling* her way round him!"

She then went on to tell Emma all about the brilliant explanation she had prepared for Mrs Glover.

"If asked!" Emma insisted.

"If asked!" Kathleen agreed. "I know: Never explain nothing if not asked!"

DESPITE HER CONFIDENCE and devil-may-care humour, Emma realized how close a line to disaster she was now treading — and Kathleen, too. If Mrs Morgan were to develop the slightest suspicion, she would only need to raise it with Mrs Glover, who would only need to look up the original character reference, and then the fat would be in the fire! She'd never find work as a stewardess again and Kathleen would be in disgrace for ever. She lay in her bed that night and shivered at the thought of such discoveries.

For relief she turned to her conversation that afternoon with Kathleen, and especially to the amusing notion that Captain Morgan might be the traditional vaudeville sailor with a wife in every port. But she could not enjoy the joke for long; always the dark fear of discovery hovered over her, driving out both sleep and diversion.

Eventually, of course, when New York itself fell into its brief nightly silence, she dropped off. When she awoke in the morning she discovered that the two strands of thought — the joke and the dread — had mysteriously coalesced during the night. As she opened her eyes, gazed around, remembered where she was, she realized she had already formed the intention of going to the Grand Central Depot that afternoon, just to see whether the Captain did, in fact, get off the New Haven train.

It was a decision born of desperation, of course, she realized that, too. The idea that the Captain might have another wife was absurd; but he might have a missy hidden away somewhere up the New Haven Line. Long shot as it was, her situation was now so dire she could not afford to overlook it. Anyway, she had two days to kill, and no better weapon to hand.

Captain Morgan expected his wife and daughter to arrive at the Pennsylvania Depot shortly after five that afternoon — some six hours after the *Pride of Liverpool* would have docked if she had not beaten her schedule. She decided to meet every train from New Haven from noon onward. Kathleen had said that she and her mother would spend the morning shopping, so there was no chance of their meeting in the meanwhile.

She met two trains between twelve and one, drawing a blank with both. Then a pair of detectives with the railroad company met her. They took a fair bit of persuading that she was not what they had assumed; only when she volunteered to go with them to the Shaw & Eggar office and be identified did they begin to believe her. That, plus the fact that she had waited near the New Haven tracks only and had accosted no one, just tipped the balance in her favour; but she had to tell them she was waiting to deliver a verbal message "of some delicacy" to the Captain before they would leave her alone.

Out of the frying pan into the fire! Now she would have to make their meeting appear quite fortuitous to the Captain but quite intentional to the two dicks. But in one small respect, fortune smiled on her, for Captain Morgan alighted from the very next train.

She took two steps toward him, clumsily dropped her umbrella, clumsily kicked it in attempting to pick it up — and timed the whole charade perfectly so that, by the time she had it in her hand again and rose to straighten her dress, the Captain, and several dozen others, were all staring at her.

She made an embarrassed panoramic survey around that circle of eyes and pretended to notice him for the first time. But the surprise she put into her own expression was as nothing to what she now saw in his — surprise and guilt. He was quick to recover, but it had been unmistakable while it lasted.

"Oh, Captain Morgan, sir!" she exclaimed breathlessly. "I'm all butterfingers today."

"Harding?" he asked, with a note of hopeful doubt. "I didn't immediately recognize you out of uniform. Are you travelling somewhere?"

She put on a slightly embarrassed smile and explained about the lack of facilities at the oyster house across the road — with a nod toward the Ladies. Then, in passing, she mentioned that Mrs Morgan and his daughter were already on the ship. Again his immediate response was not the undiluted joy she might have expected; just for a moment there was a touch of fear in his eyes. But then he laughed and said it was capital news. "Have you spoken to them?" he asked. "Was Chicago not to their liking?"

Emma explained that, too. "Boston, eh!" he said heartily — rather more so than a humble stewardess would have expected from so exalted a personage. "Why, they'll have seen more of America than I have! What a pity I missed them. I was seeing an old shipmate in ... La Rochelle."

When he had gone she went to one of the porters and said, "Pardon me, I was expecting to meet a friend from La Rochelle. But he wasn't on it." She pointed to the train from which the Captain had just descended. "Can you tell me when the next one from there is due?"

He told her a quarter of two — and added that the train which had just arrived hadn't stopped at La Rochelle, anyway.

That decided it. Immediately she bought a round-trip ticket to New Haven — though she was on the train and crossing the East River before it struck her that she hadn't the faintest idea what to do when she got there. The Captain had some secret, of that she was now quite certain. And New Haven was the obvious place to start trying to ferret it out. But how — and in so short a space of time, for she'd have to be back at the Fallen Angels by ten tonight.

Did they have anything like *Kelly's Street Directories* in America? Or electoral registers? Somewhere she could look up a household under the name of Morgan, anyway. But that wouldn't work. When Larry had kept her, the rooms had been in her name, not his. So if his father had a missy out there somewhere, the house or apartment would most likely be in her name, not his. She fretted over the problem all the way to New Haven, which she reached around dusk, just after four that afternoon.

As she came out of the depot she tried the longest shot of all. She went up to a gaggle of cab drivers and said in her poshest voice, "Pardon me, I was hoping to call on a friend of my father's, a Captain Morgan, but I find I've left his directions in my hôtel room in Manhattan."

The cabby she addressed shook his head, but another, a Negro who was shaking oats into his horse's nosebag, turned and said, "Frankie Morgan?"

"That's him!" she said delightedly, thinking she was now home and dry.

But the man, a freed slave by the name of Harold Martin, who had spurned his forty acres and a mule, was now a New Englander to the bone. All he said was, "You can't remember no detail, miss? Like what's the Captain's house called, f'rinstance?"

Lord! What would Captain Morgan call his house? Highbury? Dunroamin? She screwed up her face. "Oh, it's on the tip of my tongue. A ... B ... C ..."

"Try P," Martin suggested.

P? The only name that occurred to her was *Putney*, a district in London that, as far as she knew, had not the remotest connection with the Morgans. Of course, there was a famous Captain Morgan back in history who'd been a pirate. Piracy? Some joke based on that? "Pie ... pi ..." she began hopefully.

"P, E," the man offered, beginning to doubt her story by now.

Then, of course, it was obvious. *"Pegasus!"* she exclaimed with confident relief — to be rewarded with the grin of faith restored. "Yes, of course! How could I forget? The ship he saved."

"Lives out in Fife," Martin told her. "Take you there and back for a dollar-fifty." He omitted to say she could take the streetcar to the Fair Haven turn and then walk — nor that he knew for a fact the Captain was not home.

A cagey New Englander dropping clues as bait on a fishing trip can give away ten times more than he imagines when the pool of information in which he is trawling happens to be the mind of a bright cockney girl — especially when that mind is already full of suspicions. Emma pricked her ears for the slightest nuance.

301

Having assured her that the Captain was very well-liked in the district, Harold Martin, asked her if she knew his folks back in England. She repeated that the two families were close but added that it was really their fathers who were closest.

"Those youngsters of his," Martin said, "they're kind of stuck-up, huh?"

Emma said they'd never seemed so to her.

"Well, I hear they live in idleness and waste their father's money," he countered. He'd heard no such thing, of course; he had merely coupled a common American delusion about rich English children with the fact that Teresa had once told him, in her garrulous Irish way, that she didn't expect the Captain's children by his first wife would ever come a-calling.

Emma told him what Neil and Lawrence did for a living — and added, "And his daughter is in New York at this very moment," as if that were proof she couldn't be so very stuck-up, after all.

"And Miz Morgan ..." he drawled, delivering the first part of his sentence while he marshalled the rest.

"I told you. Just now."

"No, Miz Morgan. His wife."

"Oh, she's also in New York," Emma said.

"Uh uhn," he replied, shaking his head. "Less'n she went ahead of him. I saw the Captain to the train this morning and she wasn't with him."

Emma conceded she must have been mistaken, adding, truthfully enough, that she hadn't seen Mrs Morgan there today. Meanwhile her mind was racing double tides.

Her joking suspicions were proving to have some foundation after all. The Captain did, indeed, have a missy over here — and, naturally, the local people assumed she was his wife. Now that she, Emma, had declared herself a close friend of the family, she would obviously have to go through with meeting this person. But what on earth was she going to say? "Hallo! I was his son's missy, you know — at least, that's what the whole world assumed. How is it with you? Like son like father?"

Very likely!

She had to know more about the woman. "In fact," she went on, picking up her previous words, "I wouldn't recognize … Mrs Morgan even if I saw her. We've never met, you know. He's never brought her to England."

Martin chuckled, saying there was wisdom in that, for she'd be 'bout the same age as the eldest boy, Neil, was it? Yes, Neil. Anyways, he couldn't have brung her, what with little Tony being on the way till Christmas — and still too young to travel."

Reeling from this intelligence she nonetheless had the wit to say, "Ah yes, Tony. What would he be now?" And she counted off her fingers.

"Jess over a year now. Born on Christmas Day."

"Really? Now that I didn't know. I'm looking forward to seeing him at last — we've heard so much about him, of course."

"Ef'n I had a half-brother, I'd sure want to see him," he commented.

For a moment Emma wondered if he'd gained the impression that *she* was the half-sister, then she realized he was referring to Kathleen. "She might come and visit while she's over here," she said lightly.

They had passed the outskirts of Fife some time ago without her being aware of it. About half the dwellings, some fifty in number, were clustered around a spacious, elm-girt green, near the church, the post office, and the general store; the rest were scattered over the surrounding countryside among remnants of what had once been unbroken forests of red and live oak. One group formed a little nameless hamlet out on its own, crowning a small rise, which was just visible against the last band of the evening twilight. Martin turned off on the track that led to it. "Soon be there now," he promised.

And she realized she still had no idea what she was going to say or do.

"That's it!" He reined in the horse and swivelled the carriage lamp to pick out the shingle: *Pegasus.* "Sure 'nuff."

She asked him to wait — which he was determined to do, anyway — and alighted. *You'll have to think of something soon*, she told herself as she stepped out toward the front porch.

But her mind was still an absolute blank when she raised her hand and gave three very confident raps on the knocker.

K ATHLEEN PROPOSED THAT she and her parents should make a great day of it. They could take the steamer from Rector Street and go out to Atlantic Highlands. But she didn't truly mean it. In fact, she and Emma planned to spend the day up the Hudson, wandering in the woods that another stewardess, Bella Mooney, had originally discovered. Emma said they were beautiful in the snow and quite safe.

Kathleen expected her mother to say it was out of the question. Her father would then say, "You heard your mother, my girl. Now there's an end to it." And then there would be an argument and finally Kathleen would suggest she'd go on her own, with, of course, one of the stewardesses to chaperone her — and perhaps they'd give way in the end. You never knew with them.

In fact, her mother was all approval from the start; she even leaped to Kathleen's own conclusion by saying, "You can call at the Christian Girls' Guild and take one of the stewardesses along, too!" It crossed the girl's mind that perhaps her mother had some bone she wished to pick with her father; in which case she'd welcome the knowledge that her daughter was safely — and respectably — out of the way for several hours. Kathleen pushed her luck a little further, suggesting she and her chaperone should go on to Long Branch by rail for luncheon and then return, also by rail, to Manhattan through Brooklyn — an itinerary that would consume most of the day.

That, too, was agreed without demur.

Emma, however, was nowhere near as pleased as she ought to have been; in fact, she was so subdued that Kathleen wondered if she wasn't genuinely sickening for something. If so, she hoped it was trivial enough not to threaten her health but not so trivial as to allow her to sail; it would be the answer to their prayers. As they turned into Park Avenue she said as much, only to be met with the lugubrious comment that she, Emma, had an even better answer than that. But she wouldn't say what it might be.

"Well, anyway, let's go," Kathleen said impatiently as she turned toward the Pennsylvania Depot, "or we'll lose the best of the day."

Still Emma hung back, dragging her heels along the eastern side of the avenue. "Where did you say your beau is going next year? Yale, was it?"

Kathleen nodded. "Why?"

"That's out New Haven way, isn't it?"

"It's in New Haven, near the depot. But what does it matter? We could hardly go there."

"Why not?"

"Well ... there'd be no point. I mean, Chuck won't be there until ..." Her voice tailed off as she caught Emma's eye. "Why d'you even suggest it, anyway? What's New Haven to you?"

The other closed her eyes and shook her head. "If I say nothing, I'll never be able to look myself in the face again. And if I tell you ... well, I shouldn't think as you'd ever speak to me again."

"Emma!" Impulsively Kathleen threw her arms about her friend. "As if I would! What could you possibly say to make me behave like that?"

"It's the worst thing anyone could ever tell a friend — that's all I know."

Kathleen, about to laugh at such an absurdity, was suddenly transfixed by the girl's expression, which was anguished beyond bearing. She swallowed heavily and repeated her earlier question, "What is New Haven to you? Have you ever been there?"

Emma nodded.

"When?"

"Yesterday. It's only a couple of hours by train."

"Oh dear!" Kathleen closed her eyes and drew a deep breath. "Does this have something to do with ... with my father?"

Emma gave a tight little nod; her look of misery deepened.

"And New Haven? There's some connection with New Haven?"

Emma turned away and grasped a nearby railing. "Oh God!" She shook it vigorously, shaking only herself. "I should never ought to have started on all this. I shouldn't never have gone there. And that's all about it."

Kathleen took a couple of paces across the sidewalk and stood in front of her. "Well you can't just leave it at that," she said. "What *did* you discover when you went there?"

"A house called *Pegasus,* for one thing."

"And?" To Kathleen this particular find was merely bewildering.

Emma's lip trembled. A tear hovered. "I can't ... I can't say it."

Kathleen breathed in deeply. "A house called *Pegasus* ... and ... someone ... a woman ... there?"

One of the tears started to roll as the girl nodded.

"Oh, Emma!" Now Kathleen, too, clung to the railing. "Oh, Lord!"

"Irish woman, she is. Not much older than you and me. Twenty-four, twenty-five ... something like that, I'd say."

"And she's his ..." Kathleen swallowed hard. "What did you call it with Larry? What people thought you were to him?"

"His missy. Yes. She says she's his wife, of course — but then she'd have to, wouldn't she."

A certain edge to the statement made Kathleen prick up her ears. "You mean there's ..." The word that occurred to her was *issue,* which was always used in the papers when referring to such dramas as this; but in real life it sounded absurd. *A baby,* on the other hand, sounded too brutal.

Emma nodded again. "A little boy. About a year old. And one of the bonniest I ..." She hesitated, thinking that such a comment was perhaps out of place. "Anyway," she concluded vaguely.

The thought, *I have a little baby half-brother!* intruded itself into Kathleen's numbed mind, bringing a ripple of pleasure that, in the context, seemed grotesque. But she could not help it — a pleasure it was. "What's the little fellow like?" she asked.

"Curly hair. Big eyes — dark brown like his ... like your father's."

"Like *our* father's! Oh God! It's too big to take in all at once." She leaned her forehead against the chill iron of the railings and rolled her head from side to side, pressing until it hurt.

A passing gentleman tipped his hat and asked if she were unwell, and could he be of assistance?

She pulled herself together and smiled wanly. "Just a bit of bad news," she told him. "Be right as rain in a minute."

When the man had gone she turned again to Emma and said, "You know how when you pour water into sand at the seaside — how quickly it vanishes? That's how I feel about this ... this awful news. It's gone right through me. Or right into my ..." She rapped her knuckles on her breast. She smiled again. "And what's *she* like? Beautiful and vivacious, of course!"

Emma gave a reluctant nod. "Are we going to Grand Central? For the New Haven train?"

"No!" Kathleen exclaimed.

"Don't you want to see for yourself? She is sort of half-expecting you."

Kathleen merely gaped at her.

Emma shifted uncomfortably and took one or two paces of encouragement in the direction of the depot. "See, I wasn't anticipating nothing like that. I mean not a house with a garden and a baby and all that. And a wedding ring and everyone calling her *Mrs* Morgan. So ... well, I mean, on the way out there in

308

the cab I just thought it'd be like an apartment and *her* in it, like what it was with me and Larry. And I thought I'd just tell her I was you — because Americans wouldn't know one London accent from another, would they. But then, when I saw it was like a family in a proper house and all — and when she opens her mouth and I hear she's Irish, well ..."

"Is she?" Kathleen suddenly found herself avid for details of this ... what could one call her? Usurper of her father's affections?

"Anyway," Emma concluded, "I knew I'd never carry it off so, on the spur of the moment I told her I was a friend of yours in London and passing through and all that, and had she any message? I mean it was the best I could do on the spur of the moment, like."

"To carry back to me in London," Kathleen said. When Emma did not confirm it she added, "Oh, you didn't tell her I was actually in New York?"

The girl nodded miserably. "I never thought. I just never ... thought."

"So of course she's 'half-expecting' me today. Oh, Emma!"

"Sorry!" she exploded. "I never thought quick enough."

"Well, I'm not going, and that's that."

They set off in silence for the Pennsylvania Depot, but after a few blocks Kathleen suddenly stopped. "All right," she snapped, breaking a silence that had lasted all that way. "I'll have to, won't I! Otherwise she's going to think I sent you to New Haven, to sound her out, and you came back with a report that damned her out of hand. And then she'll complain to my father about what a devious and stuck-up little prig he has for a daughter — and that *will* put the cat among the pigeons!"

"Sorry!" Emma said again. "I know I'm useless."

Kathleen linked arms and spoke with deliberate cheer. "You know nothing of the sort. What you actually are is the cleverest person I've ever met. I think you're cleverer than Miss Kernow even. She'd never have had the gumption to find out all this, not off her own bat. And as for me, I wouldn't even have known where to begin."

Emma's step lightened.

But Kathleen was already having second thoughts. "Perhaps if we just asked the cabby to drive past the house?" she suggested. Then, after a short silence, "Really, it's none of our business, is it." She screwed up her face in astonishment and peered at her friend. "Isn't that amazing? You'd think that if a girl's father provided her with a half-brother, it would be — in some way or other — you'd think it would be her business, too. But it isn't. I have no right to go barging into their lives like this."

Emma stopped and sighed. "So what *are* we going to do?"

Kathleen shrugged. "We'll go, nonetheless, I suppose. We must. The main thing is somehow to stop her from mentioning any of this to Papa."

"How?" The very tone of the question revealed her sense of futility in even attempting it.

"I don't know. It all depends on her. I mean her idea about my father. What sort of man does *she* suppose him to be? I mean ... just think of the Captain Morgan we know, you and I. Can you, by any stretch of the imagination, picture him doing something like this? He must be a completely different person to her, don't you think?"

"Well, I can tell you about that," Emma replied, "on the train."

ON THEIR WAY to New Haven, Emma told Kathleen all she had learned from the garrulous, effervescent young woman who called herself Mrs Morgan — their meeting on the *Pegasus,* how it had been love at first sight for both of them, how the Captain had shielded her from the rigours of the steerage dormitories, how she had heard of his widowhood from the first officer ... and then the Great Storm and the miraculous saving of the ship, and how she had "stowed away" when all the others had gone ashore ...

"And then — according to her — your father proposed to her that very night. And ... well, she never said no more, but that was it."

Kathleen was silent a long while, staring at the vaguely familiar landscape as it went flashing by.

"Penny for them?" Emma asked at length.

Kathleen shook her head. "Thoughts that are unthinkable," she answered. "I wouldn't speak them for a million pounds." After a pause she added, "Describe her. I want to know what she looks like."

Emma closed her eyes briefly, summoning up pictures. "Green eyes," she said. "That's what you notice mostly. Pale green eyes that seem to burn. And curly red hair."

"A bit fragile-looking?"

"No! Just the opposite. Like my old dad always says, she'd be useful in a fight. Good and sturdy. And that's about all, really. Very friendly and ... well, you know the Irish."

Kathleen made a bitter face. "Too friendly by half! She was the one who stowed away — or hid — when

311

Pegasus ran aground, wasn't she. My father didn't ask her to do that. I'll bet he was horrified. She's the one who set her cap at him by the sound of things."

"Come into my parlour said the spider to the fly!"

"Just so. The more I think about it, Emma ... I mean, the shock's wearing off now — but the more I think about it the more savage I feel. This situation cannot be allowed to continue, can it? It's not just a matter now of persuading her to say nothing to Papa about your visiting her yesterday. She's got to be made to understand that the whole ... *thing*, this absurd connection with Papa ... I mean, it's just got to stop. With a proper settlement for her and the baby, of course. But it can't go on."

The other gave a noncommittal shrug. Then she grinned and said, "It's a bit like back in Highbury New Park, isn't it — you picking the locks on Larry's drawers and reading his diaries and looking at his form book."

Kathleen stared at her aghast. "I never did such a thing in my ... how did you know about it, anyway?"

Emma pointed at her right eye, then her left. "And did any good come of that?" she asked.

Kathleen returned her gaze to the snowbound landscape for a while before she replied. "I think so. Yes, I do believe it did. I learned how much he loved you, for instance. And still does."

Emma's eyes raked the skies. "Should have kept my mouth shut!"

"He does, you know."

"I *know!* But I'm not going to ruin his life by doing anything about it."

Kathleen licked her lips hesitantly. "He said in one place that you said why didn't he make you his missy in the proper sense. You know — *do* it."

"Oh, is that what I meant? Fancy that! I am a naughty gel, ain't I?"

"Emma!" Her tone was both vexed and cajoling. "Don't be like that. I want to talk about it."

"Well, that makes one of us." She went on staring out of the window.

"How would it ruin his life?"

"'Cos he could be chairman of the Baltic one day, just like his grandfather. But not if he went and married a skivvy like me."

"Skivvy! You're no skivvy, believe me. If you just had a bit more faith in yourself you'd run circles round most of the Baltic wives. Anyway, he's not going to stay on the Baltic for ever and a day. He's going to go to sea."

Emma gave out a single sarcastic "Ha!"

Kathleen stared at her in surprise. "But he is."

The other shook her head sadly. "Haven't you copped on yet? Your brother will still be talking about running away to sea when he's thirty. The other one's different, I grant you."

"Neil?"

"Yes. He won't stay at sea much longer. But Larry won't ever swap."

"Oh, but that was just a madcap idea — changing places."

"Well, he won't never go to sea, neither. I wish he was here. I'd bet him on it — and it'd be one bet he'd surely lose."

Kathleen's eyes narrowed. "How can you be so sure?"

Some of Emma's coolness deserted her. "I can. That's all. I just know."

"It's only because of you he's delayed so far, you realize? The thought that he might be gone for six months to Australia while you're in London twice a month — he couldn't bear that."

Emma said nothing.

"And you do love him, too."

Emma nodded.

"Is that why you were willing to ... you know — with Larry — do that ... what you suggested?"

Emma's eyes hardened. "Let me ask you, then. What if your darling Chuck was to go and suggest it. Not marry you, but the other thing. Would you?"

While Kathleen faced the shock of the question — and honestly sought for an answer to challenges that had never occurred to her before — Emma fed her the most tempting morsels: "Nice apartment in a nice neighbourhood? Nice income? Nice gold ring on your finger, even if it's only for show? Nice little babies all well provided for? All endowed, good and legal? One, two, three ... would you?"

With the air of one who announces a painful discovery she said, "If Chuck were to make such an offer ... well, he wouldn't be the Chuck I love. Therefore I couldn't do it."

Emma laughed harshly. "You should be a lawyer! You don't want to admit you'd agree to it with the man you love, so you say the man you love could never make such a proposal, and if he did, he'd stop being the man you'd love at once! You should be Lord Chief Justice!"

Kathleen hung her head and wondered how she'd allowed the conversation to drift so far from where she'd intended it to go.

"So," Emma said, as if announcing an interesting discovery, "there's two kinds of women, it seems. I'm one — and you're the other. And the question now is, which kind is Teresa Morgan, as she calls herself?"

THE CAB CIRCUMNAVIGATED the green in Fife and set off along the track that led to *Pegasus*. "It's the one on the hill up there," Emma said. She had to shield her eyes from the noonday sun, though the reflection off the fresh snow was just as blinding. "She's coming down to the gate. She must have heard us, or kept an eye out."

Harold Martin, the same cabby as had driven her yesterday, chuckled and said, "Folks in these parts get a kind of an ear for strangers."

"What's that glasshouse-thing on the roof?" Kathleen asked.

"Widow's walk, they call it — where the wives can walk and keep lookout for their menfolks' ships. Lotta houses got 'em hereabout."

"*Widow's* walk!" Emma gave a gallows laugh.

When they pulled up at the gate, Kathleen could only sit and stare at the apparition that now stood before her, rubbing her hands in the chill of the air and smiling in the warmest of welcomes. She was certainly no stranger. She was Jenny Bright to the last little curl on her forehead — but Jenny as she had been a quarter of a century ago. How was such a thing possible?

Her mind was in a whirl as she descended from the cab and allowed Emma to lead her forward to be introduced. The scene moved around her like drifts of seaweed when you open your eyes underwater in a brilliant rock pool.

It could not be a coincidence — Jenny Bright and her father, smiling at each other in the fading photograph in Aunt Daphne's album, and her double standing here, seemingly not a day older, and claiming to be Mrs Morgan. Since it was impossible for her to be Jenny herself, she must be Jenny's daughter. The thought hovered in her mind for a moment — mere words whose meaning seemed elusive — before they took hold.

Jenny's daughter? Yes, indeed, why not? The more she thought about it, the more plausible it became. And what a difference it made, too! Why, it shed an entirely new light on the whole affair.

But Jenny's daughter by whom?

By Papa?

It almost had to be, otherwise why was he keeping her and shielding her? Assume it, anyway.

"I'm after hearing so much about you, and your brothers," said the woman. Kathleen refused even to *think* of her as "Mrs Morgan."

"Ah!" She remembered fragments of the lines she had prepared for this situation. "I wish I could say the same, Mrs ... ah ..."

"Oh for the love of God, it's Teresa, of course. And I'm sure I may call you Kathleen, mayn't I?"

"Oh, please, I'd like that. As I was saying, Teresa, *officially* my father still hasn't mentioned you to us. We know, of course. And he knows we know. But ... oh, you know what a complicated sort of man he is."

Teresa frowned in bewilderment. "Sure, that doesn't sound like him at all. And why wouldn't he tell you?"

"Pride, I suppose. He was so proud of his ... what can one call it? His sufficiency. Like Robinson Crusoe. To admit he'd caved in and married again after so many years would be like confessing a weakness to us."

Teresa remembered Frank had said something of the sort around the time of their marriage. "Sure, I can

316

believe that," she allowed.

If she was Jenny's daughter by Papa, then the little boy was by someone else. Of all the many unthinkables connected with this affair, the notion that Papa was the baby's father was now the most unthinkablest of all. Papa was shielding her from disgrace by pretending to have married her and so lending her his name.

An enormous sense of relief flooded through Kathleen at this conclusion. Of course! It was so clear now. And so like Papa, too. So noble. The very existence of this girl — the result of some impetuous and youthful indiscretion, no doubt — would have weighed on his conscience all these years. And then when she, in turn, "broke her ankle," as the polite phrase had it, he must have arranged for her to travel to the New World under his protection. Yes! That's why he saved her from the horrors of the steerage dormitories, of course. Oh, how well it all fitted now. And what a fool she was for ever having allowed Emma to divert her mind onto other, more scurrilous explanations!

She relaxed completely then. There were one or two loose ends, still. The idea that her father would go so far as to pretend to be married to Teresa, merely to shield her good name, did not feel quite right. Still, it was on the right lines — she was sure of that. It just needed a little more investigation and it would all fall into place.

She could sense other little objections lying untidily in the corners of her mind, but no doubt they'd *all* succumb to a little thought, a few more facts — when she had the time. But for the moment she could sit back, mentally, and enjoy an imposture of which she now approved. Indeed, if put to the test, she would fight with all her breath to preserve it.

She could even call her Mrs Morgan — tongue in cheek, to be sure.

Tongue in cheek, she admired the wedding photograph so prominently displayed on the mantelpiece. Next she admired Anthony Francis, and quite sincerely, too, for he was one of the most dazzlingly bonny babies she had ever seen. It gave her quite a pang to cuddle him in her arms and stare down into those big, dark eyes (so like Papa's — Emma was right there) and to realize he was *not* her half-brother but only a half-nephew; not a relation at all, really.

"I want five more," Teresa exclaimed, and then laughed. "Six of the best, your father says!"

Kathleen smiled, though she thought this was carrying imposture a little far. She longed to tell the woman how she'd worked out the whole thing, but she fought shy of it with Emma there. She'd have to explain it quietly afterwards to her friend, before she spread the misunderstanding far and wide. Meanwhile she'd just play along with it.

"Oh, Kathleen — me darlin' one!" Teresa held out both hands to her. "I think I can understand why Frank is shy of your knowing about him and me. We could never be stepmother and step-daughter, could we. Will you look at us!" She pulled her into a loose embrace and turned them to face the glass. "More like sisters, wouldn't you say?"

"Half-sisters, anyway!" Kathleen gave her a sly dig in the ribs.

"If you like." Teresa seemed slightly bewildered at this jocular pedantry. She let Kathleen go and, since jokes were in the air, said, "So — I passed your inspection, did I?"

Kathleen frowned.

"Ah, g'wan!" Teresa cajoled. "Didn't that colleen"

— she nodded at Emma — "come to see had I horns and a tail yesterday? She must have told you I haven't."

"Honestly, Teresa," Kathleen protested, "I promise you I hadn't the first notion she was going to call on you at all."

Teresa gave the sort of shrug which implied that, while she took their word, she nonetheless found it hard to believe. She changed the subject by inviting them to stop for a bite of dinner, which the two girls gratefully accepted.

When they were seated, however, Kathleen returned to the topic. "In fact," she said, as if the conversation had been continuing in her mind all this while, "I think it would be best to say nothing to my father about this visit — not for the moment, anyway."

Teresa's face fell. "Sure I've never kept a word from him since the day we met. I couldn't agree to that."

The other sighed.

"Why d'you ask it?" Teresa went on.

Any answer would have to be a lie, so Kathleen decided to go the whole hog. "Because he'd beat me black and blue if he ever found out."

"Not at all!" Teresa said stoutly. "Frank? Sure he'd never lay a finger on you. That's not his way." She glanced from one to the other. "Surely?"

Kathleen gave a reluctant shrug and looked to Emma for support. Emma nodded gravely, but did not look too happy about it.

"Well! It's not the Frank Morgan I married," Teresa said. "Nor the Captain Morgan who commanded the *Pegasus*, either. Isn't he famous on all seven seas as the master who never struck a man — and who never needed to, either. There's seafaring men who'd sooner take twenty from the cat rather than one lashing from his tongue. And that's the Frank Morgan I know." She gave Kathleen an encouraging smile. "Isn't that the way of it? Wouldn't he lash you black and blue with the rough side of his tongue?"

Kathleen gave an embarrassed shrug. "He's changed greatly since he met you," she said feebly. "All three of us have remarked upon it."

"Ah, you mean Neil and Lawrence, of course. Tell me about them, now. Oh God, I hope we all meet soon and become the firmest of friends." She laughed gaily. "There's one thing I could never be to the three of ye, and that's a stepmother! Neil would be older than me, would he not? I was twenty-four this August."

Kathleen briefly rolled her eyes up into her skull; her fingers went pitapat on her chair. "No," she announced. "You beat him by a year and a half. And Larry's only a year behind him. And I'm …"

"Lord, wasn't that quick!"

Kathleen smiled weakly. "And I'm eighteen." *Soon*, she added mentally, being aware of a slight stir from Emma, who actually was eighteen.

"Tell me about the boys," Teresa urged. "Your father says he sent the wrong one to sea and kept the other wrong one ashore."

Kathleen stared at her in amazement. "Well, I wish he'd tell *them* as much," she replied. "They're both miserable where they are."

"No," Emma put in. "That's not right, love."

Kathleen smiled at Teresa. "We differ on that point. She thinks Larry just enjoys complaining about being kept ashore."

"And so he does," Emma insisted.

"Now I want to meet him more than ever," Teresa said, watching Emma closely. The way the girl seemed to claim some kind of proprietorial right over Lawrence, but not Neil, interested her. "Have they sweethearts at all — the two gossoons? Surely they have."

Emma's elaborate display of indifference persuaded her she was right.

"They wouldn't tell us anything like that," Kathleen replied.

"You're not saying you need to be *told*?" She put the challenge to Kathleen before giving an amused lift of her eyebrows to Emma.

Emma closed her eyes and slumped; her cutlery clattered to her plate. "He supposes he's in love with me," she admitted wearily. "Larry, that is."

"He is," Kathleen insisted, then, turning to Teresa: "Honestly he is. That's the only thing that's keeping him ashore — because otherwise he'd miss seeing her every two weeks."

"Kathy!" Emma cried in dismay.

"Every two weeks?" Teresa asked. "I don't quite follow that." She glanced from one to the other, provoking either to explain.

Kathleen struggled to devise some reasonable lie, but Emma, miffed, no doubt, at her friend's earlier indiscretion over Lawrence, said simply, "I'm the one as goes away to sea, Mrs Morgan. It's ..."

"Oh, Teresa, please!" Their hostess smiled benignly. "After all, if what Kathleen says is true, couldn't you be my step-daughter-in-law one of these fine days? But I don't understand what you said about going away to sea."

Staring at Kathleen rather than at her questioner Emma said, "I'm a stewardess. On a passenger ship. On the *Pride of Liverpool*, in fact."

"Lord save us!"

"But I told no lie yesterday when I said as I'm a friend of the family. I'm a friend of *her*, anyway." She nodded at Kathleen.

"Or was," Kathleen said darkly. "Wasn't there a motto you told me once? Something about '... if not asked'?"

Teresa was on to her meaning in a flash. "Well, let me ask, then — for I'm the next nosiest parker to the Recording Angel himself — are you not a friend to the *whole* family? You wouldn't be on the *Pride of Liverpool* if you'd fallen out with Frank. You wouldn't be here if you'd fallen out with that one." She gave a cheerful nod in Kathleen's direction. "And you wouldn't be detaaaining Master Larry ashore if you'd fallen out with him. So who does it leave? Except Neil. God, aren't I only awful! Tell me to m-m-o-b. I shan't mind a bit." She leaned forward avidly to hear the explanation.

"The housekeeper," Kathleen put in — as if it were a confession wrung from her.

"Mrs Johnson?" Teresa turned to her. "Your father told me she rules the roost in London. The Holy Terror, I call her." She bit her lip in parody of a girl who knows she has said something naughty. "Is she really so bad?"

"Not if you keep the right side of her." Kathleen now wished she'd never let herself be talked into this dreadful visit. Was there *anything* this woman didn't know about them all? The painstaking thoroughness of the imposture depressed her. That was her father's handiwork, all right. "She fell out with Emma over a complete misunderstanding. I mean, she was completely in the wrong — Mrs Johnson, I mean. But she's one of those people who can never yield, you know. Not once they've put their foot down."

Only then did she recall she was talking about her mother.

"Weak, you mean," Teresa replied. "Lord — but don't I know the type. There was a teacher like that in Philipstown." She turned to Emma. "I'm sorry for you now, Miss Harding, so I am."

Kathleen suddenly saw a way out of all their difficulties. "To cut a long story short," she said enthusiastically, "Larry and I were so angry at the unfairness of everything that we decided to make it up to Emma, between us. Larry had some money he won on a sweepstake in their office and he gave that to her, and I" — she swallowed desperately at having to confess to something so heinous — "I forged a character reference for her when she applied for the post of stewardess with the Shaw & Eggar Line. And *that*, Teresa dear, is why we'd be ever so obliged if you somehow forgot to tell my father about this visit next time you see him."

Teresa turned to Emma. "And has he never recognized you? Did you change your name or something like that?"

Emma shook her head. "He was only ashore the once when I worked at Highbury New Park."

"The thing is ..." Kathleen wanted to ram her point home at all costs. "It was a very stupid forgery. I used my own Christian name and the surname of an aunt of mine by courtesy."

Teresa grinned. "Mrs Dowty, would that be? Daphne Dowty?" The grin broadened still further when she saw she was right. "Your father's old flame! He told me about her." She laughed, a silvery peal. "Isn't it only the strangest thing ever? I feel I know all about you, and life in Highbury, and all that — and really I never set eyes on you before today. That's a good omen, surely? Wouldn't you say that's a good omen?"

Kathleen just stared at her, wide-eyed. "Old flame?" she murmured.

"Did you not know that?" Teresa was mortified. "Lord, you'd best forget I ever told you — next time *you* meet him!"

"I knew they were all friends together before any of them married, including Uncle Brian. But I never knew he and she were sweethearts!" Kathleen turned to Emma. "Can you imagine it?"

Emma nodded, annoyingly superior. "I did wonder, once or twice."

"You didn't!" Kathleen insisted. "You're only saying it now." Casually she turned back to Teresa and said, "The only old flame he ever mentioned to me was a Miss Bright. Jenny Bright. Did he ever tell you about her?"

The woman's self-control was amazing. Not by the smallest flicker of an eyelid did she betray herself. She just shook her head and encouraged Kathleen with a smile to tell her more.

"That's all I know," the girl had to admit lamely. "Except that she was the daughter of a sea captain."

"She must have been before your Aunt Daphne, so," Teresa said. "Because your mother, God rest her, was next and last — until me. 'Daphne passed me on to Hilda like an old, unwanted glove,' he told me. Between the three of us and that old horse" — she glanced conspiratorially about them — "I think he still had a bit of a soft spot for her. Miss Daphne Troughton, as was."

After their lunch Kathleen said they really ought to go; she explained what she'd told her father (she almost said parents) about the day's arrangements.

Teresa got out her gig at once and said she'd drive them into New Haven to catch their train. On their way she began to tease Kathleen. Larry and Emma had each other; so did she and Frank. "And sure Neil's a sailor. He'll have a sweetheart in every port. Aren't you the one left out in the cold?" she asked. "Or is there someone I *haven't* heard of at all?"

She laughed at the blush on Kathleen's ears. "Well, ah decleah! Aren't you the dark horse. What's the lucky fella's name?"

"Oh ... it's nothing certain," Kathleen insisted.

"Kathy!" Emma chided.

Kathleen turned on her. "You just keep quiet, miss!" she began, quite angrily. But she could not keep it up. "Oh botheration!" she exclaimed as she dissolved in laughter.

Teresa saw it would be in order to consult Emma. But before the girl could reply, Kathleen broke in. "If you absolutely must know, he's a young fellow called Carleton Burgoyne — Chuck to his friends — and next year ..."

"Not the soda-fountain Burgoynes?" Teresa asked. Her eyes prepared to be mightily impressed if Kathleen answered in the affirmative — which, of course, she did. "My my! We shall be a grand family then."

"He's at Yale next year," Emma blurted out.

"Oh, you!" Kathleen said angrily.

"Well, that's what you were going to say."

"Never mind all that," Teresa interrupted. "If he's going to Yale — why, there it is! You can see it over there. Then you *must* tell your papa, me darlin' girl, and you must get him to bring you here to stay for a good long while. Wouldn't you like that?"

Kathleen stared in amazement and then threw her arms impulsively around her. "Oh! Darling Teresa —

if only I could! D'you think I could? Wouldn't it be perfect."

"Whoa-boy!" Teresa calmed the horse, whose mouth had been chucked by Kathleen's gesture. "Well, I know it's not for love of me!"

"Oh, but it is! It is! I'd think it marvellous of you even if I didn't know Chuck, or anyone else at Yale. Honestly. Honestly, honestly, and truly." She sobered a little as the hurdles ahead took shape in her mind. "But let me be the one to tell him. I know how to put it. I'll write and let you know when you can mention it — and how I wheedled him into it. It's not that he'd enjoy denying me the pleasure, but he sets great store by what Mrs Johnson says. And she'd say no like a shot, without a second thought."

Reluctantly, Teresa agreed — though privately she was sure she could outtalk a dozen Mrs Johnsons to her own darling Frank.

Kathleen sent Emma in with the money to get two footwarmers for the train. It gave her the chance to hug Teresa one last farewell — and to murmur, "Don't worry, my dear. I've worked out exactly what's behind all this. But your secret's safe with me."

Teresa laughed at this girlish nonsense. "What secret, for the love of God?"

Kathleen put a finger to her nose, a gesture she had picked up from Lawrence, and, with the two words, "Jenny Bright!" dashed into the station. "I'll write!" she added when she was fifty yards away. "*Mrs* Morgan!" And her laughter rang on in Teresa's ears.

All the way back to Fife she pondered the extraordinary events of these last two days. The only firm conclusion she could draw was that she must be older than she realized. She had always thought of herself as one of life's permanent juveniles ... still wondered what she'd do when she *really* grew up ... but she only had to spend a few hours in the company of those two to realize how far along that road she had travelled already.

Jenny Bright?

An old flame of Frank's, my eye!

He must have been teasing her. The name was probably out of some old English saying. Or nursery rhyme? Like "Jack Sprat could eat no fat ..."

Jenny Bright was always right.
It made her family scream ...

She chuckled. Sure there were possibilities there. She'd have to start learning all those old pomes now. Goosey Gander. Georgy Porgy. Wee Willie Winkie. Why not one of her own about "Jenny Bright" for a change?

The railroad car was almost deserted, so the two girls had a fair space to themselves. "Well!" Emma said heavily as they settled themselves into their seats and footwarmers. "What d'you say *now?*"

"Sorry?" Kathleen suggested.

"No — about her! Is she like what you thought she'd be?"

A slow smile spread over Emma's face. "Yes," she said at last. "If I'd had my wits about me, or was just a little bit brighter than I obviously am, well then she's *exactly* what I would have expected."

Emma frowned. "I thought you went a bit ... easy, like. I mean, I thought you was going to read the riot act to her, or scratch her eyes out, or something — before you met her."

"Ah, before I met her! Yes, it was most necessary for me to meet her. What an ass I'd have made of myself otherwise!"

"Oh, come on! You obviously know something." An accusing glint came into her eye. "You never met her before, did you?"

Kathleen smiled. "In a way. If you'll just listen, I'll tell you." And she went on to describe the photograph she had seen in Aunt Daphne's album. "There was something about the way my father and Jenny Bright were looking at each other that made me remember it," she concluded. "And if I tell you that Teresa back there is the absolute living image of Jenny Bright, you'll believe me when I say it's a face you wouldn't easily forget."

Emma was intrigued and mystified in equal proportions. "But it can't be," she objected. "I mean, when was the photo took?"

"Of course it can't be," Kathleen agreed. "So what's the next most likely explanation? Let's see if you come to the same conclusion as me. If it's not Jenny herself, then …?"

A glimmer of understanding made Emma smile. "Aha! She's Jenny's daughter. Is that what you think?"

"Otherwise the coincidence is … I mean, my father staring deep into the eyes of someone who looks just like her, twenty-five, thirty years ago — I must find out exactly when that photo was taken, by the way. And now pretending to be her husband …"

"Pretending?"

Kathleen laughed. "Of course! That's where we went wrong from the start. Very understandable, of course. But don't you see? Papa's only doing it to protect her." And she went on to outline her new explanation of the mystery.

As Emma listened her spirit sank. At first she wanted to interrupt after every other sentence, putting in all the obvious objections — beginning with, "Why would anyone as sensible as the Captain do anything so stupid, especially when there were half a dozen easier ways to the same end?" And then, "How could anyone, after such an encounter as today's, imagine that Teresa Morgan did *not* believe herself married to the Captain?"

But as she watched and listened she detected a certain fanatical glint in her friend's eye — a glint she recognized from her father's sister's side of the family, "the religious Hardings," as the others called them. And then she knew that no amount of reasoned argument would ever shake that faith. Nor did she blame Kathleen for it. To relinquish this moderately absurd explanation and face reality — that her father had, in some fit of insanity, contracted a bigamous marriage with Teresa — would be, for her, to plunge into the abyss. Even to oppose token objections would be no kindness.

The most she could do was set a little time bomb in Kathleen's mind — something the Captain would or would not detonate, depending on the truth of the situation. "Well that's all right then, isn't it!" she said brightly. "Once your father knows that *you* know all about it, his reasons and all, I should think he'd be only too delighted to let you stop there, along of Teresa, next year. I mean, every little helps, as the sailor said."

The thought had already struck Kathleen, of course; but, out of kindness to Emma — who, to be quite honest, had been just a little dimwitted about the whole affair — she pretended it hadn't. "Yes!" she exclaimed enthusiastically. "Clever you! I hadn't thought of that." A dreamy, faraway contentment filled her eyes as she gazed out over the darkling landscape. "It's just a matter of waiting for the perfect moment to let him know."

A few daydreams later she burst out with, "Oh, she's such a *nice* person, my half-sister — don't you agree?"

"Yes." Emma nodded. "Very genuine."

FRANK AND HILDA spent most of the day on Staten Island, where several charities supported by the Shaw & Eggar Line were situated. Chief among them, of course, was the Sailors' Snug Harbor, an asylum for aged and infirm seamen; but there was also the Home for Sailors' Children, the Marine Hospital, and the Seamen's Retreat, a convalescent home. Frank recognized several inmates in the Snug Harbor, though not all of them remembered him; they were past remembering anyone.

He found this particular duty dismal beyond words, though nothing would keep him from performing it — nor Hilda, either.

"That man saved my life once," he told her as they left the bedside of one of them, a wizened little dwarf who looked more like a hairy gray ape than anything human. "And the life of everyone on board. Old Keelhaul Joe. One of the few men to be keelhauled in the old navy and live to boast of it. We were in the South China Sea, in the middle of a typhoon, shipping 'em green and as close as *that* to foundering. The old *Cathay Voyager*, remember her?"

"That's going back," Hilda said. "That was only your second command, wasn't it? Kathleen was no more than two."

"Aye." They paused at the door of the ward and stared back at the old sailor. "She was almost dipping her yards. Men were falling out of the shrouds like ripe apples. But that old fellow there clung like a leech and close-reefed the main top singlehanded. The only sail she was carrying." He shook his head forlornly. "And look at him now — he couldn't tie a bootlace."

He clenched his fists and squeezed them tight several times. Holding his arm, Hilda could feel the muscles rippling and she knew he was relishing the strength that was in him yet — and, perhaps, wondering how long it might be before he fell into the same wretchedness as that poor old sailor. "At least he's dry and warm in here," she told him.

"Aye," he agreed, but with little cheer. "Yet I hope I may go some swifter way than that."

"Oh come, dear!" she tried to encourage him with a laugh as they went out into the corridor. "It's a long time before such wishes need fly."

"It seems it, I know. But when you said just now about Kathleen being only two, and yet I can remember that typhoon as if it were yesterday — and what's the girl now? Nearly eighteen. She'll be married before we know it. It's all just flashed by, hasn't it."

"Oh dear, oh dear!" Hilda shivered and took out her watch. "We've done our duty, don't you think? Let's go back to Manhattan and see if there's a theatre show or something."

He stopped and stared at her in surprise. "Theatre?" he echoed. "You?"

"Why not?" she asked. "We could go to the Winter Garden. We could get a bite to eat there, too. Or Barnum's Museum. I've heard that's very instructive. They've lots of exhibits of ..."

"Whatever pleases you most, my dear." The tilt of his head and the look in his eye conveyed that he still found such suggestions extraordinary, coming as it did from her.

"Talking of Kathleen … and getting married, and so on," she remarked when they were on the ferry back to the Whitehall pier.

"Yes?" he replied guardedly.

"Well, probably nothing will come of it," she said, as if she were already soothing ruffled feathers, "but you remember that Mrs Burgoyne who played such a large part in organizing our visit? Well, she has a son, Carleton — though everyone else calls him Chuck, which I think is extremely undignified. Anyway, he's just six months older than Kathleen and … well, they became rather sweet on each other over Christmas."

"How sweet?"

"A little bit in Chicago and quite a lot in Boston."

"Hm!" He sank into his thoughts for a long moment. "Eighteen-year-olds!" was all he said when he emerged again.

"I know." She gave a sympathetic sigh. "It's absurdly young to be considering anything serious — but of course they don't see it in that light. To them it's the one great passion of their lives. We were so much more sensible in our day."

Eighteen? He thought of Jenny. He thought at once of Teresa, and tried not to. "Weren't we just," he said. Then taking his cue from her tone, seeing what was expected of him, he went on, "The question is do we allow it to die a natural death? Or do we artificially prolong it by saying no at every turn?"

"It's a terrible dilemma. I wonder what Daphne would advise? I sometimes think she understands Kathleen better than anyone. Perhaps we'll postpone any decision until we're back in Highbury?"

He understood then that she had merely wanted to alert him to the problem and to leave it simmering in his mind for a week or so. He was quite willing to oblige. "Perhaps we'll let it run," he said. "It might even fly. Quite a catch for her, eh? I suppose he'll be taking over the family business sooner or later? Chicago."

"That seems to be the idea. After he comes down from Yale."

A twitch in his arm startled her. "Is anything the matter?" she asked.

He gave an awkward laugh. "Somebody walked over my grave. Oh, it's visiting all those old hands … staring death in the face."

The rest of the day passed pleasantly enough; they particularly enjoyed the American curiosities in Barnum's Museum. They were walking west on Forty-Second Street, down to the Shaw & Eggar pier, when he reverted to the subject of Kathleen and her new beau.

"In the normal course of events," he said judiciously, "I'd be inclined to let it burn itself out. I mean, if he lived round the corner in Highbury. But, what with absence making the heart grow fonder and so forth, and all the Atlantic between them, I think we'd better put our foot down at once and tell her there can be no question of pursuing this American liaison. We simply cannot permit it."

"If you think so, dear." Hilda knew better than to oppose him head on; there were more effective ways to change his mind without his realizing it. Daphne would most certainly have to be called in now. Suddenly she gave a little skip and a laugh. "Well, talk of the devil! Coo-ee! Kathleen!"

They were more on Shaw & Eggar territory now than in Manhattan proper; she felt able to call out like that. But a moment later she stopped dead and the smile left her face. "Well, I'll be damned!"

That stopped Frank in his tracks, too; he could not remember the last time he'd heard his wife use such language.

The two parents stood in the pool of one street light; the two girls in the pool of the next one down; between them, a gulf of darkness. Hilda waved them to go on, implying they could meet more congenially on board.

"What was all that?" Frank asked.

"Didn't you recognize her?"

"Kathleen?"

"No, the other one. I *knew* there was something familiar about her ..."

"Emmeline Harding? The stewardess. She must have been Kathleen's chaperone today."

Hilda turned to him in astonishment. "You mean Emma! Emma Harding. You even know her name and you still don't recognize her? Oh, if I hadn't been so anxious to discover *your* whereabouts yesterday — no, Tuesday!"

"Of course I recognize her. She's been with the *Pride of Liverpool* since her maiden voyage."

"Oh, Frank! She used to work for *us!* She was an upstairs maid at Highbury New Park. I gave her the boot two years ago." She bit her lip.

"I can't believe it," he told her. Not a flicker of a muscle betrayed him but the electric juice of fear ran through his veins like heady wine. "The line would never have employed her. She must have produced impeccable references."

"Yes, references," Hilda muttered. "That must

certainly be looked into."

"They'd be in the Liverpool office, not here." He could not help remembering that it was the same Miss Harding who had accidentally bumped into him at Grand Central the day before yesterday — except that now he could not be so sure it was such an accident.

"Kathleen must surely have recognized her," Hilda said icily. "And yet she said nothing. This is some conspiracy between them. Oh!" She stamped her feet in fury. "I have never, never trusted her. I know she's our daughter but there's some streak of deceit and treachery in her. She's too clever by half. I'm sorry to say this, Frank, but I think our voyage home is going to turn into a misery for all of us."

"Are you sure about this, my dear? One glimpse under a street lamp ...?"

"And the name Emma Harding! Don't ask me if I'm sure."

"What do you propose doing, then?"

She thought rapidly, licking her lips like a cat — or that was the image it conjured in Frank's mind. "The minute we get on board, you distract Kathleen. Take her and show her the bridge, or the engine room, or something. Show her your cabin. I want to have it out with young Miss *Emmeline* Harding before she realizes the game is up!"

THE BRIDGE AND ITS miraculous instruments did not seem to capture his daughter's interest. Frank, knowing that his wife would make quite a meal of poor Miss Harding, began to cast around desperately for some other distraction. "Would you care to visit the engine room?" he asked. "You could see the other end of this telegraph system."

"Is it different?" she inquired.

He had to admit it was identical. "What then?" he asked. "I know! You never saw my cabin, did you! Would you care to take tea with the captain, Miss Morgan? I tell you, there are ladies on this boat who would fight for the privilege — or there will be by tonight."

Proudly she offered him her arm and let him lead her below. He asked her what sort of day she'd had, and she, forgetting that her original suggestion about taking the ferry out to Atlantic Highlands had been a ruse to cover an excursion up the Hudson to Emma's favourite woods, blurted out what a wonderful walk they'd had beneath the trees, and the deer they'd seen, and how crisp everything had been in the snow ... and she only managed to keep it up, after she realized her error, because, incredibly, he didn't seem to notice at all!

He was distracted over something; she wondered if this wouldn't be the moment to tell him what she knew. After all, to save it for a later day might smack of duplicity when the truth finally emerged. On the other hand, he of all people, would also appreciate her ability *not* to speak of it, even to him. She decided against it for the moment.

The rituals of tea time were sufficient diversion for a while; then, when the steward had withdrawn, her father said, rather sternly, "I can't pretend to know what's going on, but perhaps you can enlighten me? Does the name Emma Harding mean anything to you?"

A slice of caraway cake was poised half-way between her plate and her teeth; it required a supreme act of will to force it all the way. "So Mama recognized her," she said flatly, in a voice that seemed remote and alien.

"Kathleen!" he barked.

She forced her eyes to look at his, which were pitiless. She forced herself not to flinch. "Yes," she said. "I did know." She smiled. "But so did you. Larry told me he told you about her."

He hadn't expected that! He shook his head. "Not her name — and certainly not her history. Otherwise, d'you think I'd have allowed her to set so much as one toe on board?"

Typical Larry, she thought glumly — always a little braver in his memory than he was in fact.

"But with you it's different." His finger stabbed the air a fraction of an inch short of her breastbone. "You *knew!* So kindly explain, miss — and you'd better have very good reason."

"I hope I have, sir," she replied as meekly as possible. "At least they seem good to me — and by principles I have learned from you and Mama."

He nodded tersely. "That much I doubt — but I'll give you the benefit of it for the moment."

She described, in the most neutral terms she could manage, the circumstances surrounding Emma's dismissal, implying — without putting it in so many words — that it had been grossly unfair of Mama not even to give Emma the chance to explain her ambiguous remark. She described Emma's movements up until the moment she set her bags down at the tram stop, and then, as if the question referred to her present tale, said, out of the blue, "Do you think members of the same family should have secrets from each other, Papa? Important secrets, I mean? Me from Larry? Larry from me?" Then, pointedly avoiding his eyes, she added, "Me from you? You from me?"

He realized at once that she knew something. The daughter he had left behind in London a month ago would never have dared pose such a question. "Perhaps not," he replied cautiously. Then he realized that the paterfamilias who had left London a month ago would never have responded so mildly to such a piece of impertinence, either. "At least I hope you would keep no important secrets from me, my dear," he added.

"I'll tell you then." At last she laid the piece of cake back on her plate; her finger and thumb had actually met inside it. She licked a few crumbs and seeds off her hand and went on to tell him how Emma, smarting with the injustice of her dismissal, had resolved to revenge herself on the family through Lawrence, who had always shown a sort of young-mannish interest in her. "Except that, alas, she really fell in love with him — and he with her."

"So it was *he* who gave her a good character. That's what he was working his way round to confessing that day!"

Kathleen drew a deep breath and said, "No, Papa. I'm afraid that was me. I gave her a reference in the name of a Miss Kathleen Dowty."

"I can hardly believe what I'm hearing."

She nodded gravely.

He shook his head at her folly.

Kathleen, who had expected a bolt of wrath from the heavens at her confession could hardly believe what *she* was hearing. She went on with the defence she had prepared against his anger. "And I'm not ashamed of it, either. I considered I was doing no more than right a terrible wrong. I wouldn't expect you, or even want you, to agree openly, but Mama *did* do her a terrible wrong. Anyway, has Emma ever let you down? Has she ever been anything other than an exemplary stewardess?"

"She has been an exemplary stewardess," he agreed evenly. "As to whether or not she has let me down ..."

"I didn't mean letting you down. I meant the *Pride of Liverpool*."

"As to her letting me down," he insisted, "that remains to be seen."

Until that moment the determination had been growing within Kathleen to tell him all she knew; but now, for some obscure reason, every instinct she possessed warned against it. He was too calm, too watchful. It was as if he had suddenly leaped ahead of her and was waiting to catch her — whether in jest or otherwise she could not tell.

"The way I judge Larry," she said carefully, "is ... all right, he had a secret to guard. And, or so he imagined, he had good reason to keep it from me. But the truth is, it very nearly led to disaster for both of them."

He licked his lower lip and nodded for her to continue.

"She had to get away from him, or they'd have destroyed each other."

"Why?"

"Because they loved each other — but expected completely different things from it. She had no illusions about marrying him. In fact, he's asked her time without number and she's always refused."

His eyebrows rose in surprise.

"Indeed she has. She thinks he'll make a great career on the Baltic and ought to marry someone of his own class."

He pursed his lips. "But he's going to run away to sea, isn't he? That's what I've been expecting."

"You should tell him that, not me."

He smiled at last — the first warm and genuine smile for some time. "I feel I've never really known you, Kathleen."

For a moment she was too moved to go on. Then she swallowed the incipient lump in her throat and resumed her tale. "I think he will run away. But Emma's equally sure he won't."

"Perhaps she'll give in and marry him now," he said. "She sounds like one of the most sensible young ladies imaginable. Just what the boy needs."

Kathleen frowned. "Why now?" she asked.

"Never mind. You were saying — about Lawrence's secret and why it almost spelled ..."

"Oh yes. She wouldn't marry him but she'd happily have settled for" — she cleared her throat awkwardly — "the next best thing."

He nodded almost imperceptibly.

"Whereas Larry ... oh, I don't know what he wanted of her, but not that. Something huge and romantic and impossible. Something she had no idea how to give him. So they were destroying each other. And I could see it happening so clearly. That was why I persuaded her to apply for the position here — and why I perjured my immortal soul to help her."

"I see." He nodded, as if he were sorting this information into the proper regions of his mind. "And ... his secret?"

"Well, don't you see? He thought it was secret from me, but really I knew it. I not only knew it, I *approved*. Absolutely. I know what the world would make of it." She smiled as if she'd made a silly error. "I mean I *knew* what the world would make of it, but even so I saw no wrong in it. So ... well, if only he'd had the sense to *tell* me, it would have saved so much heartache." After a silence she added, "Or d'you think that just shows how young I am?"

She heard the breath rushing in and out of his nostrils. "Sometimes it's not nearly so easy as that," he said at last. "Suppose that instead of telling you flatly all about it ... suppose Lawrence had merely given you to *understand* that he knew that you knew. Wouldn't that have done just as well?"

"I suppose so," she replied dubiously.

His smile broadened still further. "Good!" he exclaimed. "I think that's one of the big differences between being a child and being grown up. The difference between the secrets of childhood and those of the grown-up world."

Her smile became equally broad at that, for at last she saw what he was *really* talking about. "Yes, of course it would have done," she said — as if the truth had been staring her in the face all along.

"And now," he added, rubbing his hands cheerily, "the trick will be to persuade Miss Emmeline Harding to marry young Lawrence after all."

She frowned.

"Because I'm afraid your mother has recognized her and taken it into her head to have her dismissed once again."

HILDA FOUND EMMA coming out of Walter Grandison's stateroom bearing a tray of dirty crockery and half-eaten seed cake. "I want you, miss!" she snapped. "And I'm sure you know why."

Mrs Glover was on the scene at once; her ears had a special sensitivity to that particular tone of voice from anywhere in the first-class area. "Is anything the matter, Mrs Morgan?" she asked anxiously.

"I fear so, Mrs Glover," Hilda said primly. "But I shall be able to tell you more before we sail." She hooked a finger at Emma and strode off toward her own stateroom.

Emma looked hopelessly at the tray, at the head stewardess, and at the departing back of her old enemy. "Well? Give it me!" Mrs Glover said furiously, as if Emma must have arranged this bit of awkwardness on purpose. "And if you give the Captain's wife any lip ..." An upraised finger completed the threat.

Emma held her head high as she strode off down the corridor — though it was more a gesture of self-encouragement than an expression of her true feelings at that moment.

"Well, Harding," Hilda said coldly when Emma was still no more than half-way through the door. "Here's a pretty pickle! I trust you have some explanation? For I'm sure *I* can't think of one. Shut the door!"

"Explanation for what, Mrs Morgan?" she replied, wondering why she was not feeling more nervous at this encounter. Two years ago she would have been quaking with terror, unable to stammer out the slightest defence. Never mind "would have been,"

342

she thought, two years ago she *was* in that condition. But not now. She was still apprehensive, of course, but quite in command of herself. She took a deep breath and gave a cold little smile.

"You know very well what for, you impudent ... and how dare you smile like that!"

"Have I given cause for criticism in my work, Mrs Morgan?" Emma asked. "Has any passenger complained? I'm told my last report from Mrs Glover was highly complimentary."

"*I* have complained," Hilda cried.

"But I'm not the stewardess for this stateroom, madam."

Hilda levelled a trembling finger at her. The girl's calm was most unnerving. "Now see here, miss — none of your clever ways with me. I know you of old."

"I beg your pardon, Mrs Morgan, but I believe you never knew me at all." Emma startled even herself at this effrontery, but, now she was committed to it, she made not the smallest gesture of withdrawal. Instead she stood calmly and waited for the explosion.

It didn't come.

Hilda opened and closed her mouth like a fish in stale water. Little gurgling noises of fury escaped her throat. She continued to point her trembling finger at the stewardess but was too apoplectic to speak a word.

Emma went to the bathroom and drew her a glass of drinking water. "Sit down and take a sip of this, madam," she said on her return. "Shall I send for the doctor."

"How dare you!" Hilda found her voice at last and dashed the glass from Emma's grasp with one swipe of her hand. "How dare you patronize me!"

343

Emma bent to retrieve the tumbler, which was miraculously intact. "What is it you wish to know, madam. Perhaps if you asked me a direct question?"

"Indeed, I'll tell you what I wish to know. I wish to know how you secured this position after *I* had dismissed you without a character for making lewd remarks to my daughter. Who was so misguided as to employ you after that? *That's* what I wish to know."

"Whoever it was, madam, it obviously satisfied the Shaw & Eggar Line. I'm sure they scrutinize such items most carefully."

"You mean you won't tell me."

"I mean it's a matter between me and the Line, madam. It's not something I'd tell any *other* passenger, either."

The door opened at that moment and Mrs Glover came in. "Excuse my interruption, Mrs Morgan, but I happened to be passing and I heard you ask this stewardess ..."

"I'm not sure I require your help, Mrs Glover," Hilda said icily.

"Oh, but I can tell you, madam. It was a Miss Dowty of Highbury. I know it because it was I who scrutinized every character sent in."

"Miss Dowty?" Hilda barked. "There's no such person — not in Highbury. And it certainly wasn't *Mrs* Dowty. That I'd swear. You say you scrutinized them all?"

Mrs Glover smiled. "Not one from Miss Dowty, of course. The name is so well known in shipping circles. A Miss Kathleen Dowty it was, if memory serves me correctly."

In the corner of her eye Hilda saw the Harding creature suppress a smirk. She remembered Kathleen walking arm in arm with her, too. Summoning all her reserves she said, "Ah yes, of course. Miss *Kathleen* Dowty. I had forgotten her. She keeps very much to herself. Very well." She even managed a tight-lipped little smile at Emma. "That is satisfactorily cleared up, Harding. But I still have one or two bones to pick with you." She turned and stared at the head stewardess. "Thank you Mrs Glover. That will be all. I shall require no further information. Nor do I expect you to invigilate our conversation. I am quite capable of dealing with this matter myself."

Mrs Glover pressed her lips into a thin line and gathered her shawl about her in an ominous manner that boded no good for Emma when this interview was over.

"So! It was Kathleen," Hilda said when the door was closed once more. "Well that young lady is going to regret the day she was born! I never heard such a thing in all my life."

"If you harm her in the slightest ... the smallest ... if ..." Emma subsided into incoherence. She began to breathe as if she'd run half a mile flat out.

"You'll do what?" Hilda sneered. "You're in no position to make threats, my girl. You should be down on your knees begging me for a second chance. Not that I'd give it you. I shall see to it that you never work again — not within a mile of decent, respectable folk. And don't think I haven't the power to carry out this threat."

Suddenly Emma's control snapped. "Oh, it's threats is it, my lady!" she sneered in as fine a manner as her former mistress. "Well let me tell you mine."

"How dare you!" Hilda repeated. But now some terrible intensity in the other's manner held her transfixed. All the more impressive was the fact that the girl spoke in the softest murmur.

"I dare because you pushed me to it," Emma told her. "I shan't say what it is, but there's *that* I know about Captain Morgan which, if repeated to the right party, would send him directly to prison."

Hilda gasped at this intolerable insult. She was about to scream for Mrs Glover when she caught sight of Emma's beady eye and upraised finger; it strangled the cry in her throat.

"Now you listen," Emma almost whispered. "It wouldn't only send the Captain to prison. Larry would have to leave the Baltic. Neil would have to change his name if he wanted to stay at sea."

"How dare you refer to them in such familiar terms!" At the back of her mind Hilda wondered why she was whispering, too. It lent such credence to the girl's preposterous theatricals.

"Lis-sen!" she went on remorselessly. "And no one will marry Kathy. And you'll have to sell up in Highbury and go and live in France or somewhere."

"Pshaw! This is absurd. It's sheer bluff."

"Maybe it is," Emma agreed with a grim smile. "But there's only one way you'll ever find out. And then it'll be too late to take it all back. You ruin my life" — her finger came to rest an inch from Hilda's nose, and it was steady as a rock — "and you'll ruin the Captain's, your own, your children's, and ... Well, it's enough to be going on with."

"No!" Hilda said — though there was now more fear than fury in her voice. "I can't accept this. I simply can't accept it. You'll have to tell me more."

Emma shook her head slowly. "I don't have to do anything, Mrs Morgan. Except my work here on the *Pride of Liverpool* — which I trust I shall continue to do to the satisfaction of all my passengers. Now, was there anything more?"

"You must tell me something," Hilda pleaded, clutching at her arm. "What possible secret could you know about a good, fine man like the Captain that would have such dreadful consequences? It's simply not possible."

Emma closed her eyes in an agony of indecision. What to say? What could she say that would give not the slightest real clue but which would enable the old bag to test her assertion. At last she said, "Ask the Captain how he feels about letting Kathy go and visit Chuck when he's at Yale."

"Ha! Got you!" Hilda was all triumphant again. "It so happens I did!"

"And he agreed?" Emma asked in amazement.

Then Hilda remembered that Frank's willingness to consider such a visit had all been when he thought Chuck would be in Chicago. Once he had heard about Yale he'd changed his tune completely and said it was out of the question. "No," she had the honesty to admit.

But by then her face had already said it for her.

ALTER GRANDISON HAD HIS eye on Hilda from the moment he saw her come aboard in Manhattan — in fact, he'd had his eye on her for the past twenty-two years. His first serious attempt to seduce her had been at a ball given by Lloyd's in the City, when they were both only twenty. Fortunately — though he had not thought so at the time — she hadn't even been aware of what was going on. What a waste it would have been, he now thought, as he watched her move gracefully about the salon, playing hostess to this tiny, glittering world. And so for the past two decades he had watched her slowly ripen, like some exotic fruit whose maturity is gained in decades rather than seasons; and now she was close to the moment of her perfection.

On that particular evening, the Wednesday after they sailed from New York and just two days before they were to arrive in Liverpool, he was especially watchful. Something had changed in her since their voyage out on the *Champlain* and their time in Chicago. There was a new light in her eye, somewhere between wistfulness and bewilderment — and a third quality, too, even more enigmatic. He trembled at the thought of possessing her now, for she posed the challenge of the unknown, and there were few women left in that category — to him at least.

Around eleven o'clock, the hour when she usually gathered her ridiculous little chirping bird of a daughter and went below to their stateroom, he saw her drift out onto the promenade deck by the starboard door, the moonlit side. She was unaccompanied. So far, so good, he thought as he slipped out on the port side and made large strides toward the glazed-in portion up forr'ard. His instinct was right. She was sauntering toward the same area on her side. There were several others about, all well wrapped against the winter's night and enjoying the brilliant moonlight upon the great silver-backed rollers. Among them, he noticed with slight annoyance, was little Kathleen Morgan, deep in earnest conversation with the sick-bay nurse, who was allowed on the promenade deck after ten in the evening. (He knew as much because she was one of his three reserve bets in case Hilda failed him.)

His manservant appeared with his coat and hat, just in time for him to settle it at a rakish angle on his head and give it an insouciant tip in her direction. "I feel utterly naked without it, Hilda," he said. "Aren't we the most absurd of God's creatures!"

She laughed. "Why d'you say that, Walter?"

So he was "Walter" now — a bit of a change since the *Champlain*. "Because of our obsession with rules, don't you know. Tell a man he's free and the first thing he says is, 'Thanks very much, but what are the rules?' Now don't you call that absurd?"

"And women? What do they say?"

"You *are* the rules, Hilda. Nay, more than mere rules — you are the Law itself. You draw the boundaries. We try to get our toes over 'em." He slipped off his coat. "Here, put this around you — just like old times!"

"You mean I still drown in it."

"Well, tell me about Boston. I was sorry to have to miss that."

She did not immediately answer.

He gave an awkward laugh. "*Some*thing must have happened."

"I wish I knew." She gave an awkward laugh, too, and laid her hand briefly on his arm.

"Here, you're shivering," he said. "Let's go back inside."

"No!" Her response was immediate. She went to the rail and pressed her forehead against the cold glass. They were immediately below the centre of the bridge. Frank must be up there, not fifteen feet above her — and yet not within a thousand miles of her, either.

"Is something amiss?" Walter asked. "You know I'd do anything to help."

349

"Dear Walter," she murmured, giving him a grateful smile. "I know you would." Anxiety crept back into her voice: "You are the very soul of discretion, aren't you? I mean, nothing I said to you would go any further?"

"If you asked it, I would carry it to the grave, my dear. So ask away."

She hesitated a long while. He knew well enough to say nothing. At last she sighed and told him, "It's so awkward."

"Not really. It's mostly imagination makes it so."

"I have to begin by asking you a highly indiscreet question, you see."

He just managed to withhold the facetious reply that rose to his throat, for he suddenly twigged that she was testing him. If he were jocular now, she would turn it all aside and they'd have a pleasant, frivolous conversation that would get nowhere. "How could anything you say be indiscreet, my dear?" he asked solemnly. "Haven't I told you already — I am the soul of discretion."

She drew a deep breath and plunged in. "You have known a number of women, haven't you." She let out the rest of her lungful with a rush; now there was no turning back.

"Too many," he replied automatically.

"Yes, I remember you said that before. But when I say 'known' ..." She swallowed heavily.

"You mean in the biblical sense. The answer again is yes, I fear."

"Why d'you say that? 'I fear.' Do you really feel so much remorse?"

Her questions were becoming awkward. These were uncharted waters for him — certainly in the kind of conversation that, he hoped, would lead to a seduction. They were now navigating on the rim of that dangerous whirlpool called Truth. And yet some madcap instinct urged him to give it a try. "No," he admitted. "I cannot lay claim to any great helping of remorse."

"Why d'you do it, then? Please, I'm not asking these questions idly or pruriently. I truly desire to know."

"Pleasure?" he offered.

"And is it? You remember on the *Champlain*, when you said you'd rather spend five minutes in true conversation with me than ... oh, I can't remember exactly, but ... you remember?"

He decided to plunge in with both feet. His usual method of seduction was to let a woman tell him all her troubles, no matter how long it took — hours, days ... weeks, even. And he never met a woman who didn't have troubles. All he needed to do was look sympathetic and make sympathetic noises — while at the same time withholding any sign of genuine approval. That was most important. The victim had to feel she was getting a good hearing from someone who understood exactly what troubled her — yet somehow she was failing to win him over. She would then redouble her efforts to please him; it was an instinct in every woman to do so. She would tease him, cajole him, flirt with him, until, in the end, it was she who seduced him, granting him the ultimate Favour as the only way to win his support.

But with Hilda, something urged him to stand the entire process on its head.

"Listen, my dear." He laid a hand on her arm. "Try to forget everything that has ever happened — and *not* happened — between us these last ... how long is it? Twenty-five years! Forget that through all that time you're one of the few women I ever really desired. Forget that even now I'm wondering by what magical-impossible-undreamed-of means I could *know* you, too. *I* do — forget it all, I mean. I set it all aside. I clear the decks of all that ancient lumber, and I promise you this: If in any way, by anything I may tell you, or any service I may perform for you ... if I can help you out of your present troubles, you never met a helper more willing and able."

Recklessly she laid her head against his arm. He, more cautious, glanced about them and was glad to see there was no one within fifty paces. Kathleen and the nurse were gone. Certainly no one could see them here, for all the lights in the sheltered portion had been turned out to enable passengers to enjoy the brightness of the moon. He bent toward her, put a finger under her chin and gently raised her lips to his.

Her mouth was soft and slack, her kiss passionate. "Yesss!" she whispered when they broke.

"Mmm?" he queried.

"You know. What you said."

He swallowed audibly. "Here?"

"Now!" She pressed herself to him and writhed like a kitten.

"Come to my stateroom ..." he began.

She fumbled at his fly.

He glanced around again. There was a stanchion behind them, and behind that a pile of deck furniture, sheeted and lashed down. And between it and the steel walls of the smoking room there was just enough room for a couple in flagrante. "Over there!" he said, dragging her with him and undoing his fly as he went. The old fellow was rampant tonight, and giving off heat like a furnace. Her fingers encircled it with a contented gasp. "Twenty years of longing," he murmured as he struggled to lift her skirts and petticoats.

There was someone coming up the deck on the port side. A man and a woman, arguing. She wanted to go back inside and continue dancing. He wanted to cool off. They would stop and dispute the matter, then walk a pace or two, then stop again.

"Oh for heaven's sake make up your minds!" Walter cursed under his breath. "One way or the other."

Had he not addressed them aloud, even though it was in a whisper heard only by her, Hilda might have gone on ignoring them. But his words raised the spectre of their reality, the threat they posed by their nearer approach.

She lowered her dress and tugged a flap of shirt over ... that thing of his.

"Eh?" he croaked. "No, no, it'll be all right."

"What'll be all right?" she asked. "I don't know what you're talking about."

For a long moment he froze; and then, with what could have been a sigh — or it could have been a mere mechanical exhalation of a pent-up breath — replied, "Nothing. Nonsense, as usual. Pay no attention."

The couple settled their argument — that is, the woman persuaded the man that if *he* didn't dance with her, she knew one man who certainly would. Walter just stood there, holding his breath yet again, praying she wouldn't blurt out the fellow's name. Then they moved off. Quick as could be, before anyone else might turn up and hang them for a sheep when they had barely glanced at the lamb, they hopped back into the fully public part of the deck.

"I wonder who that woman might have been talking about?" Hilda mused.

Walter cleared his throat tendentiously and they both laughed — not because it was so funny but because they needed a laugh at that moment.

"Thank heavens I didn't tell her," Walter added, almost under his breath.

"Tell her what?" Hilda was forced to ask.

"Oh," he replied airily, as if it were a very trivial matter, "I know a very *tactful* hôtel in Maidstone. I sometimes spend an idyllic Fri-to-Mon there. Thank heavens I didn't tell *her!*"

HILDA LAY IN HER bed, as far from sleep as she had earlier felt she was from Francis. Curiously enough, now that she had betrayed him — in her mind, anyway — she felt a little closer — which sounded mad. Perhaps it was. If one were going mad, she mused, would one even be aware of it? Her image of a madwoman was of a naked, hairless creature with her limbs all contorted, crawling in the straw and laughing at nothing. She remembered her grandmother telling her of being taken as a little girl to see the mad people in the Bedlam; it had been a sort of Sunday treat in those days. That was where the image came from, to be sure, for she herself had never seen a madwoman. Or never knowingly seen one — and there was the rub. How *would* you know?

They would do mad things without believing them to be mad.

Well! And what had she and Walter Grandison done, or nearly done, that evening? If that was not madness itself, then nothing was. But did it feel mad? She had to admit it did not, neither at the time nor now, thinking about it in calmer mood. Then what had it been, she wondered? Exciting? Certainly. Novel? Beyond a doubt! Thrilling? Yes, it was the most thrilling few minutes she had ever known.

She tried to imagine that discreet hôtel in Maidstone — the discreet room with the discreet furnishings and the discreetly turned-down bed.

"I will!" she said out loud.

"Mama?" Kathleen turned over beside her and rose on one elbow.

"Sorry. I was thinking aloud, that's all. I didn't mean to awaken you."

"First sign of madness," Kathleen joked. "You didn't wake me, actually. I've been lying here listening to you grunting and sighing for about half an hour. You shouldn't have stayed out on deck so long. I'm sure you must have caught a chill."

"Chill!" Hilda threw the coverings off her side of the bed. "It's more like a fever. I wish they'd go away. You wait! Your turn will come!"

"Poor Mama!" She reached hesitantly across and patted her mother's shoulder, ending with a reassuring squeeze.

Hilda clutched at her hand. "I love you very much, Kathleen," she said out of the blue.

"Oh!" The girl was nonplussed. Her mother had never said such a thing to her before.

Hilda gave a little laugh, awkward and hesitant. "Sorry. I didn't mean to embarrass you."

"Oh, you don't embarrass me," Kathleen lied. "It's just so ... I mean, I love you, too, only we're usually too stiff-upper-lip to say things like that in our family, do we."

"We don't say anything, really," Hilda sighed.

"What is it?" Greatly daring, Kathleen leaned across the space between them and kissed her mother's cheek. Half of her hoped it was what she thought it might be; half of her dreaded it.

"I was thinking how demonstrative Mrs Burgoyne is with Chuck, demonstrative of her affections, I mean. No English mother would behave like that, would she. Not in Highbury, anyway. We'd all be too afraid of turning our sons into milksops. Yet look at Chuck! You'd think of a hundred other words to describe him and never come near 'milksop'!"

"A thousand!" Kathleen agreed. She grazed her mother's shoulder with the cold tip of her nose. "So that was your New Year's resolution, eh?"

"Not consciously. I'm beginning to wonder if our consciences are any guide — no! I don't mean consciences, I mean conscious*nesses*, or whatever you could call them. Our conscious minds … oh dear, I've lost the thread now. We've seen so much and … done so much. My head's all in a whirl."

"Can I ask you something?"

"What?"

"About Emma Harding."

"Oh dear."

Kathleen groped for her mother's hand and lay down again, clasping it to her breast. "You needn't answer if you don't want to. I mean, it's none of my business."

"Isn't it?" For the first time Hilda laughed — a little dry chuckle.

"Papa told me you were bent on dismissing her again. I was going to throw myself overboard if you did."

Hilda shivered suddenly and pulled the clothes back over herself — rather awkwardly since Kathleen would not release her left hand. "Why does she mean so much to you?" she asked.

"She's the best friend I ever had. And she's such a wise and sensible person. Has Papa told you about her?"

A little squirt of fear erupted in Hilda's innards. "Papa? What does he know of her? He was hardly ever home when she …"

"Only what I told him. I thought he might have told you, that's all."

"Oh!" Her tone spoke of the forlorn nature of such a belief.

"You know Lawrence wants to marry her?"

Hilda gave a start and struggled to sit upright in the bed. Kathleen pulled at her hand to make her stay down. "Don't worry. She won't accept him. She's turned him down scores of times."

"She's turned *him* down?"

"Yes. I think she's wrong, because she loves him too, you know, but she says it would never work. It wouldn't last."

"Well!" Suddenly Hilda felt so weak she was rather glad to be lying down. "But how do they meet? If these proposals are so frequent."

"She has rooms in Upper Street."

"Oh, has she indeed! Well, I suppose she can afford them. They make a small fortune these stewardesses, you know. But do you mean she entertains Lawrence in these rooms? He actually pays calls on her?"

"Don't worry. It's nothing like you imagine."

"I'm surprised *you* even know about such things. When I was your age …"

"Oh, Mama!"

"What?"

"Don't pretend you were so ignorant at my age."

"At seventeen? I most assuredly …"

"Jolly nearly eighteen."

"Until the day I married your father, I knew nothing."

"D'you think that was good?"

For a long time her mother was silent; when at last she spoke it was to an earlier point: "So, all that sort of thing has been going on behind our backs all these months and months. I do think *you* might have trusted me enough to tell me something of it."

"Why? You couldn't have stopped it. They're both earning their own keep — and you know what your opinion of Emma was. Incidentally, you didn't answer my question. Why *did* you change your mind about her?"

Her mother's tone was so offhand, so dismissive, that Kathleen knew she was lying. The realization came with something of a shock. She knew parents told little fibs to their children — white lies to avoid all the unpleasant and seamy things in life. But not lies like this. "Oh," Hilda said with a yawn, "she told me I'd been unfair to dismiss her without even giving her a chance to explain — which, on mature reflection, I saw to be true. So I gave her the chance there and then and, I'm ashamed to say, she showed me I had, indeed, been wrong all the way. Still, if I hadn't dismissed her, she wouldn't have got this rather splendid position on the *Pride of Liverpool* — so there was a silver lining after all." After a pause she added, "There's just one thing I forgot to ask her. Perhaps you know."

"What was that?"

"How did she manage to get a character? I must look it up if I remember when we get to Liverpool."

Kathleen was silent a while and then said, "Let sleeping dogs lie."

"Perhaps you're right. I still can't get over Lawrence.

All these months! Treachery inside a family is so complicated, isn't it."

"Treachery?" Kathleen objected to the word.

"Betrayal, then. You can't deny it was a kind of betrayal." She sighed and added, "But by no means the worst."

That settled the affair! Short of actually putting it into words, her mother could not make it plainer that she knew all about Papa and Teresa — or, rather, she *didn't* know all, but just enough to make it seem like a betrayal. Kathleen decided there'd never be a better moment to set her mother's mind at rest. She clasped her hand tighter yet and said, "If you think it's a betrayal, Mama, you've got completely the wrong end of the stick. I thought it was, too, but the moment I met her I saw it couldn't be. You'd know it, too, if you could only see her."

"See who?" Hilda gave a nervous little laugh. "I'm sorry, dear, but I assure you I have no idea what you're ..."

Kathleen chuckled and shook her mother's hand. "Honestly! There's no need to pretend. I've met her. I know all about it."

"Again I have to ask — met who?"

"Teresa! Jenny Bright's daughter. The girl who calls herself Mrs Morgan."

Hilda froze.

Kathleen shook her hand even more urgently. "You think it's a betrayal, don't you. But it's not. Papa's shielding her — pretending to be married to her because of the baby. But she's Jenny Bright's daughter, so she's the last person on earth Papa could *really* marry, isn't she."

Out of the silence Hilda asked, "How do you know all this?"

"Oh, it's too complicated to explain. But I told Papa that I thought what he'd done was so noble — and he laughed, just as you'd expect him to."

"How do you know about Jenny Bright?" her mother asked. "She died years before you were born."

"Oh," Kathleen said casually, "there's a picture of her in Aunt Daphne's album, or one of her albums."

"Of course." Hilda came close to laughing, though with relief rather than any humour.

"Why 'of course'?"

"Didn't she tell you? No, I'll bet she wouldn't. Jenny was intended for Brian Dowty. I mean, that was their parents' intentions. But Aunt Daphne had already set her cap at Brian so she persuaded your father to cut in, even though she knew he and I were more or less betrothed."

"But I thought she was your friend!"

"So did I, until then! It led to quite a long estrangement, I can tell you. But of course I learned to accept she didn't *intend* for your father to fall in love with Jenny Bright."

"But he did?"

She felt her mother nod — and then give a brief, silent laugh. "Betrayals, betrayals, all around I see."

The word was much kindlier than "treachery." It had an almost festive ring, like the name of a party game. "Let's play Postman's Knock!" "No, I'm tired of that. Let's play Betrayals!" She went on repeating the word in her own mind while she tried to picture a discreet little hôtel in Maidstone ...

There was no difficulty picturing the man on the discreetly turned-down bed, though. And it wasn't Francis.

T|HE BRIDGE OF the *Pride of Liverpool* had a projecting portion of open deck on either side of the hull. Merseyside humour had dubbed them "bugger-lugs" at first sight, which polite maritime circles had then translated as "side-whiskers," the meaning being the same. At seven bells of the middle watch — or half past three in the morning to his unsleeping wife and daughter in their stateroom below — Frank was standing alone on the port side-whisker, gazing at the setting moon through his binoculars. It was not his watch — the middle watch never is the captain's. Nor was it Wheeler's either; he was deputizing for the third officer who was down with a touch of malaria. It made for a distinct tension on the bridge to have the captain *and* the first officer there at a time when both should be sound asleep.

It is a tradition of the sea that when a captain moves to one half of the bridge, all officers and hands with no instrument to tend in that half move to the opposite side. So Wheeler murmured "Permission, sir?" as he stepped out of the bridge house onto the open deck.

"By all means, Wheeler," Frank said without turning round.

The officer joined him at the rail. When he was "Wheeler" they could talk; when he was "Number One" it was strictly business. "Nothing the matter, I hope, sir?" he said.

Frank grunted.

"Very calm for January."

"We'll pay for it at the equinox. There's a bill for everything in the end." After a pause he lowered his

361

binoculars and, with a brief glance over his shoulder, said, "I've been a bloody fool, Wheeler. Hybris, that's what it was — tempting the gods. What's your opinion?"

"I thought it incautious, sir."

Frank gave a small, humourless chuckle. "A cautious judgement! Did you read that case in the papers last year? An old fellow who died at the age of eighty in Hackney, in the arms of his wife, whom he'd married at the age of eighteen. And all that time ..."

"I remember it," Wheeler said. "It turned out he had another wife ..."

"In Dalston! Only a mile away! Married her at twenty. And for sixty years he'd hopped between them, raised two families — and no one ever twigged."

"I wonder what happened to them."

"The two widows? They moved in together."

Wheeler cleared his throat.

"I know," Frank agreed. "Not much hope of that in my case. Why did I do it, man? D'you remember the old *Pegasus*?"

"Not so old, sir. She's bound for Rio at this very moment."

"It was a different age. D'you remember standing on her deck after we ran her aground — the day before we refloated her? It was a world on its own." After a pause he repeated the phrase: "A world on its own, outside of time. And that was my undoing. It came to an end the very next day, and I didn't realize it."

Wheeler drew a deep breath and said, "Has Mrs Morgan discovered anything, sir?"

"It wasn't for carnal reasons, you know," Frank went on. "It was just that, if I'd lost her then, I ... well, I don't know what I'd have done. Eh? Mrs Morgan?

No. No, she doesn't know a thing. It's my daughter, as a matter of fact. But I'll tell you the most extraordinary thing of all: *She approves!* I was so taken aback I could hardly ..."

"But how on earth did she discover such a thing, I mean learn ... I mean, she's hardly out of the nursery herself, sir."

"I'm not quite sure. We haven't had much chance to talk about it — as you may imagine! One of the stewardesses had a hand in it. Used to be a housemaid of ours. Very 'thick' with Kathleen, as they say in Ireland."

"And she approves, you say? Isn't that extraordinary, sir? May I ask — I hope I'm not trespassing now — but may I ask *how* she conveyed the fact? I mean, did she just out with it?"

"Exactly. Almost the moment they came aboard. I was showing her the bridge and my cabin and the speaking tubes and things and ... out it all came! She'd visited Teresa that very afternoon, seen the baby — everything. And she thoroughly approved! It's put me in a quandary, as you may imagine. I'd almost got over my fear of discovery. And then to find I'd been unmasked by two slips of things like that — barely out of rompers, as you say. And *then* to be told they approve! It beggars the imagination."

"Can the stewardess be trusted, sir? It's the Harding girl, I presume?"

Frank nodded. "I believe so. She didn't have too happy a time of it when she was our housemaid. Mrs Morgan took against her rather hard. She recognized the girl at once, of course, as soon as she came aboard, and was all set to have her dismissed. So if ever there was a time to blurt out what she knew about me, that was it. Yet she held her tongue."

"*And* kept her place here," Wheeler pointed out skeptically.

"That's what I thought, too, of course, but it wasn't so. I haven't told you everything, yet. My younger son, Lawrence, wants to make the girl my daughter-in-law. I'm beginning to think he's a better judge of character than any of us."

"It, ah, mightn't be a bad idea, sir," Wheeler suggested. "Keep it in the family. Give her a vested interest in it."

Frank laughed and clapped him on the shoulder. "You're a tonic, man. Sound, practical advice and no tut-tutting. That's what's called for now. For instance, my daughter has fallen for a young American lad, heir to quite a fortune. And he's going up to 'varsity this autumn. To Yale."

The significance passed the officer by.

"Yale is in New Haven, just a few miles from Fife. Kathleen wishes to go over there and stay with Teresa."

"Aha!"

"You're wrong. I don't believe that's her only cause for approval — though I agree it is very ..." he hesitated.

"Convenient?" Wheeler offered.

Frank nodded. All his good humour deserted him. For a while he stared at the sea, which was now swallowing a bloated, reddish moon. "Love!" he exclaimed. "What a terrible, destructive thing it is! There's Kathleen, not yet eighteen, not old enough to understand one hundredth part of it — yet already it's perverted her moral judgement ... all the values we've struggled to teach her. Yet who am I to talk! It's going to destroy me, too."

THEY DOCKED AT Liverpool the following noon, Thursday. Kathleen and her mother caught the first train to London and, having had almost no sleep the night before, slept all the way, arriving stiff and sore and ready for a proper bed. Frank and Emma caught a later train but travelled at different ends of it. It arrived at Euston close to midnight. Moments after he alighted he caught sight of Lawrence skulking behind a pillar. "She's in the second class, at the back," he told him in passing. "I wouldn't take no for an answer, if I were you."

Emma found Lawrence standing there with his jaw still open. "Catching flies?" she said wearily. "What are you doing here? As if I didn't bleeding know! Why do I bother?"

Lawrence pointed at the barrier, where his father was just surrendering his ticket. "D'you know what he said to me as he swept by? He told me you were farther up the train — and he said I wasn't to take no for an answer."

"Ohmigawd!" She dropped her bag and slumped wearily upon it.

"What?" he asked, filled with sudden concern for her. "What's been happening?"

"Oh, piss off!" she said, in a voice barely above a mumble. "I'm sick to the back teeth with your lot."

"Emma?" he cajoled. "My darling?"

"No!" She closed her eyes as if in pain.

He touched her shoulder hesitantly. "Whatever anyone else may have done, surely you know that *I* mean you no harm?"

"No one means me any harm. D'you think that makes it easier for me?" She stared around listlessly;

the anonymous crowds pressed on, ignoring them both. "That day your mum kicked me out — I should have gone straight down the shirt factory and asked for work. Or the Star and Garter, pulling pints. I should have gone on the game. *Anything!* The worst day's work in my life was standing there, just waiting for you."

"You're hungry," he said confidently. "I'm a bit peckish myself. Let me buy you some supper."

She stared at him in amazement. "Didn't you hear me?"

He grinned and blew her a kiss.

She shook her head but could not suppress the first twitchings of a smile. "My God, you're like the froth on a pint of Whitbread's," she said glumly as she rose, first on one leg, then on the other, groaning and favouring her hips like an old woman. "Come on, then."

"You know the worst thing about you?" she asked after they had gone through the barrier.

"What? There's too much choice."

"You *think* you're going to beat me. You think you're going to wear me down. But you won't, you know. I can be just as stubborn as you."

"The Holborn will still be open. I've never taken you there, have I."

In the cab he seized her hands and pressed them to his lips; she could feel him trembling. "I love you, Emma," he told her. "I think of you night and day. You're all the world to me."

"Do they do a good steak and kidney pie at the Holborn?" she asked.

He lifted one of her knuckles to his eyelid, where he managed to scoop just enough water to call it a teardrop.

"Oh, Larr-ee-ee!" she exclaimed in a perfect mixture of anger and compassion.

"I can't help it," he replied. "Every minute we're apart I'm miserable. I can't do anything without relating it to you. I go through the manifest of a dirty little tramp steamer at East Wall and I think, *Oh, wouldn't Emma love to be here!*"

She pushed him away brusquely, but she laughed, mostly with relief. "You can never be completely serious, can you."

"Can you?" he countered.

She said nothing.

"People who can be utterly serious," he said, sitting up and pulling his glove back on, "are really just a little bit immature, don't you think? Neil, for instance. I mean, if there were gold diplomas for solemnity, he'd sink his ship with them. And yet there's something ... not-quite-grown-up about him, don't you think?"

"You know what I think about your brother, Neil."

"Well, that was a case in point, wasn't it."

"And what about your dad? He can be solemn enough when he wants."

"I used to think so. But now I believe it's all tongue-in-cheek. Or mostly, anyway. The look in his eye when he passed me just now!"

Emma said nothing.

"He's certainly changed since they made him captain of the *Pride of Liverpool*," he went on. "I know you hardly saw him when you worked at Highbury New Park, but surely the other servants told you what sort of man he was?"

"D'you know Kathleen's read all your diaries?" she asked suddenly.

"Eh? What's that got to do with it? Oh — immaturity. I see." He sighed, and then the full implication of her announcement struck him. "I say — has she? The little swine! All of them?"

"So she claims."

He dug her craftily in the ribs. "And she told you. Well, of course, she would, wouldn't she! Since you're the star of them." He chuckled. "So you and she have been discussing me, eh? Well, well now. I must say — that bucks a fellow up, don't you know."

They drew up at the Holborn Restaurant then, a huge edifice on several floors. At that hour of the night, or early morning, it was full of theatre people — from both sides of the lights — gentlemen of the press, and contented revellers stoking up for the long journey home. Lawrence and Emma took a small table in an alcove on the second floor, which was noticeably less crowded than the others. They ordered a mixed grill: sausage, kidney, bacon, lamb cutlet, and fried eggs. As soon as they were seated and alone he returned to the subject. "What did you say about me, eh? You and my inquisitive little sister, the wretch."

She surveyed him coolly and then asked if he really wished to know.

He answered with an uneasy affirmative.

"We were talking about men in general. We just used you as an example."

"How charming."

"Did she write to you about Chuck Burgoyne?"

He nodded. "From Boston — I mean, that's where she wrote from."

"She said he wasn't like any English boy she knew. He'd ask her opinion on something or other and he'd really want to hear the answer."

"I'm sure there's lots of English boys like that. How many has she met?"

"I told her you were the same."

"There you are, then! You're right — she is immature."

"I said it was the worst thing about you."

He laughed and patted her arm.

"Straight!" she assured him. "I mean it. Where I come from, if a man doesn't belt you round the mouth once a week, you begin to think he doesn't love you no more. No one ever taught me how to deal with a man who thinks I'm worth as much as what he is."

"More," he murmured.

"I mean, when you ask my opinion on this or that, or what I think we ought to do, I just get all paralyzed."

"But why?" He laughed weakly, begging her to confess she was joking.

"Because, like I said to her, it frightens me silly. It's like you're asking me to decide for us — and I'm not trained up to it."

He licked his lips and grinned. "You mean, if I grabbed you by the hair and dragged you off to my cave and told you to consider yourself my wife, and don't you dare speak until spoken to ... that would do the trick where all my present wiles fail?"

She considered the question; a faraway look stole into her eyes. "No," she replied at last, with the faintest of sad smiles. "You've spoiled me for all that, too. I can't go back, because I know there's better things in life. And I can't go forward, because they frighten me. I'm not brought up to them."

He felt every last drop of jocularity drain from him. "You know what you're really telling me," he said at last.

"What?"

"You're saying that if I stop pestering you and being calf-sick and stupid and all that sort of thing ...

if I just give you time, you'll probably agree to marry me in the end."

She nodded forlornly, as if to say that good New Year's resolutions were one thing; February the first was another. "I'll tell you something for free," she promised. "It won't be anyone else."

After that the atmosphere between them changed markedly. The tension just seemed to evaporate, and they talked like a pair of cousins who endlessly flirted with the possibility of an affaire between them, though both knew it would never actually begin. They ate their meal with new relish while she told him of amusing things that had happened in New York and on the voyage back. But of her escapade with Kathleen she said nothing.

They had a slight tiff in the cab on the way back to Upper Street, when he told her he was perfectly willing — not to say eager — to go on paying the rent on the rooms and she insisted she was quite able — not to say eager — to look after it herself these days.

As she slipped the key in the lock she glanced quickly up and down the deserted street and then asked him in for a nightcap. "I still got the *same* bottle of port," she announced proudly.

When they were up in her room, she nodded toward the bed and said, "Come on! You know we both want to."

He took up her left hand and, consulting her ring finger as if it were a watch, replied, "No, it's not time yet."

Their eyes met and locked.

"Tell you what," she said. "You spend the night with me and I'll marry you. There — can't say fairer!"

He closed his eyes and shivered. "Reverse the order," he said, "and we'll shake hands on it. Promise."

She laughed and wriggled her hand free. "It's just got to be a battle between you and me, hasn't it!"

He opened his eyes again and found hers still glued to his. In the soft lamplight he thought her the most beautiful creature who ever breathed. He wondered that his heart could manage to go on beating, it was so congested with love and longing and lust for her — tender, ardent, and fierce. "So it would seem," he said at last.

T HE FOLLOWING MORNING, while her parents were dealing with all the correspondence that had piled up in their absence, Kathleen slipped over to her Aunt Daphne's, "just to say hello, and we're back, and what a lovely time we all had," she explained as she tripped to the front door.

"And to tell her all about darling Chuck," Hilda commented to Frank after she had gone.

"And about Emma Harding," he added.

"Yes, I wonder if Daphne knew all along about Emma?" Hilda mused. "I'll bet she did. If Kathleen knew, then Daphne did. She tells her everything."

A little knot of fear curled and uncurled itself in the pit of Frank's stomach. He knew he was alive again.

Kathleen stayed to luncheon; it took that long just to exhaust the wonders of the *Champlain*, the railroad to Chicago, Chicago itself, "Yuletide" in America, the marvel of the Pullman dining car ... Manhattan ... Boston. They had reached the semolina before she even mentioned the name of Chuck Burgoyne. But when she did, the floodgates opened and Aunt Daphne was left in no doubt as to the width, breadth, height, and depth of her feeling for the young man.

After this feast Daphne declared that she must either prostrate herself for two hours to digest it all or they must go for a brisk walk in the snow on Highbury Fields to blow the cobwebs away. Kathleen naturally chose the brisk constitutional, though she sneered that London snow was rather dirty compared with what they had in *New* England.

Just before they left the house, Kathleen, as if it were the merest afterthought, said, "Oh, there was just one thing. You remember that album of old photographs I borrowed from you — years ago?"

"Oh, yes, dear," Daphne replied in her fluttery tone.

"Could I just have another quick peep in it, please?"

"Now? Can't it wait? We're all dressed to go out."

"Just a quick peep? Dear Aunt Daphne? Please? I'll forget it if I don't."

"Oh, very well!" With impatient grace, yet intrigued at the girl's earnestness, she went off to fetch it.

Kathleen turned directly to the photograph of Jenny Bright — and saw at once that her memory had not played tricks with her. The resemblance between Jenny, twenty-five-odd years ago, and Teresa today was uncanny. "What's the fascination of that old photograph?" Daphne asked, watching her closely.

"Just the way Papa's looking at her."

"At whom?"

"Jenny Bright."

"Ah!" Daphne clasped hands in an apparent rapture. "*That* was her name! I've so often tried to remember it. Jenny Bright — of course! But how clever of you to know it! Come on, let's go out. You've seen it now, and I'm starting to roast in these furs."

They went out into the crisp, sulphur-laden air. A

gang of schoolboys who were shying dirty gray snowballs at a party of superior schoolgirls paused in fretful respect for them to pass by. "That's not a very chivalrous thing to do," Daphne told them.

"They started it, missis." One of the boys showed her his satchel, which bore the marks of several impacted snowballs.

"Tut tut! And you fell for it!" she replied. "When I was a little girl, young men your age were much too clever to fall for tricks like that."

Dubiously they weighed their new-minted snowballs against their burgeoning dignity and decided she was right. They pelted a dog, instead, which dodged them nimbly, looked deeply hurt, then followed them, hopefully panting for more.

Watching them go, Daphne murmured, "Give me the right fulcrum and I'll move the world, said ... someone or other. Aristotle."

"Archimedes," Kathleen told her.

"It works with men, too," she said delicately, ignoring the correction. "A useful little fact for any woman to know."

"Can you tell me about Jenny Bright?" Kathleen asked as they stepped into the Fields, where patches of snow were still virgin. "Is there some family secret about her?"

"How d'you know her name at all?" Daphne countered.

Kathleen shrugged. "I've just heard it mentioned from time to time."

Daphne laughed. "I'll believe anything but that."

"Oh all right!" She owned up at last to having lifted the photograph so as to peek at the name on the back. "And you knew I did, too," she accused, "because you saw it was straight when I returned it."

"Honesty is like traffic, dear. It flows in both directions."

Kathleen sighed and promised to try and remember that. "Anyway?" she prompted impatiently.

"D'you need me to tell you that your father was once rather sweet on her? I should have thought the photograph made that clear."

"How did they meet? It sounds so romantic."

"He sailed as cabin boy on her father's ship, the *Hiawatha,* I think she was called. They traded between Tilbury and the Baltic. Actually, he was a bit more than cabin boy — certainly by the time he finished. He got his papers under old Billy Bright on that vessel. A three-masted schooner, she was. A beautiful vessel."

"And what happened to her — Jenny, I mean?"

"She went down on the Goodwins. There was a terrible storm one night — eighteen-sixty, if I recall."

"Good heavens! I never heard of that. Was Papa there, too?"

"No, he had measles or something — one of those diseases it's rather nasty to get when you're grown up. Mumps? I really don't recall. Perhaps it was 'sixty-one or two. My memory isn't what it was. But she certainly drowned. Went down with all hands."

"Poor Papa!" She paused and ran her eye over the long terrace of elegant houses that made up the Crescent, all cream and ochre and silvery grey in the watery afternoon sun. The scene could have changed little over the past quarter of a century. Perhaps he had stood here, too, after that fateful storm, grieving his heart out for poor lost Jenny — and vowing that, come what may, he would shelter and look after her child. Their child.

"Did you know them very well?" she asked. "The

Brights? Did she always sail with him?"

"From the time her mother died. She'd have been sixteen or seventeen then. She sailed as ship's cook. On coasters the hands bring their own grub and take turns in the galley. But on tramps the master is responsible for their vittles and for providing a cook."

"And did she always sail with them? I mean, was there ever a period when she didn't? A few months, perhaps?"

Daphne halted and grasped her by the shoulder. "D'you mind telling me the point of all these questions, dear? You've obviously learned something about her and you're trying to see if it fits. Why not just tell me?"

When it came to the point Kathleen found she simply couldn't. She pretended that Neil had been told the yarn by an old shipmate and he had passed the story on to her during his last spell ashore. "According to this old salt, you see, Jenny had a daughter. And ... gracious!" She rolled her eyes and swallowed hard. "It's jolly awkward. Could the baby possibly have been ... you know?"

Daphne sank into thought, delicately caressing her lower lip with a lavender-gloved finger. "What a question, Kathleen, dear!" she said at last.

"I know." The girl made a hang-dog face.

"My every instinct urges me to say no, yet I have no reason to be so certain. There were quite long periods when I never saw either of them. So — in a court of law, now — I couldn't swear it was impossible." She smiled sweetly and then added, "But in any case, why should such a tale agitate you so? It was all a long time ago, and surely you must know that we, too, were young once, and made lots of silly mistakes?"

Kathleen drew a deep breath and said, "Promise me you won't tell anyone? Only it's such an enormous discovery. They *did* have a daughter, you see! They called her Teresa, and ..."

"But how can you know such a thing?" Daphne asked — in just the right sort of dismissive tone that would egg the girl on to tell more, tell all.

And sure enough Kathleen produced the coup de grâce at once: "Because I've just met her! In America. A week ago yesterday I had luncheon with her. Emma Harding and me, so you can ask her if you think I imagined it all. And you'll never guess what! She is the living image of her mother — down to the last little freckle! I recognized her at once, just from seeing that photo."

"Well-well-well. I can understand your interest now."

"So you think it's possible?"

Daphne nodded her head judiciously. "I have to confess that everything you say makes it sound more and more likely. But how did she manage to end up in America?"

"Papa must have arranged for her to be brought up by relatives in Ireland — though she always believed they were her true mother and father, of course. And then, d'you remember when he took the *Pegasus* over to America? Well, as luck would have it, that was the voyage on which he'd arranged to collect her in Cork and take her to America, where she has family. He even put her in a special cabin. And then when the Great Storm came ..." She stopped in her tracks and rolled her eyes heavenward. "Lord!"

"What now?"

"Don't you realize? It must have seemed to him that history was about to repeat itself. First the Goodwins, then that bit of wild New England coast. How awful to have brought her safely through her first twenty years only to see her drown, too! Poor Papa!"

"But obviously history *didn't* repeat itself."

"No. When he deliberately ran *Pegasus* aground and sent everyone ashore bar himself, he kept her back, too. Secretly."

Daphne cleared her throat. "I wonder what she made of that!"

"Well that's when he told her the truth about her parentage. He told her he was her father."

"I see. And she, in turn, vouchsafed all this to you, did she?"

"Not a word of it," Kathleen said triumphantly. "She's as tight-lipped as could be. No, I worked it all out for myself!" She stuck her thumbs in her armpits and fanned her fingers, the way Lawrence used to when he boasted of some bit of cleverness.

"What a convoluted tale it is, to be sure," Daphne said, making sure to caress her with admiration. "And so now she's living over there with her adoptive family, is she? Do they know of it?"

"No. The only family she spoke of to me, over there, is a brother — Ignatius — and he obviously doesn't know. I didn't meet him, mind."

"Ignatius? Goodness gracious, are they Roman Catholics? The Brights, I remember, were as staunch Protestants as you'd ever hope to find. They won't be resting easy in their graves. Or in Davy Jones's locker. Is she not living with this brother, either?"

Kathleen chewed her lip anxiously and said, "I'm starting to feel a little cold. Can we go back?"

"By all means." Daphne obliged her at once by turning round. "Heat is in the very sod," she added, consciously stepping in Kathleen's footprints. "Did you hear what I asked?"

377

"Yes." The girl sighed. "That's the awkward bit. You see, in a way history *has* repeated itself. The fact is, Jenny was expecting a child when she boarded *Pegasus* that time."

"Oh dear!" Her pace slowed to a saunter. "But the baby must be … what? Eighteen months or something by now? Yes, just about eighteen months, I'd say. And *Pegasus* ran aground in March 'eighty-five, didn't she. My memory at least reaches back that far."

"Actually," Kathleen admitted with reluctance, "one can't be sure. He was born on Christmas Day that same year. So, er, it *could* have happened just *after* she landed in America."

"Or …" Daphne's pause seemed to last a year, "… just before she embarked, as you said."

"Yes," Kathleen agreed with relief. "Anyway, it means Papa is still keeping her, still shielding her from her shame."

"It would be so like him."

"He's allowing her to syle herself 'Mrs Morgan,' you see. It would avoid so many awkward questions."

Daphne almost choked at that opinion.

"Locally, I mean," Kathleen explained. "In New Haven."

"Ah, locally!" Daphne echoed. "New Haven's where they live, is it?"

"Just outside. It's a little township called Fife, near the ocean."

"Fife."

Kathleen laughed. "And the house — you'll never guess — the house is called *Pegasus!* Isn't that sweet?"

"Positively cloying!" Daphne agreed.

Kathleen's laughter redoubled and she hugged her aunt's arm. "Oh, you!" she scoffed. "You like to pretend to be such a cynic and really you're as soft-hearted as any of us."

Daphne's laughter agreed with her. "So all's well that ends well," she said, wrapping the topic up for the day. "Now tell me another thing. What about little Emma Harding ..."

"She's not so little any more."

"Oh dear! Is Lawrence following in his father's footsteps, then?"

"No!" Kathleen collapsed on her arm in embarrassment. "Don't be so awful! I don't mean like that at all. I mean she's a grown-up now. You wouldn't call her 'little' Emma Harding if you knew her."

"Is Lawrence still keeping her in those rooms in Upper Street?"

"No!" Kathleen said scornfully, as if that were another of those childish things she'd laid aside.

"Ah." Daphne's tone was crestfallen.

"She pays the rent herself now. Out of her own pocket."

"Ah!" She became much happier at that.

D APHNE HAD PICTURED Emma's rooms so often, though she had never been beyond the street door, let alone up the stairs. They were, of course, rooms out of a penny dreadful confiscated from a scullerymaid. From the second-hand linoleum on the floor to the chipped plaster antlers over the door, they were every Abigail's dream of the sort of rooms a Ruin'd Maid might expect her nice kind gentleman to provide.

The communal hallway and stairs did not disappoint Daphne; nor did the outer aspect of Emma's door, whose cheap paint had sagged before drying and now hung like the hide of a sickly elephant, gathering London's grime in its folds. But the moment Emma opened that door, first three inches, then three feet, the scullerymaid tales were forgotten. Now that the rooms were hers, Emma lavished all her earnings upon them. The floor was stained and polished round the edges, like any gentleman's drawing room, and, Daphne noticed, the Turkey rug that covered its centre, though not new, was of better quality than some of her own. The plaster antlers had gone. The heavy velvet winter curtains were of the same dark caramel as the art-silk counterpane and both had identical crimson fringes and tassels.

That was all she had time to notice in her first rapid survey of the apartment from beyond its threshold. But it was enough — especially as it was reinforced by the pleasant aroma of lavender wax, which wafted out to greet her. It bore Emma's greeting, too: "Come in, if you please, Mrs Dowty. I expected you might call. Excuse the mess this place is in."

"Thank you, Miss Harding," Daphne glided past her, peeling off her gloves. "It is a raw morning, but at least we have the sun." She gazed about her and smiled with genuine pleasure, for the place was as neat as a new pin. "Oh but this is quite charming. You have a wonderful touch." She laid her gloves on a lace runner on the table and surreptitiously felt its quality.

"Irish," Emma told her. "I bought it off of one of the other stewardesses who was a bit hard up. Bit of luck for me, anyway. May I offer you a cup of tea? I was just about to make one myself."

"Well, if you're sure it would be no trouble."

"The kettle's boiled."

Emma drew the curtains that shut off the bedroom

half of the large room before she busied herself in the cubbyhole that served as her kitchen. Daphne conducted a more leisurely survey of her surroundings. She saw nothing expensive and nothing cheap; it was good, middle-class value in all senses of the phrase. Now she saw Emma at close quarters again, she could just remember her at the Morgans' — a moon-faced little hoyden with freckles and an elfin sort of smile, always cheerful. That such a person could create a place like this on a mere pittance astounded her. It also gave her a vague sense of unease as she thought of her own servants at Highbury Crescent. She'd always considered servants in general to be essentially savage folk, tamed only by their association with people of a superior class, and then only with reluctance, tempered by the necessities of life. Left to themselves, she thought, they'd surely revert to the orgiastic ways of their rural forebears.

That was frightening enough — to live among people in whom you sensed there lurked a wild creature, and not too far beneath the skin. Yet here was one of them, left to herself, and what had she done? She had created a very passable middle-class nest — not a gimcrack imitation full of tawdry gewgaws masquerading as respectable, but one of taste and discrimination. In a way, that was more frightening still.

"You said you were half-expecting me to call," she remarked. "Did you know that Kathleen visited me yesterday?"

Emma emerged with the tray. Now that the topic was broached she relaxed and could smile properly. "It would have taken an earthquake and two floods to stop her, I'd say." But she grew solemn once more as she set out the teacups and took the doyly off the seed cake. "It won't spoil your luncheon," she promised. "It's very light."

"Did you make it yourself? How clever you are. The only thing I *ever* learned to make was egg custard. I make it for Mr Dowty when he's poorly. He says it cures him in half no-time, but I'm not sure he intends it as a compliment to my cooking."

As Emma busied herself with the usual rituals she said, "I don't know why I was smiling just now. It's a very serious business, this. I don't mind telling you, I lost a good bit of sleep last night, thinking about it all."

Daphne cleared her throat delicately. "I'm not sure I know precisely what has happened. Kathleen told me the most extraordinary tale yesterday. Does she actually believe it herself?"

"Oh!" Emma slumped with theatrical hopelessness. "I don't know." She stared out of the window awhile and then repeated herself. "I don't know. Sorry, d'you take milk and sugar?"

"Milk, please. She *seems* to believe it. The light in her eyes! It's what one sees in the faces of young missionaries and those funny people who think the earth is flat."

Emma smiled again, despite herself. "It's in that class, all right."

"Would you mind telling me what really has been going on? It's not idle curiosity, you understand. I'm expecting Mrs Morgan to luncheon today. Perhaps I'll give *her* egg custard?"

For the next ten minutes, in as calm a manner as she could manage, Emma told Daphne Dowty all that she knew of the affair. She did not exclude her confrontation with Mrs Morgan on the *Pride of Liverpool*. "I'm sorry I had to say even that much, Mrs Dowty," she concluded. "But if you've ever stood out in the street with all your worldly goods in two cardboard cases and no roof over your head, and no prospect of respectable work, you'd understand."

"I understand it even without that, my dear," Daphne replied. "I think, in the circumstances, you were a model of restraint." She raised the last morsel of cake to her lips but absent-mindedly bit the knuckle of her thumb instead. She replaced the cake, uneaten, on her plate. "The question is, what do I say to Hilda Morgan? She's bound to want to talk about it. And what if Kathleen has told her this same preposterous tale?"

"Oh, I shouldn't think as she's done that," Emma remarked. "She'd have no call to on the boat." Her expression was suddenly puzzled. "They never talk much in that family, do they. Not to each other. It's all nods and winks and understandings. I know my own mum and dad talk to each other mostly through the dog, but that's different. Did Kathy tell you how she let the Captain know she approved of what he was doing?"

"Not in so many words." Daphne leaned forward with interest.

"I couldn't hardly believe my ears when she told me. She said they talked about Larry and me, and why Larry tried to keep it a secret from her. Only she knew about it anyway, 'cos she used to walk up and down outside here, spying ..." She faltered, for she had suddenly remembered who Kathleen's companion was on some of those occasions.

Daphne gave a contrite, mischievous little smile and said, "Go on."

The more Emma got to know Daphne, the more she warmed to her. It was astonishing because, on the face of it, you'd say they were the last two women on earth who'd be able to find the slightest thing in common. But there it was; such things happened.

"Anyway," she went on, "Kathy knew all about us and Larry thought she didn't. She explained all that to the Captain and then asked him if he understood how awful she felt not being able to talk to Larry about it and tell him she approved. And then, or so she says, he twigged she wasn't talking about Larry and me, not really. She was talking about *him*, the Captain, and Teresa! That's the way they go on in that family, see? They never come out with it, straight up. So anyway, then the Captain asks her wouldn't it be the same thing if she'd managed to let Larry know she approved but without putting it in so many words. But if Larry sort of twigged her meaning anyway. Wouldn't that be just as good, he asks? Of course, she thinks he's telling her he's got her point."

"Oh dear!" Daphne closed her eyes and looked ill. "*She* approves of her father shielding his chance-daughter and the chance-child. But *he* imagines her approval is for his ... well, we can't mince words, can we — his dubious marriage to this poor Teresa creature."

"And because he's so happy, she thinks it only goes to show she was right about what's going on in ... the other Morgan household."

Daphne smiled. "You are discretion itself, Miss Harding. But I already know that the house is called *Pegasus* — God save the mark! And it's in Fife, near New Haven, in Connecticut."

"A right little babbling brook!" Emma commented.

"Not really," Daphne replied. "Indeed, I had to lower the bucket several times before it came up full." Her smile faded. "But what will happen now? The

Captain will very happily allow her to go to New Haven to see this Chuck person. Can one really call a young man Chuck? It sounds so minstrelsey, don't you think: 'Prithee, Chuck, pluck me that air upon thy lute!' However ... he will happily permit Kathleen to stay at *Pegasus*, Fife, population eight-hundred and fifty — or fifty-*one* now — because he thinks she knows all about it and approves."

"*And* it will soothe Mrs Morgan's suspicions if whispers ever get to her."

"Precisely! That hadn't escaped me, either. Mrs *Hilda* Morgan — we shall have to start differentiating between them now. But what is it going to do to Mrs Teresa Morgan? She'll think she's playing mother to her half-orphaned step-daughter! How long will that delusion last, with the babbling brook running through every room in the house?"

Emma nodded morosely. "That's what kept me awake half the night."

There was a dainty pause before Daphne said, "And what does Lawrence make of it, may I ask?"

Emma shook her head. "I never told him. And I won't, neither."

"Ah." Daphne nodded approvingly. "You not only have good taste, Miss Harding, you have excellent judgement to go with it. I think you are right. Men are savages. There's no knowing what they'll do next." She emitted a humourless little laugh. "D'you know the most extraordinary thing about this whole affair?"

Emma raised her eyebrows.

"We both know where our moral duty lies in such a deplorable business. We both know what we *ought* to do. But instead of doing it, we more or less join in the conspiracy and scheme out ways to cushion the various parties and reduce the damage to a minimum."

Emma gave a complicit smile. "D'you know how I ended up thinking last night? I thought, what's he done wrong, really? As long as one stays in America and the other stops here, where's the harm? I mean, Mrs Hilda Morgan is very happy, if you ask me — *very* happy to have a husband who's not there ten months out of every twelve." She fidgeted with her napkin and added, "I don't think it's what you might call a very *conjugational* marriage, if I may so phrase it."

Daphne gave a single delighted hoot of laughter and said, "Perfect!"

"And there's Mrs Teresa Morgan, happy as a dove in her nest over there, with the bonniest baby you ever saw — and she can't wait to have half a dozen more. And there's Captain Morgan himself with enough put by and enough coming in to keep them all afloat for ever. So where's the harm?"

"I'm so glad you feel like that, my dear," Daphne said solemnly. "It makes it so much easier to break the news to you."

"Break the news?" Emma repeated. "To *me*?"

"About Lawrence's *other* sweetheart — The Honourable Miss Tomasina Goodbody of Highgate Manor — or do you already know about her?"

She was so convincing that for a moment Emma could only sit there and stare at her in horror.

"Where's the harm?" Daphne asked mockingly.

Emma saw her point then and laughed. "Oh, you did give me a turn, Mrs Dowty. That wasn't fair."

"But it's what we're up against, Miss Harding. Good heavens, is that the time? I must go, or I'll never make that egg custard. Just before I do, though ..." She opened her bag and drew forth what Emma at first took to be a visiting card. It gave her a little thrill to think that she was about to be honoured with that

most powerful symbol of middle-class acceptance —
for the first time in her life.

Then Mrs Dowty turned it over and she saw it was a
photograph — or part of a photograph — of Teresa
Morgan; the gentleman standing at her side had been
crudely cut away with curved scissors. Just a sleeve,
clad in a rather strident Donegal tweed, remained.
The hand that protruded from it rested on the young
lady's shoulders in a most proprietorial fashion.

"Is that the one Kathy saw?" she asked.

"No, it's one I happened to have in an old box in the
attic. Is it very like her?"

"I tell you — I'd stand up in any court of law and
swear it *was* her. That's how like they are."

"How extraordinary! Aren't men extraordinary?
But for that accidental likeness, none of this would
have happened!"

"It is accidental?" Emma asked. "I mean, we can be
sure of it?"

"Oh yes. Since yesterday I've gone back through
my diaries … I've practically relived each day of those
years. One hears of girls who've managed to conceal
their unfortunate condition in astonishing ways but
if Jenny Bright is among them, hers would be the
most astonishing of all. And besides … Ireland! I ask
you! The Brights had no connection with that country,
and certainly not with any Roman Catholics there."

Emma was amazed. "So it's just the look of her!
That's all he did it for. 'Extraordinary' isn't the word.
And Captain Morgan of all people!"

"Ah!" Daphne began pulling on her gloves again.
"Now that *doesn't* surprise me. Jenny Bright told me
once that she saw him walk overall for a bet. D'you
understand 'walk overall'? I don't suppose it means
anything in your sort of merchant vessel?"

Emma shook her head.

"It means shinning out along the bowsprit — the thing like a toothpick that sticks out from the sharp end — then up the royal-mast stay to the very tip of the foremast, down as far as the futtock shrouds, up the next royal-mast stay to the top of the main, down to the shrouds, up to the top of the mizzen, then hand-over-hand down the standing backstays. It's dangerous enough in harbour. In the middle of a Bay of Biscay storm it's suicide. But Frank Morgan did it — and lived!"

Emma gasped but Daphne's upheld finger promised more. "The very next day, she told me, they were going into Cadiz, I think, and it was a question of making a short but slightly risky run over a sandbar or a longer one around it — in which case they'd lose one whole tide for their departure. Frank Morgan had the helm and he refused to take the risk — not without a direct order from old Billy Bright. And Billy was too canny to give it. There's the Captain for you. Not an easy man to understand."

I F HILDA MORGAN HAD lost any sleep the previous night, she showed no sign of it as she bustled across the Dowtys' threshold, stamping the snow from her boots. She remarked that it was very dirty compared with the pristine snows of New England.

"Are you and Kathleen on some sort of retainer?" Daphne asked as she helped her out of her coat. "Or is there an open competition with a prize for everybody at the end of it?"

"From whom, dear?" Hilda asked absently as she patted her hair back into place, surveying the effect critically in the hall mirror.

"I don't know — some New England acclimatization bureau or tourist committee. You both wax so lyrical on the purity of its snows, I wonder you don't emigrate tomorrow. Indeed, why not? Frank's as often over there as he is here. *And* you'd have all that beautiful snow to admire when he's away."

"Don't be silly, dear." Hilda laughed. "How could I? My home is here. All my friends are here."

"And Kathleen?"

"Aha!" Hilda turned and gave her nose a playful little tweak — which nonetheless made Daphne's eyes water. "So she has told you something!"

"Something indeed!" Daphne agreed as, rubbing her nose, she led the way to the morning room.

"And so has Mary Abercrombie, who called just before I left. She says she saw you entering one of those slums in Upper Street this morning."

Daphne pulled a face. "One of our Rescued Magdalens has been ever so slightly naughty."

"Oh." Hilda wanted to hear no more of that. But Daphne decided that if a little gentle badinage was to be the order of the day, she could give as good as she got, even if she had to invent it. "I hear you were quite the belle of the voyage," she gushed. "Everyone is talking about how vivacious and charming you were. The Shaw & Eggar should take you on permanently."

"Oh!" Hilda pretended to fan her face at an embarrassment she did not feel. "People are so silly. Anyway, I bet you're just making it up."

"Not at all," Daphne assured her. "Indeed, we had John Harbison to dinner last night — the Harbison Line, you know."

"I know John Harbison," Hilda replied.

"And he said a certain party on the Baltic was waxing most lyrical."

Hilda smiled acidly. "I don't suppose he mentioned the party's name? That would be too much to expect."

Daphne thought quickly. She had read the passenger list of the *Pride of Liverpool's* latest voyage, of course; she read all the passenger lists. The question was, which name would embarrass Hilda the most? One absolutely stood out. "Walter Grandison, of course," she replied.

She had expected to draw blood, but in the form of anger, not in the form of sudden rush of scarlet to the tips of Hilda's ears. She turned away at once, busying herself with the curtains, so as to allow Hilda the hope that her embarrassment had gone unnoticed. It was the least one could do for so dear a friend, she thought.

But Walter Grandison, eh? The very last name she would have coupled with Hilda's — which was, indeed, why she had chosen him in the first place. Such a dreadful old satyr, with such a commonplace patter when he tried to seduce one. Surely he had more sense than to attempt it on Hilda? And surely she had more sense than to ... but just look at those ears!

"The swine!" Hilda exclaimed. "I danced with him *once,* that was all."

To Daphne it seemed a very schoolgirlish counter-argument but she said nothing further.

"Eurgh!" Hilda exclaimed. "He smokes those dreadful gaspers all the time and to disguise it he chews cloves. Can you imagine anything worse?"

"Yes. My egg custard. But you shall have a chance to make the comparison for yourself."

"Oh no," Hilda said morosely. "Not your egg custard!"

Daphne grinned. "Perked you up a bit, though, didn't it! There *are* worse things in life than Walter Grandison. Not many, but you can count on me to find at least one. To be quite serious, we have a new Madeira, a Sercial — would you care to try it?" She was already pouring a measure.

All through luncheon and beyond, she had a replay of Kathleen's enthusiasms of yesterday. What intrigued her most was how similar the two accounts were — and that was odd, for she had never thought of Hilda and her daughter as being remotely alike in their tastes and interests. Even odder, Hilda had changed far more than Kathleen in making this accommodation; she was younger, more vivacious, less censorious than Daphne had seen her in years. It was an uncanny revival of what she had been in their girlhood.

Eventually she was driven to remark upon it. She held up a hand to stem some particular enthusiasm of Hilda's. "I must say I'm beginning to regret I decided not to accompany you ..."

"Oh, I do wish you had, Daphne dear. It was the only thing to mar our pleasure. I lost count of the number of times I said to Kathleen ..."

"The *only* thing?" Daphne picked up the word. "Well-well!" She didn't wish to make her feeds too plain.

The smile faded from Hilda's face. "Actually, there was one more. Something that quite marred the whole visit. If I tell you, will you promise me it will go no further?"

Daphne smiled winsomely. "You know how utterly hopeless I am at that sort of thing."

"No, seriously, my dear. It is something quite dreadful. I don't know if you remember a beastly little maid we had a couple of years ago — face like a pudding basin all splattered with freckles. I gave her the boot. A sly, deceitful little minx if ever ..."

"If I saw her again, I'd probably remember," Daphne cut in. "Anyway, what of her?"

"Well I did see her again, and I did remember, too. I dismissed her without a character for some odious insinuation she made to Kathleen. So you may imagine my astonishment when I saw her in the uniform of a stewardess on the *Pride of Liverpool!*"

"She'd stolen it?" Daphne guessed.

"No, no. She secured the job in the usual way — only her references were forged. By herself or some friend."

Daphne pulled a face. "Such unpleasantness. I hope she left quietly. Or did you have to bring her back to England in irons? I don't suppose the Americans would welcome ..."

"No, it was nothing like that. I do wish you'd stop guessing and let me tell you what really happened. It's infinitely worse. I cornered her at once, of course, the minute I spotted her. But instead of taking it like a man — or on the chin, anyway ..."

"I was going to say ..." Daphne murmured.

"Instead of meekly accepting her dismissal — her *final* dismissal, this time — she had the temerity to tell me she had some private knowledge which, if made public, would send Francis to prison and make social pariahs of me and the children."

Daphne gave a silvery laugh. "Sheer bluff," she snorted. "But what pluck!"

"I thought it was bluff, too."

"And you called it, I hope?"

"Alas, no." Hilda shook her head solemnly. "I didn't dare risk it."

Daphne was shocked. "But that's tantamount to saying you believe there might be something in this grotesque threat."

"I know."

Daphne swallowed her surprise and, feeling rather pleased with her display of innocence, said, "Why? What more did you learn? There must be more to it than that to make *you* even consider such menaces seriously."

Hilda shook her head. "It was just ... that dreadful light of certainty in the girl's eyes. She truly does know something so heinous, so ... She convinced me of it, anyway."

"Well! It's hardly something you can tax Francis with, not outright. What did you say the girl's name was — Peggy?"

"I didn't. It's Emma. Emma Harding."

"Oh yes, Emma! I recall her now. Come to think of it, I've seen her around the village, quite recently. I meant to tell you." Not a flicker, Daphne noticed; so Hilda probably knew nothing of Lawrence's dealings with the girl. She continued. "Anyway, you could hardly say to Francis, 'Guess what Emma Harding has told me!' But surely ... *in*directly, somehow?"

Hilda stared out of the window a long time before she replied. "I didn't need to. The fact is, Kathleen let slip something, quite innocently, that made me realize what it was."

"Good heavens! Does she know about it too?"

Hilda shook her head. "Perhaps she does, in her heart of hearts. But she refuses to admit it. Poor girl! How can she? I can hardly admit it to myself even now. At her age ... impossible." She turned to her friend with a rather wan smile and said, "I'm sorry, this can't be making much sense to you. I take it Kathleen said nothing to you?"

"I wouldn't say *nothing*, dear. I could practically rebuild the *Champlain* if someone mislaid it. I could walk blindfold in Chicago without feeling lost."

Hilda laughed and said she didn't mean that.

"And if something like a cross between Adonis and Lord Byron walked into the room, I should recognize Chuck Burgoyne in the twinkling of an eye."

"Oh yes, I believe you there. But nothing about how *noble* her father is?"

"Ah!" Daphne's smile turned sentimental. "Bless her! What an example to her generation!"

Hilda suddenly changed tack. "I don't suppose you have any photographs from the old days? In particular, d'you remember a dinner given by your father's firm to the crew of the *Hiawatha* — old Cap'n Bright?"

"Billy Bright!" Hilda exclaimed in rapture, as if she had not thought of the name in more than a quarter of a century. "Didn't he have a daughter? *She* was called Peggy. Yes, I knew someone was called Peggy."

"She was called Jenny — and well you know it. Your father-in-law wanted her for Brian, and you weren't having it, so you steered her and Francis together as only you know how. Peggy, indeed!"

Daphne pinched the bridge of her nose between thumb and forefinger. "*Such* an age ago! I do envy people with good memories. It's all a blur to me."

"Perhaps a photograph would refresh it all for you. Have you kept any?"

"I wonder? Let's go and see!" Daphne's smile suggested it would be a new kind of naughtiness.

After letting Hilda leaf through two of her father's albums, in which she knew her friend would draw blank, Daphne allowed her to find the picture she was seeking — the one Kathleen had discovered eighteen months ago.

Hilda stared at it a long while and then sighed. "Yes! We never stood a chance while Jenny was around, did we."

"What has this to do with what we were speaking of earlier, Hilda dear? D'you think Francis still has a soft spot for Peggy Bright? Reprehensible, I know, but hardly the stuff of which penal servitude is made."

"But suppose he found her — *Jenny?* What if he found her again?"

"Why, *then* we'd have a chance at last!" Daphne responded brightly. "Twenty-five years in salt water is a grand cure for beauty, I'm told."

Hilda stared in exasperation at the album, wondering why she and Daphne were still friends, why she had ever expected a serious, sympathetic hearing in this house, and how she was going to force her to take this business in earnest.

But Daphne had an unerring instinct for the moment when her friends were beginning to wish they had come armed. She obliged Hilda by turning sober and pensive. "It doesn't make much sense to talk of him *finding* Jenny Bright, my dear. Her death is beyond all doubt."

"Then let me tell you a most extraordinary tale — told to me in the most artless fashion by Kathleen, the day before we docked in Liverpool. Or in fact it was the night before that — in the wee small hours. A fine tale for a daughter to tell her mother in the hope of getting her off to sleep, I must say!" And she repeated Kathleen's story, word for word, as well as she could recall it.

Again Daphne was struck by the similarity of the two accounts. When it was done she gnawed the knuckle of her thumb for quite a while before she said, "And you think this is in some way connected with the Harding girl's threats to you?"

"Ha!" Hilda exclaimed in a bitter kind of triumph. "You see! You don't consider Kathleen's explanation seriously either. You're like me — you think it's bunkum."

Daphne nodded. "But how could Harding have found out? Surely Kathleen didn't tell her?"

"No, it was the other way around. I've managed to piece all that together from disjointed bits of what Kathleen told me and my own knowledge of Harding's atrocious character. She *knew* I'd spot her at once, the moment I came aboard — as, indeed, I did. And she'd twice seen Francis either getting on or getting off the New Haven train in the terminus, Grand Central station. Apparently one of the stewardesses' favourite haunts is an oyster bar beside the station and they use the railway companies' conveniences. And obviously there was something about him … some air of guilt. It was a slender chance, of course, but what choice had she? Nemesis loomed. It wouldn't take long for a sharp little vixen like that to catch the train to New Haven — it's only eighty-odd miles — and inquire among the cabbies there to discover the whereabouts of a Captain and Mrs Morgan — *if* such a couple existed."

Daphne fluttered a hand at her breast. "When you say it like that, it sounds so … I don't know. Doom-laden. 'Captain and Mrs Morgan'!" She shivered. "What are you going to do?"

"Kill him, of course," Hilda said calmly.

Daphne blinked, but recovered quickly. "I know

that, dear. I meant after. You could hide in our attic. No — the servants would be bound to talk."

"I mean it," Hilda insisted. "The only question is how? You don't suppose I could ask Mary Abercrombie to ask her husband about what poisons to use? Where *can* one find out about such things?"

"Captain Frith was killed in the South Atlantic by a cobra," Daphne offered cheerfully; then her face fell. "No, that was on the Calcutta run. What snakes do they have in New York?"

"You don't think I mean it, do you."

"On the contrary, dear. I thoroughly approve. Half the wives in England would give their eye teeth to have as good a cause to murder their husbands as you have."

"It wouldn't be murder."

"Well … only in the technical sense, perhaps. They'd only send you to the gallows in the technical sense, too. You know — bolts and hinges and weights and calculated drops. Why not murder *her*, instead?"

Hilda shook her head vigorously at that. "Poor thing, she's as much his dupe as I. No, he's the one who must pay for it."

"Don't you think he is already doing so? It can't be cheap, running two establishments. Is he starting to curtail your allowance? Is he beginning to check your extravagances?"

"I have no extravagances!" Hilda protested.

"No woman ever does, but when did that stop our husbands from checking them? Is he starting to pinch the pennies?"

"No," Hilda admitted reluctantly. "I have to give him that. He's never been censorious in that way. I have as free a hand as anyone could wish — and, of course, I've never abused it."

"Still," Daphne said consolingly, "I'm sure you'd soon accustom yourself to living on a greatly reduced income. After you've got rid of him, I mean — and assuming you don't get found out. As you say, your tastes are not extravagant. I was in one of those slums in Upper Street, as you call them, only this morning. I think you really would be surprised at what a person of taste can make of such unpromising material."

Hilda frowned, only half-catching her friend's drift.

"Perhaps Upper Street would be a little too close to all your *former* friends and acquaintances. But I am reliably informed that there are similar apartments in Dalston and Hackney. And if you pulled in your horns and kept a really tight rein on your budget, I'm sure you'd manage splendidly. You could give piano lessons and so forth ..."

"Daphne," Hilda said wearily. "I know what you're trying to do and it's becoming rather tiresome. You won't talk me out of my intention to kill him."

Daphne smiled warmly. "I wouldn't even try, darling. I know you far too well. No, as I said at the very beginning, it's not the murder itself that concerns me. That's your affair. But *after*. What do you do *after*? What does Lawrence do? And Neil? And what becomes of dear little Kathleen? That's what we've got to plan for. Compared to all those questions, the murder itself will be child's play, I'm sure."

WALTER GRANDISON'S KNOWLEDGE of human nature was narrow but deep. He knew exactly which levers to pull, which heartstrings to tug, which carrots to dangle, which sticks to brandish — and, more important still, which of those devices to leave alone — in order to get his way with his fellow man ... and woman. In that limited field none could master him. He was *slightly* interested in understanding why this or that stratagem worked, but only insofar as it might help him better his performance. Beyond that, however, his curiosity faded sharply to extinction. For him, the world was a vast machine that some unknown designer had carelessly left lying about, waiting for someone smart enough to come along and discover its uses; miraculously, in his case, its principal use seemed to be the unending increase in the pleasure and profit of one Walter Grandison. In short, there was very little to distinguish the man from ninety-five percent of his fellow humans.

What elevated him up among the top five percent, however, was the sheer determination, the persistence, the stamina he deployed in this most common pursuit of all. As far as his shipping line went, he gave it about one hour out of each twenty-four; but the butterflies and drones who preoccupied most of the remaining twenty-three would have been astonished to see him at it. He strode into the offices in Leadenhall Street, trailing the sparks of an unmistakable aura; everyone knew when the Chief was in the building. His mind was sharp as a surgeon's lancet, his power of command formidable, his decisiveness a legend. He left his principals and underlings feeling their very souls had been massaged in this daily encounter. And when it was over they would stand at their windows watching with faint contempt the swell who sauntered off with his mauve gloves and lovat-grey topper, making for the West End, from the Land of the Cockney to the Land of Cockayne; and they would at the same time wonder how they could also feel willing, almost, to die for the man.

A similar quandary gripped Hilda as she lay in his arms at last in the discreet hôtel in Maidstone; he was, at the time, massaging something more corporeal than her soul, though that, too, she had placed in his hands — from Fri to Mon, at least.

Every instinct told her Walter didn't give a hoot for Hilda Morgan. She was no more than another feather in his cap, one more notch in his roll of battle honours ... or however warriors recorded such triumphs. But her sense of logic and fair play asked when had he ever pretended otherwise? His fingers wandered at will over her body, drawing forth pleasures whose very existence she had never previously suspected. Yet he knew where they lurked. He knew what mixture of caresses and tweaks, of fondlings and squeezes, would lift her on an upward cascade of thrills and delights to an ecstasy that, he claimed, was as old as time. To her it remained as novel as tomorrow, no matter how often she experienced it.

But the gratitude she felt toward him for this shattering revelation was — appropriately — no more than skin-deep; for even in her wildest moments, caught up in the whirl and fire of it all, something within her knew he did it ultimately for his own sake, not hers. It was a kind of conjuring trick, as a jesting father might pay his son's pocket money by apparently producing the coin from the lad's own ear — only with Walter there was an element of genuine magic, too, in that the coin in which he bribed her to give her all to him *was* somehow produced from within her own body.

And when it was over (for the moment, and for the fifth or sixth time since their arrival the night before last), and she lay there exhausted, seeking the bits of her that had exploded to the far corners of the universe, and wondering if her cries of joy had really been so loud as to require him to half-throttle her with the pillow like that ... in short, while she rebuilt her mundane personality out of the wreckage of her orgiastic self, it occurred to her that if she owed him any debt of gratitude at all, it was not for the fact that he had given her a new Hilda to live with, but for his very callousness in the giving.

Never for one moment did she entertain the slightest hope or wish for a lasting liaison between them. To her he was no more than a foreign country. You paid it a brief and pleasurable visit. You enjoyed its quaint, exotic customs — all the more for the contrast they offered to everything you cherished at home. You sampled its strange fruits and enticing cuisine. And then you returned to your native haunts and put it all behind you. She felt no intimation that she was beginning a new life with him; quite the contrary — this was a time *out* of life.

Yet even as she reached that satisfying conclusion, her honesty would not let her sustain it. This Fri-to-Mon adventure was more than a brief tour in a foreign clime; it was also a savage and gleeful revenge on Francis. How could she possibly deny that? This frantic coupling of two bodies — whose frenzy she at last understood — was so important to him. She could remember the desperation with which he used to plead for her to overcome her reluctance and distaste and let him have his "rights"; only now did she begin to understand why.

It was the first crack in the pillar that sustained the temple of her righteous indignation, upon whose altar she hoped one day to cut out her husband's heart — the nagging little weevil of suspicion that some small part of the blame might rest with her.

And Walter, for his part, lay there beside her, wondering, as always at this stage in the proceedings, what on earth was going on in her mind — *her* being a kind of cypher to which an entire lexicon of female names could be applied. His chief fear was that *she* might be scheming how to get away for another Frito-Mon like this ... and another, and another. One or two he did not mind, but any suggestion of a longer-lasting liaison sent a frisson of terror up and down his spine and quite ruined his performance. Why, when their bodies were so predictable, were their minds so alien and unknowable?

"We should get up and go to Evensong," she murmured, not having the slightest intention of doing so; it was just part of her slow reconstruction, a promise for next week to honour.

"If I read Providence correctly," he drawled, "we have just completed the profoundest act of worship available to mere mortals."

She pinched him lightly. "What a dreadful blasphemy, Walter! I'm surprised a bolt of lightning doesn't come in through that window and strike you dead."

"The fact that it never has must count for something."

"Why do you do it?"

"What? Blurt out the truth?"

"No. You know ... what we just did. Why d'you go on and on at it, and with so many women?"

He chuckled at her unwillingness to name "it."

Women of enormous passion, he had noticed, were often the most reticent; the ones who were most frank were those to whom it was no more than a pleasant tickle. Maude Harbison, who had almost died of her pleasure (and in this very bed, too!), would not undress — not even kick off her slippers — if he were in the room.

"Why?" Hilda insisted.

"It's the only important thing in life," he told her, as if explaining the obvious to a dim pupil. "Everything else is a mere filling-out of time, a recharging of the reservoirs."

"Do you only pick married women?"

"Of course." The question shocked him; then he added a concession: "I sometimes make an exception for spinsters over thirty. Confirmed old maids, you know."

"How many say yes and how many say no?"

"Of the old maids? None. They all say yes. Of the wives, almost all say yes. And most of the decliners yield to subsequent assault. Mind you, I only pick those with a certain look in their eye. My reputation helps there. When a woman's eager for it, she gets that look in her eye and she makes no attempt to conceal it from me."

She gave a baffled laugh. "What a view you have of us! It's the exact opposite of the received notion."

"The received notion is a fiction dreamed up by men who cannot fully satisfy their wives — and are terrified their wives will discover the fact. Fortunately, you women know so little of the world, and are so desperate for *some* Higher Ideal, you'll believe anything we men tell you in that line. You even police the system almost unaided by us — like little clockwork marionettes when someone trips the lever. I regard it as my duty to spread the truth of the matter among you — to liberate you. It is my little contribution to the grand cause of female emancipation, which is gathering such momentum lately. Not that I claim the credit for that!"

"Oh, Walter! You are so impossibly perverse! You know your motives are nothing like so high-minded as that. You do it entirely for your own pleasure. Be honest, now."

"But when have I ever denied it? You miss the point, Hilda. You seem to think that pleasure and duty are incompatible. But just imagine — if you were Creator, and you wanted to stop your little creations, your little people, from damaging their brains, wouldn't you make it extremely painful for them to bang their heads on rocks and shelves and so on? Similarly, if you wanted to encourage them to do certain other things — eat nice food, take warm baths … stay together long enough at least to bring up a family — well then … do I need to finish the question? Pleasure is to duty as hand is to glove."

Hilda realized she was hearing the authentic voice of the Serpent in Eden; briefly she wondered why the Bible laid so much of the blame on poor Eve. She said nothing, however.

He, disappointed that one of his more polished monologues had roused so little response, said, "Eh? What?"

She, having thought of nothing to reply, said the first thing that came to mind: "To stay together long enough to bring up a family, eh!" She immediately regretted it, of course, but it was too late.

He licked his lips and bated his breath; this was a novel response, indeed.

She rushed on. "I suppose you get your best trawls

among women who've done that? Women like me, whose little chicks have flown the nest, or are about to. We must be just about ripe for the plucking!"

"Is that how you feel?" he asked.

She fell upon him with a sudden kiss. "No. I feel angry. I feel savage that I have been forced to wait until my life is half over — probably — before discovering ... what you have shown me."

"Well, now you know it's there," he said nervously (for it seemed she might be about to ask him to take her away from it all), "you can change all that."

"Can I? Francis, in case you don't know it, has a *mistress!*"

He laughed, unable to stop himself; then he apologized.

But she was mortified — swore she'd never speak to him again.

He made a desperate lunge to repair the situation. "The only reason I laughed, little bird, was at the tone of finality in your voice. You spoke as if a mistress were some kind of *impediment* to your purpose! In fact, she's your strongest trump."

His assurance had the most relaxing effect on her. She lay back and a dreamy smile played about her lips. She reminded him of a child about to be told a bedtime story. The child knows it's not "true," but anticipates it with even greater pleasure for that very reason. "How?" she murmured.

He cleared his throat delicately and admitted he now found himself in a powerful dilemma. "Ever since we arrived here you have been fishing for little crumbs about my previous amours in this hôtel."

She drew breath to protest but he caressed the tip of her nose with one gentle finger and said, "Don't worry, that's not an accusation. I merely wish to point out that I have not yielded the smallest detail. Nor would I give the slightest hint about you to anyone else — not even if it were my only way to the couch of Venus herself. The same discretion also applies to *your* amours."

"My amours?" she echoed scornfully. "You are the first and only one, I can assure you of that."

"The second," he insisted quietly.

Reluctantly she saw his point; she was about to turn her scorn on Francis when he went on: "That is how you must think of it now. Morgan is your *first* amour. If he has, indeed, taken a mistress — ask yourself why? Where did *you* fail him?"

"But I didn't know anything about ... all this, until I met you. Until that night on the *Pride of Liverpool*, in fact. How can it be my fault?" She was losing the thread of the argument; he seemed to buffet her in a different direction each time he opened his mouth.

"Does it matter whose fault it was, or is?" he asked. "The important thing now, surely, is that you *do* know. From this moment on, I cease to matter in your life. I've served my purpose in the much larger warp and woof of your existence. An accidental grace note, a happy little trope — that's all I can ever be to you now — compared, that is, to the mighty challenge that lies ahead."

"Challenge?" she echoed faintly.

"To get him back, now that you *do* know. D'you mean to say you think you couldn't do it? Good heavens, Hilda, of all the girls in our generation, you're the one to rise to that challenge. And the one most likely to succeed. You stand head and shoulders above all the rest — or so I would have said."

She could not deny that the prospect filled her with an extraordinary pleasure; her heart was already beating double. One small doubt assailed her: "But I'm no longer sure I even like him," she complained.

"All the better," he said smoothly. "It means you've lost your Achilles heel, every woman's worst enemy."

"What's that?"

"Her susceptible heart. It is the drunkard's friend, the faithless husband's spy — the skeleton key that every loving woman freely hands to the man who will destroy her. You've lost it. He'll search you inside out and never find it."

"Yes!" She inhaled deeply, experiencing yet another novel ecstasy.

Watching her, watching the smile split her lips, watching her tongue lick them, watching the bubbles it left behind as they burst, he felt the rarest of rare emotions — for him: Pity for another man.

D O THE HONOURABLE THING, *do the honourable thing, do the honourable thing* … the wheels tapped out the refrain on the steel rails all the way to New Haven. Tell her. Beg her forgiveness. Promise you'll make it up to her. Assure her she'll never go in want, nor the child … or children? Frank's own train of thought derailed at that point. The realization that he would have no more children by Teresa if he confessed his crime brought his impulse to cleanse himself to a halt. It was impossible for him to let her go.

His thoughts of her were a mosaic of snatched images. No doubt when his guilt was published to the world … no, he must not start thinking like that. No doubt, *if* his guilt were ever to be published to the world, cynics would say he'd done it for one purpose only — to secure himself a juicy young bedmate to keep him warm on the lonely side of the Atlantic. But, though images of the pair of them in the extreme of passion were in that mosaic, they formed only one insignificant corner of it. Far more prominent were memories of Teresa in more public moments — standing at their gate with that genial smile of welcome on her lips ... Teresa bent over her baby, his tiny hands pummelling her breast to yield more, more ... Teresa holding the little lad above her head in the evening sunlight last fall, raising him among boughs weighed down with crimson apples, and the threads of their laughter spinning a golden cocoon around them ... Teresa running her eye over this room or that in the house, checking, not that it was tidy (as would be the case with Hilda), but that it sparkled with the proper welcome — for these blessings, and a thousand others beside, he would do it all again, even with the certainty of discovery at the end of it all. And, incredibly, it was still no certainty.

These thoughts and images held him with their grand sonorities; but every now and then, darting and flashing among them, he glimpsed a little minnow of a notion that refused to rest and be identified. Something to do with himself alone. Something he had not yet understood about himself.

People had often said of him that he was "born to command." Indeed, they had said it so often he had idly drifted into believing it himself — or at least into accepting it. But he remembered how, when they had first started talking like that, something within him had rebelled at the notion. It wasn't so much that he was born to command as that he was born to be alone; you could see how most people — who are born to neither condition — might easily confuse the two.

But he could feel the difference. Command had been steadily thrust upon him; and, he had to admit, he had taken to it well enough — but only because it had provided that essential aloneness which was his natural state. Even his treasured images of Teresa were those of the observer rather than of the participant.

So much he already knew about himself, and had known for some time. But that scurrying minnow of a thought lay somewhere just beyond this familiar territory. He tried to stalk it now, feeling it so near to capture; but still, for all his efforts, it eluded him.

He gave up — too easily, he realized. His need to grasp that ephemeral notion was too weak. But why? Perhaps because it would threaten the already shaky foundations of his divided world. But it could also be because he was too old to believe it would provide the Key to Everything; in fact, he was old enough to know there is no such thing. The Key to Everything was a chimæra that helped him endure the first half of life; between now and his death it remained only to explode the myth.

At the New Haven depot Harold Martin was among the waiting cabbies. A citizen of Fife and a neighbour of the Morgans, he was accepted among his fellows as the Captain's personal chauffeur. They set off into the gathering dusk of the late-March evening, Frank riding outside.

"I'm glad to see you back in circulation, Martin," he remarked as they rode off down Water Street. "That must have been a nasty bout."

"Took a long time to shake her, Cap'n," the man agreed. "And I'll tell you another thing — I don't heal a cut so fast as once I did, neither."

"I know that feeling …"

They meandered on, past the tall-masted ships in the harbour, which he eyed with a certain nostalgia; then over the bridge, where he watched a crew of Yale oarsmen returning exhausted to their boathouse. The talk meandered, too, as comfortable as the cab and as uneventful as the town-and-country sprawl around them along the East Haven road. Then Martin said, "I never seed that girl of yours again. I thought she was fixin' to come over here and annexe herself to her step-maw."

"Oh ..." Frank gave a dismissive laugh. "At that age ..." He left the sentence hanging in a dozen ambiguities.

Martin picked up one of them. "I reckon she must have a lot of friends over there in England."

"Almost all of them," Frank agreed.

"'Ceptin' one." He hawked a thumping quid of tobacco juice into the road. "I heered her and that frenna hers talking about some fancy beau? Fresher at Yale next fall?"

"Aye," Frank agreed lightly. "It'll be a different story then, I expect."

"She'll be good company for Mrs Morgan."

Frank heard an anxious hesitation in the last few syllables of the remark and he realized the man feared his words might be taken to imply that he, Frank, was something of a cradle-snatcher. He chuckled to put the fellow at his ease and replied, "She may have it in the back of her mind that Mrs Morgan, being so close in years, will prove a mite indulgent of her canoodling with her young freshman. If so, I think she's in for a disappointment."

The cabby then remarked, apropos nothing, that his wife said most of the women in Fife envied Mrs Morgan; the choice between having a husband around the house every day or just twice a month for forty-eight hours each time was a no contest.

Then Frank realized the man's awkwardness had nothing to do with implications of cradle-snatching; he had simply regretted the suggestion that Teresa might be lonely.

Frank wondered why he fanned the embers of this particular conversation when he could so easily divert it to neutral matters. That elusive thought darted through his mind again.

Teresa was waiting, as usual, at the gate. "Good evening, Mr Martin," she called out as they drew to a halt. "That chill on your liver has finally gone?"

"Thank the Lord — and that liniment you sent round. The man who could lie in bed with *that* on his skin would be past all curing. Essence of angry termite, I called it."

"I'm glad it worked."

"What was it?" Frank asked as they strolled hand-in-hand up the path.

"Wintergreen, double-strength. My aunt said it's a grand cure — for *men.*"

She laid such stress upon the word he asked her what she meant.

"Sure, when a man has a sniffle doesn't he promote it on the spot to double pneumonia."

"And a woman doesn't?"

"We can't afford to. Oh, Frank!" She leaned her head tenderly against his arm. "Every time I see you coming up that rise, I think of that first evening we had alone on the *Pegasus* — remember?"

"As if I could ever forget!"

She laughed, as if he had said something amusing. Then she said, "The look on your face when you realized I was there!"

They were approaching the porch. He drew her aside, behind the concealment of a large mahonia bush, and crushed her to him, drowning his senses in the warmth and nearness of her. "Every minute with you preserves the magic of that time," he murmured. "I was thinking on the train how you are the one person in my life who has ever got near me, truly close to me."

"Dadada …!" came a plaintive wail from within.

"Not Kathleen? Not your sons?" she asked — meaning "Hilda" but not wishing to be so blunt.

"None of them," he assured her. "I don't know why. It seems that if you don't start right with them, you can never … hey, is he saying dada?"

She chuckled, "And mama and baba and wawa and yaya …"

"Never mind." He released her and made for the door. "He's saying dada at this moment. I'll start right with this one!"

"Frank?" she pleaded, standing her ground.

"Later," he promised in a tone heavy with single entendre.

And later he was as good as his word. At the very climax of their bliss she flung her legs up over him and dug her heels tight into his buttocks, as if she would press all of him into her. His chief surprise was that, apart from the suddenness of her gesture, it did *not* surprise him. She would never say outright, "I want another baby" — not because she was too reticent but because she had some profound feeling that such things were better managed without words. All evening, from the moment of his arrival, she had bristled with little signs and gestures that, he now realized, had been the prelude to this, the grandest gesture of all.

But even as he joyfully submitted his flesh to her will he caught yet another glimpse of that elusive thought which had plagued him all day. This moment, too, had some bearing upon it.

He cradled her in his arms and settled into that mock sleep which precedes the real thing. "'Tis the twelfth today," she whispered.

"For another few minutes," he whispered back — until the significance of the date struck him. "Lord!" he said, waking up again. "I never thought."

"And me dropping hints all evening, like whales on pedestals!"

"Two years ago this very night, eh!"

"That's when we started Anthony."

"So that's what it's all about!"

"And what'll we call *her*?"

He chuckled. "You're as sure as that, are you? She's not five minutes formed and you're all set to name her."

"I was thinking of Grainne. There was a great Irish woman sea pirate called Grainne once. And Morgan was a great English pirate, wasn't he?"

"He turned respectable in the end. They made him governor of Jamaica, where he hanged every last one of his former shipmates. I don't think we want to start delving too deep into historical precedent — not on my side of the family, anyway."

"Well, I like the name for itself: Grainne Morgan, so you just be thinking it over and getting yourself used to it."

"Grainne," he murmured experimentally, pronouncing it *graw-nyer*.

"No!" she protested. "*Graw-nyuh* — and very short on the *nyuh*." She made him repeat it until he had it to her satisfaction. Then he asked how it was spelled.

When she told him, he said the other children would all call her "Granny" Morgan.

"Well," she said defiantly, "if that's the worst they can think of, she'll 'scape lightly, so."

A little thrill of fear twisted in his belly. "Females!" he exclaimed vaguely.

"I'll tell you one female who may well bewilder you into such a cry," she said. "And that's your own daughter. I'm after getting the strangest letter from her."

He yawned, though he could feel his ears physically twitch at her words. "I must look at it tomorrow."

What an oddly compulsive woman she was! She could have mentioned the letter and shown it to him at any moment during the evening, but no — her entire being was consumed with one purpose: to be quickened by him into bearing another child. Nothing had been allowed to occur that did not, in some way, conspire to that end. Was it only her, or were all women like that? Was Hilda the exception? How could one ever tell? Who on earth could he ask such a thing?

Funnily enough, though he had posed himself the question in a purely rhetorical, almost despairing fashion, the image of Emma Harding came at once into his mind. It was absurd, of course. He and she had barely exchanged more than a dozen words in their lives — all of them entirely formal. What tiredness did for you.

"She calls me her sister," Teresa complained.

"Well," he pointed out, "you are more or less of an age — as I thought old Martin was hinting as he drove me out here."

"What's that mean — 'thought he was hinting'? Was he or wasn't he?"

"Not at all." And he went on to explain what had happened.

She kissed him tenderly in the neck as he finished. "God, I hate meself for it, Frank, but I'd say Mrs Martin has the right of it. There's no time for brawling between you and me. You're never here long enough. Did we ever have a cross word now?"

He kissed her in return and inexpertly stifled another yawn; would she never take a hint? Now she'd fulfilled her purpose, she was set to talk the night away. And then he saw that was the answer. Make her purpose serve his. "Listen while I tell you," he murmured seductively. "If you want to make sure of Grainne, we'd better give it another go tomorrow morning, Sabbath or no. And tomorrow night, too. And for that I need my sleep."

She chuckled. "Lord love you, Frank, but you're a man who knows what he wants — *and* how to get it!"

But she let him be, and soon he was deep asleep. His final thought before oblivion was that Hilda might have voiced precisely the same sentiment — except that her tone would have been laced with contempt and disapproval.

T HEY WERE FOUR AND a half days out of New York; the old salts on board swore they could already smell the Mersey on the air. It had been an oddly subdued crossing. Normally, people treated the half-dozen days afloat as a sort of holiday from life and all its demands — indeed, as a holiday from just about everything, including the usual restraints of civilization, or even of common prudence. In the eighteen or so crossings Frank had made since

Pride of Liverpool's maiden voyage last August, he had seen folly on an undreamed-of scale. Men who, ashore, would not have hazarded a fiver on the next pope being male, would calmly place fifty on the turn of a card, and at odds that even a child could see were appalling. Ladies of unblemished character would brazenly ask for the corridor illumination to be dimmed at night because, they claimed, the little sliver of light that crept in at the threshold kept them awake!

At first it had shocked him, such behaviour from the aristocracy and people he'd been told all his life were there to be looked up to. But then Walter Grandison had told him it wasn't just because they were on a voyage that they behaved with such abandon — they were at it all the time, at home and in private. "If I weren't such a confounded man of honour," he added, "I could name you at least three titled hostesses who ring the stable bell at half-past six each morning, to enable everyone to get back where they ought to be before the shaving water arrives."

After that Frank had caused the identical hour — five bells of the morning watch — to be rung at its full daytime volume, and was sourly amused at the glances of approving complicity he received on his rounds thereafter.

It was Grandison, too, who put him right on another matter. To Frank it had seemed caddish that it was always the women who flitted back to their own staterooms and cabins around five bells, never the men. "Work it out for yourself, Morgan," he chided. "A gentleman spotted leaving a lady's cabin might as well paint a whacking great sign on her door: *No better than she ought to be!* But a fleeting shadow, vaguely female in outline, with its face all veiled, could be returning to any one of two dozen rooms, what?"

"But if she's spotted actually leaving the said gentleman's cabin," Frank asked, "isn't that like hanging up a sign: *No better than* he *ought to be?*"

Grandison shrugged. "Hardly worth pointing out, eh, old fruit? Might as well say, *This fellow shaves.*"

But there had been little of such shenanigans, as Teresa would call it, on this particular voyage. The passengers consisted for the main part of youngish, rather earnest devotees of Old World art, who spent their time poring over the Baedekers in the library, plotting itineraries that would maximize their intake of "sights" and making announcements like, "Well, honey, we can go *half*-way up Mont Blanc!"; or they were frail, elderly couples who were more concerned with getting through the night at all than with finding a new partner to assist at the achievement.

So it was all the more extraordinary when, on making an unusually lonely round one evening, he saw a stewardess leave a first-class stateroom about twenty paces ahead of him and scurry off toward Mrs Glover's cabin in obvious agitation. "Is something the matter, miss?" he called in a stage whisper.

She turned, recognized him, and ran to him. He saw it was Emma Harding.

He stopped outside the stateroom from which she had emerged in such a lather; it was occupied (nominally, at least) by Lord and Lady Merton, eighty-eight and fifty-three years old respectively.

"Oh, Captain Morgan," Emma gasped, hammering her breastbone with a clenched fist, as if there were no other way to calm her heart. "Something awful. Lady Merton's been and gone and ..." Her eyes rolled heavenward.

"Snuffed her deadlights?" he asked, hoping an easy maritime colloquialism might help to reassure her that this was all in the line of duty.

It worked, too. A brief, wide-eyed stare was followed by the ghost of a smile. "Yes, sir."

"You're absolutely sure?"

She nodded. "Not a pulse anywhere, nor any cloud from her breath on a mirror. And you can shine a light in her eyes and ..."

"Very well. I remember now — you did first aid, didn't you. Very good."

"Only the difficulty is ..." She swallowed heavily.

All this while she had, from time to time, been glancing not at the Mertons' stateroom door but over his shoulder at the first-class cabins, some way down the corridor. "Well, I think I know what the difficulty is," he assured her with a backward tilt of his head.

She nodded.

"Which one?"

"Mr Jervis's." She gave a sigh of relief at being spared an explanation. "What shall we do, sir?"

"Well, I don't think we need involve Mrs Glover — or indeed anyone else. And fortunately there's no *Mrs* Jervis — or at least none aboard. She's not a large figure, Lady Merton, would you say? How strong are you feeling? Or, better still, nip along to the sick bay and bring the sedan chair from behind the door. Get the doctor and nurse, too — it'll look better. I'll see to things here. Is Lord Merton ... er?" He nodded at the stateroom door beside them.

She shook her head. "He must have taken opium or something. I didn't try to wake him, but you've only got to look at him."

"I think we'll let him sleep it off in peace then. What point would there be in waking him just to tell him that? Poor old boy, eh! The nurse can take her ladyship straight to the fog locker. How is Jervis taking it?"

"Very calm, considering, sir. Says it's a great inconvenience to him. I left him trying to get her nightie back on. I should ought to have offered to help, I know, but … somehow …"

"No, you did absolutely the right thing. Cut along and get the medicos now. Bring them directly to Jervis's cabin."

Jervis was, indeed, taking it very smoothly. "Can't wipe that bloody smile off her face, Captain," he said in a morose tone as they surveyed the reclothed form of Lady Merton. "No warning at all, you know. Cries of delight one minute. Next minute — that."

"It's Merton one must feel sorry for," Frank pointed out. "Not many octogenarians can expect to outlive a wife thirty years their junior." The comforting thought flitted through his mind that he and Teresa would never be more than a quarter of a century apart.

"We shall just have to hope he doesn't notice," Jervis said seriously. "It's quite possible he won't, you know. He's been calling her by all sorts of names out of his past for months, poor girl."

"Well, he's sound asleep at the moment. I'll have her taken straight to the mortuary …"

"Two grand pianos *and* a mortuary! What a ship this is, eh!" the man said in genuine admiration.

The doctor came in first, followed by the nurse, followed by Emma Harding. He repeated all the tests Emma had described and confirmed her conclusion with a dour nod. "Good teeth," he commented after he, too, had failed to turn her smile into something more appropriate to her new condition.

Captain and stewardess followed the chair to the door, not really intending to leave at once but feeling the departed lady's departure deserved some mark of respect from *someone*.

"You can leave the light on," Jervis called out affably as they stood at the doorway. He was climbing back into bed and reaching for a book from his bedside alcove. "Don't feel much like sleep, somehow," he explained. "Most upsetting business."

They closed the door on him and stood awhile in respectful silence, at least until the little cortège had turned the corner at the end of the passage.

"I was going to change his sheets," Emma remarked. "Fancy going on sleeping in sheets in which someone has just died!"

"You deserve a brandy, young lady," Frank told her. "We'll go to the wardroom. There won't be anyone there at this hour."

She looked hastily all about them. "D'you think that would be wise, sir?"

"We have a lot to talk over," he said evenly. "We'll never find a better chance than this. Go and wait for me there." She drew breath to protest but he said, "I'll tell Mrs Glover what's happened and explain I wish to speak to you about it."

A few minutes later a nervous, wide-eyed Emma stepped gingerly across the threshold of the officers' wardroom. Wheeler and a junior engineer were sitting near the bar playing backgammon; they stared at her in astonishment. Wheeler asked who she wanted.

"If you please, sir," she replied, "the Captain sent me here. One of our passengers has died in ... unusual circumstances, and he wishes to speak to me about it."

"Ah." They rose and left their game frozen as it was. "Do take a seat — Miss Harding, isn't it? No need to stand. Quite a shock, what? Who was it?"

"Lady Merton, sir." Emma seated herself near the door.

Wheeler's manner changed subtly. "Oh. When you say 'unusual' circumstances, you mean fairly *usual* ones, in fact?"

"Yes sir." She could not suppress a smile.

"With Mr Jervis?"

She nodded.

"Thought so. I had my eye on them all through dinner tonight. Thought there was something brewing there. Well, well — it had to happen to us sooner or later, I suppose. How's his lordship taken it?"

Frank came into view at the end of the corridor; Wheeler stilled her reply with a waft of his hand. "I'll hear about it later," he promised. "Rum do, Cap'n," he said as they passed.

"Prefer brandy," he replied without stopping. He shut the door on their laughter and told the barman he could stand down for the night. "Just leave us a bottle of that very smooth cognac and a couple of balloons."

When they were alone he poured her a modest measure and a slightly larger one for himself. "Well, young lady," he said jovially as he handed it to her, "when are you going to make an honest man out of my younger son?"

She almost dropped the glass. "Eh?" she exclaimed.

He laughed. "I know what you're thinking — or soon will be. It's a fine way to buy your silence. Keep it in the family. But I hope I'm a better judge of character than that. If you were bent on talking, you'd already have done so by now." He cradled the balloon in his hands and took a deep sniff of its bouquet. "You're not drinking. Would you prefer something else?"

She grinned dourly. "There was a time I lived on this stuff, sir."

"Well at least you had taste."

She took a sip and relished it; not until she breathed out its heady fire did she realize how exhausted she had been made by this evening's excitements. "What you asked me just now, sir," she said, "I mean ... were you serious? Wouldn't you mind?"

He shrugged noncommittally. "I won't pretend it's the match I'd have arranged for him. But then" — his smile became wan — "arranged marriages are not all they're cracked up to be, either."

"Is that why ...?" she began, and then thought better of it.

He smiled but did not take her up. "The next thing you're going to think is that I'm throwing Lawrence to you like some kind of reward."

She frowned at him in bewilderment.

"For being so ... *tactful* with Mrs Morgan when she recognized you in New York that time. I don't know what you told her, but you could obviously have said a great deal more than you did. So if I assure you I am not offering to hand over my son as any kind of reward, you'll probably find it hard to believe. D'you know what *I* believe? Drink up."

She obeyed and waited for him to tell her.

"I believe you're actually too good for him. He's a bit of a waster, don't you think? Rather shallow?"

"He is *not!*" she asserted with some passion.

"I see." He smiled again. "Well, there you are, then. If, however, you decide against marrying him in the end, I give it as my opinion — and I say this quite irrespective of any other matters that may lie between us — I am quite certain that in five or ten years' time, you could be head stewardess on one of our sister ships. The first of them will be launched this autumn, as you probably know? But even that is not the limit for you, or so I believe. However, if I continue in this vein, you will think I am trying to surround you with bribes. Oh listen, I'm weary of telling you what you're about to think. Why don't you tell me what you actually think, instead?"

The suddenness of the question panicked her. Since her mind was feeling particularly blank at that moment, being filled with the rapidly dwindling shock of Lady Merton's death and the rapidly increasing effects of the brandy on her almost empty stomach, she said the first thing that came into her head, which was: "What I'd really like to know, sir, is why you did it at all?"

"Did what?" he tried.

When, to her amazement, he did not explode in wrath, she gave an involuntary giggle of relief — which he took for one of incredulity that he should try to fob her off in so clumsy a fashion. She was another Wheeler, he decided: didn't know the meaning of fear. "That really would be telling," he went on. "I wish I knew why, myself."

She laid down her empty balloon and said, "Shall I tell you what I told Mrs Morgan, sir? It's what you really want to know, isn't it?"

"Phew!" He winced as if he had played the king and she had trumped it with a measly two. Then he laid his empty balloon beside hers and, taking her hand between his, said, "We must be on the same side, you and I. I would not be comfortable to have you anywhere else. You are far too astute."

423

He held her hand just long enough for the novelty of it to thrill her; then, before her embarrassment could grow to outweigh it, he let her gently go and added, "Of course I want to know what you told her."

"And if I do tell you, will you, in return, tell me why you did it, sir?"

He nodded. "Insofar as I know at all," he promised.

She told him word for word as much as she could remember of her confrontation with Hilda Morgan, offering none of the excuses he must already know she could put forward in her own defence; nor did she rake over more ancient history. His admiration for her dignity and coolness increased still further. "Thank you," was all he said when she had finished.

"Is that all?" she asked.

"What more is there to say? You were provoked to the farthest limit yet you said the very least that would have been credible." He refilled her balloon. "There are no words for my gratitude, Miss Harding." He toasted her.

She waited.

He stared at the blanked-off porthole and sighed. "Stuffy in here," he said. "Care to go out on deck?"

She rose, smiling grimly to herself. If he thought the cold would drive her below with half his tale safely untold, he was about to learn her blood was at least as thick as his.

But that was not his intention, as he showed the moment they were on deck, when he sent one of the watch below to fetch her sweater and cape. "And hat?" he asked, turning to her.

She shook her head. Perhaps he truly did intend to answer her question fully. For the first time she began to feel afraid. To know a secret because you'd teased it out for yourself was one thing; to know it as a matter

424

of trust was quite another. She was not sure she wanted to cross that divide.

A few minutes later, after the seaman returned with her gear, she lost all choice in the matter. They leaned against the railing, a careful six inches apart, dangling their brandies and staring at the chill, almost tar-black sea, over which a gibbous moon had already begun to set. Seven bells rang; the middle watch would now be groaning into wakefulness — "showing a leg" in the old tradition — getting ready for their midnight muster.

"It's curious you should ask that particular question," he said. "For the first year of my marriage to …" The name, or the precise naming, gave him difficulty.

"Miss Teresa?" Emma suggested.

"Of course. You know her, don't you! For all that year, the question hardly crossed my mind. There are things we do in life that just seem utterly right, and that was one of them. It still is. I have not begun to doubt it. But I have begun to ask myself why, and just recently the question has almost obsessed me. Do you have any thoughts on the matter?" he asked, then immediately added, "No, that's not fair. I've run through all the obvious reasons — the romantic ones, of course. Ans also all the ones that men will snigger over in barbers' shops if word ever gets out. And so forth. And there's a degree of truth in them all — I mean who on earth does something as important as that for a *single* reason?"

"And as risky, too," she offered.

"Ah! Once again, Miss Harding, you are there almost before me. The risk! You have the very word. Are there perhaps gamblers in your family? Do you know the lure of it?"

"Not really, sir," she confessed. "They say an uncle of mine was carved up by the bookies once, but I never knew him."

"We're the same, then," he said. "There are no gamblers among the Morgans, either, nary a one — which is why it took so long for me to twig, d'you see? There's gambling and gambling. It's not all just money on horses, you know."

He took a gulp of his brandy; she did the same. She was getting her second wind, if there is such a thing with liquor. It occurred to her that she had acquired a better head for spirits than he; not that he was drunk — his speech was not even slurred — but there was an excited edge to his voice that was new. She tossed her glass back and said hopefully, "I could do with more of that against this cold."

He handed her his hipflask, which he had taken the precaution of filling before they came up on deck. She poured each of them a generous measure and popped it back in his pocket.

"When I first went to sea," he began …

"Seven bells of the first watch and the glass rising slowly, sir," the mate reported from a little way off. "The helm steady at north by northwest and a fresh breeze."

"And royals and flying jibs taken in," Frank murmured when the man had gone, "and two reefs in all tops'ls. God, how I miss those days! You know — when I ran *Pegasus* aground, I knew in my bones they were done. My sailing days were done."

"You mean, you thought they'd take your command from you?" she asked.

"No!" He laughed. "I meant I'd never manage a finer bit of seamanship than that. There'd never be anything to stir the blood again like that. There'd be

426

other moments of danger, yes, but nothing to equal that."

Up on the bridge Wheeler said to the mate, "Well?"

The mate shook his head. "He's a master man, our skipper," he said. "He's telling her about his early days at sea. A great man like him, taking all that trouble over a frightened little nobody like her!" He sucked a tooth in amazement.

"I'll tell you why he's a great man," the First Officer replied. "Because to him there's no such thing as 'a little nobody.' Every man and woman in this crew is somebody to him."

Emma nudged the Captain's memory. "You started saying something about when you first went to sea, sir?" she murmured respectfully.

"Oh yes. D'you know what the term 'running overall' means?"

Emma remembered Mrs Dowty's tale but all she said was, "I know *dressed* overall means flags hanging from all the stays."

"That's it. Running overall means going hand over hand up those same stays and down those same topmasts. Nothing between you and the clouds all the way but the rope you're dangling from. Well there was an old seadog on my first ship, the *Hiawatha*, a fellow called Tarheel Jack, who took a great dislike to me. Quite rightly too, probably, for I was a bumptious little cove. And he challenged me one day to run the *Hiawatha* overall. Everyone told me I was insane, but I accepted. They told me it was almost certain death — and the thing is, you see, *I agreed!* I knew it was as near to certain death as makes no odds. Thinking about it now, I realize that was why I accepted the challenge. But I didn't take it up at once — we were in Grimsby at the time, in port."

He took another gulp of brandy and breathed out ecstatically. But now it struck her that the drink had as little effect on him as it did on her; if he was drunk on anything, it was on the remembered excitement of that escapade.

"I bided my time, see," he went on. "I endured the taunts of Tarheel Jack and the others, telling me how yellow my liver had turned and so on. But I waited until we were out at sea. I won't say it was a storm, but it was rough. Bay of Biscay, it was.

And then, in the second dogwatch, when we were all sitting in the fo'c'sle, sipping cocoa and swapping yarns, I suddenly tapped old Tarheel Jack on the shoulder and said, 'Right-ho, matey! Now's the time!' Even he turned pale, I may tell you. But I did it. With *Hiawatha* bucking beneath me like an unbroken stallion, I did it. The last stay was the worst, of course — the mizzen backstay. How I clung on, I'll never know. You could see the bones in the palms of my hands when I came back to deck, and there was blood to my armpits, but I clung on."

Emma winced so violently she almost snapped the glass in her fingers. "Why?" She no more than breathed the word.

"I say the mizzen backstay was the worst. It was also the best. I never felt more alive than I did then — laughing at death. And I felt it again that night I ran *Pegasus* aground — running her aback with not a fathom to spare, between rocks that would have planed the keel off her like paper. D'you understand it? This feeling I'm trying to convey?"

"I do when you talk about it," Emma replied. "You make it real, but it's not a feeling I've had myself."

"No. Women have more sense," he responded jovially. "It's not just a matter of risk, you see. Not just plain danger. Of course, risk and danger are exciting enough in their way. But this is something as far beyond that as ... as, I don't know — the moon to a seagull."

She stared at the far horizon, where the moon had been; only the last small arc of its ice halo now marked the spot.

"It must be *certain* death, you see. To face certain death, to take it by the throat and shake it into submission ... that's the ultimate excitement."

The hair suddenly prickled on the back of her neck as she realized why he was telling her all this. "You mean ... that's why you ... you and ..."

"Yes. Discovery is certain, of course. Mind you, I didn't believe it was at the beginning. I thought ... two wives, thousands of miles apart ... different continents ... a whole ocean between them. I couldn't see the slightest risk." He laughed at his simple-mindedness and then asked, "D'you know when the truth of the situation first struck me?"

"It must have been in New York?" she guessed. "When Miss Kathleen ...?"

"Yes!" he exclaimed. "That was when I knew discovery was certain. And yet I also know I shall cheat my fate this time, too. The excitement of it is every bit as great as on those earlier occasions — greater, because it goes on and on and on. It's so relentless. I wake up every day and it's waiting out there for me."

She took the flask from his pocket again and filled up both their glasses, emptying it entirely.

"Why not," he said, feeling the weight of it. "Now do you believe me when I assure you I'm not seeking to bribe or reward you for your continuing silence? Not in any way."

After a thoughtful pause she gave an awkward little laugh. "There's a funny thing, sir," she replied. "I never did believe that."

"Why not?" he asked abruptly, but with the sharpness of curiosity rather than of suspicion.

"I never believed you was that ... *simple* a man."

Indeed, she thought to herself, it would be better for him if he were. Such an elaborate disguise to throw over an act so elementary! Why could he not just admit he'd lost whatever love he'd felt for his wife and been bowled head over heels by Teresa — and then went and did the obvious, short-sighted thing? Why couldn't he admit it was as common and as ordinary as that? Instead, he had to go and mix it up with a daredevil moment or two from his past — not to say act of folly, in one case — and make it seem like some grand challenge to the Fates themselves! The brandy had loosened her inhibitions to the point where she almost blurted out these thoughts; but at the last moment a further notion intervened. It suggested that to shatter his delusions would be as painful and destructive to him as it would be to have overturned his daughter's equally lofty absurdities on the train back from New Haven.

That the two sets of illusions were destined to collide, she saw at once, but no way of deviating either of them occurred to her.

"To hubris!" He raised his glass in a wild and jovial toast to the dark elements all around him.

"To a safe anchorage," she said, as if it were a correction.

He laughed. "And in that order!"

They drained their glasses and, moved at last by a common impulse, flung their balloons far out into the Atlantic.

ILDA MOVED. It had never happened before — well, once, when she got a cramp — otherwise, never. It was so shocking, it quite put Frank off his stroke. "Go on!" she urged. That was unprecedented, too. He went completely limp then. "Oh?" she said plaintively. And he just lay there, too shattered to speak for a while. In any case, they had never developed a vocabulary to deal with this sort of thing; it had always just sort of happened in a wordless flurry, followed by a few contented grunts and slumber profound. What could he now say, anyway?

The entire evening had been extremely bizarre. "Hilda," to him, was the manager of this house. "Hilda" was the organizer of his social life whenever he came ashore. "Hilda" was the provider of certain basic comforts — the uncomplaining provider, except in one particular department, the one that had no lexicon. And a superb job she made of it all. She had forced him to accept her on those terms, to think of her in nothing but those terms, to become accustomed and even mildly fond of her as no more than that "Hilda"; and a superb job she had made there, also. So to find her stepping outside the bounds she herself had so rigidly drawn for the past twenty-three years was unnerving to say the least.

How different it had been before they tied the knot! Then, if they had been able to discuss such matters, he would have told her he didn't mind what sort of a fist she made at the housekeeping, or at managing his life; a loving smile and a welcoming bed would have compensated for the worst. He still could not understand how a woman like her, so beautiful to look at, so voluptuous in her body, could nonetheless be so utterly cold. It had been a disaster from the beginning, from the very first night, when she had lain there, trembling with terror — which he, in his untutored haste and arrogance, had mistaken for passion. It was a gulf that none of his later penitence and attempted tenderness had been able to bridge.

Over the past few years — and certainly since he had married Teresa — he had resigned himself to the situation and considerately left her more or less at peace. So to come ashore now and find her wearing a new perfume (when she had never worn perfume at all), and squeezed into new corsets (which exaggerated every curve her previous busks had flattened), and humming snatches of light opera (the habit she most detested in Daphne Dowty), and suggesting they dine out for a change (and in a chambre privée at the Café Royal, of all places), the misgivings rolled like Biscay swells. And as for the nightdress she had put on when they finally got to bed — its daring would have caused some comment even in a New Orleans sporting house. Where had she acquired such a thing? Hilda of all people!

Even so, for her to have *moved*, and to have given out those little sounds of actual pleasure, was so unprecedented, so profoundly shocking that he could only lie there and … well, wonder which side of the Atlantic he was on!

Hilda giggled and put her lips to his ear. "Poor old fellow," she whispered skittishly and then, without another word, turned her back on him and fell fast asleep.

He eventually achieved the same merciful release two nerve-racked hours later. But an hour after that, just before seven bells of the middle watch, he came suddenly wide awake, fresh as new paint, and consumed with a lust for her that had been stoked and damped, stoked and damped, these past twenty years and more. Nothing could withstand it.

"Yes-s-s!" she gasped as he took her from behind, for she was awake, too.

He did not awaken again until the maid brought in their early morning tea. For a second or so he wondered why Hilda did not follow her invariable habit by sitting up at once and testing its heat; then he remembered.

She ignored the tea. The moment Walker withdrew she insinuated one thigh over his and said, "Mmm?"

Lexicon or no lexicon he realized he would have to say something. "What is all this?" he asked. "I mean why now?"

She shrugged and moved her head onto his chest. "I love you," she said.

"Hilda?" There was a monitory edge to his voice now.

"What?"

"It's not like you ... all this."

"I'm at a funny time of life for a woman."

"Funny!" he echoed.

"Funny-peculiar."

"Is that all you're going to say on the subject?"

"What else *can* I say?"

"Sorry, for instance?" He pinched her with a strength half way between jest and anger. "For twenty-three years, all but a week or two, you've behaved as if my desire for conjugal pleasure were nothing but the crudest and most ..."

Suddenly she heaved herself off him, but only to resettle where her lips could close on his and silence his words. To his horror he saw she was crying. At least, there were tears on her cheeks — something he had never seen before. At last she settled her face in the crook of his neck and, breathing into the pillow, made a small furnace round his ear. "Will sorry do?" she whispered. "Don't you understand?"

"Understand what?" He turned away from her at his waist so she would not feel his arousal, which was painful rather than pleasant after so much exertion last night.

"One gets set in certain attitudes. One wants to change but one doesn't know how. We never discussed it, not once. How could we? Even now ... we can't seem to."

She wriggled herself into a more comfortable position upon him, discovered his condition, gave a cry of pleasure, and devoured him in one clean thrust.

And as his body rudely shouldered him aside and took over he felt himself consumed by an enormous anger. Why now? Why wait all this time?

At least, those were the immediate, the uppermost targets of his fury; but behind them he felt a more insidious thought take shape: How dare she just *use* me like this?

DAPHNE GAZED ABOUT her, not once but several times. "D'you know, my dear Emma," she said sweetly, "I'm not at all sure I'm glad to have made your acquaintance. Until the beginning of this year I would have said *I* was the most contented woman in England."

"Oh yes?" Emma responded guardedly.

"Well, if you're not, you're a naughty girl and deserve to be whipped. Just consider all the advantages you have! These beautiful rooms where no one else can come unless you invite them. Your life on the ocean wave. Your complete independence ..."

Emma cleared her throat to show she knew that Mrs D. (as she was now permitted to call Daphne) had some ulterior purpose in all this flattery — though she could not yet guess what it might be.

Daphne continued, "You can have no idea of the lives that we poor birds in our gilded cages lead." She smiled sweetly.

Emma took a chance, knowing that you could hardly ever go wrong if you read Mrs D. by opposites. "If this is winding up to some argument that I should marry Lawrence ..." she began.

"Marry Lawrence?"

Daphne's innocent eyes did nothing to persuade Emma she had guessed wrong. "Anyway," she concluded, "I don't want to start on all that ... Lawrence and that. I had enough of it from the Captain on this last voyage back from New York."

Daphne's eyes went wide with shock and pleasure. "Do tell!" she cried.

And so Emma related every last detail of her extraordinary encounter with Frank that night. "Of course," she concluded, "when he told that story about running *Hiawatha* overall, I kept mum about hearing it from you. But you was right, you see. It is the idea of risk what excites him — or so he believes."

Daphne pricked up her ears at that qualification. "D'you think otherwise?"

Emma pulled a dismissive face. "To me there's a much simpler cause. I don't think ... you know ... life at Highbury New Park ..."

Daphne twigged. "Ah yes. I remember your saying it before. Not a very *conjugational* marriage! Brilliant! How I wish we moved in the sort of circles where I could dine out on jokes like that. It's worth a dozen dinners at least. But the only man I've dared tell it to is Walter Grandison. Well well, you may be right. Tell me, what sort of a woman do you suppose Mrs Teresa is. I mean, one knows how she looks, but what is she like?"

Emma shrugged awkwardly. "How do I know? I only ever had tea with her — that sort of thing."

That sweet smile again. "You know because you're a woman, and women know such things."

"Maybe." Emma gazed unhappily out through the window. "But should they talk about them? That's what I ..."

"Ah! Because you suppose I'm being merely prurient! In that case, I see your difficulty, my dear. But no, it's much more than that, believe me."

"Is it?"

"Of course it is. Don't you realize, Emma, that we are the only two people in this whole sorry business who are capable of keeping a level head. One day there is going to be an almighty explosion — and the way things are going, it'll be sooner rather than later, I believe. Without our help they haven't a chance of surviving it. So if we don't share our impressions and ideas ..."

"All right!" Emma nodded firmly. "What d'you want to know?"

Daphne smiled and breathed more easily. "Tell me first about Walter Grandison. He was on that fateful return voyage from New York last January, was he not? Did something, ah ... how may I put it delicately? Did something *untoward* take place between him and

Mrs Hilda? I thought I saw you give a little twitch. When I mentioned his name earlier."

"Why d'you ask?" Emma still did not feel entirely easy in the rôle the older and wilier (if not wiser) woman was seeking to force upon her. "I mean — you're acting like you already know ... well, a thing or two."

"Aha! So there *is* something! I can see it in your eye. The reason I ask is because when I teased *her*, immediately upon her return from America, about being 'the pride of the *Pride of Liverpool*,' she asked who had told me such nonsense. Of course, nobody had told me any such thing. However — since I habitually read every passenger list, I simply picked the name most likely to annoy her: Walter Grandison. And believe me, if I'd had a bag of chestnuts, I could have roasted them at her ears! And I'll tell you another thing: Twice since then she's been plagued by mysteriously sick relatives down in Sussex — always conveniently between Friday noon and Monday morning. And on the second occasion I took it into my head — on the merest whim, you understand, mischief could not have been further from my thoughts — to call upon Walter Grandison and, strange to relate, he, too, was away from Fri to Mon!"

"In Sussex?"

"Kent." Daphne smiled triumphantly, for she had at last stirred Emma out of her uncommunicative reticence. "But in places, I'm told, the two counties are hardly a yard apart, while in others they are promiscuously contiguous! There now, I've told you my all. What do you know?"

Emma made several reluctant movements of her head and shoulders before she confessed that, in her opinion, something *had* happened between those two. "But nothing I could swear to in a court of law, mind," she added.

Daphne shuddered. "Thank heavens it hasn't come to that yet!" A frown creased her brow. "But I can still hardly believe it of Hilda — of all people!"

"Unless …" Emma put in.

"What?"

"Kathleen may have driven her to it, accidentally like. I was just thinking. On the train back from New Haven she was so full of her papa and how noble he was being for Teresa's sake. Sometimes she's that close with a secret, no one would worm it out of her. And sometimes she tells anyone who comes along. But I was just thinking — they shared a stateroom, of course — mother and daughter in the same bed — lots of time to talk the night away — nothing to get up for too early — see what I mean? If Mrs Hilda dropped a hint about what I said to her, that might be all it needed to start …"

"… the babbling brook," Daphne concluded for her. "Yes, well, I'd better confess that's precisely what did happen. I'm breaking a confidence, I know, but sometimes it becomes a duty to do so — more! It becomes a pleasure. Even so, knowing Mrs Hilda as I do, I still find it hard to believe that that would be enough to drive her directly into the arms of that awful old rake, Grandison."

Emma gave a significant sniff but said nothing.

"Come on!" Daphne encouraged.

"Well, I was only thinking …"

Daphne rubbed her hands delightedly. "I do love it when you 'only think'!"

"What's the *other* thing Walter Grandison's got?"

Daphne's laugh was like a crowing cock. "A

shipping line! Of course! How else would Mrs Hilda get to America without the Captain knowing of it! Oh, Emma, what a waste of brain it is, your being a stewardess! Marry Lawrence and let me bring you out!" She grinned and returned to the earlier topic with relish. "But what a minx Mrs Hilda is, eh!"

There was a heavy footfall — indeed, bootfall — on the stair.

"Larry!" Emma said at once. She glanced at the clock and said, "Yes."

And there he was at the door, bright eyed, breathless — and astonished to find his Aunt Daphne there.

"Lawrence!" she said in a voice that would have cured warts, if he'd had any. "How long has this been going on, may I ask?"

Emma played along, making her eyes go wide with apparent fear.

"Oh!" he exclaimed. "I … er … that is … it's not what you think, you know."

"I hardly know what to think!" she exclaimed in sepulchral tones.

"Tell her, Em?" Lawrence pleaded.

Emma burst into laughter at that. "Tell her what?" she asked.

"You may advance and kiss me," Daphne said primly, disappointed at not being able to wring more out of his discomfiture. Then she saw another way. She turned to Emma and said, "How can you *not* marry such a man? You must be mad."

The smile vanished at once from Emma's face, but Daphne persisted. "He even looks guilty when his conscience is absolutely clear. He will *never* be able to deceive you for a moment — and you know how insidious deceit can be, once it gets a grip on a family. Lawrence, dear" — she rose and drew on her gloves

— "do your best to persuade her. I can't think why you haven't done so long ago. You used to have such a golden tongue! Stay where you are. I'll find my own way out somehow."

She kissed Emma warmly, though the girl just stood there, both frigid and fuming, and wafted herself out on a cloud of promises to return as soon as she had thought over all they had been talking about.

Lawrence held his tongue until he heard the front door slam behind her; he even went to the window to make sure she was on the far side of it before he asked, "What was all that about? D'you know her? What did she mean — 'all you've been talking about'?"

"Quite finished, have you?" Emma asked. "I don't know why you think I've got to answer to you for anything."

"Friendship's often like that," he told her easily. "Oh, I could kill for a drink. Got any beer?"

Saying nothing she went to the sideboard and thumbed out the cork on a bottle of stout.

"I'll pour it," he offered. "You're still shaking with anger. I can see it."

She put the bottle and glass on the table, beyond his reach and, seating herself daintily on his lap, put her arms about his neck and hugged him as hard as she could.

"I do love you," he whispered in her ear.

Her lips grazed his neck. "Why do I need to hear you say it?" she asked.

"I don't know. Why? You'd jolly well better marry me, you know. There's no one else who'd put up with you for a minute."

She chuckled. "I know. The thing about you, Larry, is you're the only person who can make me feel clean."

"D'you want a beer, too?"

"Come on! I want to talk to you about it."

"What — cleanliness?"

"You're no innocent. You're a man of the world. You know your way about. But you haven't let it *stain* you. Everyone else is … stained. I can't think of another word. Do you really want to marry me?"

He drew back from her, but only to the point where he could take her face between his hands. "How can you doubt it still — after all this time?" He swallowed hard. "Are you saying yes?"

She closed her eyes and nodded. He almost burst into laughter for he thought he had never seen a face so miserable. But a moment later he learned the cause — and the impulse to laughter died.

"You think this long wait has been a kind of test, don't you," she said bleakly. "Well, my old pal, it's nothing to what's coming now. Shall I just tell you the facts? Or the way it all happened?"

Deciding on the latter course, she sprang from his lap and began to pace about the room. He poured out his stout and waited for her to begin.

It took about fifteen minutes, though to her it seemed like hours. At first he interrupted every other sentence with gasps and interjections of incredulity; then he tried quizzing her closely on every particular assertion. But each time she waved him to silence and continued doggedly with her account, exactly as it had happened. Her conclusion to it all — the conversation she had had with his father the previous Friday night — answered every question and copper-fastened all she had said.

He was so shattered by it, he could think of nothing but the most trivial questions. "Did you tell him about my betting on the horses?" he asked.

She shook her head; the agony in his eyes was heart-rending. "He didn't mention you at all, nor Neil, nor Kathleen."

"Nor my mother?"

Another shake of her head, this time wordless.

"I'll kill him!" He thumped the table hard enough to make his glass jump and foam over, though it did not tip. Her fingers itched to wipe up the spillage but she managed to check herself.

"I think everyone feels that to start with ..."

"How can he treat my mother like that?" Now he, too, rose and began to pace about the room.

She sat in the chair he had just vacated and surreptitiously wiped the overflow of foam with her handkerchief, pretending to sip at the glass to cover the action. "You don't know how she's taken it," she told him. "Would you say she's all down in the dumps? I saw her going for a drive in the carriage with your father this morning. Talk about the cat that swallowed the canary!"

"What d'you mean?"

"I mean I think you're insulting your mama when you go on about it like that. She's not some wilting little ..."

He turned almost apoplectic. "*I'm* insulting her? What about him? Insult is too mild a word for it. He has traduced her, maligned her."

This time she really did take a sip. "You and your foreign words! I don't know what they mean, but I'll tell you this — I never saw a woman more radiant than your mama this morning. And she *knows*, remember. She knows exactly what he's been and gone and done."

He ran his fingers through his hair and stared wildly at her. "Are you implying she's happy with this … situation — for want of a better word?"

"Lord love a duck, Larry — don't you never listen to nothing? Of course she's not happy. Leastways, not in the sense that she accepts what he's done to her. But I think she's happy to be fighting back. I think she's happy she's going to win in the end." She took a gulp and belched — mainly to shock him, to bring him back to earth. "What a common wife you got, eh?"

"Well!" He glared balefully at her. "You've had months to grow accustomed to this … this appalling business. But I don't see any cause for humour at all."

"Nor do I," she shot back. "But I think it makes even less sense to carry on like what you are. I'm beginning to feel sorry I ever told you."

He drew breath to protest but she stopped him with another question. "What do *you* think your mama ought to do? What would you advise, if she asked you?"

"Cut him dead, of course. Expose him for the blackguard he is."

"Send him to jail?"

"Yes. It's the least he deserves. There should still be public floggings for crimes like that."

"And then?"

"What d'you mean?"

"I mean *and then*?"

He shrugged in bewilderment. "She lives without him, of course. She'd be free of him."

"Where? Didn't you listen to what I said when I told her why she shouldn't go warbling about me to the Shaw & Eggar?"

He stared at her as the vaguest of memories began to filter down. Now she was relentless. "And you? Still going to turn up on the Baltic every day, are you?

Hear them whispering, 'There's young Morgan. His father is *that* Morgan, you know!' You wouldn't stick it a week! And then there's Kathy!"

He put his knuckles to his eyes and rubbed until stars began to swirl.

"They're going to flock to marry her, aren't they! Eligible young bachelors from Edinburgh even, I shouldn't wonder!"

"All right! All right!" he cried. He opened his eyes and blinked at the light. "What *is* going to happen, then? How on earth is my mother going to 'fight back,' as you put it?"

"I don't know," she told him simply. "But I do know this — nothing you do, and nothing I do, can possibly stop it. We've just got to be ready when …"

He waited to hear no more. With a strangled, formless cry, he flung himself from the room.

She stood there a long moment with her eyes closed, listening to his boots take the stairs three and four at a time, listening to the front door slam, listening to his dwindling footfall on the pavement outside. At last she opened her eyes, saw his glass, and drained it to the dregs.

She tried to belch again but couldn't. Instead she slumped into the chair, laid her arms on the table and her head on her arms, and wept every last drop from her eyes.

IF LAWRENCE HAD not, at long last, carried out his threat to run away to sea, Neil would probably have stayed afloat, at least until he got his master's ticket. Then he might have taken a maritime place in some large port, in the harbourmaster's office, perhaps, or as a marine inspector with the Board of Trade; and in that way he would have satisfied his two main desires in life: to go to sea and not to go to sea. For, despite his inauspicious beginnings, he had, over the past year or so, felt the lure of the sea taking hold of him. Indeed, on his last voyage, from Cardiff to Valparaiso, as *Swallow* had pulled out of the bay and headed into the setting sun, and the black and golden hills of South Wales had dwindled into darkness, he had felt a sense of awe at what he and his shipmates were about to do — pitting their puny three thousand tons of steel against an ocean whose vastness he could still not comprehend, even after half a dozen crossings. He had to admit then that nothing ashore could offer such a direct confrontation between the bold littleness of man and the uncaring grandeur of Creation; and so he was bitten at last by the worm that gnaws at the soul of every true seaman, who may curse the sea, the elements, the ship, the master, the company, the grub ... but whose soul dies a little each day these scourges are not there to plague him.

It helped that, when he signed off the *Swallow* back in Cardiff, her next cargo was to be of Welsh anthracite to Spain. They were already filling the number one hold as he went ashore, and a drab, dirty hulk streaked with black rain was his last view of her. He arrived home late that evening. His telegram preceded him by a mere two hours, so there had been time to air his bed but not to kill the customary fatted calf.

"Neil! How wonderful, my darling!" His mother almost bowled him over in her delight, throwing her arms around him and kissing him warmly, many times, on his lips and cheeks. "And home for the whole month! Oh, this is going to be a wonderful Easter. All of us together again!"

She certainly bowled him over in the emotional sense; he could not remember a time when she had been as demonstrative as this. "What's the matter?" he asked.

"Matter?" She laughed. "Nothing. Why?"

"Well!" He shrugged — and then caught sight of Lawrence up on the landing. "Hallo, Beast," he called out jovially.

His brother made a painfully obvious effort, forced up a smile, and came gladhanded down the stairs two at a time. "Hallo, Beast! They're still not feeding you too well then."

Neil slipped from his mother's arms and pulled a punch on his brother's gut. "And you're none too plushly padded, either, shipmate." He saw the word kindle a little glow in Lawrence's eye as he drew breath to reply; but then he thought better of it — or, rather, changed it to an empty, though jocular, "Shiver me timbers!"

Kathleen came skipping up the passage, crying her brother's name and saying how lovely it was to see him.

"Kathy?" he teased. "Not at sea yet? What's gone agley?"

"Papa says I can be Assistant Nurse on the *Pride of Liverpool* starting next ..."

"All right, all right!" Hilda clapped her hands. "Goodness gracious, the boy's not a minute in the house and you want to tell him six months' news. Give him a chance!"

"Where's George?" Neil asked.

Faces fell. "We had to put him down," Lawrence explained. "Trouble in all departments."

They drifted into the drawing room and sat down; Neil noticed that, for once, his mother did not reprimand those who sat on rather than in their chairs. He said, "I *almost* brought a monkey back with me this time."

"Oh do!" Kathleen begged. "Next time. Bring a monkey, promise? What was his name?"

"Mickey Monkey." He pulled a face, apologizing for the poverty of invention. "He was very amusing but, in some ways, a little too human. Well, what's all the rage in Highbury?"

And from then until dinner time, and on through the meal, they brought him up to date with all the local, and family, and local-family news — or all that was fit for publication. Then there was Chicago and Boston and the wonders of a voyage on the *Pride of Liverpool* — all of which had taken place since last they saw him. Yet, though they laughed a lot and there was never an awkward silence, he could hardly help being aware that some profound change had overtaken all three of them.

Lawrence seemed his old, laconic, jovial self — until you caught a glimpse of him when his guard was down. Then there was a dark, brooding in his eye and the muscles at his temples rippled incessantly.

Kathy, who had always tried to seem mature beyond her years, was now on the other tack — behaving with a simpering girlishness that was clearly uncomfortable, even to her. Did she imagine it an appropriate way for a young girl to behave on first falling in love? It was an easy, obvious explanation but he did not feel it to be the right one.

But Mama's was the most amazing transformation of all — in fact, she was the only one for whom the word was truly appropriate. Gone was the rather remote, serious, and above all dignified woman who had controlled this household with a nod, a lift of the eyebrow; in her place was someone much ... *sharper* was the word that immediately occurred to him. It was not that she watched more or listened more, for she had always been observant in a dutiful sort of way; but now she seemed more personally engaged in things, as if it would matter to *her* if some small detail passed her by. At one extreme it shaded over into shrewishness. She was quite peevish at times, particularly with Kathy, who, for her part, was far more submissive than he remembered her. But at the other extreme it revealed a bright, engaged woman, looking for the funny side of things.

Later that night, when they had all retired to bed, Neil drifted into his brother's room for a smoke, giving as his reason that the wind was on his side of the house and would blow the smell of it indoors.

"Oh, you needn't bother about that any longer," Lawrence told him. "Mama's given up minding about smoke. She even puffs the occasional gasper herself now."

"Good Lord! All evening I've been aware of some changes, but that takes the biscuit. Mama smoking!"

Lawrence made no reply.

"You remember Mrs Fiorelli?" Neil went on. "How Bianca and Antonio could get away with murder — not because she was neglectful or careless or anything like that but because she always had some business or other on her mind — those warehouses she owned down in Wapping, and the shop in Soho, and the properties in Chalk Farm. What did Antonio's muddy boots matter if she was paying five quid a day demurrage at Wapping because her manager hadn't cleared the shelves?"

"Bianca was the first girl I ever kissed," Lawrence said. "We were only six."

"That's who mother reminds me of now — Mrs Fiorelli. She's got that same something-more-important look in her eye. Did it come over her suddenly? In fact, what has come over everyone here? Kathy's changed, too. And so — to put it bluntly, young Beast — have you."

"You should have seen me yesterday," Lawrence replied.

"You mean you were worse?"

"No! I was happy. Blissfully, ignorantly, happy. I only learned about it this evening — from Emma Harding."

Neil cleared his throat delicately. "I owe you an apology there. I did a very foolish thing. I don't suppose *she'll* ever forgive me — no reason why she should — but I thought you ..."

"Oh, put a sock in it for God's sake," Lawrence cried out in disgust. "If you knew how trivial all that is compared with ..." He shook his head, unable to find words adequate to the situation.

Neil decided his brother had obviously fallen out with Emma — not something he wished to probe any deeper. "Is Miss Harding in London?" he asked. "How can that be if Papa isn't?"

"Oh, they have to patch up one of the boilers. Sailings are postponed three days. He's gone to Belfast to look at the *Pride of the Mersey*, the sister ship."

"Why? Is he going to take her over when she's fitted out?"

"That's the big question. She's a finer ship but he's grown fond of the old *Liverpool*. Actually, Beast, I'm thinking of going to sea myself at last. I know I've

449

threatened it often enough, but this time I'll do it."

"Well, there's a place going on the *Swallow*. Nice lot of Welsh anthracite for Genoa. You'll spend half the voyage swabbing decks."

"Why? Signed off have you?"

Neil blew a thin wreath of smoke out into the night. "Thought I might spend a month or so ashore, put out a few feelers ..."

"Down on the Baltic? There's a place going there, too!"

He gave a reluctant shrug. "Something in a port, I thought. I don't believe I could leave the sea entirely behind me now. Be warned, Beast! It'll fasten itself in your blood if you're not careful. Would you think of going on the *Swallow*? I could send them a wire tomorrow."

"I have a place any time I like on the *Horsa*. Captain Rogers. Good man. Got to know him quite well. Good ship, too. Eighteen hundred tons."

"Would you sail before the mast to start with?"

Lawrence grinned for the first time. "Straight in at third officer. Luck of the devil, eh?"

"If the hands don't find out. If they do, your life won't be worth living."

"What's life without a bit of risk?" Lawrence asked in jocular superiority — and then felt sick again.

N EIL HAD COME HOME on the fourth Tuesday in March; on the Thursday morning of that same week, Lawrence went down to Tilbury and signed on as third officer on the *Horsa*. Neil went with him. In fact he had hardly let his brother out of his sight from the moment of his return; it intrigued him that he made no reference to Emma nor any further attempt to see her. He kept up his silence on the matter until the very last moment, when, with one foot on the gangplank and the bosun fingering his pipe, he pulled an envelope from his pocket and mumbled, "Take this to Emma for me, there's a good sort."

The address was there — the same one in Upper Street, he noted as he tucked it away. So the little idiot was still paying her rent! "Gladly," he said and then held out his hand. "Well, Beast, speaking as an old salt to one still wet behind the ears …"

He got no further for Lawrence offered playful violence if he dared utter another word. But the good humour soon died behind his eyes — so swiftly, indeed, that Neil felt bound to ask, "What is it? Something *is* up with you."

His brother just stood there, racked by some mighty indecision for a moment; then he shook his head and said, "Nothing. See you in a week or so."

Neil did not look back; that was the tradition. He fingered the letter in his pocket and talked himself into the moral rightness of steaming it open — to such good effect that he did not even hesitate when he arrived home. "I have a chill coming on," he told Mrs Johnson. "I think I might just nip it in the bud if I can have a kettle and some Friar's Balsam in my room."

He put enough of the liniment into the water to support his charade and then applied the steam to his main purpose, which was soon achieved. The gong rang for lunch but, having an excellent excuse not to obey it at once, he sat there and read:

My Darling Em,

What you told me of my father's actions I can no longer doubt. The shame of it is more than I can bear. I am going away to sea for a while and will try to come to terms with it. By the time you read this I shall be Third Officer on the *Horsa*, which I have spoken of, I'm sure. She runs regular cargoes between Tilbury and Hamburg, so I shall be back every week or ten days and we are bound to coincide often.

You see, I am not saying farewell to you, only that I need time to myself and a change of air, to adapt myself to what I am and what sort of family is mine. I have tried to tell Neil but cannot, perhaps it's better he not know. That is no accusation against you for making me know, for I know why you did it, directly after you accepted my proposal, was it not? I realize you could not agree to marry me with that secret inside you. But you will also understand that I do not hold you to anything said or done before that. I love you more than ever and will be desolate to lose you, yet I cannot in honour ask for your hand, not after this.

Let us decide nothing until I have had a chance to accept the situation. You are right. If Mama were to expose Papa for the foul monster he is, it would send him to gaol, which he so justly merits, but it would thrust her into exile and us three, his children, into oblivion, which none of us deserve. Yet I could not stay at home and face him, either. Surely you understand that? I do not think I could even face Kathy, day after day. Her childish explanation of his crime, making him seem so noble, sickens me. I'm sure she is beginning to see through it herself and has retreated into a kind of smirking immaturity that can only grow more desperate as she struggles to maintain her idiotic fiction …

As Neil read these words, the hair rose all down his spine. What a ghastly business! What a dreadful revelation! Why had the Beast said nothing while he was still ashore? He glanced at his watch but the *Horsa* had already sailed. He stamped his foot in frustration.

How could it be so obvious to him what had happened — while, clearly, not even the faintest suspicion had crossed his younger brother's mind? That young woman must be the devil incarnate to have bemused and bewildered him so. Larry was no fool, yet she clearly had him soaking up every foul bit of poison she poured in his ear!

That had been her purpose all along, of course. Hadn't she admitted it herself? When Mama had dismissed her that day, she'd vowed a terrible revenge on all the Morgans — beginning with Larry. Of course, she'd pretended to fall in love with him — which gave her the most perfect reason to admit her original motives and make everyone believe she'd abandoned them in the cause of True Love. The clever, vicious little witch!

Reading between the lines of his brother's pathetic drivel, he could see exactly how she had set about it, too. First she'd fed her insinuations to Kathy, but in such an artful manner that the poor girl could respond in no other way than by defending her beloved father with every ounce of reason she possessed. Then she had fed the same lethal diet to Larry, the same appalling lies, but making it sound much more credible this time. And thus sister and brother had been set at loggerheads! And thus, atom by atom, she would prise this entire family apart. Unless someone stopped her.

He laughed, for he suddenly realized he was the fly in her woodpile. The one thing she could not have planned was for him to return home at this most delicate juncture. Well, he'd soon show her he was her equal in cunning and her master in setting right all she had so assiduously put wrong.

Still chuckling, he tore his poor, deluded brother's letter into tiny shreds and threw them into the fire.

A MAN OF ACTION and simple morality, Neil wasted no time in tackling the problem of Emma. He went to Upper Street immediately after luncheon. But there was no answer to his knock. Disappointed, he decided to call on his Aunt Daphne and do a delicate bit of sounding out the ground ... see what way the wind was blowing there. Aunt D. had her own strange way of looking at things, but, with a bit of skillful reading between the lines, a fellow with his wits about him could usually work out what was what and what ... well, wasn't.

He began to realize how serious matters had become when, on being shown into his aunt's dining room, he discovered her hobnobbing with none other than Emma Harding herself! Indeed, they were doing more then merely hobnobbing, they were actually seated at table, finishing off a late luncheon.

"Neil!" Daphne cried in her fluttering tones. "My maid told me the scullery maid heard from the greengrocer that Mrs Williams's maid had heard from your maid Walker that … oh dear, now I've forgotten what I heard. Oh yes — that you were home, of course! Well, isn't it splendid to be surrounded by so many truthful people, suddenly!" She offered him both perfumed cheeks. "I'm not sure I can stand it."

Emma giggled and said, "Mrs D. — really!" Then, turning and proffering a hand to Neil, she added in a much cooler tone, "Mr Morgan, it's been some time since we met."

It made him want to vomit — to see this viper in the family bosom, giving herself airs and sitting at table with her betters. He only shook her hand because he didn't want to give his game away. He even managed to smile at her and to comment that she was looking quite well.

"Considering," she said coldly.

"We've been *shopping*," Daphne said, making it sound like an activity in its own right. "Consoling this poor maiden in her tragic loss. I keep telling her — *all* young men between the ages of eighteen and … how old are you, now?"

"Twenty-two."

"Yes, between eighteen and twenty-three are utter idiots. I know I can count on *you* to support me there, dear. I wish you could have known your father at that same age. I promise you, he was far from being the *wise* and *upright* gentleman he is today."

She watched closely for his reaction as she enunciated the two adjectives with more than her usual fastidious emphasis. There was none. Either Lawrence had told him nothing, or his time at sea had taught him better control of his expression than she would have believed possible. Knowing the Morgan family's preferences when it came to sharing information among themselves, she decided to assume the first explanation. Oh dear! It was going to be pretty much uphill from here on.

He glanced at the Harding creature when his aunt spoke about his father; the light in her eyes made him shiver. It was the stare of the basilisk, the hypnotic gaze of the python as it prepares to sting the rabbit. He began to understand, too, how she had ensnared his brother, for there was no denying she possessed an undoubted … well, you couldn't call it beauty — and to talk of mere prettiness was too feeble. The word that occurred to him, the word he shied away from using, was *character*.

He could hold her merciless gaze for no more than an instant, but it was long enough to realize that she had changed most of all, these past two years. Loth though he was to admit it, she had grown immensely in stature. Merely to look at her was to want to know her; she seemed to be surrounded by a special aura, a warmth, a limelight, that drew him to seek her company. He shivered and felt a light sweat break out in the small of his back. It was going to take all his strength of character and all his intelligence to defeat this Jezebel. Fortunately he had plenty of both.

"Do join us for a little demitasse, Neil?" Aunt Daphne invited. "Or a small liqueur — the sun's over the yardarm, *well* over. Perhaps we can linger here until they bring us our tea — just move on one place, like the Mad Hatter."

He seated himself opposite the Harding. "You've

heard about Larry, then?" he asked his aunt. "He's done it at last. Third Officer on the *Horsa*, Hamburg-bound." He pulled out his watch and consulted it. "Just about dropping the pilot, I'd say." He smiled at his aunt. "I gave him the address of the von Kraemers. I hope he has time to look them up. Gisela von K. is such a charming young lady." He turned to the Harding. "Perhaps you know them? Have they sailed on the *Pride of Liverpool?*"

Daphne winced. She moved her foot toward Emma's, preparing to give hers an encouraging nudge, when the girl said, "They sail on the *Berlin*, of course."

It wasn't the words so much as the emphasis; Daphne herself could not have done better in suggesting that no one in their right minds would sail on the *Pride of Liverpool* when they had the choice of the *Berlin*. The encouraging nudge turned into two gentle taps of applause. Emma shot her a grateful glance — which nonetheless hinted she was well able to handle this idiot.

"Ah. Yes." Neil said.

He straightened his tie and stared into the high polish of the table, trying to read the girl's expression in it, like Hercules and the Gorgon. Or was it Jason and the Medusa? Or were the Gorgon and the Medusa the same? Anyway ...

Suddenly, literally from nowhere, the most dreadful image seized his mind. He saw himself in that room in Upper Street, being strapped to the bed by the Harding. She pulled the ropes, which were of silk, as tight as she could.

"Did you say liqueur?" he asked in a panic, before that awful scene could develop any further. What was she doing to him? How did she manage to take control of his mind like that and put such monstrous suggestions into it?

"And you're staying ashore now?" Daphne said as she rang the bell for the maid. "I'm sure you're wise. I couldn't help noticing the way you consulted your watch just now."

"Eh?" he responded.

"It made me think at once, *Yes, this young fellow belongs in a nice, comfortable office in the City.* I've seen them on the Baltic, you know. They all look at their watches in exactly that way. Of course, you'll need to put on another five or six inches in girth, but the stodge they call 'food' down there will soon do the trick." She smiled at Emma. "Isn't everything turning out well!"

It was her turn for the basilisk stare. But her smile only broadened as she reached across and patted the girl's hand. "Don't fret, my dove. He'll be back, more sensible than ever. The sea gives people an e-*nor*-mous amount of common sense. Amn't I right, Neil? And look at yourself, dear. You're ten times the young lady you were a year ago — not that I knew you then, but I have an instinctive feel for these things. It's quite uncanny. And then there's Captain Morgan! Need I say more?" She told the maid to bring the tantalus with the liqueurs.

"Aunt Daphne," Neil said severely, "I think you have already said too much. Your levity is admired and treasured *within* the family but" — he smiled apologetically at the Harding — "I'm not sure it is to Miss Harding's taste. No one will be more sensible than she of the fact that he is the captain of a vessel in which she holds a comparatively menial rank."

Daphne did her best to contain her mirth but eventually it exploded out of her. "He doesn't *know!*"

she said to Emma. "Lawrence hasn't told him!" She turned back to Neil and, ignoring his thunderous mask, gave a fond shake of her head. "I don't know what it is about your family, dear, but you tell each other nothing! Did Lawrence really not tell you?"

"Tell me what?" he barked, even angrier that she had forced him into the position of seeming to want to know the answer.

She turned back to Emma. "May I?" Below the table the pressure of her foot turned it into an urgent plea.

Emma shrugged.

"Poor girl, she's too modest to tell you herself, but your brother has plagued the ears off her, night and day ... well, morning and evening, anyway — begging her to marry him. And at last he's quite worn her down. Rather foolishly in my opinion — because, believe me, she's worth a hundred of him — she yesterday accepted his offer." She faltered on the last words, aware that her mask had slipped, allowing her anger at Lawrence, and her contempt for his cowardice, as she saw it, to show. She had intended to suggest it would be in order for him to embrace his future sister-in-law, just to rub his nose in it, but the momentum had gone. She merely favoured him with her indulgent, slightly pitying smile. The maid brought the liqueurs.

Emma felt a lump rise unexpectedly into her throat. Mrs Dowty was such a brittle lady, so forbidding and unknowable behind her jocular exterior, that it had not seemed possible for her to entertain genuine emotions and sympathies; to be granted a sudden, unintended glimpse of them like that was poignant and moving.

Neil felt it, too, but, having not the first notion as to why Aunt Daphne might feel like that, he put it down to the fact that she was, after all, a woman-god-bless-'em, which fully entitled her to be irrational and opaque.

Of course, such a marriage would be out of the question. *He'd* see to that. Meanwhile, just to lull her suspicions, he'd play along. "Capital!" he said with a broad smile. "Congratulations! I hope you'll be very happy."

"Ah!" Daphne was ecstatic. "You have such discrimination, Neil. It quite takes my breath away. Usually, as you know, it is considered extremely bad form to congratulate the lady. It cuts a little too near the bone, with its suggestion that she's been angling after the man for years. But, since the very reverse is true in dear Miss Harding's case, you immediately reverse the etiquette in the matter! So *precisely* right!"

Neil just sat there fuming, not least because he was unable to find a chink through which he could stab at his aunt's inflated self-esteem. "Curaçao," he murmured, sipping his drink. "I never sailed there."

He looked up and was unnerved to find the Harding staring at him, weighing him up. The meeting of their eyes, forced her to some conclusion. "Larry said he'd give you a letter for me, Mr Morgan," she said evenly.

"Ah." He sat up and patted his pockets in a rather perfunctory manner. "No, he must have forgotten."

It was so artlessly done that Daphne twigged at once what lay behind this exchange. "Oh, isn't he the most vexatious young man!" she exclaimed lightly. "If I were you, Miss Harding, I'd write to him care of the *Horsa's* agent, Lumley and Co, in Cheapside. I'll give you their directions before you go. Tell him what his brother has just said and remind him how important that letter is to you."

Emma thanked her and promised to do so that very night. She herself would be sailing on Saturday but, as Larry would return next Monday or Tuesday, it would give him ample time to remember.

By now Neil's spirit was at its nadir. He knew she was possessed of bags of cunning, but to see it deployed on this diabolical scale was frightening. Not only had she warped Kathy and Larry to her will, she had even suborned someone as powerfully independent as Aunt Daphne. Clearly the situation called for more thought.

Or — it suddenly struck him — perhaps it called for *less!* Indeed, perhaps it was time to seize the initiative and take some direct action. He realized that, if he waited for the Harding to leave, he'd be bound by the etiquette of the situation to offer to escort her home — during which time she'd put out all her snares and draw him into her vile web, too.

He finished his drink with indecent haste, made his excuses, and left. Daphne saw him to the door. "I'm so glad you're home for a nice long spell now, Neil," she said. "There's so much to tell you. Don't go popping off again, will you? Come round and see me again, and soon."

He promised he would. Then he skulked around Highbury Fields, waiting until the Harding came out. He hid himself behind the public lavatories until she went past. Then he followed her down Upper Street to her apartment.

S HE OPENED HER door no more than a crack. "Oh, you," she said warily when she saw who it was. "What d'you want now?" Instinctively she pulled the door a little tighter, until it and the jamb simply bracketed her head. To him it suggested a degree of vulnerability, as a woman who feels herself threatened might pluck even a well-buttoned dressing gown yet tighter to her. "I'm not going to let you in," she warned, as if she had just read his mind.

Their eyes dwelled coldly in each other's and a ripple of fear passed through her — not fear of him but of herself. She disliked him intensely. She could not think of one good feature, one saving grace, to throw into the weighing of Neil Morgan's soul. And yet some small part of her felt irresistibly drawn to him. It begged her to take that smug face between her hands and smother those imperious, arrogant lips with her kisses — even though the very thought of doing such a thing filled the rest of her with disgust.

"You know what I want," he said.

She slammed the door in his face and stood with her back pressed tight against it, her heart hammering like mad. It infuriated her that she could not control this feeling within her. It was purely physical — the sort of thing she'd learned to control years ago. Why should it be giving her so much trouble now? And with Neil, of all people?

He pushed the door open, using his superior brawn to shoulder her aside. Then, with his foot in the door, he said, "I want to know what poison you've been spreading about my father."

"Oh, that!" She walked away from the door and went to the far side of the table. Her dispirited tone and the dejected slope of her shoulders suggested he was no longer any threat; she was using her body to fight itself, with what success she had yet to discover. "So Larry did tell you, after all," she added.

"No!" he snapped. Then, just as swiftly, "Yes! That is to say, er …"

"Aha!" she sneered. "It was in the letter, wasn't it! There *was* a letter after all. Oh, Neil!" She sighed and slumped into a chair. "You're such a simple, stupid … I don't know."

He wanted to tell her he did not recall having given her permission to address him so intimately, but the words, marshalling themselves in his mind, sounded strangely pompous.

She went on: "I don't suppose he said anything important. Nothing I couldn't guess?"

"If you mean has your poison done its work, the answer is yes." He remained at the door, reluctant to venture too far inside this witch's den. "All I want to know is what you've been saying — to Larry, to my sister, and even, it would seem, to Mrs Dowty. My God! I've come home just in time, haven't I."

"If you say so." She stifled a genuine yawn, glad only that her desire for him seemed to have evaporated as swiftly as it had come over her.

"I do. If it weren't for me, Harding, you'd have completed your revenge by now, wouldn't you! So let me tell you — I'm jolly well going to put a spoke in your wheel, young madam."

"Yes, Neil. I'm sure you're a one-man Charge of the Light Brigade once you get going."

"So come on, out with it! What lies have you been spreading, eh?"

She shook her head sadly. "I'm ashamed of myself. It's obvious to me I've met my match in you. In fact, there's no point in telling you. You'd see through me at once." These last words gave her an altogether new idea. "Yes!" she exclaimed, brightening considerably. "You would, too, wouldn't you! You see clear through me — through everything. So why don't I let you — see it all with your own eyes?"

"Eh? What trickery is this? I warn you …"

"It's very simple, Neil. All you do, Neil, is get across the Atlantic somehow without your family knowing. And judging by the way you all tell each other your thoughts and feelings and what you're doing every minute of the day — that's going to be the hard bit, Neil. But then comes the easy bit. Once you're over there, in New York, you go to the Grand Central Depot on Park Avenue at Forty-Second Street and you catch a train to New Haven, Connecticut. That's about eighty or ninety miles, Neil. And when you …"

"What *is* all this tomfoolery?" he asked. "And who said you could call …"

"When you get off at New Haven, take a cab to a little township called Fife, like in Scotland, only smaller. Can you remember that? Ask the cabby to drop you at a house called *Pegasus*."

He had drawn breath to speak, but that stopped him dead.

She grinned. "Yes, I thought that would check your gallop. *Pegasus*. You'll remember that, I daresay?"

"What are you … what is all this? I don't understand a word you're saying."

She dared to go nearer him, dared even to lay a hand briefly on his arm. "I'm confessing, Neil. I'm shopping myself to you. I'm telling you how to gather the evidence that will unmask me. When you get to this house called *Pegasus* in Fife near New Haven, Connecticut, all you need do is introduce yourself to the lady of the house. Tell her your name, Neil. Tell her who your father is."

"And then?"

"Why, she'll give you all the ammo you need to sink me like a stone."

He laughed scornfully. "You're bluffing. You're sailing to America yourself in thirty-six hours. You'll get there before me and make sure all I find is one big red herring. You just want me out of the way."

It was the first intelligent point he had made all afternoon. "Very well," she conceded, "if you'll promise to go, I'll cry off sick ... no, wait a moment! Better still! Your family's on good terms with Walter Grandison, aren't you?"

"What of it?"

She tweaked his watch out of his waistcoat pocket. "You've got time. The *Burgundia* is sailing from Southampton at midnight. Take a passage on her and you'll be in New York twenty-four hours ahead of me."

Stubbornly he shook his head. "It must be something you've already arranged, then. Otherwise you wouldn't be so cavalier about sending me there. I know you and your tricks by now."

"Ohmigawd!" She sighed hopelessly. "I am a devil, aren't I! All I can suggest, then, is that you ask Kathy who she met when *she* went to *Pegasus*."

"She has ... visited this place?" he asked in horror.

"Ye-e-es!" She said, as a teacher might say to a dim pupil who has finally grasped that two and two make four, most of the time.

He squared himself to the decision. "Then I most certainly shall go. Whatever trickery you may have used to deceive her will hardly take *me* in, but it is imperative I know the poison so that I may devise the antidote — with all dispatch. Yes." He plucked forth his watch again. "With all dispatch."

"Neil!" she cried as he turned to go.

"What?"

Unable to stop herself she grasped his head between her hands and pulled him to her, smothering his lips in hard, passionate kisses. Then, when he was just beginning to recover from his surprise, she thrust him from the room, slammed the door, and bolted it.

She just stood there, trembling with anger and ... something else, something she did not wish to name. How *could* she! What on earth possessed her to do such a thing?

He was not moving, either. Soon there came a hesitant knock at the door. "Emma?" he said.

She made no reply.

He went after a while. She crossed to the window and watched him all the way up the street; no feeling about him remained in her. He no longer seemed worth even her distaste.

When he had covered some thirty paces he stopped and raised a tentative hand to his lips. He half turned to look back at her window, but then thought better of it. After that, he strode out more purposefully.

"What have I been and gone and done?" she asked herself out loud.

But she had no need to answer. She knew exactly what she had done — she had killed two birds with one stone.

W ALTER GRANDISON WAS charm personified; he spoke as if the *Burgundia* had been built especially to perform this trifling service for the son of one of his dearest and oldest friends in an hour of need. Neil was to consider himself a guest of the company — and naturally he, Grandison, would not breathe a word of it to a living soul. Overwhelmed with gratitude, Neil took the letter to the captain in which his status was confirmed, raced to Victoria Station, which was fortunately just down the road from Grandison's house in Eaton Square, caught his train in the nick of time, and sank with relief into the plush velvet of one of its compartments. The greatest adventure of his life had begun. His family, meanwhile, believed he was helping a friend refloat a ketch that had sunk in the Norfolk Broads — a bit of an emergency that would keep him out of easy reach for as long as he liked … certainly for three or four weeks, what with having to careen and caulk her, into the bargain.

Burgundia, though not so palatial as the *Pride of Liverpool*, was nonetheless luxurious by the standards of five years ago — and certainly far beyond anything Neil had experienced afloat. It was bliss to lie in state in his stateroom and listen to the bells toll away the middle watch, knowing he could snooze on until six bells of the forenoon watch if he wished.

All the way over he kept thinking of the Harding creature and her strange behaviour at the moment of their parting. Being only human, he devised two contradictory explanations for it, both of which he was able to believe simultaneously. Indeed, being only Neil, he managed to combine them into one, super-contradictory explanation. The first was that, like all women — all women of her class, anyway — she was desperate for a good bit of the old jolly roger. He could hardly believe it but his little idiot of a brother probably hadn't raked her innards through even yet. That fact alone could explain her vengeful behaviour; perhaps she started out wanting to spite herself on Mama but then really did fall for the young Beast, just as she claimed. Women of every class were notorious for such emotional inconsistency. Naturally, if the little Beast didn't respond as females of that type expect a man to respond ... well, case proven.

The other explanation was that she was devoid of tender feelings of any kind, being consumed with hatred and a lust for revenge. Cold as ice, she calculated every move. That kiss had been no accident. Its timing, its apparent passion, its duration, and the way she had expelled him immediately she broke contact — all had been precisely contrived to throw him into confusion. In that, she had succeeded, for a time at least — until his superior morality and intellect had reasserted itself and he had been able to see through her wiles.

And as for that frightening image in which she had tied him down with silken ropes, that hadn't been magically projected into his mind by some witchcraft of hers. The very idea! No, it had been a warning. His cunning old brain had been warning himself — of what she'd do to him if he foolishly dropped his guard.

The Burgundia docked in Manhattan just before midnight on the last day of March, a Thursday. He was up betimes the following morning and, having assured himself that the *Pride of Liverpool* had not made another Riband-stealing voyage and arrived ahead of him, caught a mid-morning train to New Haven. Now, for the first time, he turned his thoughts away from the past, away from the Harding creature and his thousand and one schemes to frustrate her, toward the future — which had suddenly become the *immediate* future for him. What, he now asked himself, was he expecting to find in this mysterious house called *Pegasus*?

The whole business was damnably tricky. Whatever it might be, his father was at the heart of it — as villain in the Beast's eyes, as hero in Kathy's. Kathy was the only one who had actually seen the place; yet somehow, in describing it to the Beast, she had got it all in a twist and sent him off at a tangent.

Or perhaps that was the Harding's doing.

Yes, it must be — and it was she, too, who made sure Aunt Daphne got her version of it rather than Kathy's.

Also there was another nagging thought just beginning to take shape in his mind — one of those small details that he ought not to have overlooked, except that when one's mind is full of higher things and having to concentrate on so many important matters of life and death, little trifles often get crowded out. It had first occurred to him on the *Burgundia*, when he had been running an interested eye over one or two of the stewardesses. He realized that Mama must have spotted the Harding at once, the moment they boarded the *Pride of Liverpool* in Manhattan; it was inconceivable she would not have recognized the creature. It was equally inconceivable she would not have had her dismissed on the spot. Yet that had not happened. The Harding still had her place on the ship, and Mama — apparently — raised not a whisper of complaint about it.

So the Harding must have threatened her in some way. That remark in the Beast's letter about Papa's richly deserving to go to jail came uncomfortably to mind. If there were anything in it, that would certainly induce Mama to swallow her objections and say nothing. But then one had to explain her general vivaciousness and cheerful attitude to things — hardly the behaviour of a lady who fears her husband's impending incarceration.

And so Neil sat on the train to New Haven and smiled to himself at the way his keen, analytical mind was able to dissect the situation and lay its many puzzles out in a neat, ordered sequence — a pleasure only slightly marred by his inability, for the moment, to find the one thread that held them all neatly together. No doubt it would come to him. The important first step was to winnow out all the dross and expose the kernel, or kernels, of the situation in all its, or their, simplicity. Then the meaning of it all would descend upon him in a flash of inspiration, the moment he grasped what was really going on in this mysterious house called *Pegasus*.

"Is it far?" he asked the cabby as they set off from the depot. He had elected to sit outside with the fellow, despite the raw April weather, in the hope of gleaning a nugget or two.

"It's a piece," the man said.

For most of that "piece" they talked of trivia — the signs of spring, the new Interstate Commerce Act and its effect on the railroads, Bismarck's call for a larger German army, the Hydro-Electricity at Niagara Falls, and the brilliant new incandescent gas mantle — which neither of them, as it turned out, had yet seen. At last, in growing despair, Neil tried a frontal assault: *"Pegasus,"* he mused. "Now isn't that rather an unusual name for a house? I never heard of a house being given that name before."

"Name of a horse," the cabby volunteered. "Used to fly, back in the days of the Ancient Greeks. A horsefly, mebbe." After a pause he added, "There's a Greek family moved into Fife last week. We passed the house a while back. I could 'a showed you if I'd 'a knowed you was interested in that sort of thing."

"I'm told it was also the name of a ship. She ran aground somewhere off the coast of Maine a couple of years ago."

"Could be." He spat into the roadway. "I heared that tale myself. You a seafaring man, are you, mister?"

Neil laughed awkwardly. "You mean you can tell?"

"Nope. The only seafaring man I know — apart from fishermen, of course — is Captain Morgan. And you've got a kind of a roll to your walk, jess like him. He's lord and master at *Pegasus*, so I guess you know him."

"He's my, er, shipmate," Neil admitted. "We're shipmates. That is, I'm third officer and he's ... well, of course, he's captain, ha ha. Yes."

The cabby squinted down at the knob of the young man's cane, where a monogram of the letters *NM* was plainly legible. "That figures," he said.

"Indeed, by jove, doesn't it," Neil replied, having no idea what the phrase might mean.

"So, you're third officer on the *Pride of Liverpool*, eh?" the man went on. "I never seen her, but the Cap'n tells me she's the finest afloat."

"Oh no, not the *Pride of Liverpool*. An earlier vessel. I was third officer under an *earlier* command of the Captain's."

"The *Pegasus!*" the cabby exclaimed in delight.

"No, no — not the *Pegasus* — earlier still." He racked his memory for the names of other ships his father had sailed in. There were dozens, of course, but only one came to mind in his panic. "The *Hiawatha*," he said.

"No," the cabby replied at once, as if they were both outsiders trying to remember something the Captain had once told them. "Not the *Hiawatha*. He never captained her. That was Billy Bright's old ship — went down off the Goodwin Sands, oh, a good whiles back. It could have been the *Swift*? Or the *Tigris*. They were his two commands before *Pegasus*."

"My goodness! You seem to know him inside out!"

"Why, he's a pretty good friend to me," the man allowed. "Many a long summer evening we've set out on his porch or mine, jawing away 'bout this 'n that ... families, where we been, what we done. He's a powerful, high larn't man, your ... Captain."

"Is he at home now? I do hope so."

"Nope. Tomorrow evening, five forty-three."

Neil laughed weakly. "You can be as sure as that?"

"Set your watch by him. The power of steam, huh? It sure is a wonderful thing. Miz Morgan's home, though. Your luck's half in."

"Ah, yes, indeed."

Miss Morgan?

"Why there she is now," he exclaimed. "I'll swear she knows the sound of these tires over all others. 'Lo, Miz Morgan. Lookit here — you'll never guess who I brung you."

Neil saw the name of the house beside the gate — *Pegasus*, right enough — and then a young woman, about his own age — perhaps a year or two older — coming down the garden path, smiling a welcome

472

and wiping her hands in her pinny.

Miss Morgan, eh? A cousin, perhaps. A never-before-mentioned cousin? His sharp eyes caught sight of baby's clothes hanging out to dry, and a reason for the family's reticence suggested itself at once to his equally sharp brain.

A *Miss* Morgan — and a child. Well, let him who is without sin cast the first stone, et cetera.

"And who would that be, now?" she asked the cabby, smiling merrily at Neil the while. A pretty good-looker, he thought. A *second* cousin, maybe.

"Why this, ma'am," the man drawled, turning to Neil and eyeing him laconically, "unless I very much mistake myself, is Mister Neil Morgan, the Captain's eldest boy. He's a tad shy right now, but I reckon, eff'n you handle him right he'll open like a clam in chowder."

"Neil!" she exclaimed in delight. "Lord save us, what a surprise! But what a pleasant one, too. You should have sent a wire. Is the *Swallow* over here? Wait till I look at you." She ran an appreciative eye from his head to his toes and back again. "Oh yes, you're your father's son, sure enough."

"Said the same thing myself, Miz Morgan, the minute I seed him at the depot. Now we met them all but young Lawrence."

"You're not after bringing your brother Larry with you, I suppose?" Miz Morgan challenged jovially.

"Er ... no. 'Fraid not." In a daze, Neil paid his fare and thanked the driver for an informative ride.

"It was, too," the man agreed before he turned and drove off.

"Sure you'll ignore him," Teresa said, taking his arm. "Harold Martin would tell you how to build a clock. Have you no bags? Have you not come to stay?

Your da will be here tomorrow night — will you not stay till then?"

"Miz Morgan," he replied, quickly dropping into the local patois, as was his habit in foreign parts, "I think I should ..."

"Surnames is it! And what's wrong with Teresa, be all the holy?" She laughed. "You'd scarce be wanting to call me Mother!"

"Indeed no," he agreed, wondering why she would make such an obvious remark. "Though I see you *are* a mother."

"Well, of course I am. And" — she leaned close and squeezed his arm — "I believe there's another one cooking. But not a word to your da about that, for I haven't told him meself yet."

He blushed. Talk about brazen! "Well, of course ... er I ... I say, what a charming ... er, holly, is it?" he remarked.

"Mahonia," she replied. "Here's his lordship now. He's supposed to be napping, of course, after his feed. Come y'on, gossoon, come say hello to ..." She turned to Neil. "Will it be Neil or Uncle Neil or what? It should be Neil by rights, of course."

"Neil," he said with a shrug.

"Good man yourself!" she said, slapping him on the back and passing him the boy to hold as a kind of reward. "Talking of feed, did you bring anything to eat on the train or will you have a bite now? I have a nice warm brack that's not ten minutes parted from the range and butter as yellow as all the gold in California. Now you wouldn't say no to that, I'm thinking?"

"I wouldn't," he agreed.

She went away to prepare it. The boy struggled to go with her and Neil put him down.

One could not help warming enormously to this … whatever she was — third cousin. Her friendliness was so infectious, her spirit so open. And so very pretty. Thus far he sided with Kathy. There was nothing here to justify the things Larry had put in that letter — but there was nothing, either, to accuse the Harding of having staged or planted. At the moment his confusion was, if anything, greater than ever. But one had to remember that the darkest hour comes oft before the dawn.

The locals all called her *Miss* Morgan, and yet she wore a wedding ring. Obviously that was to satisfy strangers, who had no need to know the true state of affairs. The locals, showing that easygoing tolerance for which Americans were so famous (at least, he seemed to remember hearing somewhere that they were), didn't mind calling a spade a spade. Equally obviously, Miss Morgan — or Teresa, as he was already rather glad to call her — was some distant relative toward whom Papa felt some kind of obligation. A fourth cousin, perhaps? Yes, a fourth cousin would be well outside the bounds of legally acceptable consanguinity.

She returned, bearing his promised repast. As he let an appreciative eye wander over her figure, he ran a swift mental check of all the male and unmarried female Morgans he knew — who would have passed on the surname to Teresa; but he gave up when he realized she might simply have adopted the name when Papa took her under his wing.

Brack proved to be a sort of cross between bread and cake — delicious with butter and a slice of cold pork and pickles. As he downed it with relish — and a glass of something she called "route beer" — he decided to test his theory about her patronymic.

"I've been wondering — what was your name before you became ..." Artfully he let the question hang.

Unabashed she picked it up. "Morgan? I was Teresa O'Dee. D'you know Ireland at all, Neil?"

He shook his head. "I was in Queenstown once for repairs, that's all."

She smiled fondly. "Isn't that where I met your father. And he wouldn't have noticed me at all, only I looked like an old flame of his called Jenny Bright." She smiled archly. "And you may thank your dear sister Kathy for me, for letting that slip."

"How on earth ...?" he began.

"Oh, she axed me not to tell your father she'd been here — some cock and bull story about Emma Harding getting the boot. But Kathy must have told him herself, for 'twas the first thing he said to me. So I taxed him with it — the likeness I have to that Jenny Bright — and didn't he tell me then I was the dead spit of her."

"I see," Neil said, struggling to assimilate this new information. So much of it — and all at once. He had come here expecting to be surprised, yes, but not bewildered; yet everything he heard only bewildered him more. He decided to start on the surest bit of ground. "It was no cock and bull story, you know," he said. "About the Harding's dismissal. Oh yes! Booted out, all right — and without a character. A thoroughly bad lot, in my opinion."

"Oh, d'you think so? To me she seemed entirely pleasant. She and Kathy are very thick."

"I doubt that's going to last," he replied with pleasurable conviction.

"Sure, didn't she write Emma's character to give to the Shaw & Eggar Line for her place as stewardess!"

476

He laughed at the very idea. "I hardly think so."

"But she did, Neil. She told me so herself. She sat there in that very chair, not three months ago, and told me the whole story. She signed it ... oh Lord, she did say the name. Dowty! Of course."

"I rather think you've confused the two females, Teresa — if I may say so," he replied calmly. "I'm sure it wasn't Kathy who told you this preposterous tale. Think back, now. It was the Harding creature, herself, wasn't it. That's much more likely. Forgery's just her mark — lying, cheating, malefaction of every kind. She's a female blackguard of the deepest dye."

Teresa chuckled. "You have a bit of a soft spot for her yourself, eh, Neil?"

"Indeed, I do not!"

"Ah, g'wan! Isn't it written all over you."

He wished their acquaintance were not so new; he longed to tell her that if he had a soft spot for anyone, it was herself — notwithstanding her ... *misfortune.* He decided then and there that he would make no further inquiries in this house. He needed time to think, time to devise a rather longer-term strategy for his courtship of this lovely, if unfortunate, young person. Perhaps he'd even talk to his father about her, though it would be better and more manly, to woo and win her on his own. She would certainly respect him all the more for it, he felt sure. As to discovering what had so upset the young Beast here — that was a chimæra. Teresa knew nothing that might reflect shamefully upon his father. The Harding had lied, of course. He ought to have realized that before he even set out.

"You should know," he told her, "that Harding is going about London blackening your character — and my father's — to anyone who'll listen."

"I can't believe that of her, Neil. Someone's pulling your leg."

"Indeed she is. I don't know what she told Larry, but he's firmly convinced that something's going on in this house which, if it came to light, would send my father to jail."

"Lord a' mercy!" she laughed. "The worst crime that's going on here is the poteen my brother Ignatius does be making in the outhouse. And with Father Hines his main customer, I doubt anyone will see the inside of a lockup, even if he's caught — which he won't be. And in any case that's him, not your father. So there. You may tell Larry to put that in his pipe and smoke it. And if he wants to come and inspect us all for himself, he's as welcome here as you and your sister."

"It's serious enough to cause him to run away to sea. So there!"

Teresa laughed even louder. "So he's done it at last!" she crowed. "That's a dollar your da owes me, for he bet me the boy would never do it." She gave him a certain smile. "And what of yourself, now? Are you leaving the marine now your brother's joined it, or what?"

"Such had been my intention, Teresa, yes."

"But no longer?"

Her smile really was bewitching. "No. I was thinking I might take a post on one of the regular transatlantic liners, you know."

"Wouldn't that be a fine thing," she exclaimed. "I'd see you as often as your father then. And if Kathy starts as assistant nurse and comes over to see this Chuck Burgoyne fella — sure, 'twould only need Larry to fall in with the rest of ye and we'd have the family complete on both sides of the ocean."

When he'd finished they walked Tony down to the store and back. Cleverly, Neil kept their talk to inconsequential matters all the way, allowing him to concentrate simply on being himself and thus leaving the all-important impression of his immense charm uppermost in her mind. Then he set out to walk into New Haven for the late-afternoon train back to Manhattan.

Teresa stood at the window and watched him almost out of sight. "That," she said to Jemima, her help, "is the quarest young fella that ever I met."

WHETHER HILDA TIRED of the same loveless gymnastics with Walter Grandison before Walter felt again the ancient siren call to pastures new neither could say; but there came a time when he suggested the following Fri for a Fri-to-Mon and she said she didn't think so really and the look of relief on his face was so plain and ungentlemanly that she could do nothing but burst into laughter — at which, naturally, he turned all mortified and apologetic.

"Don't be so downcast," she chided, giving the tiniest kiss to the tip of his nose. "You have done a great and noble thing. I shall speak up for you at the Last Trump."

One eyebrow rose a fraction of an inch — a sign of enormous interest in Walter Grandison.

"You have revived a flagging marriage and, let us hope, secured it for the rest of its natural course."

"Ah."

"Well, you needn't sound so blasé — or do all your wives tell you that?"

"I don't have any wives."

She laughed richly.

"You know what I mean," he grumbled. "And, yes, as a matter of fact, they do. It's how they salve their consciences."

"And how do you salvage yours?"

"Conscience? It's one of those words I have to keep looking up in the dictionary."

"Oh, diddums!" She scratched him playfully under the chin, in the little channel he shaved between his two luxuriant sets of whiskers. "Does it annoy you to be told you're nothing but a restorer of antique unions? Actually, you haven't quite finished the task in my case."

"Oh?" His flagging interest revived.

"Yes." The tip of her little finger went on with its lazy tickling. "There is one teeny-weeny little favour you could do me — quite a big favour, actually."

"Yes?" He became wary; he had not marked her down as a potential blackmailer, emotional or otherwise.

"If I take passage on the *Burgundia*, could you ensure that I travel absolutely incognito? I could go under my maiden name, Watson, I thought, and travel in the second class."

"You'll do no such thing!" he asserted. "Travel second? I never heard such nonsense. You'll travel as my guest and in my stateroom."

"Oh Walter! Dear, sweet man — it's lovely of you, and so characteristically generous, but it won't do, you see. Mrs Burgoyne … did I tell you about her son and Kathy? Yes, of course I did … but Mrs B. studies all the passenger lists. She's worse than Daphne Dowty, if you can believe it."

"Pick the first name out of *Kelly's Street Directory* for Southampton or … Hereford … anywhere. How is she to associate that with you?"

"Don't be tedious, Walter, dear. Let me do it my way, please? To go as an unknown lady travelling solo under an obvious alias in the stateroom normally reserved for the owner of the line is not *my* idea of travelling incognito. Especially when *you* are that owner. But who is going to bother with a Mrs Hilda Watson travelling second?"

He yielded at that, pausing only to fire one rearguard shot. "You'll have to share a cabin, you know. Some have two bunks, some four."

"I was coming to that. I'm thinking of asking Daphne to accompany me. If she agrees, we'll take a two-berther."

"Let me know which sailing," he said, trying to remain as nonchalant as she would expect him to be. He'd been trying to get Daphne into bed with him for years; the chances of doing so on a voyage or in a foreign land were about a hundred times better than in London — which wasn't saying much since in London they had so far proved zero.

"Oh, I can tell you already," she said. "It has to be the sailing of the thirtieth of April, because the *Pride of Liverpool* will be sailing from New York on the third of May — which will give me a clear field."

"Not that it's any of my business, I realize, but how will you explain your absence to Frank?"

"Oh, I'll tell him I'm going down to Norfolk to see Neil and this friend of his who are trying to refloat a ketch. They're having the most dreadful difficulty with it, so he says."

"Ah, so that's where he is," Walter remarked. "I wondered why we hadn't seen him about town."

T HE TROUBLE WITH the boilers delayed the *Pride of Liverpool's* departure from that city for several days further, and the need to run in the repaired set made for a slow crossing, so she did not, in fact, dock in New York until the morning of May the sixth — the same day as that on which Hilda put her request to Walter Grandison. Company business, including the problems with the engines, made it impossible for Frank to go to New Haven this time. The *Burgundia,* meanwhile, had delayed her departure, hoping to pick up disgruntled transfers from the *Pride of Liverpool,* whose return sailing from New York was, similarly, put back. The two vessels were tied up at adjacent piers.

If Emma had any hope of avoiding a meeting with Neil, they were dashed the moment she saw him standing at the foot of the crew gangway. She drew back into the shadows of the after deckhouse, but his loud bray, "Ahaa!" and his triumphantly levelled finger drew her forth again before he could make an even greater spectacle of them both.

She forced a smile onto her face and stepped down the gangway with all the dignity she could muster.

"I'm sure you're highly pleased with yourself," he called out jubilantly when she was only half-way down.

"Can't it wait?" she called back in desperation. Then she had a better idea. "Your father's on his way," she warned.

He scuttled off at once to put a large net of baggage between him and the side of the ship.

"Isn't that the Captain's son?" one of the junior officers asked her.

She nodded and said bleakly, "Not that you'd think it, sir. He's about as much use as a stepladder on the fo'c'sle deck."

The man laughed and let her ashore without further question.

"Well?" she asked in exasperation when she caught up with him — meaning that she supposed he was proud of that little exhibition.

But he took it as a crow of triumph over him for what she imagined he had been told in Fife. "You failed utterly," he sneered, gripping her arm fiercely. "But then you didn't expect to achieve anything, anyway — did you! It was a red herring. You sent me on a wild goose chase ..."

"Let go!" she hissed, struggling to free herself without drawing too much attention to them both.

"Trouble, Miss Harding?" Long Jack Bowling, a leading seaman who'd taken an avuncular liking to her, moved his impressive bulk to where he could easily interpose it between them.

Neil threw out his chest. "I say, my good fellow, don't you know who I am?" he asked haughtily.

"I do, indeed, sir," Long Jack replied (having just heard it from the officer by the gangway). "I was about to ask *you* to remember it also."

"Hmph!" With ill grace Neil released Emma's arm and said, "Satisfied?"

Long Jack raised an inquiring eyebrow at her. "May I escort you to the hostel, Miss Harding?"

She smiled gratefully. "I'd like nothing better, Mr Bowling. But he'll only hang around and pester the life out of me, so I'd best get it over and done with. There's no actual harm in him. He's just a nuisance."

"I say, *you!*" Neil cried at her in dismay, "I'll thank you to ..."

Long Jack ignored him. "If you're sure, Miss Harding?"

She nodded and gave him another grateful smile. He moved a little way off, eyeing Neil with undisguised contempt. He made a ball of his right fist and a socket of his left hand, massaging his clenched knuckles with obvious menace; when Neil and Emma set off, he fell in some fifteen paces behind.

"Impertinent hound!" Neil muttered as they went up the slope into Forty-Second Street.

She said nothing.

"I suppose you thought Miss Teresa Morgan would send me off …"

"*Miss* Teresa Morgan?" she interrupted.

"Not to me, of course," he replied impatiently. "She's Teresa and I'm Neil, so put that in your pipe and smoke it! I suppose you thought she and I would fall out or something? Indeed, I can't imagine why you sent me on such a wild goose chase — but whatever it was, I can tell you now, it's blown right up in your face. All your wiles have had exactly the opposite effect of what you intended — whatever that was."

She laughed, but more in exasperation than humour. "If you don't know what I intended, how can you possibly say the effect is opposite? Opposite to what, may I ask?"

"All I know is you certainly didn't wish me well."

"Listen — my only wish was for you to learn the truth. And since you wouldn't believe it from me even if I was to tell you in words of one syllable … and since you don't talk to your brother, nor your mum, nor your Aunt Daphne … what else could I do but send you to learn it for yourself? Eh? D'you understand it now?"

484

"It's no business of yours what I understand. I didn't come here to tell you about me, or about Miss Morgan, or about any understanding that may ..."

"You keep saying that!" she accused him — then she heard the echo of his half-finished sentence in her mind and said, "No, go on."

"It doesn't matter. In fact, I've said all I wished to say to you ..."

"Which is nothing — as per usual! Talking with you is like swimming in a great lake of sago."

"But I'll tell you this for nothing," he added, feeling suddenly brave. "Don't be surprised if one fine day you see our wedding announcement in the paper! That's all."

"You!" she snapped. "I wouldn't marry you if you was the last ..."

"Not you!" he interrupted scornfully. "Lord! D'you think I'd even contemplate it for a second?"

"Well, who then?" she asked, thinking that this could not really be happening. It was surely some new kind of highly realistic nightmare.

"Who d'you think?" he asked petulantly.

"Not ...?" She pointed vaguely eastward.

"Ha ha!" He nodded in triumphant confirmation. "That stung you, eh?"

"Ohmigawd!"

"Yes! It must really show you my opinion of you — that I'd sooner marry a fallen woman with a bastard child than I'd even consider the likes of you!"

"Ohmigawd!" Emma repeated. "You *did* talk to Kathy, then."

"I did not." The suggestion offended him. "I come from that stratum of society where no true gentleman would dream of discussing such offensive matters with his sister."

"Kathy's only eighteen," Emma said bleakly. "But what's your excuse?" She waved him to silence and added, "I know. *I'm* your excuse. I should have known better. Well," she smiled wanly at him, "I think I owe *someone* an apology for the damage I've done."

"Accepted," he responded with brisk satisfaction.

"Gawd, I hope it will be," she murmured some twenty minutes later when, having got rid of Neil and thanked Long Jack for his solicitude, she crossed the concourse of Grand Central and made for the New Haven line.

A T ANY MOMENT of that tortured journey to Fife, Emma could have turned back. In her mind she fought over the pros and cons all the way. The greatest argument against what she was about to do was, of course, that it was none of her business; on the other hand she could claim that fate and the Morgans had unwittingly conspired to thrust her into the centre of it all. But, even allowing that it had, willy nilly, become her business, could she honourably interfere further when she had no idea where it might lead? Her only answer was that the alternative — to do nothing — looked even worse.

There was dear Kathy, blithely going the social round in Highbury, letting it slip from time to time what a noble fellow her father was — but in terms that made it obvious to any man or woman of the world what was really going on. Meanwhile her mother was, by all accounts, tripping round the same bailiwick with a certain glint in her eye, singing light opera like battle hymns. At her side was Daphne

Dowty, whose genuine concern was tempered by an attitude more common among savage schoolboys toward captive houseflies — "Pull off their wings and see if they can still go." And now there was that idiot Neil dreaming of marrying his stepmother, under the illusion she was a polluted angel. Someone had to pull the cork on this brew before its fragile container exploded in their faces — and few containers are more fragile than those composed chiefly of silence and convention,

And who better to do it, she thought wryly, than the one who first stirred that brew?

And so, in that somewhat fatalistic mood, she emerged from the New Haven depot, passed the waiting cabs, and took the East Haven streetcar, instead. But an attack of cold feet made her get off at South Grove and walk the rest of the way — anything to postpone the evil hour.

It was a glorious spring afternoon. The earth had shaken off its mantle of snow and now basked in the slant of the descending sun. She could almost feel the sap stirring in the trees, like a green fuze sputtering its way toward an explosion of leaf buds some weeks hence. Squirrels eyed her with blasé caution as she passed; pigeons fussed grudgingly out of her way, parting before her, closing behind, as they scratched among the leafmould underfoot. Once a skunk crossed her path. From her wanderings in the woods above the Hudson she knew enough to pause and let it go at its own good speed. Briefly she envied these creatures their uncomplicated obsessions, for she could remember a time when an equally simple imperative to keep body and soul together had ruled her life, too. "Those were the days," she told a giant robin, conveniently forgetting the aching limbs and bruised cheerfulness she had dragged into bed on many a night.

Just before she reached the outskirts of Fife, Harold Martin caught up with her. "It is, isn't it?" he called out. "I thought it was. Friend of Miss Morgan's? Come here back in January?"

"I can't afford a cab," she replied.

"I'm going home anyways," he replied affably. "You kin set up and ride shotgun. You're heading for *Pegasus*, I guess?"

"Not a bad day for a walk, all the same," she told him as she climbed up. That was to show him there'd be no tip, either.

As they set off he said, "You ain't no Morgan, though."

"Harding," she said, holding out her hand. "Emma Harding."

"Harold Martin," he replied, shaking hers vigorously. "I know."

"You're an old family friend, huh?"

"Old? I'm nineteen!" she protested, adding no more than a couple of months to her age.

"You look twenty-six," he replied, thinking it would flatter her. "You know the younger son at all? Lawrence?"

"We've met."

"Wish we could say the same. Would be kinda nice to say we met all three." He glanced sidelong at her to see the effect of the remark.

"Oh?" she responded. "Has Neil been here, then?"

"Yes, siree!" He grinned, glad to be ahead of her. "Last Friday. Come to see Miz Morgan for hisself, I reckon. Set in that very seat — fancy you missing him by less 'n a week."

"Shame," she said. "Is the poor old horse lame?"

He clucked it to go a little faster, though he was more and more despairing of getting anything useful out of her before they reached their destination.

"I missed him too, in a way," the man told her. "Brung him out, sure 'nuff, but he walked back all by hisself."

"He can be a bit of an oddity at times," Emma agreed.

Martin chuckled. "I'll believe it. Wouldn't let on as he was Frank Morgan's son. Claimed he and the Captain were shipmates. And him almost poking out my eye with a cane with his initials on it — *NM* — in fancy writing, and a seaman's walk you could tell at half a mile, the spit of the Captain's."

Emma smiled. She could just picture Neil doing his level best to keep a secret. There was something stupidly endearing about that man.

"The reason I hung on at the depot," the man added, "was I was kinda expecting the Captain hisself. It said in the papers that the *Pride of Liverpool* was delayed till today."

"I believe I saw her slip into her berth this morning," she told him. "He could be on the next train."

They arrived at *Pegasus* a minute or so later — and Emma still had not yielded a single fact of significance, or even of interest to him. He spat disgustedly into the roadway as he turned back down the hill.

Teresa called "Come on in!" from the window. Emma found her busy feeding Tony, with all the usual rituals: "A spoon for your da ... a spoon for your ma ... one for Aunt Emma ..." and so forth. She just stood and watched in amazement, thinking that if any child of hers refused a spoonful, that would be his last until the next meal — and it would be the same spoonful then! Perhaps she wasn't intended for the business, anyway. Watching Teresa, with her endless loving patience and goodwill, she felt inadequate.

It did nothing to make the prospect of the next hour or so easier, either.

"I was half expecting the Captain," Teresa said.

Emma told her the news about the boilers.

"So he sent you to tell me?" Teresa guessed.

Emma admitted that was not the case. "Matter of fact," she said, "I come because I knew he *wouldn't* be here."

Teresa caught the tone in her voice, looked at the lad, and said "Oh."

Her patience grew markedly shorter after that. Tony, seeing he was no longer to be indulged, burst into bitter tears. When they didn't work, either, he dried up, just as swiftly, and sulked. Jemima came in and took charge.

Teresa took Emma's arm and led her downstairs. "Are you in some kind of trouble, dear?" she asked under her breath.

Emma nodded. "And I wish I was the only one. But it's all of us." The normality of everything in the house and its dedication to a regime that was so domestic oppressed her. "Can we go for a walk?" she asked. "Somewhere no one can overhear us?"

Teresa smiled and closed the parlour door behind them. "This is safe enough, I think," she said.

Emma shook her head. "I doubt it."

"What d'you mean?" Her tone acquired a slight edge.

"You're Irish. You got red hair. I doubt it's enough."

The fact that Emma spoke the words without a trace of humour — not even gallows humour — made Teresa turn pale. "Does it concern me?" she asked. "And the Captain?"

Emma nodded. "Most of all."

Teresa grabbed her hat and cloak from the hallstand as they passed. Outside she pointed west, toward the sun, which was now three-quarters down in the sky. The land sloped gently down across a couple of fields before rising to a wooded ridge that cut off their view of the ocean. "There's a nice walk through those oaks," she said. "Will that do?"

"I hope so," Emma replied solemnly.

Teresa gave an anxious laugh. "April Fool has come and gone, you know. Though I thought when Neil turned up on the day itself ... well!"

"I know what you mean," Emma agreed.

She had not planned what to say, not word for word, but she had formed a general outline of it at the back of her mind. She knew she had to start with something arresting but ultimately beside the point — something that would seize Teresa's attention and distract her long enough for her, Emma, to make the point. Now she realized she had been handed the perfect opening.

"I met him in New York this morning," she said. "That's why I came out to see you straight away."

"Well, I 'clare to God! What ever made you do that?"

"I don't know what happened when he was here, but ..."

"He did strike me as, you know, a little ... well, *odd* is the only word for it."

"I'll tell you how odd he is," Emma said grimly. "He told me he is in love with you and hopes you will ..."

"What?"

"Oh yes! And he hopes you will one day do him the honour of becoming *Mrs* Morgan! *His* Mrs Morgan, of course."

Teresa halted in her tracks, stared at Emma open-mouthed, and then gave a nervous, cajoling sort of laugh, begging her to admit this was some kind of delayed April Fool's prank.

Sadly Emma shook her head.

"But he *knows*," Teresa insisted. "We talked about his father ... the baby ... everything. I told him there might be another on the way and he didn't ... in fact, he called me 'Mrs Morgan' to start with."

"Did he?" Emma asked. "Are you sure?"

"Sure there's more gold in that fingernail" — she held it forth dramatically for inspection — "than there's doubt in the full of me."

"I think he called you *Miz* Morgan — the same as Harold Martin called you just now when talking with me."

Teresa shrugged at this pedantry. "Same thing."

"You know that. I had to stop and remember it. I'll bet you all Lombard Street to a china orange Neil has never heard the word. To him 'Miz' would be the same as 'Miss.' He thinks you're not married."

"But the baby ..."

"He thinks he's being very noble about that."

Teresa closed her eyes; still reeling under the shock she murmured, "What's Frank going to say when word reaches him?"

"That's what I want to talk to you about. The Captain. I want to talk to you about him, much more than about Neil. Is that all right? Well, even if it's not, I've got to. I want to tell you a conversation he had with me on our last voyage back to Liverpool."

They picked their way down a ragged path that skirted the two fields and gave out onto a much broader walk beneath the oaks. As they went, Emma told her everything Frank had said on the subject of risk and his addiction to it. And, although Frank had never spoken to Teresa in those terms, she heard nothing that sounded out of character. And when Emma reached the bit about running the *Pegasus* aground, she remembered the light in his eyes and knew it was the truth. She had not the faintest inkling what dreadful revelations were to follow, yet a sense of heavy foreboding overtook her spirit. The little Irish encouragements of "I know" and "Is it so?" and "You're right enough there!" dried up and she listened on in a brooding silence.

"For a long while I never believed him," Emma admitted. "I mean, you know how some men — *all* men — like to swing the lead a bit. And if you ask any sailor, from Hudson's Bay to the China Sea, what's the last word they'd use about Captain Morgan, half would say dishonest and the rest would choose reckless. The thing is, you see, he'll go a thousand miles to avoid a risk to his passengers, crew, vessel ... anything like that. But if it's just himself or his family, then he can't say no to it — he'd go a thousand miles to take it on."

"He's a very ... what's the word? He's not an easy man to understand," Teresa agreed. "Just when you think you have him, when you say to yourself, 'That's Frank Morgan, sure enough,' he'll do the opposite — and you realize that's the man, too."

"Can I ask you one thing?"

"Sure," Teresa replied affably, then added: "Maybe." Then she laughed nervously and said, "See, I've caught it now!"

"What — if anything — did he tell you about the first Mrs Morgan?"

"Hilda?"

Emma nodded.

493

Teresa sighed. "That theirs had been a very happy marriage … that she'd given him three fine children. Indeed he's told me more of Kathleen, Neil, and Lawrence than about herself. He always talks about them. He's very proud of them. I'll tell you a secret, Emma. 'Tis my dearest hope they'll one day think of this as their new home." The path had led back to the edge of the oakwood; she swept a hand vaguely over the landscape before them and smiled fondly. "Though whether I could ever be a second mother to them is another matter, what with being no more than two years older then Neil."

"A hundred and two," Emma corrected, tapping her cranium to show where the seniority lay. She gazed up across the fields to where the red shingle roof of *Pegasus* jutted above the skyline. So much happiness, so much pure contentment was enshrined beneath its kindly shelter — could she now bring herself to speak the words that would shatter it? She felt her resolution falter. Before that movement could gather pace she forced herself to ask, "Did he tell you exactly when Hilda Morgan died?"

"He doesn't like to talk about it much — and, sure, that's only natural. Why? Was it a painful case?"

Emma closed her eyes, clenched her fists, drew a deep breath — and heard a cry of "Ahoy!" from across the fields.

She opened her eyes again and saw a familiar and unmistakable figure trotting toward them down the path.

"Frank!" Teresa cried happily as she ran like a hare toward him. "You got away after all!"

A DOZEN TIMES and more over the next twenty-four hours Teresa found herself on the point of taxing Frank with what Emma had said, or hinted at, or started to say ... but the foreboding that had overcome her at one point down there in the oakwood lingered on and made her keep silent. A profound sense of her own unworthiness, reinforced by the weekly imperative of confession and atonement, also held her in check. Whatever it was that Emma had come to tell her, she knew it would leave her feeling more wrong than wronged — if, indeed, there was anything of that sort in it at all. What could it have been?

She thought back over the little that Emma *had* let slip. It obviously had something to do with Hilda Morgan's death — the time of her death or the manner of it. Some dark secret surrounded it, something that affected Frank and herself and, more puzzlingly, even Emma Harding, who had been no more than a servant in the Highbury household. But there lay a further mystery, for, although Frank had never actually mentioned how long ago Hilda had died, he always gave the impression it had been many years ago — long before Emma would have been old enough to be employed in the house. Had she ever, in fact, been a maidservant there, or was that just a story they put about to cover some other connection between her and that house?

It was baffling, right enough. And there was no hope of learning more from Emma herself, not while Frank was there, for he watched her like a travelling rat and never allowed the occasion for them to be alone together. On the other hand, his powerful character and genial manner so cheered her that Emma's hints began to fade in significance. And when she whispered in his ear that night that "the cardinal" was now three weeks late, so things were looking hopeful, he was so unaffectedly joyful that her forebodings slipped even farther into the background.

The balm of his joviality continued its work until the middle of the following day, Thursday, when he announced that they had to return to New York and the *Pride of Liverpool*. She was quite her old bonny self as she waved them out of sight in Harold Martin's cab.

A gentle rain was falling, so Emma rode inside. She sat there and listened to the cabby (who must have been dying to know what was going on) and the Captain (who must have been dying to know what had been going on) talking of hunting, steam engines, and possibility, widely canvassed at that time, that life existed on Mars. Men, she decided, were not just unknowable — they were absolutely unknowable.

"You'll travel with me," Captain Morgan said grimly as soon as they were inside the depot.

Her spirit hit rock. She remembered a picture book in the Morgans' library, *Cassell's Illustrated History of Europe* in six volumes, bound in Leatherene and offered at a concessionary price to readers of the *Morning Post*. One picture in particular came to mind: "To The Guillotine — 21st January, 1793!" ... the expression on one of the women's faces. Emma knew it was the very model of her own face at that moment.

Theirs was a large, open Pullman car but they had one end of it to themselves, at least until the next stop at Bridgeport — long enough, she realized with leaden heart, for him to roast her. He had been nice as pie while anyone else was around. Down in the oakwood he had behaved as if it was the most natural thing in the world to find her there and had insisted that she stay overnight and go back to the ship with him today. Now all that charm was pushed aside. She glanced briefly into his eyes and saw nothing but two black vaults of anger; it was her first encounter with the legendary Morgan who could quell a riot with one stare from those same pitiless eyes.

But she was no longer the little Emma who, two years ago, had stood so weak and wet before this same man's wife, seething with an outrage she dared not express, meekly pleading for a mercy she had done nothing to occasion. So, when Frank asked her, in a voice that would stop the heart of a leaping tiger, what the hell she imagined she was doing in his house, her desperation prompted her to the same trick with which she had stilled Teresa long enough to begin her revelation. "Neil wants to marry Teresa," she said. Five little words.

Six words and her voice would have broken. And through that breach would have poured all her terror, all her eagerness to apologize, confess herself utterly at fault, cast herself on his mercy … promise the world away. But for five words she could just hold herself in poise, just meet his eye, just breathe evenly.

Deep within him something thrilled at her daring, as if he had created it in secret some time ago and now had called it forth from the neglected corners of her soul where its very existence had gone unnoticed by her. He felt himself becoming, as it were, a third party to their conflict, caring nothing who won as long as it was battle royal. Indeed, if she could come through it unscathed and emerge with the realization that she was ten times the woman she had so far imagined herself to be, he would count it one of the grandest days of his life. That curious third party within him settled comfortably to watch their duel and applaud her every advantage.

Then, a hundredth of a second later, the actual meaning of her words overtook him. "What the devil?" he barked.

For that same brief interval the fire of his rage was dimmed and she saw in his eye the glint of panic — the food on which his love affair with risk was nourished. It was enough to sustain her, too, through one more reckless statement, again just five words long: "He told me so yesterday."

"I don't believe you," he said, levelling an accusing finger at her, like a pistol, right between the eyes.

The bridge of her nose began suddenly to itch, maddeningly, but she forced herself to sit stock still.

"You're trying the same trick on me as on Mrs Morgan," he went on. The ghost of a flicker of a momentary smile on her lips forced him to add, "You know very well which Mrs Morgan I mean."

She felt like a fallen climber, hanging over the abyss, who suddenly finds a new handhold and uses it to inch one step nearer salvation. She dared to breathe again.

"But this time you're bluffing," he concluded. "You're daring me to call it."

Some instinct told her she should give him more time for her words to take hold; it was reinforced by the pain in her lungs, for she had held her breath so long that her single inhalation had only served to reinforce the torture she now felt. She, too, needed time — to take a dozen deep, surreptitious breaths before she embarked on the tale whose telling she had now made inevitable. "Got any brandy, Cap'n?"

she asked, disguising one deep breath as a jocose sort of sigh. "I don't know whether I need it more now than you're going to when I've done." A dozen words or more! It was progress.

His hand shook a little as he set the two silver cups, like outsize thimbles, between them and filled each to capacity. He pushed the cork back into the hipflask and left the choice to her.

At any other time she would have taken the smaller; but now, to emphasize her point, she chose the larger, instead. "We'll swap when I've finished telling you," she said grimly.

He fought himself not to smile. That impartial third party, who was still there, though he had shifted the focus of his interest, had to allow that she was magnificent. Did she know what power was in her? He doubted it — and regretted the loss of this opportunity to prove it to her.

She downed the cup in one, thumped it back on the baize between them, covered it with her hand, and breathed out grateful fire. Then, having taken several deep breaths in the meantime, she told him what conversation had passed between her and Neil the previous morning. She funked it slightly by leaving him with the impression that Neil had learned of the existence of the house called *Pegasus*, and of its fair mistress, from Lawrence — though not, obviously, of her connection with their father. In passing, she also told him that Lawrence had run away to sea at last; but the Captain hardly considered life on a tramp between Tilbury and Hamburg to be anything of the kind. "Just a further postponement," he called it contemptuously. "So Lawrence also knows, eh?"

She pushed her empty cup forward and said, "Swap?"

He accepted the offer with a grim chuckle. "What's more, I'm almost sure Hilda knows, too."

She gave a baffled laugh. "Sometimes you talk as if it wasn't happening to you. I don't know!"

"I thought she'd be the one to bring down the curtain when she learned of Teresa." There was an odd note of disappointment in his voice, which intrigued Emma.

"What makes you think she knows, sir?" she asked as she watched him refill their cups; this time his hand was rock-steady again.

He shook his head. "I couldn't possibly go into that. But when you've shared a ... home with someone as long as that, you get to know ... certain things. She's learned what's going on, I'm sure of it. I'll bet Daphne Dowty told her. May I ask you a question, Miss Harding? What would you do in her place?"

It was, of course, a question to which Emma had given much thought. She answered without hesitation. "I'd plan two dozen ways to cut out your heart and liver and feed them to the cat. And then I'd start thinking for meself. I'd think of the nice house in Highbury New Park — which I'd have to leave for some shabby little hôtel in France, once the truth got out. I'd think of the nice young daughter no one would marry, once the truth got out. And the two fine young men who'd never get to the top of any tree, once the truth got out. And the income that would stop coming in, once the truth got out. And then — being me — I'd look for the silver lining."

"You think there is one?"

She nodded and gave him a rather sour smile. Somehow, miraculously, she had wrested the emotional upper-hand from him; the realization challenged her to make the most of it while it lasted. "I'd think what's sauce for the gander is sauce for the goose, as well."

He started up. "Good heavens! You don't suppose *she's* gone and ...?"

"No, of course not," Emma said scornfully. "*She's* got more sense."

"What do you mean then?" he asked, his alarm beginning to shade over into anger again.

"I mean, sir, that any woman between my age and hers — and beyond — is aware of ... what? — half a dozen gentlemen who'd take them off to a quiet hôtel for a night or two at the drop of an eyelid."

"Not Hilda!" he exclaimed; there was an odd mixture of amused scorn and bitterness in his voice.

She shrugged. "As you say, sir — you've shared her ... home for a long time." She put the same pause into the words as he had done. She knew very well what word had been in his mind. Now it gave her the confidence to hold his gaze.

He looked away from her and licked his lips anxiously. "My God!" he murmured. He jerked his head back to her and once again his eyes were ablaze with anger — which redoubled when he caught her smiling. "Oh, you are a very superior young miss!" he said, with that same scorn and bitterness in his tone. "Think you know it all, don't you!" He half-rose in his seat and craned his neck to peer about them, checking they were still alone, or at least out of earshot of the people at the far end of the car. "Women!" he exclaimed as he resettled himself. "You have no idea what it's like. Sauce for the goose! Sauce for the gander! Sauce, eh? Is that all it is? I can believe it." He downed his brandy and stared at her. The anger was gone. So, too — surprisingly — was the bitterness and contempt. She found herself eye to eye with a hunted soul, a man possessed.

501

"Please?" she whispered — having no idea what she wanted of him, only that his pain, the sudden exposure of his vulnerability, was unbearable to her.

"I'm not talking of lust," he said, "but of longing. I don't expect you to know the difference. *I* didn't know the difference until I married that woman whose life you so nearly destroyed yesterday. There is a cleanness and an innocence in *longing* that is gold, pure gold, beside which your 'sauce for the goose' is … is worse than trash. I would rather sit out the rest of my life in jail … I would rather live through a thousand ages of purgatory than *not* to have done what I have done, or not to know what I have learned. And if her idea of revenge is a night on the tiles with" — he reached through a ragbag of names and came up with the first — "Walter Grandison, then I don't even consider her to be part of the human race!"

He saw her frown at the name and added. "Or someone like him. He's been sniffing round Hilda like a street mongrel ever since she came out." He smiled wearily and without humour. "Why? Was it a bullseye?"

Emma shrugged. "How would I know that, sir?"

"You seem to know everything else." He became serious again. "But do you know what *I'm* talking about? What d'you feel for Lawrence, eh? What does he feel for you? A bit of sauce in a quiet hôtel? Would that cover it? If it does, you might as well get married, because it's as much as most people ever discover. But if you know what *I'm* talking about — a longing that is pure and sweet and will not give you rest — then do not hesitate about it, for you have found the key to the rarest treasury on earth. Sell your very soul for it." His finger tapped the table twice, ramming home his words. "Take it from one who knows."

NEIL RETURNED ON the *Burgundia* by the next sailing and, on arrival at Southampton, went directly to Walter Grandison, this time in the Grandison building in Leadenhall Street — for his business now was official. He wanted a position of some kind in New York, he explained. Of course, he could walk into any situation with the Shaw & Eggar Line, but he had always rather despised chaps who used family connections and friends to secure themselves a place; he wanted to do it off his own bat. So what did Walter Grandison suggest?

Walter Grandison suggested that Neil should make a clean breast of it — show himself to be the honest fellow the world took him for. In short, what was his *real* reason for wanting to forsake the sea, with all its high romance, for a dull place at a desk ashore?

Neil, finding himself with a true man of the world, over whose eyes no wool could be pulled, confessed it was an affair of the heart — or, as he put it, tapping his breastbone, "an affliction of the old ticker, I'm afraid."

Uncle Walter's sympathetic smile begged for more.

Uncle Walter learned that she was an Irish girl, a vivacious, red-haired beauty of great charm and refinement.

Uncle Walter remarked that there must be thousands such far closer to home than New York. Very well — New Haven. Ah, Fife, was it? No, he didn't know the place. Population, eight-hundred and ninety-six — well, that explained it. All the same, his original point stood: There must be thousands of vivacious, red-haired beauties of great charm and refinement within just three hours' sailing time from Liverpool.

But Miss ... O'Dee was perfection itself, absolute perfection.

Ah! Then Neil would not be seeking a *permanent* situation in America. It was Walter's experience that romances with girls who were "absolutely perfect" tended to endure a much shorter while than those with girls whose characters were known in a more rounded fashion — "warts and all," as someone once said. He himself could name (if he were not such a howling gentleman, of course) several dozen absolutely perfect women he had known for a comparatively brief period.

Neil swelled with pride and said that if it was warts his Uncle Walter wanted, what did he say to *this*? And he told him.

Uncle Walter replied that it was certainly beyond the curative power of the usual country charms — blood on halved potatoes, incantations to the frogs, and so forth. He regretted his earlier flippancy, for he could now see that Neil had, indeed, found the love of his life. What he suggested was that Neil should take a *temporary* position in the New York offices of the Grandison Line (alas, they had none in New Haven); he, Walter, agreed that fellows who traded on the ties of family and friendship for a permanent box in the theatre of life were little short of cads; *temporary* assistance, however — he stressed the word again — was quite another thing. Three months, should he say? That should be long enough for a sprightly young blade to find a permanent place by his own effort.

As before, Neil was almost overcome with his gratitude. He was quite sure three *weeks* would be sufficient.

Uncle Walter said he was to consider himself free to

504

leave the Grandison offices the moment he found such a place. He would write to Mr Kilroy, the chief clerk in the New York office, at once. And, indeed, he did, as soon as Neil had left. It was a terse letter, confined to two instructions. Neil was to be given a position where he could do no damage to the line. And he was to be paid on the lowest going scale. "If he objects, remind him he is a gentleman, not a junior clerk. Also make daily inquiries as to his luck in finding *real* work."

It was, he thought, a small price to pay for such an interesting nugget of information: old Frank Morgan's eldest boy in love with a Fallen Woman in Connecticut — *and* defying his illustrious father's wishes by taking a post ashore! He felt sure Daphne Dowty would give her eye teeth to hear of it — though it was not really the yielding of her eye teeth that interested him. Never mind. At last he had the nucleus around which to construct a campaign to get at the parts that did.

F OR DAPHNE IT WAS going to be the struggle of a lifetime. She now had to overcome her deep-seated aversion to meddling in the lives of those around her — for she drew a stark line between the merely passive acquiring of scandal about her friends and the active use of it to try to change them and their ways.

She had already put a toe in the water — and over this same business, too — when she had gently pointed out to Hilda the consequences of shooting Frank or of exposing him to a term in jail. Now she had to persuade her that to let Kathleen continue in her ignorance much longer was akin to leaving a loaded revolver lying about in a crowded nursery — a practice to be recommended, she thought, only to mothers of *excessively* large families.

Her chance came when Hilda suggested they should go to one of the cheap little tailors in Upper Street to purchase costumes for their rôles as second-class passengers. The choice was so limited that the expedition was over almost as soon as it began. Hilda, for whom shopping was more an emotional than a commercial experience, felt rather deflated. It was like finding the plate full of crusts when you had looked forward to bourbon creams. She gazed about them for something else to do — and heard herself saying words she would not have let pass her lips in any other circumstances: "That dreadful Harding creature has her lair somewhere in this vicinity, has she not?"

Daphne pounced. "Would you care to see it? I'm sure she'd be only too happy."

"What d'you mean — would I care to see it? Is she here? She can't be. The *Pride of Liverpool* is ..." Her voice tailed off as she saw the key Daphne was now dangling before her eyes.

"Following Lawrence's desertion," Daphne explained, "her poor aspidistras and spider plants had no one to water them."

"You?" Hilda was appalled.

Daphne gave an apologetic nod. "I know we don't see eye-to-eye on her, dear, but I actually admire the girl. If the word *sterling* has any meaning at all, it was coined for people like her."

"You mean ... you are acquainted with her?"

"I hope I may claim we are friends. However, that is beside the question — which is, would you like to accompany me while I sprinkle the tradescantia?"

"Absolutely not!" Hilda said firmly.

Daphne smiled as if to say she quite understood and *almost* approved. "Then we'll go straight home and have a nice cup of tea. We should practise pouring it into the saucer and fanning it with our hats. Or would that be steerage? One's ignorance of the finer gradations of social class is quite shame-making. After all, we practically invented the whole business, didn't we — people like you and me."

As they were passing Emma's place Daphne flashed the key again and said, "Sure? It'll only take a minute."

Hilda stared at the door with distaste. It had been newly painted and looked rather smart. "Such vulgar mouldings," she remarked.

"Home, then," Daphne said.

"Just to water the plants?" Hilda asked.

"What else, dear?"

Daphne led the way. The hall had been painted, too, and the stairs freshly varnished — depriving Hilda of such comments as she might have hoped to make. Daphne, remembering her own preconceptions when she had first trod those steps, said, "You must know what to expect. Plaster trinkets from the Caledonian Market ... patched linoleum ... paper-lace doilies ..." She kept up the litany all the way to Emma's door.

Hilda stood transfixed at the threshold, jaw agape.

"Yes!" Daphne exclaimed brightly. "I fell into precisely the same error. I wonder what you are thinking to yourself now, Hilda, dear? Could it perhaps be crossing your mind that you have misjudged the dear girl in other ways, too? More important ways, eh?"

"Dear girl? I wish you wouldn't say things like that." Hilda stepped gingerly inside and ran an

507

experimental hand over the deep polish of the tabletop. "Are those real watercolours?" she asked, taking a few more steps to peer at two pictures on the wall beside the window.

"Yes. She bought them on her last visit to New York, in a village there called Greenwich. The Americans are streets ahead of us, aren't they — one couldn't buy anything half so good in *our* Greenwich, I'm sure."

While Daphne watered the plants, Hilda completed a slow, critical survey of the rooms; when she had finished she said nothing.

"Talking of Emma Harding," Daphne said, "I thought it rather extraordinary, didn't you, how little she actually told you about Frank and the Ginger Colleen — especially when you reflect on all that she *could* have said."

Hilda wondered if she dared pull open a drawer or two.

"She could really have 'rubbed your nose in it,' as vulgar people say. We *must* practise being vulgar now, you know."

Hilda's lips vanished into a thin line. She pressed the wood of the wardrobe, pretending to feel its quality, hoping its door might just happen to fall open. It didn't, even when she pressed harder.

Daphne was remorseless. "I believe she could have reduced you to tears. There's almost no end to the humiliations she *might* have heaped upon you — yet she chose to say so little that you didn't even ..."

"All right, Daphne, dear! I think you have made your point. She didn't rub my nose in it. What an example to us *all!*" She added these last words with an acid smile at her friend.

Behind her the wardrobe door swung quietly open.

"Ah!" she exclaimed, turning back in delight.

Daphne came and stood at her side. "Yes," she sighed after they had taken stock of its contents, "we can hardly pass on this morning's purchases to Miss Harding when we've done with them!" She smacked her lips. "Would you like a cup of tea here? Emma brings back the most delicious lapsang from New York. So sensible!"

"Really?" Hilda's tone was still disbelieving.

"Yes, because you drink it without milk, you see — no matter what hour of the night she gets home. Such a practical young girl! Actually …" She drifted away toward the kitchen alcove and lit the gas to boil the kettle. "Talking of young girls, practical or otherwise, I was rather hoping to have a word with you about Kathleen. So I think we shall, in fact, stay here and have a cup of tea, after all."

"What about Kathleen?" Hilda came to peek over her shoulder at Emma Harding's cooking arrangements. An unease she had felt ever since entering these rooms suddenly crystallized itself into a pang of … could it be … envy? Yes, there was no other word for it. This tiny space, where every cubic inch was precious, seemed filled with the deepest sense of calm she had ever felt. She pictured Emma Harding arriving on the Liverpool train at Euston, taking an omnibus out here to Highbury, opening that newly painted front door, coming up those stairs, opening this door, closing it behind her, and standing there a moment, leaning against it with her eyes closed, breathing deeply and enjoying the utter serenity of this place. This inviolate space that was her own, her very own.

And the envy she felt lay in her realization that never in her life had such an experience been open to her, nor even the possibility of it. She had never known a place she could call her own. She was mistress of her own home and she had her own boudoir within it, but they were not hers as these rented rooms were Emma Harding's. Suddenly she felt like a marauder.

She shivered lightly and took a grip on herself. "What of Kathleen?" she asked. A delicious aroma of China tea filled the apartment.

Daphne smiled. "Ah, I jumped the starter's gun a bit there. I meant to ask you first what Walter Grandison said when you put this rather strange request to him?"

Hilda knew perfectly well that Daphne never did anything by mistake. She had dangled some petty worry concerning Kathleen before her as a feint while she now trawled for something more susbtantial about Walter G. She smiled a knowing smile, to let Daphne know her little plan was discovered, and said, "He was courtesy itself, of course, and forbore to ask even the most trivial question."

Daphne gave a silvery laugh.

Hilda asked what she meant by that.

Daphne replied as she handed out a cup of tea, "Oh, Hilda, you are such a very *dear* friend, otherwise I could not possibly tell you." She gave a brief demonstration of not-telling-Hilda.

It lasted long enough for Hilda to have to say, "What? Tell me what?"

"Well think, dear! Think of old Walter's reputation."

From the way Hilda licked her lips and tried to sip her tea, even though it was still scalding hot, Daphne knew she had touched a raw nerve; she was careful not to show it.

"I know his reputation with *other* ladies," Hilda

said coldly. "I do not regard myself as vulnerable in that respect."

"Nor do they, of course," Daphne pointed out.

"Do you include yourself among them?"

"He has tried. Oh, he has tried!"

"Anyway, what does it matter what he said? The point is, he agreed. What were you going to say about Kathleen?"

"I didn't explain why I laughed just now. If I don't, you will think me utterly heartless — and, what is even worse, rather impolite. I laughed because I cannot think of any other woman who could have delivered such a remark. Only you."

Hilda brought her cup to her lips again and, again, winced. "I have no idea what you're talking about."

"I'm saying that if *any* other woman of our acquaintance delivered such a remark, then *every* other woman of our acquaintance would know at once that dear Walter's agreement to our arrangement was in the way of a reward for favours granted — that is to say, The Favour, granted in the plural. Whereas, of course, *no one* could possibly think that of you! My laugh was the laughter of pleasure to realize it. Now, as to Kathleen ..."

Hilda drummed the table with angry fingers. "Why could no one possibly say that of me?" she demanded. "Why do you persist in making me out to be so different from all the other women of our acquaintance? And where do you place yourself, incidentally?" She lifted the cup only half-way to her lips this time before she set it down again.

"Among the virtuous, naturally." Her eyes twinkled. "But for the basest of reasons, alas: I cannot stand the man. Or let me be precise. I adore him at my dinner table; I should hate to grace his bed."

"And d'you suppose he'd give you the chance?"

"Oh!" Hilda raised the back of her hand to her forehead as if she had an attack of the vapours. "Twice a year, at least, for the past twenty years I have had to repel him. I have almost — now don't let this go any further, will you — I have almost yielded, simply to make him desist, for I'm told that, like lightning, he never strikes in the same place twice. You don't know how lucky you are — to have such a cold … or rather virtuous, yes, virtuous — reputation. It has spared you such ennui."

"Oh has it indeed!" Hilda declared angrily. Her lips vanished again and her jaw muscles writhed.

"Ask anyone," Daphne suggested.

"Well, it just shows how ignorant people can be. Ignorant and utterly *silly*. They know nothing. They understand nothing."

Daphne stared at her in amazement. "No!" she exclaimed at last, her eyes going wide with horror. "Not you!"

"Why not? Why d'you think I'm so different? If husbands appreciated their wives a little more, people like Walter Grandison would have to go sniffing elsewhere, I can tell you that."

"And is he … appreciative?" Daphne asked. In that moment her mask slipped. If she had put the question in her usual supercilious manner, Hilda would have responded with some dismissive remark and insisted on a change of subject; but there was such a wistful light in her eyes that Hilda felt quite touched. She smiled, nodded, blinked, and said, "Very!"

Daphne gave a little sigh.

Hilda could almost feel the subject being packed carefully away — but she felt sure it was in a box marked WANTED ON VOYAGE! She sipped her tea, which was of a drinkable temperature at last.

"Anyway," Daphne said, "it makes my point about Kathleen all the more urgent. Walter G. is no fool. If I may put my cards on the table at last, it's my guess he has made as many fruitless attempts on your uxorial virtue as he has on mine, down the years — and with as little succes, *until* this year. Now put yourself in his place. He has no idea what's happened to change your mind but he knows something's afoot. Hundred to one it concerns you and Frank — what else could it be? If there's any doubt left, you remove it with this extraordinary request to get yourself to America incognito. So now he *knows* it concerns Frank and ... something else over there. Some *one* else — that's also a hundred to one. Then he realizes you've left young Kathleen behind ..."

At that Hilda laughed. "If you're going to suggest he'd make an attempt on Kathleen's virtue ..." she began.

But Daphne waved her to silence. "Of course not. Wives are his game. Mature wives whose husbands don't much mind who sires the tail-enders as long as the little woman's kept happy."

"Daphne!"

"Well, it's the simple truth. But the danger with Kathleen is that Walter G. will pay a courtesy call on Highbury New Park, be utterly astonished to find the lady of the house away, stay the regulation ten minutes with her worthy deputy, *Miss* Morgan ... and find some occasion to provoke her to explain just how noble and selfless Frank is being over there in America. Walter would twig it faster than any of us."

"Oh, Lord!" Hilda closed her eyes and sank her forehead into her hand.

For once her cup of tea lay untouched.

HAVING FAILED WITH one Mrs Morgan, Emma decided that the only honourable course left to her was to confront the other. But Fate saw it differently. The trouble with the *Pride of Liverpool's* boilers, fortunately now cured, had thrown her sailing schedule out to such an extent that, instead of leaving Manhattan on Saturday the 30th of May, the day the *Burgundia* sailed from Southampton, she actually arrived in Liverpool. Both Hilda and Daphne knew it, of course, for the papers had reported every twist in the saga. But there was nothing they could do about it now; the die, as is its habit, was cast. At the very moment that the *Pride of Liverpool* was tying up, the two women were standing on *Burgundia's* second-class deck, waving at the crowd in general. Between them stood a somewhat bewildered Kathleen.

The *Pride of Liverpool,* slowly recouping her schedule, would then perform a rather swift turnaround and sail back to New York on the following Monday. If both vessels kept to their usual speeds, *Burgundia* would arrive on the Friday, just a day ahead of her swifter rival. Hilda and Daphne resigned themselves to a steady diet of fingernail.

Emma had her fair share of the same delicacy on the train down from Liverpool. She arrived in London just before five that evening and, knowing she could neither relax nor eat until she had done what she must, stopped by her rooms only long enough to drop her bag, and then walked directly to Highbury New Park. As she turned at the circus and went along St Paul's Road her heart began to race, just as it had done on the day of her dismissal — the last occasion on which she had walked this way, though then she had been coming from the house, not going to it. She had barely turned into Highbury New Park when she saw Lawrence, striding toward her, head in the clouds.

She stopped. It brought his attention back to earth. He saw her and paused; then he ran the remaining two or three dozen paces between them. There was so much he wanted to say that he found he could not utter a word. He caught her by her forearms to check his momentum, swinging her round until both were facing the way they had come. "You don't half look daft when you grin like that," she told him.

He hugged her briefly but they were too aware that this was his home street. "What are you doing here?" he asked as they separated again.

"We docked this morning."

"No, *here*. In Highbury New Park."

"Oh, I'm on my way to see your mother."

"Ah." He ran an awkward finger round his collar. "That was a pretty silly letter I wrote you."

"I never got it. Neil tore it up — after reading it, of course. If you think *you* were silly, you should …"

"Hang on." He frowned. "What were you going to see my mother about?"

"Not were, *am*. Oh, it's too difficult to explain. Although … I don't know." She eyed him quizically. "Maybe if I was to tell you, you'd advise me if I'm doing the right thing at all. My head's all … pfft!"

"She's not at home, anyway."

Emma shrugged. "I can wait. I certainly couldn't settle to anything else until this business is …"

"I think it'd be quite a long wait, love. She's *really* gone."

"Where?" Emma had visions of a family break-up — Mrs Morgan gone back to her mother or something.

He pulled a wry face. "I have an awful suspicion. I just hope I'm wrong. Mrs Johnson won't say a thing, nor any of the others. There's a sort of conspiracy among them."

Emma came to a decision. "Go back to my rooms. Got any money? You can buy some leek and bacon at the corner and start cutting them up. I'll make your favourite when I get back. I won't be long."

She wasn't, either. Mrs Johnson had always felt a little guilty at the way she had been dismissed. They had met from time to time since then, in this shop or that, and the housekeeper had always gone out of her way to be affable. It did not take long to get the complete story out of her.

"They've gone to America," Emma told Lawrence the moment she let herself in.

"Oh no! That's what I feared."

"Oi, that smells good. I didn't mean you to cook it as well."

"No cook on the *Horsa*," he explained as he took her in his arms and hugged her tight. "I'm sorry," he whispered in her ear. "God, how I've missed you!"

"Me too." She swallowed hard and thrust him away before the disorder within passed beyond her control.

As he watched her push by him, shed her coat, tie on her apron, a new feeling of happiness overcame him, though it was a second or two before he could pin it down; then he realized it was a sense of something almost infinite between them: time! It suddenly seemed to him that an infinity of time now stretched all around them, enveloping them both in its protection and reaching out in all directions.

He went and stood behind her, lifting his hands to her shoulders, lightly massaging her neck.

"Ye-e-ess!" she sighed as she stirred the leek and bacon fry-up, sizzling in the pan. "You can do that for ever!"

"You know the moment when you steam into port, when you make fast and the engines stop pounding? You know what a wonderful sense of *arrival* you get at that particular moment?"

"What of it?"

"I feel it now with you, Emma. The voyage is over. It really is over. The doubts, the uncertainties, the dangers ... they're all over. They're all behind us." He pushed his lips among the wisps of hair on her neck and kissed her gently there. "What I'm saying, my darling, darling, darling Emma, is — if I come ashore again, will you? For ever?"

She dropped the fork and turned to face him, slipping her arms around his neck and hugging herself against him with a force that took his breath away. "Yes," she said, slipping one hand behind her to turn off the gas.

But he, knowing what was on her mind, got there first and held her off.

She bit the lobe of his ear, rather harder than he would have wished, and said, "Ooh, you are stubborn!"

While she buttered the bread that would form a bed for the fry-up, he slipped down to the jug and bottle for some ale, and an apple pie from the bakery across the street. It proved to be the best meal either had enjoyed since they had last sat together at that same table. It gave them heart enough to face the many unpalatable decisions that now pressed upon them.

She told him first of her encounter with Neil and the fantastic ambitions he had formed.

"How did he even know of her existence?" Lawrence asked — then struck himself on the forehead. "My letter to you! He's a swine to have opened that." Then he frowned. "But I don't think I mentioned her name even. Lord, I was in such a state, I don't know what I wrote."

"I told him," Emma said quietly.

"You?"

"He came to me, demanding an explanation. Can you imagine trying to explain something like that to someone like Neil?"

He made a glum, sympathetic face.

"He let me say half a dozen words and then he started jumping to all sorts of conclusions … shouting at me … insulting me. In the end I just lost my patience and told him to go and see what was going on there for himself — names, directions, everything."

He reached across the table and squeezed her hand. "No one can possibly blame you for that, my love. I certainly don't."

"I've not finished telling you, yet. After I met him in New York and heard what madness he's up to now, I saw how unfair it was on her, so I went out to set her straight, like."

His eyes lit up with hope. "And did you tell her?"

She held up a finger and thumb, a fraction of an inch apart. "I was *that* close to it. Then the Captain turned up."

Lawrence whistled and flapped his hand as if he'd burned his fingertips.

She told him what had followed and of the conversation she'd had with his father on the train between New Haven and Bridgeport. "The thing is," she concluded, "when he tells you a tale like that, and looks at you with those eyes of his, you find yourself thinking he's right! *He's* got the vision. The rest of us are just blind."

"I know. We were steaming down the Elbe the other night, down to Cuxhaven, and there was an incredible moon. I was off watch but I just stood there and gazed at Germany, slipping by. And suddenly I got the feeling it wasn't just a foreign country out there, it was a foreign … *place!* A foreign planet, almost. As if everything had been wiped clean and it could all start again — the way it must have been when God showed Adam the world and told him he could start giving names to everything." He laughed, a little embarrassed at his own earnestness. But the memory of his feelings at that moment still gripped him and impelled him onward. So did the light in her eyes. "I mean to say, can you imagine what it must have been like to be Adam in that time before God told him to start thinking up names? Can you imagine looking out at a world full of *things*, and none of them's got a name yet? That's what I felt like, going down the Elbe the other night. It was like a waking dream, really. It was all connected somehow with Papa's … you know. *Bigamy!* let's start saying it. It was all tied up with that. And I suddenly saw that it didn't help one bit for me to go off on my high horse like that. It didn't even help *me*. And it certainly didn't help you! And so I realized I had to come back here and … I don't know. Do something."

"Do what?"

"I was going to tackle my mother with it — see what her attitude was, and, sort of, take it onward from there." He stroked her arm in apology for the feebleness of his notion. "Why do you think she's gone to America? Did I say she's taken Kathleen with her?"

"No!" Emma sat up, eyes wide. "Mrs Johnson never said that."

"I'm pretty sure she has. Kathy's not there, anyway."

"She just said she'd gone together with your Aunt Daphne. Second class on the *Burgundia*." She hit herself on the forehead, exactly as he had done earlier. "Of course! Walter Grandison!"

"That's right. He owns her. Why that tone?"

"Because your Aunt Daphne predicted it. I should have realized. Your mum's been palling up with old Grandison lately and Mrs Dowty said it was to get a passage to America without anyone finding out. But she never said as she'd be going along, too, the sly old minx! And Kathy too, eh?"

He nodded unhappily. "But why? That's what I can't make out. What's she going to *do* when they get there?"

"What d'you think?" Emma asked as if it were obvious. Indeed, it was obvious to her but she doubted that Lawrence had the first inkling.

"Horsewhip this Irish girl? Horsewhip my father? I don't know."

"Oh, Larry!" She laughed and gave him a kindly pat on the arm.

"What?"

"You men! You think you're the most logical, reasonable creatures ever invented. You think women are just a bundle of emotions and ... and vapours. And really it's the other way round. The women in this business are the only ones who've used their common sense."

"Like Kathy?" he jeered.

"She's not a woman yet. She's a girl — and anyway, she showed a sight more common sense than you!"

He covered his head as if against shrapnel.

"What was the first thing I told your mum, in New York that time? I didn't tell her your dad had gone off with another woman. I never said a word about bigamy and that. I just said he'd done that which, if it come out in the open, would send him to prison. And if you think about it, Larry, that's the only thing what's important in the whole business. If this ever gets out, your dad'll go to prison. And I'll bet — when your mum found out what he'd done — I'll bet there was five minutes of fireworks when she wanted to skin him alive and denounce him to the beaks and all that. And then I'll bet she remembered what I said. And she thought of her boys, and Kathy, and the nice house up the road, and all her respectable friends and neighbours …"

"That's right!" His jaw fell open. "No one would marry Kathy then."

"And d'you suppose you'd be able to continue on the Baltic?"

He shook his head. "And then?"

"And then — well, put yourself in her place. You've settled down to the fact that you've just got to go on making everything seem nice and normal. And then you start thinking to yourself as you're not the only one with this secret. There's a young Irish woman with red hair four thousand miles away who could lose her rag and spoil it for everyone — herself included."

"So they've gone over to" — he turned pale. "No! Not … not … poison or something? Oh, my God!"

She closed her eyes and counted to ten, just loud enough for him to hear. "No, Larry, darling. Not poison — leastways, only as a last resort."

"Hell!" he ignored her jibes and thumped the table, making the plates rattle. "Why am I not over *there!*

You won't be back for another two weeks. How can I live through it until then?"

She eyed him speculatively, her tongue lingering on her lip. "What are you like at peeling potatoes?" she asked. "Scouring pots and pans?"

O N THEIR FIRST day at sea Daphne decided it was really rather like a picnic. On their second day she began to realize that a picnic lasting six or seven days was too awful to contemplate. On their third day she was caught out of bounds in the first class and escorted back below the salt; she said it was an exciting experience but she did not try to repeat it. After that she turned her pent-up energies upon the Morgans, mother and daughter, but most especially mother.

Her strong hand was her ability to plan; Hilda's was not. That is to say, Hilda could plan the daily routine of her house down to the last flick of a feather duster, but she would sail impromptu into the great occasions of life, trusting to instinct and a gift for improvisation; Daphne, on the other hand, was hardly aware that the household needed any sort of roster — her housekeeper saw to that — but in all other departments she could have scored points over General von Clausewitz himself.

It annoyed Daphne that Hilda could barely state her objective in going to America and confronting the other Mrs Morgan on her home ground; instead she took refuge in vague terms like "sounding out the ground" and "seeing the lie of the land."

"And then?" Daphne pressed.

"Why, then I'll decide, of course. How can I be

expected to decide until I know which way the cards are cut? It's like asking me to bid three no trumps on an unseen hand that might hold a grand slam — or nothing at all."

"Yes, granted, but at least in bridge you know the object of the whole exercise, which is to win the number of tricks you bid for. What's your object here?"

"Oh I know that," Hilda replied scornfully. "We've got to stop *her* upsetting the applecart."

"Good!" Daphne's tone suggested that Hilda was a bit of a backward child who had just passed a lesser milestone in Book One. "And," she pressed on in the same kindly tone, "have we any idea how we're going to set about it?"

Hilda shrugged and stared at their cabin door, hoping desperately for Kathleen to come and rescue her from this inquisition.

"What, no idea at all?"

"Well I did sort of think I might call upon her, pretending to be Mrs Johnson, don't you know. Apparently the Ginger Colleen, as you call her, thinks Mrs J. has been bringing up the Captain's children — or bringing up Kathleen, anyway."

"Ah!" Daphne exclaimed. "I'm so glad someone has brought up Kathleen at last. You do realize, don't you, that by taking her along with us you have more or less committed yourself to telling her the truth? I mean, you can hardly sit there with the Ginger Colleen, amicably carving up Frank's time and income to your mutual advantage, and hope that the dear girl won't twig what's going on."

Again Hilda stared at the door; would the girl never come back? "She might not be there at all," she offered.

"Ah, then we shall need some rope," Daphne replied, in the tones of one compiling a shopping list. "And something to gag her with, too."

"No! She sent a cable to Chuck Burgoyne before we left. He might come down to New York and take her off our hands. It's only for one day."

"*If* we're lucky," Daphne reminded her. "And who will chaperone them?"

Hilda smiled sweetly at her.

"Oh no!" Daphne exclaimed. "I am not enduring an entire week of this squalor simply to become a wallflower in New York, thank you kindly." She gave her tinkling laugh. "Especially not now that I know you intend doing your Mrs Johnson impersonation. It's not one I've seen before. In fact, my dear, and quite between ourselves, I've never seen you impersonate *anyone* before. And if one or other of our acquaintance were to suggest you possess such a talent, I should suspect her of drinking. So I certainly intend to be there. I wouldn't miss it for ..."

"Oh," Hilda sneered, "it's so easy for you, isn't it! I've no doubt you'd go sailing through it all and you'd have the Ginger Colleen eating out of your hand and calling down the blessings of God and all his saints upon you ..."

Daphne sat up at that and asked, "Why? Is she a Roman Catholic, then?"

"I'm sure she is. They mostly are, aren't they — colleens of every hue. She must be. Yes, come to think of it, I'm sure Kathleen said something about a rather gaudy dissection of a naked heart. A painting. That's the sort of thing they like, isn't it?"

"And d'you suppose they were married in one of *their* churches?" Daphne pressed, her eyes bright and eager.

A wild hope flitted through Hilda's breast, as if her friend might have discovered some quaint legal catch that would make all smooth. "If Francis could swallow the camel of this unlawful marriage, he'd hardly strain at the gnat of solemnizing it in the wrong church, would he."

"Oh well," Daphne settled herself more comfortably, "that's a relief."

"Why? D'you mean it's not unlawful after all — if one marriage is Protestant and the other RC?"

"No, no. I wouldn't go so far as to say that. But it is more reassuring, somehow, don't you think?"

Hilda shook her head. "In what way?"

"Well, haven't you ever been to one of *their* weddings? It's all smoke and Latin. Quite fragrant and pretty, mind you, but somehow it's not a *real* wedding. I mean nobody tells them it's a remedy against sin and to avoid fornication. At least, not in good old Shakespearean English they don't. It works, too — an admonition in Shakespearean English, I mean. Brian has grown wonderfully adept at avoiding fornication recently."

In all their years of friendship, that subject had never once cropped up between them; now Hilda did not know how to respond. Fortunately, at that moment, Kathleen did at last return to their cabin.

But whether Hilda continued to think it quite so fortunate was doubtful, for the moment Daphne saw the girl, she turned to Hilda and said, "You really must tell her."

"Tell me what?" Kathleen asked eagerly.

Hilda sighed and heaved herself from her unsteady wicker chair. "Let's take a little walk on deck, dear," she said. "There are one or two things you ought to know before we dock."

THE BOOTS MADE BY the Otis Brothers of Winnetka were reckoned to be the finest in North America. The firm sent you a special device, with which you took a dozen or so measurements, which you wrote down on the order form, which you returned with the device. Four weeks later they sent you the boots. In this specific case they sent them to Ignatius O'Dee, Teresa's brother, since it was his feet that had been measured and his dollars that had paid for them. He had the parcel delivered to his sister, since he and his wife were not always at home to receive the mail and there were one or two folks he didn't trust.

To prevent the fine leather from creasing and buckling in transit, the Otis Brothers packed their wares out with old, scrunched-up newspapers — Chicago newspapers, New York newspapers ... anything that came to hand. Teresa started to read them and then asked herself why, since she barely had time to read today's paper, she was bothering with prints almost six months old. So she put the better quality ones to be cut up for the privy and the others to wrap garbage and light fires.

Jemima, however, was made of more inquisitive stuff. After lunch she came to her mistress with a scrap she had clipped from the *New York Times*. "I never knewed you was in New York back last January, Mrs Morgan," she said, almost accusingly.

"Sure I wasn't. And if I was, it wasn't January."

"Says here you was. You and the Cap'n both." She handed the clipping over. "I already used the rest of it for garbage but what's here is plain enough. The date was January seventh. You can see it there."

Teresa took it. The part of the clipping that Jemima had managed to save was tantalizingly short:

> Yesterday was a busy one for both Captain Francis Morgan and his wife. They visited Staten Island, where several charities supported by the Shaw & Eggar Line are located. Captain Morgan is, of course, Commodore of that line and his wife, ...

"They got the date wrong," she said, dropping the cutting as if it were of little interest. When she saw that a certain skepticism still lingered on in the maid's eye, she added, "It was before Christmas. Because of the charities, see. Always before Christmas. There'd be no point after. They must change the date to make the news sound less stale."

"Just cain't depend on nothin'!" Jemima said disgustedly as she returned to her shredding.

Teresa "remembered one or two messages in New Haven" and set off for the town shortly after. She was actually beginning to remember little oddities in the behaviour of the two girls — Emma's bewilderment at their first meeting, and Kathleen's extreme awkwardness. Then, too, there was Emma's distinctly strange behaviour just a few weeks ago — the hints that she was about to reveal something dreadful concerning her and Frank, indeed, touching them all ... and the way she had clammed up the moment Frank appeared ... and the way he never allowed the girl to be alone with her after that. It all pointed the one way — to the one awful conclusion.

She could not believe it — and yet, as minute succeeded minute and fragments of remembered scenes, moments of awkwardness, nipped-off phrases, rapid changes of the subject ... all returned to haunt her, it became only too believable.

An unmutilated copy of that issue of the *New York Times* was easily located at the library. The item read:

> Yesterday was a busy one for both Captain Francis Morgan and his wife. They visited Staten Island, where several charities supported by the Shaw & Eggar Line are located. Captain Morgan is, of course, Commodore of that line and his wife, Hilda, is a daughter of the late Mr Victor Watson, who is still well remembered in New York shipping circles as Chairman of London's Baltic Exchange. Among institutions favored by the Captain and his Lady were the Sailors' Snug Harbor, the Home for Sailors' Children, the Marine Hospital, and the Seamen's Retreat. Mrs Morgan, who, with her daughter, Kathleen, spent Christmas in Chicago with Mrs Eunice Burgoyne, are this day steaming home on the *Pride of Liverpool*, the premier steamship of the line, under the steady hand of Captain Morgan himself.

That evening, by the time Ignatius cried in to check his poteen still and share a bite of supper, she knew that her life now lay in ruins.

"Begod, girl, there's a stepmother's breath in that welcome of yours this evening," he commented.

"Wait till I tell you," she said grimly and placed the cutting Jemima had rescued before him. She then told him what she had discovered in the library that afternoon.

As she spoke, the colour rose to his face, his hand began to tremble — until at last he could contain himself no more.

Her recitation ended with the words, "I'll kill him, so I will. By God, I'll put all Ten Commandments on him!" She showed her nails like a tigress. "I'll kill him. I'll kill him!"

"I'll be there before you!" Ignatius roared as he ran out the door.

For a moment she stood there, stunned. Then, realizing he meant it all too literally, she shouted after him, "No! Ignatius, for the love of God, no! That's not what I mean!" She ran to the back door but saw no sign of him. Then to the front parlour, whose window gave the best view of the road that led down the hill into Fife — but there was no sign of him there, either. She went out to the hall to put on her hat and coat when he came bursting back into the house waving a pistol.

"Here!" he shouted excitedly. "I'll do it with this. You hold him down and I'll put all six through his brain."

"Are you mad?" she screamed at him as she made a lunge to seize the gun.

He jerked it out of her reach. There was a deafening report. Bits of plaster stung her cheeks, narrowly missing her eyes. Then the sickly reek of burned cordite filled her nostrils.

And then the silence was shattered by a cry of pain from above.

They stared agahast at each other. The colour left Ignatius's cheeks as swiftly as it had risen there. "Mother of God!" he whispered, sinking to his knees and hurling the gun from him as if it were red hot. "Jesus, Mary, and Joseph! Not that!"

She sprang up the stairs, four at a time, and dashed into the nursery. A moment later her scream almost took the roof off the house.

Like a slipped greyhound Ignatius vaulted from his devotions and raced to his sister's side.

It *looked* awful, but a closer inspection showed there was more blood than wound. The bullet had grazed little Tony along two inches of the fold where right thigh and buttock meet; already the flow of blood was stanching itself. Teresa was hugging him to her, trying not to jog him up and down, patting his naked back and telling him it was all right, Mammy was there, he'd just had a bad dream …

"What'll I do?" Ignatius kept repeating. "Tell me what to do."

"Boracic, lint, cold water," she said — and then she added the strangest words of all: "Frank'll kill me for this!"

Jemima, who had come to the door during this last exchange, went off in search of the boracic and dressings.

"Go for Doctor Hebble," Teresa told her brother, mainly to get him out of the way.

By the time he returned the house was calm once more, not to say subdued; the closeness of violent death was still heavy on all their spirits. The doctor looked at the wound, dressed it again, leaving the bandage somewhat looser than Teresa had done, and said, "If he never gets worse in *these* woods, he'll be one of life's lucky young men." He took a bottle of Ignatius's poteen by way of payment and declared himself one of life's lucky *old* men.

His cool humour did something to restore their own. When he had gone they even managed a slight laugh, though with precious little humour behind it, at the narrowness of Tony's escape.

Ignatius was just wondering would it be tactless to ask had his supper spoiled in all the excitement when there came a further knock to the door. It was Father Hines, whose housekeeper was in cahoots with Mrs Hebble — which allowed him to get to the afflicted, both faithful and wavering, ahead of the competition.

He looked in at Tony, who had now dropped off to sleep again — though of a rather exhausted, restless kind — and then led them through a decade of the Rosary. After that, of course, he wanted to know what had happened.

They told him — and showed him the cutting into the bargain. They watched his expression keenly for a reaction of some kind.

It is said that if you confess murder to an Anglican parson, he'll jump out of his skin and throw a fit; but if you confess the identical crime to a Roman Catholic priest, he'll merely respond, "How many times, my son?" Father Hines now displayed something of that calm as he considered these dreadful tidings. He had the advantage of them in that this would not be the first case of bigamy to come his way; indeed, it would not even be the tenth. That milestone had already come and gone — taking with it his latent impulse to stick to a simple, moral line. Nowadays he took a broader, more pragmatic view of what was, after all, a rather commonplace sin.

"This Mrs *Hilda* Morgan," he began, "would she be a Protestant, now? The Captain is a Protestant, as I recall. What is the daughter, Kathleen? That would be the guide."

Teresa recalled how Kathy had turned up her nose at the painting of the Sacred Heart. "She's a Protestant, Father. I'm sure of that."

"Ah, well, then …" Father Hines's smile suggested that the worst of their troubles were now behind them. "If the Captain was to divorce her — which

531

they can according to their particular heresy, as you know — the Church would marry you and him without a qualm."

"But the Church has already done so, Father."

"Just so, my child. You surely see the point? The Church would marry you because, according to Canon Law, that heretical marriage has no validity at all in the sight of God. A Protestant marriage and a Protestant divorce are just empty bits of play-acting to Him."

"D'you mean, in the eyes of Mother Church, I'm his only true wife?" Teresa could not believe her luck.

"That's my reading of the affair. Mind you, the civil powers might not quite see it in that way, so we'll have to box a little clever there. But you may set your mind at rest on the main thing: When you and the Captain stand before the Judgement Seat, ye'll stand there as man and wife in the eyes of that Judge." He licked his lips cautiously and added, "There is one thing would go a long way to soften the Aweful Verdict you'll face that day."

"What's that, Father. Anything! I'll say a million Hail Marys — anything."

"If *all* the offspring of this marriage were to be brought up in the True Faith now — Jaysus, that'd look good!"

Teresa glanced at the cutting and said she doubted she'd have much difficulty there.

The priest rubbed his hands delightedly and continued, "So now it's just one or two little practical matters that call for our attention. First, to be sure, is to keep all whiff of this situation from the ears of the civil powers and the populace in general. Keep it in the family. Do you suppose the other party is aware of what has happened?"

Teresa shrugged. "We've never met — of course. Until five hours ago I knew for a certainty she was dead! But does Kathleen know? I really couldn't say. Her friend, the one who came here with her, Emma Harding — she certainly knows. So it's more likely than not that Kathy does, too."

"Yet she was friendly to you?"

"Oh God, she was."

"And you don't find that strange?"

"Strange is it?" Teresa gave a crafty smile. "Ah well now, Father, I want to tell you about that."

Father Hines licked his lips and turned a hopeful gaze at Ignatius.

While her brother took the hint and went to fetch a drop or two of the craythur, Teresa told him what one or other of the girls had said in passing once — about Chuck Burgoyne's going to Yale next Fall. "That little colleen wouldn't want to be falling out with one who had a house so handy, now would she!" she said triumphantly.

Father Hines clapped and rubbed his hands delightedly. "Well, I can't tell you how glad I am to hear it so. For it shows you're thinking in *practical* terms, too — as Kathy surely is. God send we can soon add a third to the tally!"

And so he led her on through a regular catechism of "practicalities," ranging from the Captain's income to her personal feelings about the having to share him with a woman four thousand miles away if she wished to go on living in the style and title to which she was now accustomed. He spun it out through three or four refills, and left her with the suggestion that she should take the earliest opportunity to go over to London and talk terms with the other Mrs Morgan.

"The Captain's supposed to arrive in New York this Saturday," she said. "I'll tell you what I'll do, so. I'll take the boy with me to see one of those fancy doctors with all the hiramglyptics after their names. And while I'm there, I'll slip into one of the other lines, not the Shaw & Eggar, and fix a passage to London. And I'll see that Emma Harding girl and make her tell me all she knows — and who else knows what. Arragh, God be good to you, Father, for you've put back the heart and liver into me."

On his way home the priest contrasted the distraught, tormented, and aimless young woman who had greeted him earlier that evening with the bright-eyed, confident, pugnacious creature who had just seen him to the gate — and he felt not the slightest doubt that he had done the right thing. Nonetheless, he remembered just enough theology to know that *lack* of doubt in such fundamentals of faith is the first step to many a heresy. It moved him to an unusual prayer.

"Forgive me, Heavenly Father," he murmured, "for I know just what I do!"

THE FORT TOMPKINS Light on the Staten Island shore was growing paler by the minute as the sun rose behind *Burgundia*. As they slipped between there and Fort Hamilton on the Long Island shore, into the calm of Manhattan Bay, the first red rim of day broke over the New World. Hilda and Daphne, who had not seen the dawn for years, were up in time to watch the daily miracle for once; Kathleen was not far behind. In fact, she emerged as the sun itself peeked above the scarlet horizon.

"What's that smoke?" she asked, yawning as she pointed a little way north of the sunrise.

Daphne raised her binoculars and stared at it a long moment. Then, with the twitch of an eyebrow, she handed them to Hilda. While Hilda adjusted the focus, Daphne remarked to Kathleen, "It's too far away to be sure, but I have the strongest suspicion."

"If she sailed early enough on Monday morning ..." Kathleen said.

"Quite. And our progress hasn't exactly been brilliant."

What none of them knew, of course, was that Walter Grandison had issued orders for *Burgundia* to make a rather leisurely crossing. He was, at that moment, a mere hundred yards away from the three ladies, travelling in his own stateroom, a world-within-a-world, not exactly incognito but certainly unbeknown to the rest of his fellow passengers.

He, too, was up at this unusually early hour, putting the finishing touches to a draft of what he considered to be the most important letter of his life. By that he did not mean what men usually mean — an unique document addressed to a single issue. This letter filled only half those requirements: It addressed itself to a single issue but, so far from its being unique, there were several dozen ladies who would have recognized many if not all of its finely honed phrases, polished and elaborated down the years. Nonetheless, the claim remained — in its many reincarnations this piece of paper was far and away the most important letter of his life.

"(This version for Daphne Dowty)" read the first line of the present draft; but the fair copy, which he began at that very moment, was headed, "My very dearest D."

Lawrence, who was, indeed, somewhere beneath that smudge of smoke on the eastern horizon, had also risen early, though in his case that was some three hours before the rest. Behind him, in the galley, a cauldron of peeled potatoes (and two lumps of coal to keep them white) stood ready for the breakfast chefs, not to mention a mountain of scoured pans and gleaming crockery from last night's orgy of cuisine. One of the other kitchen porters had advised him to open the porthole and "sling the lot." He said that in a couple of years' time a man with a good diving suit would be able to walk from Manhattan to Liverpool, stepping on Shaw & Eggar crockery all the way.

Now, with his pre-breakfast chores behind him, Lawrence was free to go on deck and scan the seas for a sight of *Burgundia* — his main purpose in making this vile (though actually rather interesting) voyage. But, of course, that was the one thing he was *not* free to do — for the only place that galleyboys were allowed to stand in the open was on the narrow space between the fo'c'sle and the hatch to the number-one hold, where he would be in full view of the bridge. Instead, he worked his way into the chain locker and peered out awkwardly through the hawsepipe. He might just have caught sight of *Burgundia* before she vanished through The Narrows, but the pipe slanted the wrong way and it required several adjustments of position before he found an angle that afforded even the merest pencil slit of a view forr'ard.

A seaman came in to check over the chains. "You'll cop it there, mate," he said affably.

"Dear, dear," Lawrence replied, craning his neck to see yet farther.

"They'll turn you off without pay."

"The bastards."

"Don't you mind?"

"I'll survive."

"Want to jump ship in New York, do you? I've got friends there. I could help you." He laid a gentle hand on Lawrence's buttocks and added, apropos nothing, "There's a Greek ship passing."

"Well, it had better not try and dock in this matelot's port, matey," Lawrence replied menacingly.

He gave up his fruitless search and returned to his station. The commis chef who was doing breakfasts said he was the best porter they'd ever had. He gave him a special smile as he asked would he like him to show him around New York when they docked? He knew all the best spots.

Emma had more luck; a stewardess can always find some legitimate-sounding reason to go on deck for a moment or two, if only to hunt for a nonexistent glove dropped there by a passenger. With the help of some borrowed binoculars, she saw *Burgundia* quite clearly, about fifteen minutes before it passed into Manhattan Bay. The sight of land after days and nights of featureless ocean was always exciting, but never more so than on that particular morning. Only a few hours to go and she'd be reunited with darling, darling Lawrence, able to tell him they were in time ... they were not too late ... they would miss nothing.

Teresa, having been persuaded by Doctor Hebble that not all the postnominal hiramglyptics in the world would make Tony's little graze heal one second faster, had left him in Jemima's capable hands and come to New York on her own, arriving the night before the *Pride of Liverpool* was due. She put up at the Marian Hostel, near old St Patrick's in Mott Street, where she was presently putting herself round a good breakfast in preparation for her vigil in nearby

Battery Park — which, she realized, might well have to last all day.

She shivered to think how often she had quelled an impulse to come to New York to meet Frank off the ship, even though he had made it abundantly clear that he would not welcome such antics. How blithely she would have sailed into the Shaw & Eggar offices and claimed the regal treatment that was her due as the wife of their commodore! And what uproar there would have been then, for surely Hilda *had* made those claims back in January?

Frank had given her the impression that his virtual ban on her appearance there was part of the folklore of the sea — that it was bad luck or something for wives to come within five miles of their husbands' ships. And she had accepted it as one of those things about seafaring men — everyone knew how superstitious they were; although now, come to think of it, how many paintings and engravings had she seen in which anxious wives waited at the quayside for their husbands' vessels to appear!

In a way, that summed up her entire life these past two years, since she had met Frank: two years, two months, and four days. How naïve and trusting she had been! Now that she had had time to simmer down, she began delicately to probe her altered feelings for a husband who had once seemed godlike to her.

That they *had* altered was beyond any doubt; yet she had the extraordinary feeling that, underneath her anger and bitterness, which were powerful enough to occupy her entire attention ... underneath all that, her love for him had somehow strengthened. Part of that was very primitive, of course. She was now in competition with another woman for affections she had assumed were exclusively hers. And yet to find herself taking up this challenge — instead of vowing she'd never see or speak to Frank again — was one of the many surprises of these past two days. If someone had asked her *what if?* about all this, before it became a reality, she would have answered without the slightest thought that she'd never speak to the man again.

It occurred to her that two quite contrary natures within her contended for the possession of her soul. One was an utterly conventional woman who was happy to trundle along, living an utterly conventional life, assuring herself of utterly conventional precepts — like "I'll never speak to him again." The other was equally happy to let the first rule almost every day; but now and then, when something truly important had to be decided, she took over and said, in terms that could not be denied, "No, my dear, now we'll take *this* road."

Was *that* what people meant by "second nature"? In any case, *her* second nature was very much the sovereign of the two at this present moment. Far from being apprehensive, she was looking forward with some keenness to confronting her darling husband, telling him how they were going to live henceforth, insisting on going to London, and there laying down the arrangements by which their joint and separate lives were now to be governed. Never before had she felt so strongly in control of her own destiny. She almost blessed the man for what he had done.

And Neil? Yes, one must not forget Neil. He, alone of all the actors in this cosmic-domestic drama, was still asleep. In his cheap rooming house just off the Bowery, he had lain awake until the small hours last night, devising an entirely new Theory of Life —

well, not entirely new; in fact, it was a sort of crystallization of all the great thoughts he'd ever had ... great *stray* thoughts which he'd at last been able to pull together.

The notion had come to him during a discussion with a ship's engineer he had met in the Grandison offices — the only man who'd ever been able to explain to him the principle of the compound engine. Apparently, it was a compound of *two* engines, one of which needed steam at high pressure, the other of which didn't; so it, the low-pressure one, could take the exhaust steam from the high-pressure one (which still had a bit of shove left in it) and put it to work. Bloody clever wheeze when you got down to it.

Neil had actually not been all that interested in the explanation. He was far more preoccupied with certain uncomfortable facts surrounding his feelings toward Teresa on the one hand and Emma on the other. When his thoughts turned to the realms of love and marriage, which they did almost every hour of the day, it was always Teresa's divine image that shone in his mind's eye; but when they veered off toward the more physical or corporeal manifestations of that blessed estate, as they did almost every *other* hour of the day, it was Emma's divine body that slipped into place beside him in his mind's bed. He realized it was something he had to master before he could honourably present himself as a suitor for Teresa's hand.

And suddenly, in a flash of insight over the third whiskey he had shared with the engineer, in the bar to which they had later repaired, it occurred to him that Man himself is something of a compound engine, with high-pressure parts and low-pressure parts ... high ideals, low ideals. He had worked it all out, greatly to his satisfaction, before he went to sleep last night.

But when he awoke it had all evaporated. Heigh-ho! Wasn't that typical? The best thing to do now, he decided, would be to go down to the *Pride of Liverpool* when she docked later today and have a good, hearty chinwag with the pater. Get the whole bally business sorted out once and for all. In fact, he could kill two birds with one stone: He could ask the Old Man's permission to start paying his court to Teresa.

At that moment *Burgundia* was going quarter-steam ahead past Battery Park. At her stern, among a growing crowd of excited passengers, Hilda was saying to Daphne, "Now you see the futility of planning these things in advance, dear. If I had been so foolish as to follow your advice, I'd now have to throw it all out the window and start again."

Daphne gripped her arm, eyes wide, mouth agape in horror. "D'you know what we forgot?" she exclaimed.

"What?" Hilda's heart raced suddenly.

"We never fanned our tea with our hats! And now it's too late. I knew there was something. Oh ... *bother!*"

And Kathleen, standing a short distance away at the very stern of the ship, stared down into the languid churning of her wake, concentrating on its very randomness as a means of shutting her mind against the whispers that echoed there. She failed, though, for the voices were louder than ever, telling her that,

whatever was about to happen in the hours and days ahead, she owned no part in it. In her fancy she raced away from her mother and Aunt Daphne the moment they set foot on dry land — all the way to the Shaw &

Eggar offices, where darling Chuck, having received her cable, would surely be waiting. And he would take her in his arms and, by the magic of daydreams, both hug her half to death and simultaneously sweep her off to the Pennsylvania Depot, where a special train was waiting to take them to Chicago, where she need never see nor speak to her father and mother and Aunt Daphne and Teresa again.

Teresa, staring idly at *Burgundia* through her (or Frank's) binoculars, actually saw the young girl at the very stern who bore such a resemblance to Kathleen Morgan; but not for one moment did she imagine it actually was her. That whole family was so much on her mind at present, she was almost bound to "see" them at every turn.

An hour later her vigil was rewarded when the unmistakable outlines of the *Pride of Liverpool* appeared in The Narrows, just beyond Owl Point from her vantage in Battery Park. She put her glasses away and set off at once for Forty-Second Street, aware that, whatever happened during the next hour or two, it was going to affect them all for the rest of their lives — herself, Tony, Grainne, Frank, Kathleen, Hilda, Lawrence, Emma … even Neil.

Wider than that she did not speculate; it was surely enough!

THE STEWARDESS FROM the first class waited discreetly in the background until she saw a chance of handing Daphne the letter from Walter Grandison unseen; she was gone again before Daphne could say a word. Then, as they were preparing to disembark, she paid one final visit to the ladies' ablutions and read what proved to be an amazingly generous, though conditional, offer of the most luxurious means of returning to England in two and a half weeks' time; it also contained several interesting proposals for passing intervening days (and nights) in America. She slipped it into her bag and joined Hilda and Kathleen on their way off the ship. Despite their business ashore they were all feeling grand — and looking it, too, since there was no longer any need to dress down to second class.

Burgundia docked at Pier 77, near the western end of Thirty-Seventh Street and less than a quarter of a mile from *Pride of Liverpool's* home on Pier 82. In next to no time the three ladies were in the Shaw & Eggar offices, where their fears about that plume of smoke in the sunrise were confirmed. A cable from the coastguard identifying *Pride of Liverpool* had been received an hour earlier; even now she had passed through The Narrows and would be docked before five bells of the forenoon watch.

"Well, that's that, then," Hilda sighed.

They returned to the outer office, with its vantage over the street that led down to the pier; there the general to and fro of the public and agents would provide some cover for them while they drew up new plans.

543

"We obviously can't get to New Haven ahead of Frank now," Hilda said. "At least, not sufficiently ahead to be of any service."

Daphne was less certain. They would have at least an hour's advantage on him. If they just caught a train and he just missed one ... Even so, an hour should suffice. Great things could be achieved in half the time, *if only they were well enough planned*.

Hilda wavered; the prospect of meeting Frank first did not exactly thrill her. But the puritan in her prevailed. They must not funk it now. Face him resolutely, fair and square.

Daphne persisted. Men were such unreliable, emotional creatures. One never knew where one was with them. Far better to *chercher la femme* and get at her first; you knew where you were with a woman.

And so the argument was batted back and forth over Kathleen's head, while she nursed her sorrow that Chuck had not so far responded to her wire. With each volley Hilda weakened until at last she said, "Very well. New Haven it is. Kathleen, dear, do stop catching flies and conduct us at once to the railway station. Is it far?"

The day being Saturday, and busy already, Kathleen said they'd do it as quickly on foot as look for a cab. They left their baggage in the care of a friendly clerk and descended the brief half-flight of steps to the street. But no sooner had Kathleen, who was leading the way, reached the door than she flung out an arm and cried, "Go back! Quick — for heaven's sake!"

Her command was so peremptory that neither of the others asked what was the matter until they had safely regained the outer office.

Even then the girl did not answer. She merely held up a finger in warning and, edging along the wall

544

toward the window, stood on tiptoe to peer out and down into the street while staying as far inside the room as possible. "It is!" she exclaimed.

Then she turned to the others. "It's all right, you can go to the window. She doesn't know either of you from Eve."

Bemused, but already half-knowing what they were about to see, the two ladies obeyed.

"Jenny Bright!" Daphne murmured in amazement.

"To the last freckle!" Hilda joined in.

For a long moment they continued to stare at the unsuspecting Teresa down below; she had taken up a rather belligerent position with her arms folded and her back to a lamppost at the very edge of the sidewalk.

"Well," Daphne said, recovering something of her usual poise, "until this moment I've been inclined to lay all the blame on Frank. But now I see her in the flesh, I think God also has a great deal to answer for, don't you?"

Hilda could not deny it. "It's like meeting a ghost," she said.

Kathleen, taking advantage of their cover, peered down over their shoulders, between their bonnets, and said, "She knows!"

Hilda laughed dismissively. "How can you possibly say such a thing, dear? Just because she's looking rather severe. It may simply be that ..."

"No, don't you see? What would Captain Morgan's wife do if she were meeting him off the ship?"

Daphne chuckled. "Clever little thing! Of course she would. She certainly wouldn't stand out there!"

They all stared at Teresa a moment longer and then Daphne added, "But it goes further than that."

"I was just thinking the same," Kathleen said.

545

Hilda had been too busy comparing herself point for point with Teresa to do much thinking, said, "What?"

"She's come to the same conclusion as the rest of us. The Ginger Colleen also knows which side her bread is buttered. The Citadel of Blind Fury has fallen without a shot!" She turned to Hilda with a smile. "Well, my dear, since you are so wedded to thinking on your feet, and deciding where to look *after* you have made your leap, what are you going to do now? I'd say you are in mid-air at this very moment."

Hilda could do nothing but shake her head. All faculty for thought seemed to have deserted her the moment she found herself staring at her long-dead rival for Frank's affections, miraculously restored to life and not a day older.

Daphne, who had been about to ask if Hilda didn't think she ought to go down and confront Teresa, switched the emphasis at the last moment — for she, too, could think on her feet when necessary. "Are you going to leave it *all* to her?" she asked in amazement. "All the running, I mean? She's obviously waiting to catch Frank the moment he comes ashore. She'll stand there the entire day if necessary."

Once again Hilda, whose every instinct was to put as much distance between herself and Jenny-Teresa as possible, felt her resolve begin to waver.

And once again the argument raged back and forth over the head of a grieving Kathleen, whose thoughts were only for … but this time she burst into laughter and clapped her hands, and did a little jig on the spot. For there he was at last! Darling, darling Chuck, red-faced, sweating, bursting his collar … he must have run all the way from the Pennsylvania Depot, bless him.

No, curse him!

Up here, you fool! Look up here — I can't come down ...

Oh, men!

Why are you standing there, panting like a walrus, drawing everyone's attention to yourself like a pickpocket on the run, staring at the empty pier down there? *Look up here!*

"Kathleen, darling, do stop jigging up and down like that. It's most annoying. Your Aunt Daphne and I are trying ..."

"But Mama, *don't you see? Look who's down* there! Do draw his attention to us. I can't let myself be seen."

Hilda did as she was bid, looked down, muttered, "The blithering fool!" and rapped sharply on the window with the knob of her parasol.

"I didn't mean like that!" Kathleen wailed in complaint.

But it was too late. The street turned visibly paler as everyone for fifty yards turned his or her face toward the sound. Kathleen found herself staring directly at Teresa, whose eyes were equally locked in hers.

Teresa smiled up at her, a smile that was only half-surprised, and then waved at her to come down. Then she saw that the lady at Kathleen's side was beckoning to a young man, all hot and bothered, not two paces from her. The young man blew a kiss up at the window.

Kathleen watched in a kind of fatalistic anxiety as Teresa tweaked at Chuck's sleeve and asked him a question; her finger pointed up at them.

Chuck raised his hat, smiled, wiped the sweat from his brow yet again, and made some affirmative reply, nodding vigorously.

They exchanged a few more words and then he sprang indoors. "Mrs Morgan!" he cried before he even reached the stairhead. "But how wonderful to meet you again, and so soon!"

They embraced awkwardly, and then Hilda introduced him to Daphne.

After the usual pleasantries he turned at last to Kathleen. "Well!" he exclaimed, holding out both hands to her.

"Well!" she replied, seizing them fervently. Then she flung herself into his embrace and cried, "Oh, thank God! Thank God!"

"Hey!" He laughed in a mixture of delight and embarrassment. "What's this? Oh! I almost forgot. There's a young lady out there who asked me to ask you to come down and talk to her. She knows your name and everything."

"Did she tell you her name?" Daphne asked a fraction of a second ahead of the other two.

"Yes," he drawled. "Miss O'Dee. Teresa, I think."

Daphne turned to Hilda. "Now you can't duck it any longer," she said.

HILDA, HER BOOTS filled with molten lead, through which her heart was sinking faster than a stone, let Kathleen take her down the stairs to a confrontation she had dreaded for months. How would she address this ... this person? What would her first words be? She watched her daughter embrace the young woman — rather awkwardly for both, she thought — and then she stepped forward, watching herself like a third party, a spectator at a play. Kathleen drew breath to make the introductions.

"Teresa, I'd like you to meet my mother ..." she began before Hilda preempted her entirely — by the simple expedient of stretching forth her hand and saying, in a voice surprisingly calm, "Mrs Morgan, I presume?"

Teresa gasped, took the proferred hand almost without realizing what she was doing, and just stood there, staring at Hilda.

For an eternity, it seemed, no one moved. Then the merest flicker of a smile tweaked at the younger woman's lips and, shaking Hilda's hand at last, she said, "Mrs Morgan, I presume?" too.

Daphne sealed the moment with her silvery laugh. "Eh?" Chuck said.

The two wives went on holding hands, staring into each other's eyes, smiling ever more broadly.

"Let me take you somewhere and explain — if I can," Kathleen told Chuck. "Aunt Daphne?"

"What dear?" Daphne asked absently, not taking her eyes off the other two for a moment.

"I need a chap-er-one!" Kathleen replied in a cheerful sing-song.

"Not a hope!" Daphne licked her lips and made it a smiling threesome.

"Yes, Aunt Daphne!" the girl said with steely insistence. "And you know it very well."

"Oh, what?" Daphne asked angrily.

"Our part in all this is over. Come on, now! We're in the way." She held out her hand for Daphne to take.

When Daphne still refused she grabbed her arm roughly and dragged her, protesting, away.

They were so deep in argument as they passed up the rise that only Chuck saw Neil trying to vanish through the brick wall between two shops at the corner of Seventh Avenue — and he, of course, had no idea who the strange young fellow was.

"It's quite a shock," Hilda said, letting go of Teresa's hand at last.

"Bedad, I'll second that!" Teresa exclaimed; her voice sounded alien and her heart was all over the place.

"It would be nice to go somewhere quiet and talk it all over," Hilda went on, settling herself beside Teresa so that they were both facing the pier. "But there's no time now." She nodded a little to their left, where the masts of a large liner, which could only be *Pride of Liverpool*, were drifting slowly above the rooftops. "May I ask how long you've known?"

"Only since last Monday."

"Oh, my dear!" Involuntarily Hilda touched her arm in sympathy.

Teresa gave a baffled laugh. "'Clare to God! I thought we'd eat each other a mile off — roaring up and down the banks! Would you listen to us! When did you find out? Lord, there's so much to be asking, I can't hear meself think! Who else knows? And how much?"

"And what are we going to say to … our lord and master? When we see him, that is."

"Lord and master is it?" she echoed scornfully. "We'll see about that! I'll give him lord and master!"

"Yes, well, I think we're agreed there!" Hilda said hastily. "We'll certainly eat *him* a mile off — what a lovely expression, by the way! To answer your earlier question — or actually, while I think of it, may I first ask if you know of a certain Jenny Bright?"

"Her again!" Teresa responded in a kind of jocular disgust.

"Good! That saves a lot of explaining. The likeness, if I may say so, is astonishing — though more so from a distance than close-to. And your voices, of course, are nothing alike. Anyway, when Kathleen met you she already knew of my ... of our ... of the Captain's youthful attachment to Miss Bright. And she also knew what Jenny looked like in those days, before she died."

"How?"

"Family photographs. Look, it doesn't matter."

"Sorry."

"No — I'm sorry. It's just that time is so short. Kathleen leaped to the conclusion — not a stupid one if you think about it — that you were Jenny's daughter, perhaps by the Captain, perhaps by someone else."

"But I told her ...!"

"I know. But she thought that was just a tale that the Captain had dreamed up to make your situation look respectable. She thought you were a mother without a wedding ring, you see. She thought he was lending you his name to cover your shame. And where was the harm in it? Considering the two 'wives' were four thousand miles apart? However, between you and me, I think she guessed the truth and simply couldn't bring herself to face it."

"But she can now?"

"Yes."

"And does Lawrence know?"

Hilda paused and smiled at her. "Why d'you only ask about him?"

"Well, Neil knows," Teresa replied.

Hilda's mouth fell open and it was her turn to ask how.

"Sure didn't he come calling on me and see the babby and all."

"But when ... I mean, he can't ..."

"All Fools' Day!"

"*This* year?"

"Yes."

"But he was in Norfolk at that time."

"Virginia?"

"No, Norfolk in England. Well, I must say! The artful young ... I wonder where he is now, then?" She turned back to Teresa, still unable to believe it. "He actually called on you, you say? What did he ...? I mean, how did he ...?"

"He seemed very pleasant about it. I mean, no shock or anything. A *little* odd, I thought to meself. Not a penny short of a shilling, you understand, but like as if he didn't sometimes listen to all you said."

Hilda laughed unstintingly. "Oh, but you have the gift of exactitude, Teresa! I think we have to call each other Hilda and Teresa, don't you? In the circumstances?"

Teresa agreed.

Neil, having already been forced to buy a loaf of bread he did not want, peered anxiously round the doorway of the baker's shop, wondering what on earth his mother, who ought to be on the other side of the Atlantic, was doing standing out there in the street, talking to Miz Morgan, who ought to be at home in Fife. They were upsetting all his plans.

The prow of the *Pride of Liverpool* darkened the Hudson river and began to cut off their view of the New Jersey shore.

"Even going at that speed, you know," Hilda said, "it would take a rope at least a foot in diameter to hold her."

"Imagine!" Teresa said.

After a silence Hilda sighed. "Yes, what are we going to tell him when he comes ashore?"

"Couldn't we take him back to his cabin and skin

552

him alive there?" Teresa suggested gleefully.

"What if he says no? We can't have an argument in the street."

"We could threaten to — then he'd have to take us somewhere private."

"Oh!" Hilda wrung her hands in anguish. "This is what I *hate* about planning everything in advance. I mean, if it came to an argument in the street, I could do it. But if we decide it in advance, I'd just lose my nerve when the moment arrived. Let's not decide anything! We'll just stand here, staring him in the face — and see what he does about it."

"Come to think of it," Teresa said, "does the Captain himself know? We never thought of that."

"What? That he's married two ..." She looked guiltily about them and left the rest unsaid.

Teresa laughed. "No. Does he know that *you* know? He can't know *I* know, since I didn't know meself until last Monday."

Hilda remained silent.

"Well?" Teresa prompted.

"I think he may suspect it," Hilda admitted reluctantly.

"Lord, aren't you great talkers though in your family!"

Hilda bridled. "There are certain things that can be conveyed quite adequately without words."

"Like misunderstandings," Teresa suggested.

Hilda's lips went very thin. "I don't think it's appropriate for us to start falling out at this moment, Teresa."

Teresa tossed her head. "And I don't think you should speak as if you were the only aggrieved party, Hilda. I'll tell you for free — I feel very much aggrieved in all this. I married Frank in good faith. If I were in your place, I'd ..." She bit her tongue off.

"You'd what?" Hilda snapped.

Teresa shook her head. "It doesn't matter."

"Oh, but it *does* matter. I want to know."

Teresa said nothing.

"Hah!" Hilda exclaimed with contempt. "And you accuse *us* of being uncommunicative."

"All right!" Teresa snapped. "If you must know, to be quite honest with you, I was going to suggest you should search your heart and conscience and ask *why* a husband of twenty-something years should even *want* to look outside and ... oh God, no — I'm not going to say it."

"Perhaps he found the first experience so sweet, it tempted him to try again," Hilda suggested.

"Sure that's it, so." Teresa now regretted her outburst very much — just when things had been going so well, too.

There was a long, cold silence before Hilda said, "In point of fact ..."

When she said no more, Teresa prompted her. "What? I'm sorry I said them things about ... you know."

"No, no. You were right." There was a much shorter pause before Hilda added, "Indeed, over the past few months I've sometimes thought *every* settled marriage should receive a jolt of this kind. D'you promise me that anything I say will never be passed on by you to ... *him?*"

"My life on it!" Teresa assured her.

There was a flurry of activity with ropes and tugs down on the pier as the *Pride of Liverpool* swung through a right angle alongside her berth.

"Well," Hilda said, "I confess I had come to take the Captain very much for granted of recent years."

"No more than he had you, I'm sure," Teresa commented.

"Yes. I think you understand me exactly, my dear."

Teresa thought back to the hunger with which Frank had devoured her body that night on the stricken *Pegasus*. "And now?" she asked.

Hilda nodded at the liner, which was now tying up, with her bows facing dead on to them. "I'll tell you one thing," she said. "Make what you like of it. I'm not going back in one of her staterooms. And *he'd* better understand that, too! He owes me some years of happiness yet."

"In London," Teresa said.

Hilda smiled and linked arms with her. "Of course."

Behind them, Neil, now holding an additional bag of doughnuts — also unwanted — smiled with relief. Mama obviously approved of Miz Morgan, despite her broken wing. Perhaps a long heart-to-heart chat with Papa was not really necessary after all. Matters seemed to be resolving themselves quite satisfactorily on their own.

EMMA AND LAWRENCE, having fewer responsibilities than the Captain, were down on the quay before him. As she followed him down the crew's gangway she cried out, "Where on earth did you get that dreadful suit?"

He looked at the left sleeve, then the right, flapping his arms like a chicken. "What's wrong with it?" he asked.

"Everything," she replied. "It's half a century out-of-date for a start. Where did you get it?"

"Aunt Daphne gave it me. It's a jolly good Donegal tweed — belonged to Uncle Brian when he was my age."

They had reached the bottom of the gangway by now. She lifted his arm and looked more closely at the pattern. Then she smiled and said, "Well well well!" He asked what she meant by that but she said there wasn't time. Then she brought him up to date with all she had seen from her superior vantage that morning. "So they've either gone racing ahead to Fife," she concluded, "or they're just up the road here, in the Shaw & Eggar offices, waiting for your father. We must keep our eyes peeled."

They had just reached the inner end of the pier and were about to step upon the solid rock of Manhattan when Emma suddenly stooped and fiddled with her bootlace, though it was, in fact, perfectly well adjusted already. "What's the matter?" he asked slightly petulantly.

"God alone knows," she muttered. "Don't look up the street now. D'you see that pile of packing cases and teachests over there? Go and stand behind them a mo. Quick as you can!"

"But ..."

"Don't argue — just do it!"

"Yes, milady," he said sullenly, though he obeyed her smartly enough. When she joined him a moment later he said, "I'm fed up with being bossed about, you know."

She looked swiftly about them and gave him a hasty kiss.

"Actually, that's a lie," he confessed. "I'm fed up with men making advances to me, if you must know."

"Me too," she agreed. "It was the worst voyage I've ever known for that sort of thing. Talk about the

556

merry month of May!" Then she frowned at him. "You? But how can …"

"Oho! You've no idea what goes on below decks up forr'ard," he assured her. "Anyway, why are we hiding here?"

She became serious again. "Because we're caught between the devil and the deep blue sea, my old darling, that's what. Have a peek out. Half way up the hill, outside the company's offices. Who's that standing there — or is it my eyes playing me tricks?"

He inched his head out and then gave a low whistle. "But hang on," he added. "That's not Aunt Daphne."

"I know. You'll never guess who it is."

Her tone, of course, helped him to hit upon it first go. "Not …?"

"As I live and breathe. That is your American stepmother, my old darling. Hang on." She fished in her bag and produced a pair of opera glasses, not as powerful as the ones she had used that morning, but more than adequate at the present range. She passed them to him.

He trained them on the two women, found the focus, and whistled again. "A right little cracker!" he exclaimed — then looked at her in distaste. "Am I beginning to sound like Neil?"

"Not half," she told him, taking the glasses back and putting them to her own eyes. "Yes — that's Teresa, right enough. But *what* is she doing, standing there with your mother, side by side — arm in arm, even?"

"Waiting for Papa?" he suggested.

"Obviously!" was the scornful reply. "I mean … why those two together? It doesn't make sense. *Burgundia* only got in a couple of hours ago. Your mum couldn't even have sent a wire saying come to New York, quick as you can. Teresa must have been here already. But why?"

"She must have found out independently, somehow."

"But how? Three weeks ago she knew nothing. And I'm sure nobody's been back here since ..."

"Neil?" he interrupted.

She shook her head. "In any case, *he* thinks she's unmarried. Oh!" She stamped her foot in frustration. "I wish I was a little dicky bird — I know just what lamppost I'd go and perch on, this very minute. It's not fair!"

"And where's Aunt Daphne and Kathleen, come to that?" he asked.

"Up on the rooftops with loaded rifles?" she suggested

At that moment Lawrence plucked her violently from her vantage and did not let go of her until they had the whole pile of crates between them and the *Pride of Liverpool*. Before she could ask what he was doing, he nodded to a point beyond where she had just been standing and murmured, "I don't think they saw us."

It was Frank Morgan and his Number One, Tony Wheeler, both out of uniform; they passed within feet of the two in hiding.

"It gets tighter and tighter," Frank was saying, "and yet, somehow, it never seems to hem me in completely. I tell you, man, I had a very narrow squeak after the last voyage."

"You told me," Wheeler replied. "The Harding girl. You must have shat your breeches."

Frank chuckled. They passed out of earshot of the two in hiding. "Actually," he confessed, "it was better than having a winner in the Derby at a hundred to one. I've never sweated so much since ... anyway, I caught her in the nick of time — and then watched her like a hawk until we left. I've had more close shaves, I tell you, than a Port Said whore."

They paused to check her moorings, as always.

"There he is now," Hilda said — quite unnecessarily since Teresa's arm had already gone rigid. "Frightened?" she asked.

Teresa gulped heavily. "Yes. And you?"

"Petrified. But listen — whatever we do, we mustn't show it."

"What'll we say to him?"

"Nothing. We decided that. We'll let him speak first. We have the advantage of surprise, remember."

"What in God's name is going to happen now?" Lawrence whispered hoarsely to Emma.

"If you'll just shut up, we'll see," she snapped back, still furious that she was not a little bird.

Now that the two officers had gone by, she and Lawrence returned to their earlier positions, with the crates between them and the two ladies, who were still standing on the slope above.

"They can't have a fight," Lawrence said in anguish. "Not there!"

"Oh, just shut up and watch," she cried, handing him the glasses to keep him quiet. "There's nothing we can do about it now."

"No, you keep them." He warded off her hand. "If they start fighting, you'll see the fastest hundred-yard dash in history."

"And what then?"

"I'll join in, pretend to be drunk, make it seem like a vulgar brawl, shout loud enough to drown out whatever home truths may be flying about ... I'll do *anything*."

559

She was silent.

"You?" he asked.

"Yes, all right," she said. "I'll come, too."

"Lord God Almighty!" Frank exclaimed.

"He's seen them!" Lawrence exclaimed.

"Oh Jesus, Mary, and Joseph!" Teresa exclaimed. "He's seen us! Holy Mother of God — what'll we do?"

"You shouldn't take such names in vain," Hilda chided.

"In vain, is it? By all the saints, but I hope you're wrong!"

Wheeler followed his captain's gaze and let out a gasp. "That's her!" he said. "But who is the rather handsome lady at her side?"

The Captain gave him a hunted look. "I'll give you a million guesses — and you'll need every one."

Wheeler frowned. "Not ...?"

"I'm afraid so. Lord, I thought of every possibility but this! What am I going to say to them?"

Wheeler was stunned. "But they live on opposite shores of the ocean! How did they get together?"

"I don't know, I don't know! And frankly at this moment I don't much care. The point is, they're there. What am I going to *say*?"

"Let them speak first," the other replied, with more conviction than he felt; it was just that no better suggestion occurred to him.

Frank shot him a glance of profound gratitude. "You're right, Wheeler! Oh, thank heavens you were here! Let them speak first — it's so obvious."

"Well!" Lawrence exclaimed in admiration. "There goes a man with guts! Say what else you like about him, but he has guts. Look at him — head up, shoulders back ... magnificent!"

"Wouldn't it scald your heart to hate that man!" Teresa muttered, on the verge of tears. "And I looking at him and feeling fit to burst with the forgiveness that's in it!"

Hilda tried to swallow down the lump in her own throat and failed. "You're right," she murmured back. "Without him there's nothing. There could be no other man. Quiet! He'll hear us now."

Frank, to stop his head from bursting, began to count down the paces that still separated them, which he estimated at only fifteen.

Fourteen, thirteen ...

Wheeler was right — Hilda *was* a handsome woman.

Twelve, eleven ...

And dignified, too. Look at her standing there, not a twitch in her features, not a hair out of place.

Ten, nine, eight ...

And Teresa! A sight to melt a heart of stone.

Seven, six, five, four ...

How could anyone, looking at her, seeing that wild, audacious beauty — how could anyone blame him?

Three, two ...

What *was* he going to say?

Hilda stared at him — what was he going to say.

One ...

Teresa stared at him. He drew breath to speak. Every fibre of her being screamed at the unbearable tension.

"Ladies," he said, touching the brim of his hat as he walked on by.

They turned and watched him, saying nothing, hardly moving even, until he reached the crown of the hill.

"I feel like a drink," he said to Wheeler. "Didn't you once tell me there's a very good bar near here?"

Only when they were out of sight did Hilda at last turn to Teresa. "Well!" she exclaimed in a tone curiously devoid of either anger or surprise. She repeated the word just as flatly: "Well!"

Teresa noticed their absence at once and relaxed a little. "When you think of it," she said, "he's right."

"Yes." Hilda's smile was a mixture of sadness and resignation. "He almost always is — damn him! Do you know anywhere nearby where they serve a good cup of tea?"

When Emma saw the two women turn away she glanced at Lawrence and said, "Well?"

"Well what?"

"Aren't you going after them?"

He shook his head. "Where would be the point? You saw what happened." Then he grinned. "Besides, I have something much more important to be thinking about."

She grinned, too. "What?"

He rubbed noses with her. "As if you didn't know! But I think I have a surprise for you yet. Come with me."

"Where to?" She tripped reluctantly in his wake, leaning back against the pull of his hand, smiling from ear to ear.

"Will you just stop questioning me for once. Wait till I show you."

He led her all the way to the head of the pier and then pointed south, toward the bay — or rather, as she soon realized, toward *Burgundia*.

"What of it?" she asked, genuinely curious now.

He waved a hand vaguely at the *Pride of Liverpool*. "Would you be sorry never to sail in her again — as a stewardess, I mean?"

"Not a bit," she said fervently. "This voyage was almost the last straw."

He turned her back to face *Burgundia*. "She sails on Monday."

"And?" The smile was returning to her lips.

"Well, I was thinking — old Walter Grandison's a good friend of our family. I'll bet he owes us a favour or two. His office here could cable him in London. I'll bet he could let us have a stateroom on her, on Monday."

"*One* stateroom?" she asked.

"Well, I don't suppose his generosity would run to two."

She dealt him a playful punch. "You know what I mean!"

"Oh that! Well, if we can't find someone to marry us in New York between now and Monday, we can ask the captain as soon as we're out of territorial waters and then ..." The rest of his proposal was drowned in her kiss, which was longer and more passionate than any he remembered.

When they broke she said, "But I'm not marrying you in that tweed."

T HE PLACE WHERE they served a good cup of tea — and what they called "English muffins" though they were nothing of the kind — was also the place where Kathleen had just finished explaining the whole business to her beloved Chuck, hindered at every step of the way by a malignantly disgruntled Aunt Daphne. However, she — Aunt Daphne — brightened up consdierably at the sight of the Captain's wives, who had just come in out of strong sunlight and were looking rather lost in the entrance way. "Coo-ee!" she called. "Over here!"

"Well?" she asked excitedly as they drew near.

"Well, what?" Hilda responded.

"Don't be obtuse, dear. You know very well what I mean. What happened?" Her eyes narrowed. "Or hasn't he come ashore yet? Did you just cut and run?"

"The Captain?" Hilda said offhandedly. "Oh no, we met him."

"And?"

She shrugged and glanced at Teresa as if for confirmation. "I think we said everything that needed saying, don't you, Teresa dear?"

"Indeed we did," the other affirmed. "Divil a word I would have added. That man knows just how matters stand between the three of us, I'll go bail."

"And now?" Daphne prompted.

"I'll catch the next train home to Fife ..."

"And I'll go back to London ..." Hilda interrupted.

"And that's the end of *that!*" A delighted Kathleen capped them both. "Chuck, darling, I'm feeling rather warm, and I see there's a little terrace yonder, so would it be quite in order, Mama, for us to take our lemonades over there where it's cooler?"

Hilda raised an inquiring eyebrow at Chuck. "That rather depends on this young man's intentions — now that he's learned our awful secret?"

Chuck nodded. "I think it's confirmed them, Mrs Morgan," he said in his slow, easy drawl. "But I don't believe my mother need hear of it."

"No?"

"No. She's a mighty busy lady and it may only confuse her."

"Well!" Hilda smiled toward the terrace. "I'm sure

the pair of you have a great deal to talk about, too."

When the three women were alone, Daphne cleared her throat delicately and said, "You mentioned something about returning to London, dear. Will you be sailing on the *Burgundia*, by any chance?"

"Never again!" Hilda answered fervently. "No. I'm returning on the *Pride of Liverpool* — in the Captain's cabin, no less! So there!"

Daphne shot a glance at Teresa to see how she took this provocation. It disappointed her to see a gleam of rather savage delight in the Ginger Colleen's eye.

"But how selfish of me!" Hilda went on. "Not to think of you, Daphne dear. Perhaps you would like to come back on the *Pride of Liverpool*, too?"

"Oh, Hilda, my sweet — how characteristically thoughtful and generous you are. But regretfully I have to decline. Only this morning I have discovered that an old family friend sailed over on the *Burgundia* with us. Think of it! And it has been suggested that we — the old friend and I — should see a little of America, now that I'm here, and then travel back on the *next* sailing in two weeks' time."

"*Burgundia's* next sailing?"

Daphne smiled. "But of course."

Hilda smiled. "But of course."

Teresa cleared her throat.

Hilda turned to her and said, a little sharply, "Now d'you see what I mean, my dear?"

"Indeed I do!" was the fervent reply.

"Of course, you know what was so wonderful about all this?" Daphne went on. "Why it's all gone so smoothly, I mean? The fact that Neil wasn't here! He's a dear, sweet young man and I won't hear a word against him, but he does have a remarkable propensity to grasp the wrong end of the stick and go

565

charging into that famous china shop where angels fear to tread."

Hilda agreed with a sigh. "That'll be my first little task on returning to England. Once I learn his true whereabouts, that is." She sighed again and laid the thought to rest.

Whether a sigh would have been sufficient if she had known his true whereabouts at that precise moment is a matter of considerable doubt. For Neil was even then upon the train to New Haven.

Having seen that his mother was a good friend of Miz Morgan's and that the pair of them were obviously waiting to greet his father off the ship, he decided that his best bet was to get to Fife as soon as possible, there to await in jocular ambush upon the Love of his Life. Lord, how she would laugh! And how her dear face would light up at the sight of him!

On his lap he had a bunch of roses and a box of comfits shaped like a heart — wilting and melting respectively. Also a half-eaten loaf of rather dry bread, which he was desperately trying to get down his gullet before the train brought him to his destination.

The two doughnuts had been easier; they had gone before La Rochelle.

THE END